A TIP *for the* HANGMAN

"This Chicago writer's fizzy debut is a Tudor espionage tale, set among spies close to Mary, Queen of Scots. One of them is Christopher Marlowe, whose spy work bankrolls a rather promising theater career." —*Chicago Tribune*

"*A Tip for the Hangman* draws you into a morally convoluted world of spies, treason, politics, romance and murder. With a witty, captivating protagonist and fast-paced adventure, it's the sort of book you should never pick up before bedtime lest you look out the window to see the sun rising. This is easily one of 2021's best historical fiction books to date." —*The Michigan Daily*

"Thrilling and romantic. . . . Epstein successfully evokes both the beauty and the brutality of sixteenth-century England." —Historical Novel Society

"Epstein's diverting debut gallivants through Elizabethan England. . . . A fun escapade." —*Publishers Weekly*

"Exceptional, highly entertaining. . . . This wonderful debut novel is solid escapism at its best." —*Lansing State Journal*

"Epstein pens a vivid, unforgettable hero in Kit Marlowe, Elizabethan playwright-turned-spy always sprinting one step ahead of disaster and talking a blue streak as he does so. . . . Simultaneously moving, unsettling, hilarious, and tragic—a debut that will linger long after the last page is turned." —Kate Quinn, *New York Times* bestselling author of *The Alice Network*

Allison Epstein

A TIP *for the* HANGMAN

Allison Epstein earned her MFA in fiction from Northwestern University and a BA in creative writing and Renaissance literature from the University of Michigan. A Michigan native, she now lives in Chicago, where she works as a copywriter for clients in higher education and the arts. When not writing, she enjoys good theater, bad puns, and fancy jackets. *A Tip for the Hangman* is her first novel.

A TIP *for the* HANGMAN

A TIP

for the

HANGMAN

A NOVEL

Allison Epstein

ANCHOR BOOKS

A DIVISION OF PENGUIN RANDOM HOUSE LLC

NEW YORK

FIRST ANCHOR BOOKS EDITION, JANUARY 2022

Copyright © 2021 by Allison Epstein

All rights reserved. Published in the United States
by Anchor Books, a division of Penguin Random House LLC,
New York, and distributed in Canada by Penguin Random House
Canada Limited, Toronto. Originally published in hardcover
by Doubleday, a division of Penguin Random
House LLC, New York, in 2021.

Anchor Books and colophon are registered
trademarks of Penguin Random House LLC.

The Library of Congress has cataloged
the Doubleday edition as follows:
Names: Epstein, Allison, author.
Title: A tip for the hangman : a novel / Allison Epstein.
Description: First edition. | New York : Doubleday, 2021.
Identifiers: LCCN 2020020637 (print) |
LCCN 2020020638 (ebook)
Subjects: LCSH: Marlowe, Christopher, 1564–1593—Fiction. |
GSAFD: Biographical fiction. | Suspense fiction.
Classification: LCC PS3605.P6456 T57 2021 (print) |
LCC PS3605.P6456 (ebook) | DDC 813/.6—dc23
LC record available at https://lccn.loc.gov/2020020637
LC ebook record available at https://lccn.loc.gov/2020020638

Anchor Books Trade Paperback ISBN: 978-0-593-31134-9
eBook ISBN: 978-0-385-54672-0

www.anchorbooks.com

Printed in the United States of America
10 9 8 7 6 5 4 3 2 1

To Laura Hulthen Thomas,

for setting the scene

PART I

Queen of Fire

GUISE: What glory is there in a common good
　　That hangs for every peasant to achieve?
　　That like I best that flies beyond my reach.
　　Set me to scale the high Pyramides,
　　And thereon set the diadem of France,
　　I'll either rend it with my nails to naught,
　　Or mount the top with my aspiring wings,
　　Although my downfall be the deepest hell.

The Massacre at Paris, 2.40–47

One

Without tobacco, Kit knew, he would never survive Cambridge. The university would have destroyed him otherwise: the relentless pace, the always-rising stakes. One arcane lecture after another, endless pages of Greek readings that became no less bewildering with time. And beneath it all, the pervasive fear of falling behind, of falling to pieces, of publicly confirming what the fellows all privately believed: that whatever scholarship the master of the college had conferred upon him, Kit Marlowe didn't belong here, should never have come. But once a wisp of smoke curled up in his lungs, none of that mattered. At least for the night.

Tobacco unwound his nerves like a worn shirt, turned soft and loose, trailing easy threads to nowhere. It changed nothing, of course. Kit's presence at Corpus Christi College remained as provisional as ever, the fellows' condescension as irritating. But as the smoke drifted between his lips and up to the ceiling, a shimmer in the setting sun, that seemed peripheral, manageable even. He settled against the bedpost with a sigh. Through the haze, his room felt more like Elysium than the half-furnished dormitory of a master's student.

Particularly given the company.

Tom slouched on the other end of Kit's bed, his back against the wall beside the window. Leaning sideways, he grasped for the dark glass bottle resting against Kit's thigh. The movement brought him into the beam of sunlight and made his almost-silver hair shine gold. His outstretched fingers missed his target by half an inch.

"Come on," Tom said, voice strained with the stretch. "Don't make me beg."

When Kit passed the bottle over, the ends of Tom's fingers brushed Kit's palm, causing a momentary thrill that Kit tried hard not to think about. Tom took a healthy swallow, then grimaced and looked at Kit as if he'd been tricked into drinking piss.

"God's blood, this is terrible."

Kit laughed. Tom was more right than he knew. "You want better, you buy it," he said, letting his next drag linger.

He expected Tom to resume his former slouch against the wall, now he'd realized the bottle wasn't worth sharing, but Tom, intentionally or not, had instead moved closer. He sat with one leg bent to his chest, his biceps on his knee, watching the bottle with suspicion. With his back against the window now, the light cast his face in shadow but illuminated his edges, making him look like a fresco or a gilded saint. There remained less than a foot between them. If Kit hadn't known better, he'd swear Tom was doing this on purpose, just to toy with him. He couldn't think straight like this.

"Do you know what this tastes like?" Tom said, addressing the bottle.

Kit did. He grinned. "Salvation?"

Tom blinked. "Communion wine," he said. "Honestly."

"God's blood indeed," Kit said. He ducked the half-hearted blow Tom aimed at his head. "If Rector Harvey doesn't notice, what's the harm?"

"You wouldn't," Tom said. "You're lying."

"I never." Kit pressed one hand to his chest in melodramatic offense.

Tom raised his eyebrows.

"All right," Kit said, ceding the point. "But I wouldn't lie with you."

The words had barely left his mouth before Kit wanted to die for having said them. What right did he have to consider himself a poet when he couldn't even form a sentence to his best friend without courting disaster? His ungodly handsome best friend. The one sitting six inches from him, backlit in gold.

As Tom tilted his head, the shadows on his face shifted, leaving one plane in shadow and one bathed in yellow. "Wouldn't you?" he asked. "Never took you for a man with scruples. I'd lie with you, if I had to."

Kit flushed. He didn't know if this was from embarrassment or something else, and he refused to interrogate the question. Tom's expression was unreadable, as if he had never heard of such a thing as double entendre.

God and Christ. To be tortured by a preposition.

"I . . ." Kit began, praying he'd find the end of the sentence once he started it.

The door opened without a knock. Kit swore through a cloud of tobacco smoke and leapt off the bed, widening the distance between them from six inches to five feet. Tom lunged across the mattress and seized the bottle of wine. He'd stashed it between his back and the wall by the time the door opened fully, admitting a copper-haired young man who seemed taken aback by the violence of Kit's glare. Kit would have given anything not to have this particular student in his room at this moment, but he took a measured sort of hope in noting that Tom looked as annoyed by the interruption as he felt.

"For God's sake, Nick," Kit said. "Man invented doors for a reason."

"Good to see you too, Kit," Nick said. He pushed past Kit and pulled out the room's sole chair, straddling it backward. "Tom. I didn't mean to interrupt."

"And yet . . ." Tom abandoned the attempt to hide the bottle and took an exasperated drink.

Kit directed his eyes heavenward. Granted, the evening had been a disaster long before Nick Skeres showed up, but at least that disaster had potential. Leaving the door open—lest Nick forget the way back out—Kit perched on the desk and folded his legs beneath him.

"I thought you were going to town," Tom said.

"I will," Nick agreed. "First, Kit is lending me his essay on the *Life of Pyrrhus*."

"I am?"

If Kit had ever made such a promise, he had no memory of it, but Nick's presumption wasn't surprising. The scholarship that had allowed Kit to attend Cambridge these past five years amounted to a sort of eternal probation. Fall behind and the college would rescind his funds, which would find him out on the street in a week. Nick, knowing this, read Kit's diligence as a standing invitation to swipe passages from any given essay.

"Yes," Nick said. He leaned his forearms on the back of the chair and rested his chin on them with an expectant air. "Now, come on. I have places to be."

"Who is it this time?" Tom asked, without interest. "Susanna? Joan?"

"Eleanor." Nick winked, which only strengthened Kit's urge to punch him. "So I'm in a hurry. Let me look at yours, and I'll be gone in a minute."

Tom and Kit exchanged a glance. *If you really would lie with me,* Kit's side of the glance said, *start now, because I intend to lie like you've never seen.* Tom smiled, a half expression Nick didn't notice, and nodded.

"I haven't started," Kit said to Nick with a shrug.

Nick stared. "This is the essay due in twelve hours, yes?"

"Kit and I are a little behind," Tom said, picking up the lie.

Kit nodded, with a stab at a self-deprecating smile. Self-deprecation was well out of his range, usually, but at a stretch he could fake it. "We were settling in for a night of Greek and—"

"Wine and tobacco?" Nick frowned, looking from the bottle in Tom's hand to the pipe in Kit's.

Kit's liar's code was predicated on a single rule: conviction. People believe a confident liar before they believe a nervous honest man. "Yes," he said, without missing a beat. "Call it inspiration."

Nick scowled. His chin slumped down farther until his arm obscured the bottom half of his face. "Don't do this to me, Kit," he said, voice muffled from within his own elbow. "Just let me copy out the less-brilliant bits. I'll pay you, if that's what you want."

Kit felt his shoulders tense without meaning them to. Money. That was all gentlemen's sons like Nick thought about. As if Kit's mind could be whored out for two groats a night because his father made shoes. Cambridge life had changed him after all: not long ago, he'd have punched Nick for the insinuation.

"I don't want your money," Kit said. "If you deserved help, I'd give it."

Tom, the tips of his ears reddening, had found something fascinating on the back of his left hand. Kit wanted to believe his discomfort came from sympathy, but it was more likely that Tom wanted a graceful way to exit before this sniping devolved into a genuine fight.

"I—" Nick began.

Tom raised a hand, cutting him off. "Listen."

Through the open door, rapid footfalls sounded against the stone beyond. Someone was coming. Someone with a purpose, judging by the pace, and someone close.

For God's sake. The smoke must have drifted through the open door. If Nick got them expelled, Kit's ghost would haunt Nick's across the centuries. "Open the window," he said.

Tom twisted around to fling open the window, while Nick snatched the bottle from him and dropped to his knees. He nearly vanished beneath the bed, re-emerging empty-handed seconds later. Kit leaned over and thrust the smoking end of his pipe into the washbasin. The scent of cheap tobacco languished on the air. He coughed, clearing smoke from his throat.

"Kit," Tom said sharply. Paler than thirty seconds ago, he nodded over Kit's shoulder.

Kit turned. Then he came to a quick and vibrant conclusion: either he was dreaming or he was about to be expelled.

A tall, gray-haired man in scholar's robes now stood silhouetted in the doorway. His severe Roman face was expressionless beneath his precise beard, which retained more black than his hair. His impeccable posture gave the impression that his spinal column had been replaced with a lance.

Kit pushed himself off the desk. "Master Norgate," he said. Whether shock or fear made his voice crack was anyone's guess. At twenty-one, he thought he'd outgrown that, but there were surprises to be had every day.

"Skeres. Watson." The head of Corpus Christi College nodded at Nick and Tom in turn, then fixed his light brown eyes on Kit.

Kit could count on one hand the times he'd spoken to Master Norgate in person. It wasn't the master's nature to mingle with students while they drowned in a sea of Pliny and Virgil. He was elusive, appearing for ceremonial purposes only. The fact that he stood here now could mean many things, none of them good. Opening the window had done nothing to dispel the drifting haze of tobacco.

Norgate's lips narrowed. "Marlowe, if you would follow me."

It wasn't a request. "Yes," Kit said, unnecessarily. "Of course."

He looked to Tom in a wordless plea for help and received a sympathetic wince in return. It was touching that Tom Watson cared whether Norgate had Kit murdered and thrown into the river, though admittedly it was more touching than helpful. But everything would end for the best, if Kit could maintain his composure. There was no reason to be afraid. He'd done nothing wrong.

There, if anywhere, was a lie for the ages.

Norgate ushered Kit down the hall toward the outer courtyard, walking fast and in silence. They passed the chapel, long emptied of stragglers from evening services. Two or three servants remained within, sweeping down the slate floor before the next morning's call to prayer. The setting sun streamed through the leaded windows to carve out jeweled shadows across the floor. It gave the servants the look of figures in a mosaic, Byzantine and impersonal.

"Marlowe, once," Norgate said, rounding a corner. "Just once, I would appreciate not having a vague sense of malaise where you are concerned. Do you think you can manage that?"

"I don't know what you mean, sir," Kit said, lengthening his stride to keep up. It wasn't easy—Norgate towered eight inches above him. "Unless it's the chapel wine, in which case—"

Norgate frowned. "What wine?"

Ah. Damn. "I have no idea."

The master sighed. "Marlowe, I'm trying to help you. I've taken a liking to you, against my better judgment."

Kit stared. Well, that was certainly news. Although then again, perhaps there was something to it. Corpus Christi accepted two poor scholars a year at most, perhaps only one in a lean term. For Kit to walk through these doors—let alone with funding for both an undergraduate degree and the master's he'd complete in seven months—Norgate must have taken some sort of interest. There was a world of difference, though, between an interest and a liking.

"There's no reason to look surprised, Marlowe," Norgate said testily. "Why did you think I let you in at all?" The master had sped up, somehow.

"Some sort of penance, I thought, sir," Kit said.

Norgate ignored this. "I remember your application. It isn't often a boy of sixteen submits something that remarkable, and Master Seymour tells me you haven't disappointed. Your skills in rhetoric and disputation are stunning, if morally flexible."

No secret what that referred to. Two weeks ago, Master Seymour, dean of poetics, had pitted Kit against a fourth-year master's candidate to debate the spiritual imperative of a celibate clergy. Kit, assigned the affirmative position, bested Francis Masterson in two minutes. When Masterson whined that Kit's obvious position gave him the advantage, Kit flipped sides without missing a beat and spent five minutes explaining why England's priests ought to fuck widely, loudly, and well. His logic had been impeccable, though Seymour sighed like the north wind when he awarded Kit victory.

"Your writing, too, is exceptional," Norgate went on. "Leaving you in the care of an illiterate shoemaker who spends half the year in prison would have been a crime."

Kit clenched his fists to keep from speaking. Leave it to a Cambridge master to conceal an insult in a forest of compliments. Granted, Kit owed Norgate everything, and the master hadn't said anything Kit hadn't heard before, or said himself a hundred times. But calling your own father an ignorant peasant was one thing, hearing the head of the college do it quite another. If this was Norgate's attempt to remind Kit to stick to his place and be grateful, he didn't need to hear it. Why bring up . . .

Oh. That was why.

God damn it all. Not again.

Likely—more than likely—his father's drinking and debts had caught up with him, landing him back in debtor's prison. But what could Kit do about it? Leave Cambridge and plead John Marlowe's case before the court, as he'd done as a schoolboy in Canterbury? Manipulating a magistrate wasn't the glorious purpose he'd envisioned for his new-lauded skills in rhetoric.

Norgate stopped walking. Though he'd never stated their destination, Kit supposed this must be it. He glanced at the closed door between them and identified it with a despairing lack of surprise. The master's office. This could not end well.

"I know prudence is not your best quality, Marlowe," Norgate said, "but please do not do anything stupid."

So saying, the master turned and knocked three times on the office door. Kit barely had time to consider the strangeness of it—under what circumstances did a man knock on his own door?—before a voice Kit didn't know answered from inside.

"Come in."

The two men looked at each other. While the master was not the companion Kit would have chosen for such a meeting, he dreaded entering that room alone.

Kit stepped into the office. The latch clicked as Norgate closed the door behind him.

Two

Kit had never been inside the master's office. Though he'd accumulated a considerable number of offenses at Cambridge, they had always been minor enough for the fellows to arbitrate themselves. Petty theft. Private blasphemy. Showing up to recitation with the stink of the alehouse on your breath, wearing the same clothes as the day before. It took something more to earn a summons to this office, something irreversible.

The room looked no different from any other modest study. Dark walnut bookshelves lined the walls, packed with volumes in Greek, Latin, and German. Two tall windows divided the shelves on the far wall. They opened onto a view of the green, where three first-form boys tossed a tennis ball in the dying light. Before the window stood a large oak desk, leafy vines carved around the legs and into the sides. Kit could imagine Norgate reading Petrarch's sonnets there, or annotating a Latin sermon. A scholar could be happy here, away from the daily irritation of academic affairs.

But instead of Norgate, a strange dark-eyed man leaned his elbows on the desk. Short hair inclining toward gray, beard fastidiously trimmed. Hands folded before him in a poor imitation of patience. His eyes, black rather than brown, turned down at the corners like a greyhound's. Kit knew the look in those eyes well enough. It was the look he saw in accountants and lawyers who frequented the same taverns as Cambridge's students, men who made their fortunes on slipped figures and miscalculations. Those eyes knew more about him than he had any cause to expect, or any reason to doubt.

"Sir," Kit said, and bowed.

"Marlowe," the man said. His heavy brow and low forehead lent him an air of permanent disapproval.

"Yes, sir." Kit rose and glanced at the chair in front of the desk, but the man gave no indication he might sit.

"Do you know why you're here?" the man asked.

"No, sir," Kit said. *Yes, sir. No, sir.* In twenty seconds, this stranger had done what five years of university studies could not: he'd taught Kit manners.

The man pressed the tips of his fingers together and pointed the resultant triangle at his audience of one. "My name is Sir Francis Walsingham," he said. "Royal secretary to Her Majesty Queen Elizabeth."

"Oh." And here Kit was, fingers stained with ink and clothes smelling of tobacco. Norgate might at least have given him a hint.

What in God's name had his father done to merit the attention of the queen's secretary? Kit couldn't imagine. John was a rat, he'd be the first to admit it, but a lioness didn't concern herself with rats without good reason. His mind raced with possibilities, each more absurd than the last. Smuggling. Blackmail. Murder. Kit had just escalated to sedition when Walsingham spoke again, severing his thoughts.

"My time is in high demand, as you can imagine," he said. "So you may take my presence as a sign of how seriously I regard this matter."

The uncertainty was more than Kit could stand. If he needed to negotiate John's escape from prison, or the Tower by the sound of it, he wanted to know the worst. "Sir," Kit said, "I swear, if my father has—"

Walsingham raised his eyebrows. Kit fell silent. With that one gesture, he knew he was fathoms out of his depth. "What the devil does your father have to do with it? My concern is with *you*."

Him? Kit was a student. A poet. The son of a shoemaker. To the queen and those who kept her counsel, he was nobody. A nuisance, maybe, but monarchs didn't send their secretaries across the country to condemn nuisances. Walsingham must be looking for someone else. William Morley, that third-year undergraduate whose father hunted deer with the lord mayor of London. Anyone.

"You must be mistaken, sir—" Kit began.

"It's my job not to be mistaken," Walsingham said, cutting him off. "You are Christopher Marlowe. The eldest son of John Marlowe, second-rate Canterbury cobbler. A poor scholar at Corpus Christi in your fifth year of study. Skilled in rhetoric and disputation, disgraceful in geography and geometry. You've been smoking all evening and hoped I wouldn't notice. And you are no fool, so do not pretend to be."

Kit stared. His mind had stopped providing thoughts germane to the situation. By the light of Christ, what did this man want?

"How much do you know of the royal secretary's duties?" Walsingham asked, ignoring Kit's evident shock.

Direct questions with simple answers were all Kit could cope with at this juncture. "Exactly as much as I should, sir," he said, "and no more."

Walsingham gave him a withering look. "Don't be clever. In addition to my public duties as Her Majesty's head of state, I am engaged in more sensitive matters. And that," he said with finality, "is why I asked Norgate to bring you to me. Between the ripples from Bartholomew's Day and the growing nest of Jesuits within our borders, we are spread thin enough. I can no longer afford to be discriminating in my choices."

There was an insult in the phrase, Kit was certain, but he hadn't grasped the situation well enough to be offended. He willed himself to stop fidgeting.

Though he had no idea what Walsingham meant by *my choices*, the first half of the phrase was clear. Kit's evenings in the White Stag with a smoke and a knack for eavesdropping had been as instructive as those in the library with Tacitus. The massacre of

Saint Bartholomew's Day was more than a decade in the grave, but the taverns of both Canterbury and Cambridge still buzzed with stories of armed Catholics filling the streets of France with burning corpses. It was only a matter of time, or so the tavern rumors claimed, before England's Jesuits and papists took up arms and did the same. Kit listened to these stories with the interest of a theatergoer, not the concern of a loyal subject. The idea of armed religious zealots, though alarming on its face, had nothing to do with him. As for personal belief, Kit's primary spiritual conviction was that any god who began services at six in the morning was too cruel for a sane man to worship. But Kit's spiritual convictions didn't seem to interest Walsingham.

"My informants have provided thorough and reliable suggestions about papist movements within our borders," Walsingham said. "But—"

Wait. Informants?

"I'm sorry, sir," Kit interrupted. Walsingham's greyhound eyes widened a fraction. Astounded, perhaps, that Kit had dared. "Are you telling me—"

"That I am Her Majesty's spymaster?" Walsingham interrupted, as if to say, *See how you like it.* "Yes, Marlowe. That is what I'm telling you. Do keep up."

Walsingham had still not offered Kit the chair, but if he dropped one more revelation of that nature into this conversation, Kit's knees would give out on their own. Spies. Double-dealing. Lies and half-truths. Papists and massacres. It sounded like madness.

"I don't understand," he said, tasting the sharp bitterness of understatement.

The corners of Walsingham's mouth inched upward. In other men, it might have been a smile. Here, it was a geographical rearrangement of facial features. "As the Catholic threat grows," he said, "we have more enemies than I have agents to monitor them. And each time we eradicate one, ten more take their place." He raised one finger for each name as he spoke them. "Robert Southwell. William Stafford. Henry Garnet. The list," he said, abandoning the count with a curt wave of his hand, "continues. And so we have begun turning to the universities to recruit. Intelligent, discontented young men with farcical and expensive degrees, facing poverty and uselessness. I'm sure you understand."

It was not the most diplomatic opinion ever voiced about a university education, but diplomacy had been thrown out the window five minutes ago.

"When I asked Master Norgate to recommend a student who might serve, he spoke of you at length. Of your ambition. Your persuasive rhetoric. Your inability to follow basic rules of conduct, manifested everywhere from the chapel to the alehouse."

Kit stayed silent, unsure of the proper response. It was decidedly unclear whether Walsingham intended this as a compliment or an insult.

"I don't wish to interfere with your education." Walsingham made the word sound like a crude bodily function. "But in addition to your work at Cambridge, I am proposing further employment."

To hell with it. Kit gripped the back of the chair in front of him. Nothing else would keep him upright. Maybe the tobacco had been headier than he thought. There was no other way to explain what he'd heard. "You want me to be a spy, sir?"

To his alarm, Walsingham did not correct him. "You will have time to prepare for your first operation," he said. "My associate will brief you before you are dispatched."

Kit flinched at the word *dispatched*—in it, he heard the swish of an axe. He hadn't forgotten the Jesuit Edmund Campion's execution, or how the Catholic conspirator Francis Throckmorton's eyes were said to have roved for half a minute while his head lay two feet from his neck. It was treason Walsingham sought out. Condemning men to the Tower. The metal rolls of the rack, coated with copper rust. The creaking branch of the gallows. Iron pikes on London Bridge, entering one end of a crimson-stumped head and soaring out through the crown. This was the world Walsingham proposed. This was a world men died in.

"Sir," he began, "I think, I, I'm not . . ."

Walsingham's look was that of a demon told in the midst of brokering for a man's soul that his customer wished to seek a second opinion. He paused, during which time Kit forced himself to stop stammering. "I understand," he said at last. "It is a great deal to absorb at once. And with so much at stake, I do not wish to employ an ambivalent man."

Kit tried and failed to meet Walsingham's eye. Instead, he looked out the window, at the shadows drowning the courtyard as Walsingham continued speaking.

"I will give you time to consider. But under no circumstances will you speak of this meeting to anyone. My associate will contact you in the next few days. Once you have met with him, we will discuss how to proceed in this business."

Business. Was that the word for it? Perhaps to Whitehall. When was the last time a courtier said what he meant? Honesty paved a sure path to the scaffold, everyone knew that. Lies were sterling, misdirection more valuable than gold. *Business.* Perhaps.

"Here."

The sound of five gold coins striking the desk drove all other thoughts from Kit's mind.

Gold crowns sounded different against wood than silver. Their echoes were louder, more persuasive. Kit had never seen so much gold in one place, and he had no doubt that, to Sir Francis Walsingham, these five crowns were nothing. He looked to Walsingham for clarification. Walsingham absorbed Kit's shock without shifting his expression.

"Consider this an advance," Walsingham said. "In expectation of services rendered."

It never occurred to Kit to refuse the money. It chilled the inside of his palm as he swept it up. An advance. Five crowns. And how much would a scholar earn in a year? How much would a shoemaker?

"You may go," Walsingham said.

His attention had already passed to a sheaf of papers resting on the desk. Kit's mute bow went unnoticed.

———

Alone in the corridor, Kit leaned his back against the closed door. He felt light-headed, as if he'd run five miles instead of walking fifteen feet. Without thinking, his hand traveled to his thigh, where Walsingham's five crowns weighted his pocket. He could still see their brazen glint on Norgate's desk, the queen's etched portrait watching him with her golden glare. Shoemakers' sons didn't receive crowns, let alone pledge loyalty to a head that wore one. What kind of service could he offer, a man like him?

The door behind him felt too near, the mouth of a cave with a sleeping wolf inside. Kit shivered and began the slow walk back to his dormitory. His steps echoed through the deserted halls. Had it always been so silent? Had Corpus Christi always been so small? The first day he'd walked through the university's doors, it had seemed like a palace. King's School, his grammar school, could have fit inside its walls six times. But Walsingham had pulled aside an invisible curtain, revealing a world of impossible size and a host of eyes watching him from the dark.

And why not?

He paused outside his door, hand halfway to the handle. Walsingham's proposition, overwhelming at first, had taken several minutes to penetrate, but it had done so now. Why not him? Who else, here? Hadn't Norgate said . . .

Norgate. That was something else. How long had the master been watching Kit, judging, evaluating, before writing to White-hall and putting the game in motion?

Too many questions for one night. He would answer none of them haunting his own room here in the corridor. He opened the door and stepped into the room, darker now as the sun sank lower.

Tom and Nick looked up at his entrance. Kit winced. He'd forgotten he wouldn't be alone, and the thought of navigating this conversation without revealing what had happened was exhausting. He couldn't tell them a word, but it was all he wanted to do, to have someone else share the whirling disarray of his thoughts.

He took a deep breath, then let it out. Two seconds, to stitch together some semblance of calm. Judging from the way both Tom and Nick watched him—one with concern, the other with curiosity—two seconds had been both too long and not long enough.

"Are you all right?" Tom asked. He frowned as Kit took up his abandoned seat on the desk. "You look like hell."

Kit didn't doubt it. "Fine," he said, convincing no one. "Tired. A long day."

"What did Norgate want?" Nick pressed, ignoring Tom's warning look.

"To discuss my scholarship," Kit said. The answer came with more speed than confidence. Tom looked at him askance. Some spy he would make, when he couldn't even lie to his friends.

It was too much. Nick opened his mouth to say something, ask some question, a question Kit didn't trust himself to answer. Time. He needed time. An hour, two, to think. After that, he could spin equivocations like a Jesuit. But now . . .

"I'm sorry." For once, the hitch in his voice played to his advantage. "I'm feeling ill." It was a convincing performance. Ought to be—the situation did make him feel sick to his stomach.

Tom's frown deepened. "You'll find me if you need me?"

For the first time, Kit wished Tom were less kind. "I'm fine."

"Christ, Tom," Nick said. "Don't go on like you're his wet nurse. If you won't help me, Kit, I have work to do. Thanks for nothing." He spun the chair back to face the desk and left. Tom lingered a moment, then followed him without a word.

Empty now, the room seemed darker, smaller. The slanting golden light was supplemented by a sputtering candle someone had lit in Kit's absence. Probably Nick; Tom knew how little Kit could afford to spend on candles. Before Walsingham and his five crowns, in any case. The evening shadows flickered and wavered, stretched beyond their normal bounds except for an untouched, quivering circle of light around the desk.

The small leather bag of tobacco waited in a drawer, the pipe on the desktop. Sinking into the chair, he rested the bowl against the candle and breathed in the scent of flames catching the leaves. It was a moment for intoxication, but where drink would leave him slow and useless, smoke smoothed the edges of his panic. In its place grew a foggy space of not-quite-calm, not-quite-fear, but something in between, parts of both and neither.

But in addition to your work at Cambridge, I am proposing further employment.

No. He wouldn't think about that now.

Kit would give anything to silence his thoughts with sleep, but it was only early evening yet, and his mind would not quiet so easily. Years of working late and sleeping later had primed him to be most productive between eleven and three, a fact that drove Tom into fits of almost parental consternation. There were hours yet to fill, and thoughts not to think.

Well, he knew one way to stop thought.

Kit took from the drawer a pen, ink, and a sheaf of paper bearing the messy, blotted beginnings of a speech in verse. With another deep pull of tobacco, he read back through the top page, letting the rhythm of the words slow his thoughts. Almost without thinking, his lips moved to form silent syllables, ghosting the poetry into half life. The play had hovered in various stages of incompletion for years, riddled with problems and gaps. But though he wouldn't finish it tonight, the act of writing was more important than the result at the moment.

The queen, Walsingham, that could wait until morning. For tonight, he would think of *Tamburlaine*. Of Persia, Scythia, of flashing swords and blinding sun-beat fields. Of this.

The candle burned lower. Only the drip of wax and the scratch of pen on page broke the silence. The hours passed like tides, and evening turned to night, which slipped away into the weak gray of morning.

Three

rthur Gregory glanced over his shoulder. The corridor was deserted, all the dormitory doors closed, as he'd expected. He hadn't chosen this hour for nothing. Five in the morning, when the students of Corpus Christi weren't expected at morning services until six. Gregory's hand hovered a moment, a hair away from knocking, before he lowered it again and shook his head. Somehow, he hoped the boy would be expecting him. That he'd be watching the door, alert and waiting, having sensed Gregory's presence from some slight noise in the corridor. If these young university wits needed warning to know someone was coming, they weren't the sort of people Whitehall wanted, no matter how dearly Walsingham needed more men.

He entered the room without a sound.

Ah, by the devil's fiery cock. This was worse than he'd feared.

The young man sprawled on his stomach across the bed, both arms wrapped around the pillow. He might have been dead, if not for the gentle undulation of his breathing under the blankets. One leg dangled off the mattress, his bare foot brushing the floor. At this rate, it would take the opening of the seventh seal to wake him.

He's young and inexperienced, Walsingham had said, before he and Gregory left London for Cambridge. *But the master of the college speaks highly of his potential. I think you'll find him useful.*

Gregory leaned against the closed door and scowled. Useful. If England's universities could produce no better than this, Her

Majesty should shut them down like her father had the monasteries. So much for the glorious superiority of the learned. Drunk men slept like this in half the public houses of London.

Well, he thought, make do with the useless shit the Lord provides.

Gregory coughed. The boy shifted and mumbled something but didn't wake. A dozen sheets of crumpled paper littered the floor, cast aside in frustration sometime during the night. Gregory stooped down, picked one up, and pitched it hard at the sleeping boy's head.

His aim was excellent.

The boy jerked upright with a gasp, the blanket fluttering down to his hips. Horror replaced confusion as he realized he sat in bed, naked to the waist, in the presence of a total stranger. He seized the blanket and yanked it back up, scanning the dim room for his clothes.

Walsingham paid Gregory well, but not nearly well enough for this.

"Good morning, Marlowe," he said.

Marlowe located his shirt, balled up on the floor, and pulled it over his head. "What time is it?"

"Is that really the question you want answered?"

He could see the laborious process Marlowe underwent to string a thought together—not a morning person, it seemed. Marlowe combed his fingers through his hair in a doomed effort to salvage his first impression. "Who are you?" he tried again.

"Arthur Gregory," he said. "Here at Walsingham's request."

This was the nudge Marlowe's brain had needed. He rose from bed and stepped into his boots. To Gregory's profound relief, he had slept in breeches. "Pleasure to meet you, sir."

"I wouldn't be so sure." Gregory turned toward the door. He could sense Marlowe's hesitation, trying to screw up the courage to follow. If there was one thing Gregory didn't have patience for—though truth be told there were several—it was hesitation.

"Come on," he said. "Unless you want to explain me to the rest of Cambridge when they wake."

The boy might be a disappointment, but at least he could follow orders. With Marlowe on his heels, Gregory left the room.

God's blood, Walsingham, he thought. I hope you know what you're doing.

Four

From Gregory's diction, Kit knew he wasn't a Cambridge man, but he knew his way around the college as if he were. Within five minutes, Gregory in the lead, they reached the green and started north toward town. Maybe that was a required skill for a spy: locating and employing the nearest exit. It seemed like a bad omen in Kit's view.

Kit chanced a glance back over his shoulder at the college. Corpus Christi loomed above, a disapproving monument glaring daggers into his back. Its two steeples stood erect on either side of the hall's enormous window: twin guardians of the college, like two professors flanking a lecture hall. Its brown stone and clear glass were beautiful, in their own oppressive way. In that moment, Kit would have given anything to go back. At least there, he knew where he stood.

Gregory led him across the river Cam and into the aptly named Magdalene Street, leaving Cambridge's academic buildings behind. Kit frowned, following. Even with his limited understanding of royal protocol, he'd expected their destination to be somewhat less . . .

Well, less surrounded by whorehouses.

A woman in a low-cut dress whistled at Kit and Gregory from an open shop window. Kit looked away. It was too early for this. Surely a man could pretend to be virtuous at least until seven.

He swallowed his nerves. "Are you lost?" he asked.

Gregory gave the woman in the window a rude one-handed gesture. "Do I look it?"

They continued their gradual drift north, the stagnant smell of the river faint in the distance. Here, the buildings leaned over the road, heavy wooden signs and rough-shingled awnings deepening the shadows. Fetid water pooled in the gutters, bringing a scent of decay and algae to mix with the musk of whole hogs' heads leering at passersby in the butcher's window. It was not yet six in the morning and a Thursday besides, so the district was empty of its traditional drunks, gamblers, and prostitutes, but their ghosts still haunted these streets.

Kit looked at the house before them and cocked his head to one side, considering. The White Stag was an unconventional choice for an early meeting, but he saw the utility of it. In its back rooms, a man could count on being left alone. That is, unless he paid for company.

"Kit!"

The call sounded before Gregory closed the door. Kit grinned, a scrap of confidence returning. Being on first-name terms with the matron of Cambridge's least-reputable tavern might not be the best impression he could make on an associate of the royal secretary, but her voice was familiar, and in a world gone as mad as this, familiarity meant a great deal.

"Mistress Howard," he said. "Radiant as ever."

She crossed the room toward them, an older woman with coarse gray hair and the canny look of a merchant. "So you're my early morning appointment?" she said, laughing. "As I hope to be saved, I expected someone important, from the way this fellow went on," she added, jerking her thumb at Gregory.

"I live to disappoint," Kit said.

"That's as may be, but you haven't come round to disappoint my girls in ages." Mistress Howard regarded Gregory with mild interest. "Is this fellow more your type these days?"

"Mistress Howard, we're here on business," Gregory said, very red about the ears. His enunciation seemed to sharpen as his embarrassment did. "You promised me that Marlowe and I could have some professional intercourse without being disturbed."

She gave them a knowing smile. "Right you are. We've a private room round the back, and there's no judgment in my house. You're welcome to carry on with your . . . intercourse."

Kit dissolved into laughter, earning a glare from Gregory. Ah, well. Some things couldn't be helped.

Without a word, Gregory turned from the tavern keeper, Kit trailing behind, and entered the small room she'd indicated behind the bar. Nothing much: a dirty-looking bed, an uneven table and two chairs, a window with the shutters closed and locked. Gregory shut the door and faced Kit with potent disgust.

"Do you always draw so much attention to yourself?" Gregory's voice made up in venom what it lacked in volume.

"It's a curse," Kit said, straight-faced. "What kind of intercourse did you have in mind, exactly?"

If Kit had been wondering where the line was, he'd found and crossed it.

Gregory strode to the table and sat down heavily. "A piece of advice, boy," he said. "The only people who succeed doing this job are the ones who shut up and keep their heads low. Do you know why?" He drummed his fingers against the table, subdividing his pointed silence. Kit said nothing. "Because if the wrong person learns your name, your face, and your business, you're dead." Gregory's full hand dropped on the table at the word. The resultant thud was quiet, but it made Kit flinch nonetheless. "You want to stay alive? When you enter a room, you're furniture. Decoration. Empty air. Understood?"

Kit inclined his head. "Perfectly."

He took the chair opposite Gregory, feeling not unlike a swordsman at a duel. Something to remember in the future: never come to a meeting with a spy unarmed. With a curt movement, Gregory removed a page from his doublet and pushed it across the table. Kit hesitated.

"What's this?" he asked.

"The terms of your service." Gregory took pen and ink from the drawer. "Should you agree to them."

Kit took the page in one hand. Under Gregory's cold, mocking eyes, he fought to swallow the panic pooling in his throat. He took a deep breath, which caught on something as he exhaled. This was mad. Dangerous. More than dangerous. Stupid. A spy? Him? Walsingham thought Kit was qualified, but Walsingham had known him for less than ten minutes. He'd be dead in a week.

But then Kit thought of the money. Of Nick's casual disdain, of the insults the fellows slipped amid their praise, of the holes in his shoes. If he wanted to make something of himself—move to London, take his poetry out of his dormitory and onto the stage— how would he do it? How could he, with nothing but a useless degree and more ambition than prospects?

And the men Walsingham tracked were traitors. Threats to the crown. Now wasn't the time to come down with a conscience. What were a few lies, to build a future?

"Marlowe?" Gregory prompted.

It was one thing to make a decision, another thing to sign to it. Anxiety rising, Kit gripped the side of the chair for balance. A jutting nail pressed hard against his palm, the sharp pain keeping him focused. A wild image of Saint Francis of Assisi flickered through his mind. If this was God's sign that he, too, was destined to suffer, he hardly appreciated the creativity. The least-devout stigmata he'd ever heard of.

Don't think, he told himself. Do it. Heart racing, hand steady, Kit scratched a slanted signature across the bottom of the page.

Gregory nodded. The distaste in his expression had not lessened. Kit suspected Gregory had hoped he'd lose his nerve and refuse the commission, leaving Gregory free to seek out someone else. Older, more experienced—someone Gregory wouldn't roll his eyes at like an ungovernable child. Well, that decided it. Kit would do this job, and he would do it well, if for no other reason than to wipe the sneer off Arthur Gregory's face. It wasn't a noble motive, but great achievements didn't always require noble motives. Just look at the Church of England.

"Right," Gregory said. "Now then. To business."

Walsingham's spies usually received two months of training, Gregory explained. An immersive program, often overseen by Walsingham himself. But the queen's agents were short of men and pressed for time, so Gregory was forced to abridge. Two weeks, not two months. It wasn't ideal, but then, as Gregory enjoyed reminding him, choosing Kit hadn't been ideal either. They'd make do.

Kit and Gregory met in the back rooms of the White Stag daily, at unpredictable hours. Though less reputable than Cambridge's trivium and quadrivium, their curriculum was no less rigorous. Gregory drilled Kit in basic codes and ciphers. How to open private letters without disturbing the seal. Lock picking—though Kit had known that since he was seven. Names and facts and state secrets, all spilling one after the other. Practical applications as well. One Friday evening, Gregory set Kit a test: eavesdrop on the room where the house's whores took their clients, then report every word to Gregory without notes. Attention, memory, and silence, the spy's trinity. In this manner, Kit learned more about Nick Skeres and the fair Eleanor than he'd ever wanted to know. He couldn't meet Nick's eyes for days.

One morning, early, they convened in their usual room. Kit leaned against the wall, arms folded and one leg crossed over the other. Gregory stood a few feet off, firing conversation like cannonballs. He'd switched languages three times in ten minutes: English to Dutch, Dutch to French, French to German, without pause or warning. Where he'd learned them, God knew. In the field, maybe. Gregory sounded too harsh and too fluent for classroom learning. The idea of the exercise was to test Kit's suitability for foreign deployment, but it felt like a cruel joke. It was seven in the morning, and Kit hadn't dealt with German declensions in years.

"No one will ever believe you, with a German accent that poor," Gregory said in perfect Greek.

Kit stared. Unless his first mission was to assassinate the ghost of Socrates, what would he need with Greek? Besides, Kit's Greek was rusty, as his recent marks in philosophy would attest. "I'll remember that next time I'm around a judgmental German," he said, conjugating abysmally.

Gregory, not listening, threw a punch straight at Kit's head.

Kit didn't think. His body moved by itself, lunging sideways and out of range. He watched his own hand fly up, catch Gregory by the forearm, and twist, wrenching the arm behind Gregory's back. Though half a foot taller and two stone heavier, Gregory yelped, both in surprise and pain.

Kit was as surprised as Gregory. He let go, breathing hard. "What in hell was that for?"

Gregory shook out his arm. "Making sure you're paying attention," he said. His voice had regained its usual pitch. "Your enemies won't give warning either. Your reflexes are good."

"They should be," Kit said. He'd spent sixteen years in his father's house, waiting for John to stumble home drowned drunk and angry. Kit—small, bookish, and insolent even then—had made an easy target for his father's fists. At this point, he certainly hoped he knew how to duck.

"Don't get too confident," Gregory said, still in Greek. "Confidence has killed better men than you." But a change had come over the spy's face. Not in his expression, but somewhere beneath it. Kit smirked.

Gregory, for the first time, was impressed.

———

It went on this way for two weeks, enough time for Kit to fall into a rhythm. If intelligence work was no more than this, a series of endless drills and isolated tests, it might be the right path for him after all. He'd always been like this: no interest at all in subjects he couldn't see the practical use of, but once he set out to learn something he'd work night and day to master it, and if someone suspected he couldn't do it he'd work twice as hard. It brought a sense of petty satisfaction, watching someone who doubted you adjust their expectations. Yes, if it had continued like this, it might even have been a pleasure.

But he'd known, really, that this part wouldn't last.

Two weeks after their first interview, Kit strode into the White Stag and made directly for their usual back room. Mistress Howard didn't look up as he passed; even the most curious practices became routine with enough repetition. Usually, Gregory would greet him with a silent nod or a terse insult, and before Kit had taken a seat would launch into whatever exercise he had planned. Today, though, Gregory was silent. He beckoned Kit over and nodded at the chair opposite. The table between them was empty except for a single piece of paper.

"Congratulations," Gregory said, and if there was no real enthusiasm in his voice, at least there was no sarcasm either.

"For what?"

"For completing your training."

Elation and terror blended in the pit of Kit's stomach. He'd known this was coming, but he'd hoped that when it did, he'd feel as if there was nothing left for him to learn. Two weeks had barely scratched the surface of everything he wanted to know. But then, this was spy work, not a master's degree. The point wasn't to drown yourself in theory; it was to take what you knew and use it, fast.

"Both of us will be on our way before the end of the week," Gregory said. "I have another new recruit in Rheims I need to look after."

Kit would have laughed if his mind hadn't been so occupied with the phrase *both of us*. Rheims was virtually synonymous with the English College: an institution that was part Catholic seminary, part recruiting ground for malcontent recusants trying to bring the pope's influence back to England. It wasn't at all surprising to hear that Walsingham had agents in Rheims, but it was something else to hear Gregory admit it, like having Odysseus confirm the trick with the bow and the dozen axes.

"I'm flattered you didn't think I could pass as a seminarian," Kit said.

Gregory sighed. "I'm not in the mood for jokes, Marlowe. Point of fact, it's safest to assume I'm never in that mood. Walsingham and I both knew you wouldn't have lasted a day with the priests."

"So where are you sending me, then?"

"To her," Gregory said, pushing the piece of paper across the table.

Kit pulled the paper forward, bringing it closer in the dim light. To his surprise, the page did not hold another practice cipher or map or list of names. Instead, the sketched portrait of a woman looked back at him. No one he knew. But someone he wanted to.

She was the queen's age, he thought, or a few years younger. Beautiful? Perhaps not, though she might once have been. Age had spread her features with lines and a softness that looked new, a woman whom time had weathered faster than her years. But even in pencil, those black-and-white eyes gazed straight through him. Sharp. Perceptive.

Dangerous.

"Do you know who that is?" Gregory asked.

Kit shook his head.

"Lady Mary Stuart," Gregory said. "Once the queen of Scots. You'll get to know her better than you might like. But ideally not for long."

Five

"Tom, don't be angry," Kit said. He sat on the end of his bed, watching Tom pace the length of his tiny room. The rain tapped against the window in double time to his footsteps.

Tom glared at him. "I'm not angry."

Kit said nothing. He bit his tongue, letting Tom work through his thoughts alone. If Kit could have told him the truth, maybe then Tom would understand. He'd know that leaving Cambridge in the middle of term hadn't been Kit's choice. He'd know that when Arthur Gregory told you to ship out to Yorkshire to spy on the erstwhile queen of Scotland, you didn't ask him to choose a more convenient time.

But Kit couldn't tell Tom that. Couldn't tell him anything but the same lie he'd told Norgate that morning. That John Marlowe had been arrested for disorderly conduct, the kind involving four pints of beer and a pistol. That Kit had to return to Canterbury to settle with the landlord and help his mother negotiate the courts. Lying to Norgate had been simple. For all Kit knew, he might even have been telling the truth. He hadn't spoken to his father in years; God knew what John had been up to.

Lying to Tom was harder, though. It always was.

"They'll have you thrown out." The way Tom stood now, chin high as if preparing to deliver a verdict in court, was not an improvement on the pacing. "It would save them money. And half the fellows hate you. You know that."

Kit sighed. "Tom. What do you want me to do?"

Tom shook his head and glanced out the window. The freezing drops battered against the pane, soliciting entrance. Not quite snow, not yet, but soon. "Your father's a hundred miles away. He can't expect you to take care of him forever."

"I think you'll find he can," Kit said, taking his bag from the bed beside him. He had to leave. He was only making this worse by staying.

"Let me come with you, then."

Kit froze.

Tom's startled expression mirrored Kit's. He seemed as surprised to have said this as Kit was to have heard it. They were close enough now that Kit could see the small hooked scar at the corner of Tom's eye, an injury from a fencing lesson in adolescence. Not for the first time, Kit wanted to reach out and brush his fingers against it, trace them down to Tom's lips, those handsome lips Tom now bit in worry. Not for the first time, Kit placed his hands in his pockets instead. It was a friendly offer, he told himself. Nothing more.

An offer no one else at Cambridge would make. An offer he wanted from no one but Tom.

"The road's not safe after dark." Tom's voice gained confidence as he spoke. "And you're useless with a blade."

Kit's social rank forbade him to own a sword, true, but he didn't need one—he could take most of Cambridge with his fists if the need arose. But though he'd have bristled at the observation from anyone else, that wasn't remotely Tom's point.

"I can keep you safe," Tom finished.

Kit's mind shuddered to a stop. Nothing remained but Tom's eyes, dove gray and earnest, and the echo of his words: *I can keep you safe.* Kit needed to leave, but his body ached to stay, stay and find safety here with Tom in this untouchable space, this little room guarded from the rain.

Don't, he told himself. He couldn't afford to think that way. Face burning, he looked to the floor. "I have to go."

Tom had been Kit's closest friend since their first year at Cambridge. By now, he could read Kit's silences like speech. At last, he sighed and stepped to the side, clearing Kit's path to the door. Kit was halfway out before Tom's strained voice stopped him.

"Kit."

He paused, turned back. "Yes?"

Tom hesitated. "Be careful." This was clearly not what he wanted to say.

Kit couldn't trust himself another moment. Without answering, he slung his bag over one shoulder and pushed through the door. He didn't look back.

He strode through the halls with his head down—the same path he'd taken with Gregory three endless weeks before. Five years he'd known Tom. Five years he'd overinterpreted innocent gestures and spun nothings into significance. And now, Tom had . . .

No, he told himself, and opened the door. A buffet of rain slapped him, but he barely felt it. It meant nothing. He wouldn't think about that now.

———

Soon, Kit burst into the taproom of the White Stag, drenched and piqued. Damn the rain, he thought, shaking his arms in irritation. A shower sluiced off his doublet, puddling on the floor. He looked around and forced his mind to focus.

The White Stag was more crowded than when he and Gregory first met, but that didn't surprise him. No one expected a public house to do a roaring trade at six on a Thursday morning. Now, on a Friday evening, most of the tables were full. The room glowed with flickering light from the hearth and the thick heat of close bodies and overlapping voices. A handful of men tipped their heads at Kit when he entered, which he ignored. He had spent enough evenings here to run into an acquaintance on any given Friday, but that wasn't his concern at present.

He stopped Mistress Howard as she bustled past, holding a

leather purse from a paying customer. "Did anyone leave a message for me?" he said.

"Your friend arranged a horse for you around back," she answered. "And also said if you make an idiot of yourself, there'll be hell to pay. So," she added, tucking the purse into the bosom of her dress, "I would recommend against that."

If Gregory reminded him once more not to be an idiot, Kit thought, he might start taking offense.

"Another pint, mistress!" came a voice from across the room.

Heeding her battle cry, she disappeared into the crowd. Each of them had business to attend to. She would remain inside, on the dry side of the soot-stained window. Kit, on the other hand, ducked back through the front door, into the wind.

Adjoining the tavern, the stable was dark, padded with straw dyed a dingy brown from the rain. A groom, wielding a pitchfork against a sizable pile of shit, looked up as Kit entered. "Gregory's man?" he asked.

Kit nodded. Already a man without a name. That hadn't taken long.

"You're late," said the groom.

"I'm aware."

"This one's yours." The groom gestured at a nearby mare, brown with a white star. "Next post is ten miles on. And take care of her, mind, or I'll feed your prick to the mules."

Gregory must have selected this groom personally.

Kit entered the stall, running one hand along the mare's neck. The horse craned round to look at him, taking the measure of its new rider. Kit didn't doubt the animal found him wanting. He hadn't ridden a horse in a decade.

I can keep you safe, said Tom's voice in Kit's head.

No. Not tonight. He would keep himself safe, starting now. Pushing Tom's face from his mind, he focused instead on the memory of a penciled sketch, watching him with sharp black-and-white eyes.

Lady Mary Stuart.

It was true enough that Kit wasn't cut out for the priesthood, though a seditious French seminary would at least have been an easier place to start. Instead, Walsingham was sending his newest spy straight to the heart of it. Mary Stuart, Queen Elizabeth's cousin and great-niece of the old King Henry. The best hope of English papists who wanted to put a ruler of their creed back on the throne. And Kit was to keep her under surveillance. Yes, Kit had been trained, but it was still quite a task for Walsingham to give a man he met two weeks ago. When he said he couldn't afford to be discriminating, he must have meant it.

But it didn't matter. If success depended on discretion, well, Kit could be discreet. Two days after he arrived, no one would remember a time he hadn't been present. He could do this. He didn't doubt it for a moment.

Confidence has killed better men than you, Gregory had said. And worse ones too, no doubt.

"Are you going?" the groom asked, leaning against the pitchfork.

Kit patted the horse on the neck with an air of finality. "Yes," he said.

"Then go."

Six

The dense rain pounded the parlor window until Anne Cooper couldn't see more than a few feet beyond Sheffield Manor. A chill seeped to her seat near the door, which made her think there must be a crack, somewhere, between the window and the wall. How these poorly built estates weathered the generations, she didn't know. But then, she had better things to think about than the history of the English manor. Anne's hands were intent upon the knitting she'd taken up half an hour ago, moving independently of her attention. That remained on Thomas Morgan, who sat at the desk beneath the window composing a letter. The snap of the hearth underscored the sound of his pen. If only she could glean the words he wrote from the scratching on the page . . .

From the couch, Mary sighed. "You must nearly be finished, Thomas," she said. Her accent—from a childhood spent at the French court, which despite everything she made no effort to shake—imbued the words with yet more exasperation.

"Nearly, madam," Morgan said. He did not look up.

"Tell him he is long overdue," Mary said. She sat up straighter, to impart her own urgency into Morgan's writing. "Tell him I do not intend to wait by the fireside, embroidering handkerchiefs and waiting for the axe."

Anne looked at her mistress, surprised. Mary had strong cause to expect persecution, but she had never yet proclaimed without prompting that she feared her own death.

Morgan set aside the letter. Anne imagined he meant his expression to be reassuring, but his temperament was ill-suited to comfort. "You are safe here, madam," he said. "Rest easy." Not for the first time, Anne wondered how Morgan rose to prominence in Mary's household, when he couldn't tell a lie to save his life.

"I do not want you to speak in platitudes," Mary said. "I want you to write to him. If you will not, I will do it myself."

Chastised, Morgan nearly upended his inkwell in his haste to resume the letter.

"Remind him," Mary said, "that Dante wrote about a special circle of hell for traitors. And that if he proves incapable, I can find others to take his place."

Anne was so much part of the fabric of life at Sheffield that Mary and Morgan had forgotten she sat near them. Listening had long since taken precedence over knitting, and her sock suffered the consequences. She had dropped several stitches ten rows ago, and the sock now shrank at a diagonal. But what did that matter, when Mary spoke the word *traitor*? Was this only irrational suspicion, or a real threat bearing down on the house?

Instead of pressing the point, Morgan set down the pen again and glanced to the door. "Madam," he said.

Anne, turning her listening ear outward, heard the footsteps as well.

"Yes," Mary said. "I am expecting someone tonight."

"Quite right, madam."

There could have been a murderer in the hall and Morgan would have said, "Quite right, madam." Anne hadn't yet decided whether Mary's confidant suffered from an excess of political ambition or a shortage of spine.

"Anne, if you would?" Mary said.

If given the choice between supporting her mistress against threats of betrayal and playing porter, Anne would have let the visitor find his own way through Sheffield. But she'd been given an order, not a choice. She rose and ducked from the room.

The manor's entryway was elegant, Castilian marble floors and wood paneling along the walls. It, like Mary, belonged better in a

Venetian palazzo than here, three miles from a village rife with pigs and straw and shit. It was a manor fit for a queen, even a displaced one, which made the shivering man dripping mud on the marble seem painfully out of place. A young man, slim in a way suggesting poverty, with short brown hair soaking wet against his forehead. He smelled of horse and rain and something that might have been incense, but was more likely tobacco.

Anne frowned. She knew enough of the world to make distinctions among men. There was an air, a way of standing, a habit of dress that united all respectable people, and this man didn't have it. A man like this had no business calling on a Stuart. He shook the water from his hair, like a dog out of the rain. Anne's scowl deepened.

"What's your business in Sheffield, sir?" she asked.

"So this is Sheffield. Excellent." He flashed her a grin. Liking him less by the second, she didn't return it. "It's impossible to tell where you're going in weather like this. I was worried I'd ended up in Southampton."

"Your business?" she said, this time without the *sir*.

"This is the Earl of Shrewsbury's manor, home to Mary Stuart, isn't it?"

Anne nodded. No use denying that, although she didn't trust the man's habit of answering questions with another question.

"I've been sent as a footman to Her Ladyship. I believe I'm expected."

This was possible. The Privy Council arranged the bulk of Mary's staff, filling it with cowards and sycophants who could pose no threat. But no savvy London politician would dispatch this insolent madman. She scanned him as subtly as she could, and while she saw no weapons, an assassin could hide a knife any number of places. She couldn't dismiss him—there was a chance he meant what he said. And Mary expected him—there was a chance he was only who he claimed to be. But Anne had no intention of letting her guard down. These were dangerous times. Mary wasn't the only one with reason to fear.

Anne gestured toward the parlor. "The lady is within, Master . . ."

"Marlowe. Kit Marlowe. At your service, mistress. In any way you might want." He winked, and Anne understood everything at once.

By the Virgin. Was that all this was? Not an assassin. Just a fool who didn't know where his flirtation wasn't wanted. Men. Every time.

She opened the door and preceded him into the room. Mary watched them enter with interest. Morgan barely mustered a glance in their direction.

"Christopher Marlowe, madam," Anne said, taking her previous seat near the door. Let Marlowe cope with Mary as best he could. She almost hoped he'd try his would-be seduction on her mistress. It would be the last thing he did on this earth.

Marlowe stood some feet short of Mary, so as not to drip mud on the carpet. Anne watched him, first with disdain, then with shock. She must have blinked and missed some change, one actor substituting for another. This wasn't the arrogant rake she'd met in the hall. He'd metamorphosed—somehow—into an aristocrat's perfect servant. His every step spoke deference, every breath an apology.

"My lady." Marlowe bowed. "I apologize for my lateness and my, well—" He made a self-conscious gesture toward his sodden clothes.

"Marlowe," Mary said. "I blame you for neither your lateness nor your wetness. I would ask if you had a pleasant journey," she added, glancing toward the deluge outside, "but it seems evident you have not."

"The rain did slow me, madam, but it wouldn't stop me."

Well done, Anne thought. Transforming lateness into a sign of dedication. Shortcomings into virtues. Someone had taught this man well.

"I am glad to hear it," Mary said. "You may retire to the servants' quarters on the third floor. Master Beton, my chamberlain, will direct you in the morning." She wrinkled her nose. "A bath, I think, may be in order before then."

Marlowe ducked his head, choosing gratitude over offense. "Thank you, my lady. With your permission?"

A small smile passed across Mary's lips. She waved a hand, granting him leave. Marlowe inclined his head at Morgan, whose terse, unwelcoming silence was an art form in itself. Then he swept a final bow, striking the perfect balance of circumspection and extravagance, and left the room.

Morgan could learn one thing from this Kit Marlowe, Anne thought. The man was the best liar she'd ever seen. She liked him better for it, and did not necessarily trust him less. A skilled liar could be either a friend or a risk, depending on whom he lied for.

Either way, he was worth watching.

Seven

K it had slept in more than his share of disappointing rooms over the years. In Canterbury, his family's two-room lodgings held eight people, leaving Kit and Meg, his next-eldest sibling, to nest on the floor while the younger children shared the bed. Then, as an undergraduate in Cambridge, he'd shared a coffin-sized dormitory with another poor scholar, an unimaginative fellow from Warwickshire who dreamed of becoming a priest, and who snored. Sheffield's servants' quarters weren't so different: a large, open space, perhaps thirty feet long, with a slanted ceiling and a scattering of straw mattresses where the rest of the male staff slept. Not luxury, but he could bear this. And after a journey of a hundred miles, any bed would do. Moments after he collapsed onto one of the open mattresses, he fell into a deep enough sleep that only a royal fanfare would wake him.

A royal fanfare, or the arrival of Mary's chamberlain the next morning, which sent the entire room into a flurry.

Kit cracked one eye open, regarding the activity around him with the detachment of an astrologer tracking the spheres. It felt as if he'd been asleep for five minutes—the room was still dark, and through the narrow window he could see the mist of pre-dawn. God help him, but it couldn't yet be half past four.

"Get up," hissed one of the servants, giving Kit's mattress a swift kick.

He winced and dragged himself upright. He was a footman to Lady Mary Stuart, he told himself, willing the identity to stick. Kit Marlowe the footman had spent his life following orders and asking no questions. The arrival of a chamberlain—in the middle of the damned night or not—was business as usual.

In the space of minutes, the staff had dressed and made themselves presentable, just as Master Beton, Mary's chamberlain, stalked into the room. A middle-aged man with a nose like a falcon and a scowl like a mother superior, Beton sized up Kit with a sweep of narrow blue eyes. His dislike shone tangibly. Kit stood silent, bewildered. He'd done nothing to earn that dislike, at least not yet.

"I asked them to send me a proper footman," Beton said. "Not a vagrant boy."

Kit scowled. *Boy.* Someday he'd reach an age where strangers addressed him as an adult. Perhaps forty. He swept a bow, deep and sarcastic. "If I find a proper footman, sir, I'll send him your way. Meanwhile, my vagrancy is at your service."

Beton's lips narrowed. "Truly, I have been blessed," he said tightly. "You'll start on silver duty. Harper will show you the way. Then, Harper, you'll join Mannox in the stables. Elliot, you'll attend Master Morgan."

The list of daily tasks was issued with curt precision, the chamberlain running through the list of male servants with the ease of a roster rattled off each morning. Finally, Beton left them with another filthy look as a parting gift, and Kit was left to follow another footman to the pantry. It was every bit as awful as he'd feared: what seemed like an Arabian treasure trove of silver plate had been spread across every flat surface. By noon, he'd scarcely made a dent, and his shoulders and arms ached until they felt detached from his body. The fumes of polish soared to his head and left him dizzy, more potent than any tobacco.

The days continued on much the same, with Beton discovering new agonizing and menial tasks to fill Kit's time. After the silver, Kit was set to dusting the rooms on the manor's second floor along with Simon Harper, the second footman who'd led Kit to his doom that first day. He was a nervous fellow, his pale skin almost as transparent as his personality, which provided no distraction from the tedious work. For God's sake, Kit thought, he'd come here to find information, put his training to use. He hadn't come to clean a year's worth of grime from the wainscoting.

Before long, he began to wonder if this wasn't an elaborate scheme, Norgate and Walsingham colluding to teach him humility. It wouldn't have been out of character for either of them.

———

Weeks passed without any meaningful variation in the routine. Kit watched Mary as carefully as he dared, but if she and the pope drafted plans of regicide in hidden corners of Sheffield Manor, she hid the evidence well. Most nights Kit spent lying awake in the dark, turning over every word she'd spoken in his presence and testing a thousand possible double meanings. It was a dangerous pastime, and he knew it—a good spy wasn't known for an overactive imagination—but it was that or go mad from tedium.

Other nights, he found a different way to quiet his mind.

He found the attic his third night in Sheffield, wandering the halls one night when the house was abed but his whirling thoughts made it impossible to lie still another moment. Nothing much on its face: a small storage space with a single window, led to by a ladder that could be pushed out of the way to avoid obstructing the corridor. But he could do what he liked there, and in the life of a servant, he quickly saw, such places were in short supply. He came back again and again, transforming the space into a quiet, lofty sanctuary.

Tonight, the countryside lay in a hushed stillness through the window, and the moon sliced a round porthole of silver through the dark. With a groan of effort, Kit pulled himself up from the last step of the ladder, thighs and knees trembling in protest. He'd gone soft during five years at Cambridge, and day after day of hard work left every inch of his body aching. He rested his hands on the small of his back and glanced toward the dark oak chest in the corner, behind a trestle table that sagged to one side like a drunk. Inside, beneath several bolts of fabric, lay his treasure, the one he'd lifted from Morgan's study with more daring than wisdom: loose sheets of parchment, a capped inkwell, a cracked pen.

As he wrote, resting the stack of pages against his thigh, the words came easier than they'd ever done in Cambridge. Straight from his head to the paper, as if his hand weren't there to mediate them. Perhaps the mindless work of the past weeks had left his thoughts free to turn over and solve the play's problems. Or perhaps days thinking of treason primed him to spend nights on *Tamburlaine*, the story of an upstart rebel snatching thrones from kings.

He could hear Tom's voice, exasperated, in the back of his mind as he worked. *As if you don't have other things to do. You're wasting time. You've found nothing. You could be doing what they sent you to do, but instead you risk everything on this. Sometimes I wonder if you want to be found out. So you can come back.*

So you can see me again.

Kit scowled at the page, irritated by the drift of his own thoughts. Tom was his friend, yes. The first person at Cambridge he felt close to, close enough to talk of anything serious. Of course he would think of Tom now, here, alone, frustrated. And even if it was more, if he blushed like a fool when Tom spoke to him, let his gaze linger a little too long, was it so terrible, that sort of thing? God put on a show in Leviticus, but after that he more or less turned a blind eye to certain thou-shalt-nots. David had Jonathan. Jesus had John. It couldn't be wrong to miss Tom, to want to speak to him, to dream some nights of . . .

He slapped the pen against the floor. "Stop it," he said aloud.

Through the window, the bells in the village church tolled twelve hollow notes, marking one day leaning into the next.

———

Gregory told Kit to expect danger on the job—that one wrong word, one wrong look could cost a spy his life. He'd failed to mention how dull it was. Kit itched for regicide, for the threat of armed traitors storming the countryside. At least as a false seminarian in Rheims he'd have had lessons in Hebrew and Aramaic to pass the time. Not his area of interest, perhaps, but certainly better than cleaning floors.

He'd been at it for hours, scrubbing flagstones in what must have been the manor's fourteenth parlor. Surely a moment of rest was called for, so long as no one caught him. Breathing hard, he sank down in one of the armchairs, letting his head drop back to gaze at the ceiling. His arms and shoulders burned from fingertip to neck. He could have stayed here, dozing in this chair, for the rest of his life.

"Thomas," Mary snapped, from beyond the parlor door. "Thomas, damn you, come here."

Kit sat up, fatigue forgotten. When as staunch a Catholic as Mary Stuart spoke of damnation, she meant it—and Kit would risk his own damnation to find out why. He pressed close against the door, ear to the crack, just as he'd practiced at the White Stag. But the words he grasped at now were more important than Nick Skeres's inelegant attempts at seduction.

"Madam?" said Morgan's voice, emerging into the corridor.

"Has the boy brought today's letters?"

A pause. "There were none today, madam," Morgan said.

"Damn him, the whoreson bastard. He might address the next letter to my grave and save the trouble."

Mary always struck Kit as being more likely to break into an outpouring of Ave Marias than violence, but something in her voice made him fear her. That wasn't the voice of a woman passing a season in Yorkshire. That was the voice of a queen. One who could command life and death, and would, given the chance.

"I confess, I begin to question the gentleman's reliability, madam," Morgan said.

Mary's laugh reminded Kit of ravens. "Do you? A letter. If we cannot count on him for that, Thomas? Write to him again."

"And say what, madam?"

"Tell him to hurry. It seems this was not clear the first time."

Mary's voice grew fainter as she moved down the corridor. "Frighten him, if you can. He tends to be more useful when afraid."

"Yes, madam," Morgan said, following.

Kit sat back on his heels. Letters. Urgent letters, and an unreliable correspondent. Hardly worth a report to Walsingham. In Mary's position, waiting for letters like a Jew for the Messiah was hardly surprising. What else was there to do in exile?

But her anger *had* been surprising. And it was as close as he'd come to news in weeks.

It was worthless by itself, but if he learned whom Mary wrote to, who could say?

———

Kit did his best, in the days following, to sound the rest of Mary's staff about whom she might be writing to and why. It was a delicate business, trickier than listening behind closed doors. Overly direct questioning and Sheffield's servants would wonder why he'd taken such an acute interest; not direct enough and his hints would fall aside useless and unnoticed. So far, he'd achieved nothing—which meant, he decided, that he'd need to change tack. No risk, no reward.

Late nights had been Kit's one moment of freedom at Sheffield, but he abandoned his practice of writing in the attic and sat up instead in the servants' wing, joining his fellows as they allowed themselves at last to relax. They'd gathered in the men's quarters that night: himself, Simon, Matthew—Mary's groom—and Anne, all sitting on the floor in varied states of exhaustion. It would be a wonder if he didn't fall asleep. Kit's limbs seemed to sink into the floor the longer he stayed still: another twenty minutes and the ground would swallow him whole. But there was something to be said for a shared state of half attention. Conversation turned looser late at night. Who knew what Mary's servants might say when at ease?

Matthew took a healthy pull on his hand-carved pipe, smoke

whispering in streams from his nose, and passed it to Anne beside him. She ventured to the male servants' quarters now and again, passing a free evening before wandering back to her own bed, though Kit couldn't say why. It wasn't for the pleasure of his company—she had enough opportunities to shoot him accusing looks during the day. And it certainly wasn't for the tobacco, as she passed the pipe to Kit without comment.

"Not much for smoking, Cooper?" Matthew asked.

Anne shook her head. "It's a vile habit. Fit for prostitutes and sailors."

Kit laughed. "Clearly you've never smoked," he said. "Transubstantiation at its finest. The breath of God from a leaf." He closed his eyes, inhaling deeply—Christ's blood, he'd gone a long time without this. "Forget bread and wine," he said to Anne, passing the pipe on to Simon. "If Christ wanted people to respect the sacrament, he should have magicked himself into tobacco."

Anne looked at him with some alarm. Her eyebrows had begun to climb at *transubstantiation* and had still not reached their summit. Before she could take Kit to task for blasphemy, though, Simon broke down in an aggressive fit of coughing, a thick plume of smoke belching from his throat.

Kit's shoulders shook with silent laughter. "Yes, well," he said, "it's an acquired taste."

"Make an effort not to die, Sim," Matthew said, arching his back in an exaggerated yawn. "I'm going to bed."

"It's early," Simon whined, with another cough to shake out the smoke. "Live a little, for once?"

Matthew stood and shook his head. "I'm off at the second bell for Cresswell, after that fellow Babington. That's more than enough living for me."

Cresswell. Kit leaned forward, reminding himself to breathe. This was the first Kit had heard of any communication outside the manor. Mary lived in exile, and in Yorkshire, and under strict surveillance by the queen. There were only so many people she might be in contact with. And Babington of Cresswell, it seemed, was one. The name meant nothing to him—or to Simon, judging by the footman's enduring lack of interest. But it was more than enough to catch his attention.

"You sound elated," Simon said drily.

Matthew sighed. "As you'd be, if you had to speak to him. I hand over his message and he barely looks at me, like he thinks his letters appear from midair. Not a word of thanks, no care for the horse, just a door shut in my face and it's back on the road."

Simon muttered an oath as Matthew slouched off to bed, cursing noblemen of that nature to an impressive variety of hells. Kit, for his part, had never felt so alive. Matthew wasn't just visiting Cresswell; he was carrying letters. Who else but Mary's unreliable correspondent? It would do him no good interrogating Matthew about the messages he carried. The groom couldn't read, no doubt in part why Mary had chosen him as her messenger. Still, it was closer than Kit had dared to dream of coming.

And there was something else to consider, too. The way Anne's head tilted at Matthew's words, the faintest display of interest. Nothing, unless you were looking for it. For a spy starved for information, it was a great deal more than nothing.

Anne was Mary's most trusted servant. If Babington was important, Mary would have mentioned him before, and Anne would know why.

All he had to do, then, was get Anne Cooper to talk.

———

Three days later, Kit found himself on his hands and knees, scrubbing dirt between the flagstones in the south corridor. Dirty water splashed up his arms and soaked his breeches, which combined with the filth under his palms to make him feel like part of the manor itself, a disembodied force that kept the household running. It was degrading work, but satisfying in its own odd way. Filth made an easy target for anger, and after almost six weeks at Sheffield with minimal progress and only a name to go on, he had enough frustration to work out on the deep-caked dirt. It made him think of his mother, the way she'd scour pots with the ven-geance of a soldier after losing an argument with his father. God knew with six children and a drunk husband, she had enough rage to vent into household chores. As he watched the cracks between the stones fade from dirty black to a pale gray, he wasn't sure if becoming more like her gratified or unnerved him.

"Kit, for God's sake, there you are."

Kit glanced up and swore. From the far end of the corridor, Matthew rushed toward him, his boots tracking ovals of mud along the tiles Kit had spent all morning scrubbing. He flicked his rag toward Matthew's muddy footprints, leaving a scattering of droplets in its wake. "Christ's light, if you think I didn't just finish cleaning that."

Matthew, reeking of horses and indifference, did not react. "Beton's called us to the servants' hall," he said, gesturing for Kit to follow. "If you don't hurry, it'll be your own blood you're scrub-bing off that floor."

There was truth to that. With a last scowl at the mud, Kit tossed the rag to the ground and followed Matthew, his own watery foot-prints behind the groom's.

They edged into the hall, where the full staff had already assem-bled, Beton standing before them like a general on a battlefield. Whatever he'd summoned them for, it had only elevated the chamberlain's overall sense of self-importance, which rolled off him in waves. Kit ducked his head and slipped into the back of the group, trying to take up as little space as possible. With luck, his delayed entrance hadn't been noticed.

"Marlowe," Beton said. The crowd shifted, putting Kit back in the chamberlain's line of sight. So much for subtlety. "Thank you for your dramatic arrival. Imagine if, one day, I had no need to ask myself where you were or what you were doing. How dull my life would seem."

Evidently Beton's repertoire of insults included sarcasm as well. It was a discovery Kit would have been happy to live without. "I can leave and come back later, sir, if you'd like to build suspense."

Beton's lips narrowed, but he gave no other indication that he'd heard. He began to pace in front of the assembled servants, his hands interlaced behind his back. "In three days," he said, "Sheffield will host a visitor. I expect the height of obedience for the duration of the visit. No mistakes. No indiscretions. I hope it's clear, Marlowe," he added, "that I am referring to you personally."

Kit inclined his head in wry acceptance. It didn't matter: Beton's manifest dislike, the obvious reputation he'd earned himself, none of it. Sheffield was to have a visitor, the first Kit had seen in all these long weeks. He couldn't imagine what sort of person might make a social call on a deposed queen under house arrest, but whoever it was, they were the sort of person Whitehall would be eager to know about.

"I will allow none of you," Beton continued, "to let Master Babington depart with anything less than an exemplary impression of this household. Or the consequences will be as severe as it is within my power to make them."

The chamberlain's threats escalated from there, with ever-increasing levels of specificity and violence, but Kit was no longer listening. The world around him ceased to matter once Beton spoke the name. Babington would be coming to Sheffield. The haughty gentleman from Cresswell, the mysterious recipient of Mary's letters, the man who irritated and galvanized Mary more than anyone else Kit knew of. Enough waiting—everything would come to a head the moment Babington set foot in the manor. And Kit would hear what the gentleman had to say to Mary, come what may. Even if—God forbid—he had to behave himself to do it.

Eight

Early in the evening when Babington was set to arrive, Kit retreated from the rest of the staff, toward his attic refuge. He would need all his focus in the days to come, and anything he could do to gain a sense of calm would, he reasoned, only strengthen his resolve. Besides, no one could fault him for a tiny respite, forty-five minutes constructing the latter half of a scene. He frowned with the pen between his teeth, then scratched out a line of verse he'd spent a quarter of an hour adjusting and, somehow, had only made worse. Outside, the storm raged on, rain battering the glass in harsh drops that thickened steadily toward snow. Every so often, a low rumble of thunder sang out in the distance. It was the perfect ambiance for *Tamburlaine*, that persistent growl evoking invading armies, though the abysmal quality of his work did nothing to show it. He'd thought poetry would clear his mind, but even as he shaped the letters, all he could think of was Babington's pen, scribbling down missives to Mary Stuart and sending them off by messenger into the rain.

Through the open door to the attic, Kit heard hurried movement and the sound of two voices hissing to each other.

"Move! You think Babington will wait for you?"

"Where the devil is Kit? If he thinks I mean to do his job and mine—"

Babington was here already? He wasn't expected for two hours. Kit swore and flung his manuscript into the trunk, then bolted for the door. There should have been time to finish the scene, hide the evidence, and arrive at the same moment as the other servants.

Of course, a gentleman was never early, his hosts only unprepared. But this felt dangerously like being ahead of schedule.

Kit tore downstairs and into the entrance hall, where a contingent of footmen waited for their guests to present themselves. Breathless, he skidded to a stop beside Simon, who made a show of not looking at him.

"I thought you weren't coming," Simon said under his breath.

"I value my life," Kit said, keeping his eyes on Beton.

With a mistress under house arrest, the chamberlain seldom had occasion to flaunt his professional skill to anyone but Mary and Morgan. Since the announcement that a visitor was en route to the manor, the chamberlain resembled a flustered hydra, sprouting new heads to berate everyone at once for trivial offenses. But now, with only minutes remaining, he didn't say a word about Kit's lateness. Watching the door, Beton shifted his weight from one leg to the other, like a child in need of a privy. Kit's nerves had been strung tight before, but the chamberlain's anxiety drove him near distraction.

The door burst open, admitting a fierce blast of rain and a howl of wind. Kit flinched, drawing back from the storm, as two men rushed inside toward shelter. Beton had led them to expect an influx of newcomers, making the pair look, in Kit's view, somewhat forlorn. A gentleman, tall and slender, and his valet, some ten years older than Kit—they both looked worse for the weather and in none too pleasant a mood. The valet slammed the door behind them, the sound landing almost in time with a clap of thunder from beyond. Kit watched as the gentleman stripped off his cloak and threw it to the valet, revealing beneath it a cerulean doublet of obvious quality. The valet caught the sodden cloak without looking and folded it over his arm, as though accustomed to having things thrown at him.

So this was Anthony Babington. Kit didn't know what he'd expected. Someone older, at least. Babington might be within a few years of Kit's age, though he carried himself with the haughtiness of a fifty-year-old duke as he approached the chamberlain.

Still, there was something compelling about this young aristocrat, the imperious set of his slim shoulders and his hooded eyes. He was almost too good-looking, so handsome it was unsettling to look at him directly. Babington had a saint's face, meant for viewing by candlelight. At once a disdainful gentleman and a noble heretic, persuaded there were worse things than hellfire.

"Sir," Beton said. "On behalf of the Lady Mary Stuart, you are welcome."

"Mm." Evidently the travel-worn gentleman was not known for his scintillating repartee. "Show me somewhere I can change. This weather's not fit for rats to move in."

"Of course, sir. Harper—" Beton rounded on Simon, who looked like his dearest wish was to sink into the floor. "Escort the gentleman to his chambers. Marlowe, show Master Babington's man to the servants' quarters."

Kit swallowed a protest. Simon was a nervous wreck under the best of circumstances. He was more likely to escort Babington into a broom closet by accident. And Kit would give anything for five minutes alone with the gentleman. Babington looked like the type who would say anything in front of his servants, considering them incapable of thought. Jaw tight, Kit turned to the valet, who smiled in return. It was the least sincere smile Kit had ever seen, and an instant flame of distrust sparked in his gut at the sight of it. Without a word, Kit started up the stairs.

A normal man would have followed several steps behind, but Babington's valet kept close to Kit's shoulder, sharing each stair with him. In the intermittent candlelight along the stone stairway, the valet glittered with energy. There was a swagger to his step that seemed foreign to his role, as though he thought he could play everyone in the manor like a lute. If his game was to irritate Kit, it was working.

"Marlowe, your name was?" the valet said.

Kit lengthened his stride, attempting to keep a stair between them. No luck. What wouldn't he have given for longer legs. "Yes."

"Charmed. Robert Poley."

Kit nodded. Lying was his profession, but telling Robert Poley it was a pleasure to meet him pushed the limit.

"You know your way around, I'll give you that," Poley remarked, as they passed the second landing and took a series of tight turns toward the servants' stair. Babington's cloak, still over Poley's arm, dripped against the floor.

"I hope so. I live here."

"True," Poley said. His smile looked like a cat seconds before it disemboweled a mouse. "You've been here long?"

A faulty understanding of personal space, Kit could forgive that. He could even ignore an unnerving smile or an insincere countenance. But a habit of asking questions was beyond the pale. Perhaps the man was merely making conversation, but Kit saw no reason to take the risk.

"Long enough," Kit said, as they reached the landing. He gestured toward the door. "If you'll excuse me. My mistress needs me in the hall."

Poley gave Kit a small bow, as false as his smile. "Yes," he said. "I expect she does. I'm sure I'll see you again."

Kit took the stairs two at a time. He sincerely hoped Poley was wrong.

———

The dining room's floor was swept to a shine, its walls papered with a green and gold pattern of vines and leaves and lilies that made Kit's head swim. In the center stood a long table: built for twelve, set for three, occupied by two. Against the wall, Kit closed his eyes and fought down a sigh. He'd never been patient at the best of times, but two hours standing here waiting for Babington was frankly ludicrous.

He couldn't have prayed for a better chance than this. Kit was the only footman in service that evening, Beton having realized that, despite his own misgivings, Kit's theatricality would suit the occasion better than Simon's twitchy anxiety. The only other servant on hand was Anne—but then, Anne was always on hand. She sat on a small wooden chair by the door, steadfastly knitting away at a shapeless square of wool. Each click of one needle against the other set Kit's teeth on edge. Mary and Morgan had managed to fill the first hour discussing the news from London—nothing of interest. The second hour had been a diplomatic tour de force on Mary's part, as she fought to keep Morgan from dragging Anthony Babington downstairs by the ear.

"You're certain Babington has arrived?" Morgan said, glaring at Kit.

"Yes, sir," Kit said, for the sixth time.

"Thomas," Mary said. If not for her unshakable poise, Kit suspected she would have put her elbows on the table and taken her head in her hands. "He will be worth your wait."

"I'm sure, madam," Morgan said, though he did not stop glaring at Kit.

Kit looked away. He could volunteer to seek Babington out. If he caught the gentleman alone . . . But before he could voice the suggestion, Mary and Morgan looked to the door. Kit turned as well. Anne shot him a disapproving glance, which he ignored. True, it wasn't his place to be curious, but he'd stood in this drafty room for two hours. Extenuating circumstances were to be considered.

Anthony Babington bore no sign of having ridden through a biblical storm earlier that evening. He had changed into another doublet, this one in bold crimson, with an elegant ruff that reminded Kit of a young lion. Babington had seen to his hair, and Kit caught a note of perfume as the gentleman walked, head high, toward Mary and Morgan. His faint smile was not apologetic in the slightest.

As Babington approached the table, taking long steps intended to showcase his legs, Morgan pressed one fist to his mouth, somewhere between thoughtfulness and loathing. After weeks in his service, Kit knew Morgan well enough to read him. Babington was a shameless dandy, but that wasn't why Morgan hated him. Babington could go, and had gone, where he pleased: Paris,

Rheims, London, anywhere. Meanwhile, Morgan—like Kit—had been trapped within these four walls, never venturing farther than a corridor's length. For a man with Morgan's aspirations, an idiot with freedom of movement must have been unbearable.

For Kit's part, everything he needed was right here. This exiled queen. Her irascible councilor. And this self-satisfied, good-looking gentleman, a peacock amid the pious, at risk of spilling his secrets.

Watching Babington take his seat across from Mary, Kit couldn't decide what feeling possessed him. Interest, certainly. Respect, possibly.

Then he saw that Babington had brought his valet. Identifying his reaction to that was simple.

Easy to see, now, where Poley took inspiration for his manner. The imitation was poor at best. The self-possessed swagger in Babington's walk was like a wild cat in motion. In Poley, who boasted neither Babington's youth nor his good looks, it reminded Kit of a tavern brawler. When Poley took his place beside him, Kit pointedly ignored him.

"My lady," Babington said. His lack of a bow visibly grated on Morgan's nerves, but he didn't seem to notice. "Forgive the delay. The weather. You understand."

"Of course, Anthony," Mary said with a barbed smile. "Clothes make the man. As you have repeatedly informed me."

In that moment, Kit liked Mary more than ever. Someone had to put Babington in his place. Two hours. Kit hadn't been able to feel his feet in ages.

"Just as they make the woman, madam," Babington said. "Might I add that you look—"

"You may not," Mary interrupted. "If I want flattery, I will pay my footman a shilling to liken my eyes to sunbeams."

She waved a hand in Kit's direction. Kit wiped the smile from his face. He'd wanted to earn Mary's trust, not her attention. Fortunately, Anthony Babington had better things to do with his head than turn it for a footman, however loquacious.

"God forbid I grudge you your pleasures, sir," Morgan said coolly. "But I'm not certain you understand our situation."

Babington found something of pressing interest on the floor. Kit, having been on the receiving end of Morgan's ire more than once, could hardly blame him. But when Babington looked up again, his glimmering courtier's smile was perfectly in place. "I understand quite well. To the matter at hand, then. I think you'll be pleased with my report."

Mary's insincere smile sharpened, until Kit feared the curve of her lips might reveal fangs. "For both our sakes, Anthony, I certainly hope I will."

"Never doubt it," Babington said. He leaned back, draping one arm over the chair. Morgan's eyes narrowed. But Babington had a trump left to play, something to justify this mad confidence. "His Most Catholic Majesty is nothing if not faithful."

Anne's knitting needles stopped clicking.

Both Kit and Poley leaned forward as much as they dared, desperate to catch whatever came next. Kit glanced at the valet without turning his head—what did an arrogant ass like this care about Babington's report? But perhaps he shouldn't have been surprised. Any thinking man would want to hear what followed an opening salvo like that.

Morgan's expression was a masterpiece of contradiction, equal parts eagerness and exasperation. He turned to Kit like a soldier sighting a pistol. "Boy, fetch a flagon of Anjou from the cellar," he said. "Master Babington must be weary from riding."

Leave? He couldn't leave now. Kit's mind was in a frenzy of connection, pulling together facts and conjecture almost too fast to follow. His Most Catholic Majesty. God's light. Spain. It had to be Spain. No ruler wore the pope's approval as proudly as King Philip. So Mary Stuart communicated through Babington with Philip of Spain. Mary, the would-be claimant to the throne, and Philip, ruler of the most powerful nation ever to loathe and be loathed by England. It didn't require a Cambridge education to put the pieces together. And he'd be thrown out before he could hear what followed.

Poley looked at Kit sideways. "Go, then," he said under his breath. Kit didn't think he imagined the pleasure in Poley's words.

The thought occurred to him, wild, half formed—could he hide? Watch through the keyhole and ...

And earn himself a dagger point through the eye. He bowed low and walked with feigned composure toward the door.

"Poley," Babington said from behind him, as an afterthought. "Run to my rooms. I believe I've left the window open, in a storm like this."

Kit could see the shock on Poley's face without turning. He smiled. It was a cruel smile for a petty pleasure, but sometimes cruel and petty were all one had.

"Yes, sir," Poley said.

Kit opened the door and stepped outside, Robert Poley on his heels. For a moment, they stood in silence.

They looked at each other. They looked at the door. They looked at each other.

"Damn it to hell," Poley said.

They turned in opposite directions and tore off at a dead run.

The wine cellar was two flights down, almost directly beneath the room where the trio in council now sat. And every stair Kit took stole another word from him. Another thought. Another plan.

Kit's breath stabbed at his side as he flung the cellar door open. This was what he deserved, for spending five years sitting at a desk. He couldn't remember the last time he'd run so hard, and his legs and lungs both burned as he skidded across the floor, raking the racks of bottles with his eyes. His body yearned to catch its breath, but every moment cost him dearly, and if a little pain was the price to pay, then he'd pay it. Kit seized the nearest flagon of wine—he had no idea what it was, and did not care—and bolted back toward the stairs. A maidservant had just turned the corner on her way to the larder; Kit nearly knocked her flat as he charged down the corridor. He stammered an apology, catching himself on the wall, and sprinted up the stairs, her angry shout following after.

Not too late, he thought. Don't let it be too late.

He halved his pace ten feet from the door, panting for breath. Composing himself as best he could, he adopted a look of total uninterest and slipped back inside.

"I will, of course, remain in constant correspondence," Babington was saying. He cast a glance toward Kit—or, more accurately, toward the sound of the opening door.

The words stripped Kit of breath. As if someone had fastened a noose around his neck and pulled. Too late. Babington had already said his piece. And every scrap of information Walsingham could have used had blown away into the storm.

"Constant correspondence would be an improvement," Mary said. "Let me remind you, Anthony, that in my circumstances I rely on you for news. I cannot wait for your convenience to know where I stand."

Babington shifted like a chastened child. But for the moment, Kit wasn't looking at him. He was watching a pair of knitting needles, dancing in and out of loops of wool.

Anne. Anne, who'd been there all along. Anne, who would have listened, even if she hadn't meant to.

"You know where you stand, madam," Babington said. "In the favor of God."

"And too soon for comfort in his presence," Mary snapped.

"Madam," Morgan cut in, with a sharp look at Kit.

The door opened, and an out-of-breath Robert Poley re-entered the room. A faint sheen of sweat coated his brow. He looked at the conversation unfolding at the table, crestfallen. Kit didn't spare him so much as a smug look. He ducked his head and filled Morgan's glass, praying none of his thoughts showed on his face. Retreating from the table, he chanced a glance at Anne. Her hands continued their thoughtless work, expanding the shapeless mass of her knitting. Perhaps she hadn't noticed anything. Politics bounced off servants' ears like light from a mirror.

But Kit had heard. *I cannot wait for your convenience to know where I stand.*

No question, then, of if. Only when.

Nine

Thomas Morgan belonged in Sheffield's servants' quarters as much as the pope belonged in Constantinople. And yet, the next morning, there he was, framed by the door like a medieval saint in a church recess, staring down the fleet of servants as they hastened to their feet. The pale sunrise washed out identical expressions of surprise on each face. In his panic, Kit could conjure only one explanation for Morgan's presence: one of the servants was on course to be hanged. And if that were the case, he had a good idea who among them it would be.

Kit could feel Poley watching him from across the room. Small wonder why—Poley had witnessed Morgan's distaste for Kit with his own eyes last night, and he seemed the type to take pleasure in another man's pain. Kit looked down at a long, narrow scratch on the floor. If he died today, he would not let his last sight on earth be Robert Poley's face.

"I wished to express my appreciation for your service last night," Morgan said. "The situation was sensitive and required precise handling, and you all performed well."

Kit almost laughed. Appreciation? From Morgan? Unlikely. But Morgan had not spoken the words so much as extracted them from his mouth like a crossbow bolt from a wound. And in any case, he wasn't finished.

"In light of that," he went on, "the Lady Mary has granted you a day's leave, to spend how you wish. She, Master Babington, and I will require nothing."

Kit chanced a look at Morgan, then looked down again. Sure enough, Morgan's glare had fixed on him. This dismissal, like last night's, was personal. An excuse to shunt Kit from the scene while priceless information still percolated through the manor. But Kit couldn't protest. None of the servants around him looked likely to argue against a day's furlough in the village, no matter what was being discussed indoors, and resenting the gift would only attract attention. He inclined his head toward Morgan, acknowledging the glare without commenting on it.

It was not ideal. It was the furthest thing from ideal. But some of his work could be done outdoors as well as in.

Outside, the air was cold enough to ache Kit's chest. Last evening's rain had turned to snow, burying the last traces of moldering leaves and muddy footprints under a crust of powder and thick ice. Free from the manor, the bulk of Sheffield's staff turned their steps toward a seedy-looking public house on the far side of the village. Kit could see the attraction: under Beton's puritanical management and Mary's moralistic rule, the servants weren't apt to find that particular kind of pleasure at the manor. But Kit had his eye on a different sort of satisfaction.

Anne watched them go, her lip edging toward a curl. In the winter light, her reddish hair reminded Kit of brass. "Animals," she said, to no one in particular.

Kit, beside her, nodded. "Sinners all."

From the elevation of Anne's eyebrows, she believed Kit would spend every waking moment in a whorehouse if given the chance. On another day, he might have been offended.

He shrugged. "Not my style," he said.

Anne still seemed unconvinced, but a faint smile crossed her face. "Well. What are your plans, then, Master Not-My-Style?"

You, Kit thought. You, and what you know. He spread his arms wide. "I'm persuadable."

Anne turned away, striking off toward the north end of the village. "Come on," she said without looking at him. "After last night, I need a drink."

Kit grinned and started after her. He might make something of the afternoon yet.

Anne led the way to an outwardly unpromising tavern across from the main square, where she palmed over a few coins for a bottle of sack. Feeling that spending the day indoors would defeat the purpose of liberty, they took the bottle back outside with them. A low stone wall circled the main square, to keep cattle from escaping on market days. Kit brushed the snow from it and sat beside Anne.

She passed Kit the bottle, and he drank, first apprehensive, then grateful. Excellent. Ages better than the cheap swill he'd been able to afford—or steal—in Cambridge. That made sense, he supposed. In a village where there was nothing to do but raise sheep or slaughter them, a man might as well be able to get comfortably drunk.

"Can I ask you something?" Kit said, passing the bottle back.

"May I live to regret it," she said.

Go easy, he thought. A simple question to get her talking. And if it satisfied his own curiosity too, well . . . "Is there a reason you hate me?"

For someone with such a fierce moral position on lechery, Anne drank like a professional. "I don't hate you."

"Really?"

"I don't drink with people I hate."

Sure enough, the dislike she'd flaunted in their first interview had faded. At least she could sit beside him now without issuing a barrage of silent threats. When had that happened? Perhaps Kit's personality was an acquired taste. He wasn't sure he liked the implications of that.

"I needed this," Anne said, taking another drink before passing the bottle. "Another day inside with Master Morgan and by the Virgin, I'll go mad."

Kit laughed. Anne's professional demeanor was unimpeachable. He'd never considered she might be acting too. But that knowledge made his job easier. In such close proximity to Mary and Morgan, the thousand petty annoyances filling Anne's days would take their toll. And a sympathetic ear was a powerful weapon, if he wanted her confidence. A spy's alchemy, turning empathy into gold.

"He's a bastard, no mistake," Kit said.

"And he hates you. We're laying bets on how long you'll last before he throws you out."

"What's your wager?" Kit asked.

Anne shrugged. "I gave you three months."

"Generous."

"Make an effort, will you? I'd like to win."

"This is me making an effort. If it isn't enough, only Mary's kindness will save me," Kit said, and waited.

He didn't dare risk a more direct transition: nudging the conversation, more than redirecting it. But Anne didn't need much to warm to the subject. She smiled—an actual smile, not her usual mocking one, as if she'd waited for him to say Mary's name. She leaned back, supporting herself on her palms. When she spoke, it carried the same cadence Kit had heard the Cambridge rector use when reading from the New Testament.

"You've enough to count on," Anne said. "She's been through so much, and somehow she's still as generous as she is. I don't know how she manages it. Sometimes I think she must be a saint."

She put a curious weight on the last word, one Kit didn't know what to make of. He thought, on a whim, of the Holy Maid of Kent, whose prophecies had haunted the king a generation before. Inspired, divine fervor. Speaking the words of a God you'd seen in person, who sat in the same room, took meals with you. Of course, Elizabeth Barton had ended with her head on a spike. It all came back to that.

"I wouldn't call her a saint, if I were you," Kit said.

"And why not?"

"Curious thing about saints when they're not protected," Kit said. He feigned interest in a pack of children engaged in an unskilled game of knucklebones in the middle of the square. "You wouldn't believe the terrible ways they can die."

Anne looked sharply at him. "Who was your teacher," she said, "who gave you faith like that? Not the queen's church."

Kit felt the conversation slipping out of his control. He wouldn't learn anything by talking about himself. "Not exactly," he said, following the thread, grasping for a pivot. "And not my parents either. The most orthodox Protestants you've ever met. I'm the family disgrace, the way I've come out."

"Is that so?" Anne's gaze was now so intense Kit could no longer pretend he didn't notice. She'd given this more significance than he'd intended, and in the wrong register, one he didn't know how to follow. If he wanted to shape the conversation, he would have to push it. Take a risk and hope it didn't cost anything he couldn't afford to pay.

"Being a disgrace is my specialty," he said. "If Morgan could have thrown me from the room last night with his own hands, he'd have—"

"Do you mind if I join you?" asked Robert Poley.

If ever Kit had been tempted to kill a man, it was now. Poley strode up behind them, hopped over the low wall, and sat on Anne's opposite side, legs splayed out to take up twice as much room as a man needed to. Anne inched closer to Kit, widening the distance between them. Clearly Kit's distaste for Babington's valet wasn't an isolated phenomenon. Well, Poley's interruption might make Anne like Kit better, comparatively. In present company, the competition for "least unlikable" was not fierce.

Kit gave Poley a smile he'd learned from his mother, one that wished its recipient an agonizing and creative death. "Yes," he said. "We mind very much, actually."

"Forgive me," Poley said, though he made no move to leave. "I didn't realize I was interrupting a seduction."

Before Kit could voice an objection, Anne took up the task. "By the Virgin, no one asked you, you nosy shit," she said. She stood up, and the movement made Kit's heart sink.

"No?" Poley smirked. "Apologies. If you're free, then, mistress, maybe I might—"

"Has that ever worked for you?" Anne asked. "Ever? Once?" She drained the bottle and tossed it with a muted thump into a nearby pile of snow. Poley watched, seemingly more impressed than put out. It was as if the idea that Anne might openly reject his company had never occurred to him. "Kit, I'll talk to you later," she said over her shoulder, already crossing the square away from them. "This part of town seems to have a rat problem."

As Anne swept back toward the manor, Kit twisted his spine to glare at Poley. "Are you satisfied?" he snapped.

Poley grinned. "Seduction. I knew it. You want to board her, boy, don't let her shake you off any time there's a ripple in the water."

Kit stood and turned his back on Poley, walking off in the direction he and Anne had come. It was that or punch the man square in the face, and though Kit could handle himself in a street brawl if he had to, his cover as a respectable servant was already on weak footing.

He'd speak with Anne again that evening. He'd have to. Start by commiserating over Poley's interruption, then nudge the conversation back to where they'd left off. He could make it look natural. It wasn't all lost, he thought, as he crossed in front of the inn again, deeper into town. All right, it was mostly lost. But there was other work he could do this afternoon. Speak with Matthew, perhaps. In staking his hopes on the meeting, Kit had all but forgotten the letters, but for want of a better option—

"Well, imagine meeting you here."

Kit jerked to a stop. The sudden loss of momentum caused him to slip on a patch of ice beneath the snow. He barely stopped himself from falling, wrenching his back in the process. The pain didn't register against the shock of that voice. And, as he turned in search of it, the sight of the speaker, a square-shouldered man in his middle thirties with short gray-gold hair. He wore a ratty brown cloak and stood in front of the inn's stable with a wry smile.

"Gregory?" Kit said.

"No, it's Edward the fucking Confessor. Honestly." Gregory's face was serious, but Kit could see the amusement beneath it. Clearly he enjoyed Kit's shock.

"I thought you were in Rheims," Kit said.

Gregory shrugged. "I was. Now I'm here. I was set to meet somebody else, but you might as well join. Come in, unless you want the world to hear."

Gregory disappeared into the stable without another word. Kit watched the empty space he'd occupied, equal parts shocked and exasperated, and followed.

The air hung warmer inside, with the nutty brown smell of straw and stagnant water. Six or seven poor-looking horses stood within, available for rent to any with an equal shortage of money and scruples. The animals watched them with eyes that glistened black like beetle shells. Kit took a step toward Gregory, who didn't edge back.

"I don't suppose you could have warned me you were coming," Kit said. "I—"

"Spare me, Arthur, I know I'm late," said Robert Poley, sauntering through the stable door. "I was trying to—"

Kit turned. Poley made it halfway to where Gregory stood before he froze. His too-bright eyes locked on Kit's. Other than the fervent dislike on Kit's end, Poley's shock mirrored his exactly.

Poley regained his composure before Kit did. "Hello again," he said. He leaned against the low stall door, resting his palms along the top.

"*You're* a spy?" Kit said to Poley.

Poley grinned. "And to think of the effort I wasted watching you."

Gregory laughed, drawing a scowl from Kit and reminding him how much he detested being laughed at. It wasn't as if he expected Walsingham to hand out the names of every agent in his employ, but the fact that Whitehall had set a spy in Babington's house-hold as his valet seemed, in Kit's uneducated opinion, like critical information. He crossed his arms, then, realizing it made him look petulant, uncrossed them again.

If Gregory noticed the five different emotions Kit had cycled through in the last thirty seconds, he ignored them. "You've exceeded my expectations, Marlowe," he said. "I thought I'd find your corpse on the side of the road."

"Did you come all this way to insult me?" Kit asked.

Gregory smiled. "No, though I might have done. London wants news of your progress. I was to get Poley's today, and as luck has it I've caught you both. If you've found anything, let me know, and I'll keep Walsingham informed."

Kit's fingernails bit into his palms. Six weeks. Six weeks he'd been on the job, proving he could do everything Walsingham asked and more. Was being treated like a competent human so much to ask? See what Gregory made of this.

"Mary and Babington are in league with King Philip of Spain," Kit said. "He came with a message too sensitive to be put to paper. But 'His Most Catholic Majesty is nothing if not faithful,' or so he says. And her maid heard every word of his plan. I spent the morning with her, until this man"—with an expansive gesture at Poley—"interrupted us."

Gregory looked at him, stunned. "They're in league with Spain," he repeated.

"Can't say I'm surprised, can you?" Poley said. "The only place you'll find more papists is Rome, and they're too busy excommunicating the French to bother with us."

"What was Babington's message?" Gregory said.

Kit and Poley looked at each other.

"We don't know," Poley said.

"Yet," Kit cut in.

Gregory groaned. "A plague on the sacrament, don't do this. You were there to know there was a message. And you were sent away. You both, specifically?"

Gregory was sharp. Kit would grant him that. "Yes," he said. No good denying it. "Us both, specifically."

"And you've been given leave? In the middle of the day? Right after—"

"Arthur, I know," Poley interrupted, raising a conciliatory hand. "The boy's new. He made a mistake. But it's nothing I can't handle."

"*I* made a mistake?" Kit repeated. "I just need more time—"

"If I'm hearing you right," Gregory said, "we don't have time. Poley, you're in too deep, but watch yourself, I won't be responsible for scraping your brains off the floor. Marlowe, you're out."

Kit stared. Out? Just when Anne was on the brink of telling him everything? Yes, the risk had grown, but this was intelligence work, not a tennis match. Risk was part of the game.

"Mary trusts me," Kit said. His voice sounded high, pleading, but it was too late to fight that. "It's not her, it's her man. It's Morgan. I—"

"You've done well," Gregory said, as if Kit were a schoolboy searching for praise. "But I won't have you kill yourself with your own stupidity. Get back to Cambridge, and we'll use you from there."

"Don't mother him, Arthur," Poley said, exasperated. "The boy knew the risk when he signed on."

"Walsingham's orders," Gregory cut in. "Pull him out if he's compromised. You think you know intelligence better than Walsingham, Robert, you go to London and tell him as much."

All this time feigning servitude, Kit had forgotten that his life was directed by a different master. He couldn't remember ever having felt this tired before. Anne trusted him. Mary trusted him. And Walsingham would throw all that away, with nothing to show for it. "How do you suggest I leave? I can hardly tell Mary I'm off to Cambridge."

Gregory shrugged. "You're a poet, don't you spend half your life spinning lies? You'll work something out. Oh. Another thing." He unearthed a folded page from his pocket and gestured with it. "Bit of a winding path to get this to you. Walsingham had me bring it on my way. Have a secret lover writing you sonnets?"

Kit held the letter in both hands. His stomach dropped. He didn't need this now.

He knew that clumsy hornbook lettering, the way the *s*'s in *Corpus Christi College* were all written backward despite the candlelit lessons he'd given their author years ago. Only one person would write to him this way, without the polish of formal education, addressed not to *Ch. Marlowe*, but *Kit*.

"Hardly," he said to the page. "This is from my sister."

Poley gave a long, lewd whistle. "A pretty boy like you has a sister? Introduce me. I'll give her a night she won't forget."

"Another word and you'll be lucky to remember your own name," Kit snapped.

Not only did Kit have a sister, he had four, and a brother not yet breeched when Kit left for Cambridge. Good solid Christians, he often said, keeping the church in business. Baptisms charged by the head, after all. He didn't want to think about them now. What he wanted was to burn the page without reading it. His eldest sister, Meg, could have written to him for any number of reasons, none of them good.

Gregory and Poley looking on, Kit unfolded the page. There were only five words. It took no time to read them.

Jane dead. Childbirth. Come home.

If Gregory looked for a response, he would have a long time to wait.

Jane. Eight years old when he'd left for Cambridge. His sister. Little Jane.

"Well, go on," Gregory said. "Poley, back to work. Marlowe, make your excuses to the heretic. Walsingham will call on you at Cambridge soon with next steps."

Jane dead. Come home.

When Kit looked up from the page, Gregory and Poley had gone. But there were enough ghosts in the stable to take their place.

Ten

The cloudy sunrise gave Canterbury the feel of linen washed once too often, soft and fading to gray. Kit arrived in the dead of early morning, when the pious were already in church and the impious still abed, but the hush couldn't mask the danger in his decision to return. When Walsingham learned of this unsanctioned detour, he'd have Kit's head. He followed the length of High Street, keeping his distance from those he passed. There weren't many to avoid. The occasional pilgrim or merchant brushed past, leaving soggy footprints in the snow. A pair of widows gossiping in lowered voices, a child chasing a cat with a broken tail, a . . .

Kit blinked, and the fair-haired man at the end of the street became only another stranger, cloaked and booted against the cold. The man turned down Saint Margaret's Street, out of sight. The dull ache in Kit's chest sharpened. He closed his eyes and let himself feel the hurt.

If it had been Tom. If he hadn't been alone.

But then, he wasn't alone. He had Jane's specter for company.

They'd walked this direction together, he on his way to King's School, she to the baker's for bread, kicking pebbles along the dusty street. He'd raced her along this road, from Saint Andrew's Church to the Bull's Stake, his longer legs leaving her behind, though in an indulgent mood he'd let her win. Here, there, everywhere, his sister had been, and now was not.

Thirteen. Married off before you could see her breasts, and

expected to carry a child. He understood, in theory. A family with more children than it could feed had to be resourceful. Sons were apprenticed out, or sent to school if they were bright enough to manage it. If a daughter could be pushed into the arms of a husband, so much the better. But Jane. It hadn't been theory for her.

The kings and saints set into the cathedral's west tower loomed overhead as he walked. Comfort, for some. Reassurance of an ever-watchful God. Reassurance for fools and the ignorant. He itched to scream, swear, anything to shake their gaze. What good did it do them, guarding the dust of a dead archbishop? Had those sainted bones ever answered a prayer? Narrowing his eyes at the church, he spat into the gutter. Let angels strike him down as a blasphemer if they cared to. If God was watching, Kit wanted to ask how he planned to answer for Jane.

His legs knew the way from here, though it had been years since he'd traced this path. Along King Street, where the way narrowed, the bulk of the cathedral disappeared behind worn shingles and the hanging emblems of shop fronts. He saw his father's sign from the end of the street, and he felt his feet falter. It would have been so easy to turn around, to claim the letter hadn't reached him. But he'd come this far. After all that, to be frightened off by a building? Even this building. The shop, and the lodgings above it where Kit had grown up, had endured as the church's carved kings had: roughened, not moved, by time. It was wedged between a tinsmith's and a shuttered building that once housed a tailor. A wooden board covered the upstairs window, where a drunk had once sent a rock through the glass when Kit was nine. Never fixed, which he supposed he should have expected. Everything Kit hated about the place had only intensified since he'd been away: its shabbiness heightened, its harsh edges harsher. Even the smell, leather and beer and sawdust, seemed to spill from the threshold, spreading its influence into the street.

But the blue-eyed man who opened the door to Kit's knock, he was new.

"Who are you?" the man asked.

"I might ask you the same," Kit said. He tried to slip past the man, but a firm hand pushed him back.

"Christ, you're from the constable. We'll pay when we can. Now get out, or I'll have your balls on a spit."

Kit ran a hand through his hair. For God's sake. John *was* back in prison. As he'd told Norgate, thinking it a lie. "Let me in," he said. "And leave my balls out of it."

The man tried to close the door, but Kit pushed forward. He winced as the door slammed against his shoulder, jolting pain down to his fingertips.

"If you want me to leave," Kit said, "it'll take more than a door."

The man's fist moved fast, but Kit moved faster. He sidestepped the blow, sending it breezing six inches from his ear. They locked eyes. Kit grinned, in a way meant to unsettle. Not thirty minutes home and here he was, his father in prison, bracing for a brawl.

"Who's there?"

Kit couldn't see the woman who'd spoken inside, but he'd know her voice anywhere.

The man didn't break Kit's gaze. "Constable's boy."

"Well, tell him to— Kit?"

Five years was a long time. Margaret Marlowe had grown, as had Kit. But in every way that mattered, she hadn't changed at all. They looked alike, she and Kit, always had. Light brown hair, upturned eyes, a delicate arch to their cheekbones. Years ago, strangers in the street would ask if they were twins.

"You came back," Meg said.

"I got your letter. You still make your *s*'s the wrong way round."

She laughed and embraced Kit. When he'd left home, he'd towered over her. They stood of a height now. It felt like he'd shrunk, not like she'd grown taller.

Noticing the man's tight fists and Kit's scowl, Meg gestured at Kit with unconvincing casualness. "Bill, this is my brother Christopher. Kit, William Bradley. My husband."

Kit knew she'd married, a year or two ago, but had never seen the man. This quick-fisted brute was her husband? Meg's sense of humor had never been cruel, but Kit wished she were joking. "Congratulations," he said.

Bradley said nothing. The promise of a blow still hung between them.

The threat wasn't lost on Meg. "Come in," she said. "Mother's upstairs."

Kit winced, exhausted at the thought. He loved his mother. A man only got one, after all. But it was a bit much, to be hauled in front of Katherine Marlowe after all this time to account for his life and behavior. After a point, silence felt easier.

"How is she?" he asked.

"Getting better, I think. She doesn't talk of it much, and I don't like to ask her. She grieves in her own way, you know."

No one had solicited Bradley's opinion, but Kit suspected this had never stopped him before. "Sorry business, but it's to be expected. Not the husband's fault Jane couldn't carry. She should have kept her legs together another year."

"Excuse me?"

Kit had never wanted to kill a man more. Not his fault. Who else would you blame for forcing a child on Jane, barely more than a child herself? Should have kept her legs together. As if that had been Jane's idea.

Meg gave Kit a warning look. "Come in," she said. Bradley, after a moment's silence, stepped aside. Thankfully, he didn't follow them in, but pushed past Kit into the street. Toward the tavern, Kit imagined, to commiserate with his fellows over the appearance of his high-and-mighty brother-in-law. Bradley had that air about him.

Encompassing the entire first floor, John's workshop held the semi-sacred silence of a chapel, dust motes suspended in beams of light. Nothing had changed since Kit's last day under this roof. He paused at his father's bench, trailing one finger along a half-constructed sole like a coroner considering a body. He'd sworn never to set foot in this workshop again, never to look back, never to return to the life he'd dodged by a hair's breadth. Until now, he'd kept that promise.

He pulled his hand away. Jane, he reminded himself, as he took the stairs two at a time. Think of Jane.

"Christopher!" said Katherine as he opened the door.

His mother looked paler than he remembered. Thinner, too, as she rose from the edge of the bed and took Kit in her arms. Her shoulder blades protruded beneath her dress like wings. Kit patted his mother on the back, itching for release. His proper name would have been intolerable from anyone but her, from whom it merely grated. Try explaining to her that *Christopher*, the name of a saint and a shoemaker's son, no longer had anything to do with who he was.

She brushed a hand against his hair. "I knew you'd come back."

It took a true master of rhetoric to make the phrase *I knew you'd come back* sound like *I couldn't be more surprised you're here*. In that regard, Katherine Marlowe rivaled Cicero.

"Of course I—"

A torrent of words beat back the rest of his sentence. His mother had stored up five years of questions, and she'd be damned if she didn't ask them. "Look at you, half wasted away. Can't you take care of yourself? Up all hours squinting at books, I'm sure, forgetting to eat, you'll catch your death. And what's taken you so long, Christopher, doesn't a degree take three years? Don't tell me you've turned vagrant."

Kit laughed. He'd never had an actual defense against his mother's accusations of vagrancy before. Was this what responsible sons felt like all the time? "I'm six months from a master's, Mother."

"Oh?" she said, just left of impressed. "That's something. You ought to tell the master from King's, what was his name?"

"Gresshop?"

"That's the one. He always liked you."

She had always been like this. His mother had the same amount of mothering to give, regardless of how many children she spread it across. That was how her grief for a lost child manifested, in a tremendous wave of concern for the ones who remained. He'd welcomed it, once, when he was small. Her sudden flashes of affection after tracing the path to the churchyard every few years, the family shrinking by inches. Mary, Kit's older sister, dead of fever before his fifth birthday. Thomas, a little squalling thing, lived barely long enough for baptism. Stephen, her name for the unchristened boy who was two days dying. And now Jane.

The difference, now, was that someone could be blamed for Jane.

Meg laid a hand on Kit's shoulder, cutting between him and Katherine. "Mother, he should go. Before the day gets on."

"You're right." Katherine sighed. "Best get that over with. They'll listen to him."

Kit winced. Of course. In this world, sons existed to serve their fathers. Financially. Spiritually. In his case, legally. As if Kit had the time. At least in Westgate prison, John Marlowe couldn't cause trouble. Well, if they wanted Kit to play savior, he would play it. Anything to leave this ghost-filled house where his mother spoke to a boy who didn't exist and his still-sleeping younger siblings, if he woke them, wouldn't remember his name.

"Come with me, Meg?" he asked.

She smiled. The weight in his chest didn't lift so much as shift sideways. He'd do it; it had always been his responsibility, and no one else was as good at it as he was. But he wouldn't do it alone.

The bells sounded half past as he and Meg left the house. Day had broken, and sunlight cast a glimmer against the muddy snow. Kit walked half a step ahead.

"Wouldn't it be nice if once we found him at morning prayer instead of prison?" Meg said, lengthening her steps to catch up.

"I'd be less surprised to see him burning down the church than praying in it," he said, then he sighed at Meg's frown. "A flaming pox on the Trinity, Meg, I'm joking." Somehow Kit's near-professional skill at swearing did not reassure her.

After they'd walked for a few minutes, the prison rose up at the end of High Street. Its two cylindrical towers were notched with crenellations from its time as a defensive outpost, and narrow windows pockmarked the walls: egress for an arrow or the barrel of a gun, but nothing wider. Between the towers, the city gates stood wide, welcoming travelers on the road from London. Westgate, a prison built into an open door. The irony couldn't have been lost on its residents.

When Kit pounded a fist against the prison's side door, the shutter behind the barred window pulled back. The pointed face of a porter peered out with a nervous air ill-suited to his profession. He glared at Kit, who gave him a smooth smile in return.

"I'll be seeing John Marlowe," Kit said. He almost laughed at Meg's surprise. His voice had leapt up a register, the voice of a privileged gentleman who could make the world jump with a word. She should get used to that. Cambridge had taught him plenty, including how to act.

The porter, too, seemed shaken, but he recovered. "Not without the provost's approval you won't, boy."

Kit's smile didn't waver. He dipped into his pocket and procured a scrap of paper, which he held aloft between two fingers. "I think you'll find everything's in order."

The porter squinted and cursed, unable to read the page through the small window. Meg's surprise turned to suspicion. Not without reason.

The page was blank.

Kit turned his head and winked, so only Meg could see. *Trust me*, said the wink. After Sheffield, a ruse like this was a grammar-school game. Sure enough, he heard the harried jangle of keys as the porter flung the door open.

"I'll need to—"

All right, Kit thought, drawing his knife from his boot.

The porter went silent, the point of Kit's blade now pressed between his ribs. Meg's eyes widened. Built small like their mother, Kit knew he wasn't imposing, but a knife could make any man look six feet tall. His hand held steady, and his smile broadened.

"Now," he said, "I think you were about to invite us inside."

"Right away, sir." The porter edged back into the prison, Kit and

Meg following. If only Kit had tried that as a child. Think of the time he could have saved. *Sir*, even. Quite a promotion over *boy*. As they followed the porter through the narrow halls, Meg made a point of not looking at Kit.

The porter stopped near the end of the hall. He indicated a wooden door identical to those on either side. "I can give you ten minutes, sir. More would cost me my job." He cringed, fearing Kit's displeasure.

It was curious, seeing men cringe before him for a change. Kit didn't mind it. "We'll only need five." He reached into his pocket and produced a shilling, which he flipped in a neat arc to the stunned porter. Meg's eyebrows rose. Unexpected confidence was one thing, unexpected capital quite another. Well, she'd do better not to ask questions. The porter inserted a key into the lock and, with a well-placed shoulder, forced the door open.

The room lacked light to see clearly, but Kit's memory of the space remained intact. The brick-and-mortar walls, the wooden board of a bed, the shallow dirt pit prisoners used as a privy. Kit would have thought one visit to a room reeking of another man's shit would be enough incentive to avoid repeat arrest. He swallowed a retch as the door closed behind them.

"Father." Meg's voice echoed off the stone. "It's Meg and Kit."

"Let me see you," said their father from inside.

Against his better judgment, Kit stepped toward the shaft of light filtered through the window. As his vision adjusted, John became clearer, seated in the corner with arms looped around his shins. Kit crouched so they were eye to eye, like a hunter inspecting a kill.

Was this the man he'd feared since childhood? This tall man folded in half, dark eyes sunken, beard matted? The slanted light caught new strands of gray in John's hair, making his bruised cheek and split lip look ridiculous. He was nearly fifty now. Kit hadn't considered that. He'd thought John ageless. The man who'd given him two legacies: a name of no value and a driving need to escape. No giant now. Only an old man in a cage.

John stood up. He wavered on unsteady legs but braced himself against the wall. Kit rose in one easy motion. He didn't move to help his father.

"What are you doing here?" John said. He still sounded drunk. Was that possible? "Thought you were too good for us now."

More than he knew. "I can go, if you like."

"Right." John stepped forward. Kit still had to look up to meet his eye. All he'd done, all he might still do, and he'd never be taller than his father. "Go. Leave. You've never been good for anything else."

Without asking, Kit knew how John found himself in prison. Sitting at his usual table in the back of the Griffin, throwing back pint after pint. A toast to Jane's memory, though after an hour he wouldn't have remembered his own name, let alone his daughter's. Rage rising as the drink did. With his bookish son off at university, John would have had to find someone else to vent his anger on. By the looks of the split lip, that someone hadn't borne it with the submission Kit used to. A better Christian might have sympathized. Kit didn't have energy for that. Saint Christopher would bear any burden on his shoulders, but Kit had never aspired to canonization.

"All right," he said, turning to the door. Meg put a hand on his shoulder, but he shrugged her off.

"You useless shit," John said.

Slowly, Kit turned back. "I'm sorry?"

John advanced another step. The move felt familiar, a childhood echo, only now, Kit didn't flinch. "You think you're better than us? Look at you. Writing verses like a damned court fool, whoring about with any slut who'll let you near her diseased cunt. I'd take my name back from you if I could, see it die rather than you carry it."

"Kit," Meg said. She had, after all, seen him pull a knife on a porter with less provocation. But Kit had no desire to threaten his father. He knew an easier way to hurt him. They were alike that way.

Instead, he laughed.

"Your name?" he said. "Twenty years from now, when men talk about Marlowe, I promise they won't mean you." He turned away from John and knocked on the door, despite Meg's protests. "Porter? We're finished."

The door opened again, easier this time. Kit stepped squinting into the light. Meg hung back. He heard her murmur something to John, didn't know what, didn't care to. Then she followed him out. The porter shouldered the door closed and locked it with a satisfying click. Ignoring Meg's half protests, Kit pressed a small purse into the porter's hand. The porter opened it and gaped, dazzled by silver.

"Have him released tomorrow, around nine," Kit said. "He can spend today thinking things over."

The small fortune eroded what remained of the porter's dedication to protocol. "As you say, sir."

"Well, Meg." Kit turned to her with a smile that sat sour on his mouth. "Shall we?"

She knew what he meant without asking.

———

Jane Moore. 18 January 1572–26 November 1585. Requiescat in pace.
Kit crouched before the small white stone, tracing the letters with his thumb. The snow soaked through the knees of his breeches, but he paid it no mind. "It's not even her name," he said. The name of her murderer. They'd laid her to rest with that.

The high hedges around Saint Andrew's churchyard shielded the plot from the late-morning activity of High Street. White graves, barely distinct from the snow, stretched in tight rows across the narrow yard. As for living occupants, the hedged-in space boasted none but Kit and Meg. A sparrow perched on the head of an eroded angel, watching them with uninterested beady eyes. It had seen hundreds of brothers and sisters, wives and mothers and husbands traverse these gates. If it lived another year, it would see countless more.

Meg held her cloak close. The snow dusting the grave rendered the new-tilled earth identical to the ground around it. Jane had been gone for days. It looked like years. "The parish donated the stone," Meg said. "Said it was the least they could do."

"It was," Kit said, not looking at her. "God spent less time in that church than she did."

"Kit, do you enjoy blaspheming in churchyards?"

He stood, and Meg took a step back. The sparrow fluttered its discomforted feathers and took to wing, a small speck against the clouds. "She was a child, Meg. Your God has killed children in his name before, but what good does it ever do?"

"Kit, please. People will hear."

He didn't mention that they were alone in the churchyard, that only the dead could hear him. "I can't believe you married him," he said. The words slipped out before he committed to saying them. If his mouth left his brain time to think, he'd have stayed silent. But his mouth had never been good at doing that.

Meg looked at him with disdain. "Why not?" she said. "You think you have the right? I haven't seen you in years. You don't know."

Kit began to protest that he did know, he knew Bradley's faults. His arrogance, his crudeness, his quickness to anger. His willingness to punch unknown visitors on sight, even when they proved to be his brother-in-law. But he wasn't given the chance. Meg was like their mother in that way—when she had something to say, she'd say it.

"I know why you hate him. I live with him. I know. He's no saint." Meg folded her arms across her chest, hugging her elbows in opposite hands. Protecting herself, Kit thought. Against what, he didn't know, and wouldn't ask. "But I won't do better. Business keeps him in London half the year. And he brings money. He takes care of us, Kit."

He kicked at the snow, scattering a small flurry across the grave. *He takes care of us.* A job that should have fallen to Kit.

But what was he meant to do? Stay in Canterbury and become, what? A man stooped decades before his time. Gray hair and a hunched back from bending over the shoemaker's bench, reeking of leather with fingers cramping around the needle. Or huddled in his own Westgate cell, tracking the days with scratches on the wall. Listening through the bars to the cathedral bells calling the faithful to the bones of a martyred saint, while not far away he rotted in a nameless crypt of his own.

He sighed. If she'd ever left Canterbury, ever thought about the possibility of something else, she'd never accuse him. She'd understand, then. "Meg, I had to—"

"Go to hell, Kit," Meg said. "We all knew you'd only come back to bury us."

He tried to respond. Faltered. She was right. Abandoning them had been the goal all along. Why accept the scholarship to Cambridge otherwise? Why embrace Walsingham's schemes? He looked at Jane's headstone but thought only of dragging himself from this living grave, by education or court favor or whatever else it took.

"Please," Meg said, hugging her own arms tighter. "Don't let her hear us like this."

The gravestone stood silent behind them. *Jane Moore. 26 November.*

"She can't hear us." Kit's voice was cold, toneless. A churchyard voice. "She's dead. That's it. Nothing after."

Meg's voice hardened. "So you're leaving again? Just like that?"

He shrugged. "I'll stay tonight. Mother expects it. And I need to speak to the landlord about the rent. But I'll go tomorrow."

"Can I get one answer from you, if nothing else?"

Who knew? The days when Kit could answer questions without hesitation were gone. "Ask and we'll find out."

"Did you rob a convent on the way here, to pay the jailer?"

Despite everything, he laughed. Arthur Gregory was hardly the moral equivalent of an abbess. No doubt Walsingham's man had discovered by now that his new protégé had cut his purse on the way out of Yorkshire. Well, it served him right for treating Kit like a child. "If it's money stolen from helpless nuns, I take it you won't want this?"

Meg, stunned, caught the purse he tossed her. She weighed it in her hand, judging the quantity of silver from its density. Kit smirked. Meg might deride him all she wanted, but anyone could see the money had impressed her. Had she known where it came from, she might not have been so quick to accept it, but money was money without context.

"Take care of yourself when I'm gone," he said. "I'll write to Mother when I reach Cambridge."

If he hadn't known Meg better, he'd have said she was almost crying. "She can't read, Kit."

"No," Kit agreed, turning. "But you can."

Eleven

Kit leaned against the doorjamb, holding his mud-splattered cloak close. The pose served a dual purpose: not only did it look casual enough to mask his nerves, but it kept him upright, which he doubted his ability to achieve unaided. He'd arrived at Cambridge fifteen minutes before, coming here directly after the irate night porter had dragged him to Norgate's office to explain himself. He hadn't even sat down yet. Every muscle in his body screamed that this could wait, until he'd eaten, until he'd slept.

It couldn't, of course. He wouldn't let it.

The dormitory looked just as he remembered it, spartan and impersonal. The bare walls, the small bedstead, the desk heaped with a whirlwind of papers. And sitting with his back to the door, the only person who could give this tiny room such brilliance, turn it from cell to shrine. Tom made an irritated noise and swept up two pages from the desk. Kit, knowing Tom's habits and the lateness of the hour, suspected they were the first draft of an essay. One not due for two weeks, most likely, but Tom was a diligent student, and his sporadic late-night productivity helped him cope with occasional bouts of insomnia. In any case, the essay wasn't long for this world, as Tom crumpled the pages into a tight ball.

"Aquinas, you self-righteous masochist," he said to the book before him—Saint Thomas Aquinas's *Summa Theologica*; Kit could just make out the title. He pitched the crumpled pages over his shoulder. They landed two feet from Kit's boot. "Just because you drove away prostitutes with a fire iron doesn't mean you can tear the joy from my life."

"That's the spirit," Kit said.

Tom froze. His shoulders stiffened. At last, he turned.

He looked the same, Kit thought, as Tom stood up from the desk. His fair hair still caught the candlelight like gold. His gray eyes still mirrored the room's shadows. Even his expression—that blend of pleasure, surprise, and exasperation Kit was so often on the receiving end of—even that was the same. Of course it was. Kit had been gone a matter of weeks. How much could a person change? Plenty—he himself was living proof. But Tom was the same. That same silence Kit couldn't interpret. The same unspoken questions thickening the air.

"When did you get back?" Tom asked.

"Just now," Kit said. He closed the door as he entered, kicking the corpse of Tom's essay aside. Rambling seemed preferable to this frightening silence. "What's that about prostitutes and fire irons? And here I was, worrying you'd become a monk without me to corrupt you."

"I'm not cut out for monastic life, you'll find," Tom said.

Kit's fists clenched tight enough to flash white knuckles through the skin. He'd never been this petrified, not even in Mary's service, but he couldn't afford to miss this chance. The risk of his new life made that clear. If he didn't ask the question, he'd spend every day wondering what would have happened if he had.

"Tom," he said—a good start, but God knew where he meant to go from there. He put his hands in his pockets, took them out, interlaced his fingers behind his back, released them. What did people do with their hands at times like this? "Can we talk?"

Tom leaned back against the desk. "Aren't we?"

"That's not what I mean." He swore. "I want you to be honest with me." Was that his voice? That couldn't have been his voice. His voice didn't sound like that.

"Always," Tom said. His smile faded. Kit didn't know how to read what replaced it.

"Do you . . . I mean, have you ever . . . when you said . . . did you want . . ."

Words. How did they work? And he called himself a poet.

Tom pushed himself off the desk toward Kit. His movements were graceful, but underneath that uncertain. Kit, in a rush of daring, took the last step forward until his right hip nudged Tom's left. They had been this close before—no boundaries in a college as small as Corpus Christi, and neither of them had ever taken an especially puritanical position on how much space God's creatures were meant to keep between them. But they'd never been this close on purpose. It thrilled and terrified him in the same breath.

"Tom, if you don't, I wouldn't . . ."

"For God's sake, Kit." Tom's voice was soft. He was smiling again. "Shut up. Yes."

Forget his own verses. Kit never wanted any kind of poetry but this. The poetry of Tom's fingers against his skin. The poetry of breath catching in his throat. The poetry of a *yes*.

Tom brushed a strand of hair from Kit's forehead, then cupped his cheek in one palm. Without meaning to, Kit leaned into the touch. Hungry. He was so hungry for this. To be held this way, wanted this way. By Tom. No point denying that now.

When Tom kissed him, he was almost too startled to believe it.

Kit had kissed and been kissed before, but never like this. At first, Tom's kiss was gentle, chaste even. Leaving the door open for a misinterpretation of Kit's pathetic stammering, a pull back, averted eyes and a mumbled apology. An apology Kit did not want. He pulled Tom closer, one hand weaving into his hair, and slipped his tongue between Tom's lips. Tom pressed back, his breath and his body together a sigh. His hips fit perfectly against Kit's, firm and warm and real. His breath in Kit's lungs was heaven.

The room around them disappeared. Nothing existed but Tom. His body was so warm, the taste of him intoxicating. Kit couldn't breathe. It hardly seemed possible.

When at last they pulled away, Kit's fingers slid down from Tom's shoulder to close on his hand.

"How long?" Tom asked.

Kit stared. As if between the two of them, Kit's feelings had ever been the subtle ones. "I don't know," he said. "Five weeks. Five years. Forever. Does it matter?"

Tom eased Kit's cloak away, tossed it over the chair. "No," he said. "You're right. It doesn't."

Kit shivered, but not from cold. "So," he said.

Tom laughed, a laugh that harbored a thousand suggestions. "Seeing as you're back," he said, his smile broadening, "what would you say to a proper welcome?"

What would Kit say to that?

Nothing at all.

No persuasion, no hesitation. The pressure of Tom's hands against his shoulders, the taste of his lips, his smile. Kit thought his chest would burst. Nothing had ever compared to this before. He would never, never be able to stop.

Tom moved fast, confident. He stripped Kit of his shirt, then his breeches—awkward and inconvenient, as it ever was, why was clothing such a damned nuisance? Fingers mastered buttons, flung aside fabric, and still Tom's eager, impatient hands caressed him, explored him, woke his body from a long sleep. Tom pushed him backward, onto the bed. Kit gasped, having forgotten how strong Tom was, having forgotten how deeply he liked that strength.

Tom shucked off his own breeches as he straddled Kit's hips— preoccupied with Kit, his own clothes seemed to have slipped his notice until now. He glowed, bared chest and strong thighs perfect in the candlelight. Tom kissed him again, and Kit felt pulled up toward him like a plant to the light. Kit heard himself whimper; God, it was pathetic, hadn't he possessed dignity at one point, some sort of self-respect?

Undressed and unapologetic, Kit pulled back for a moment, just to look at Tom. Every curve and line and inch, everything he'd imagined under cover of darkness, a hundred times more beautiful for being real. Tom was real. And smiling, that smile, impossibly broad, shot through with a spark of mischief.

"Is something wrong?" Tom asked, smile dipping at Kit's hesitation.

Wrong? This? "It's not fair," he said. "For you to be this perfect. How dare you."

Tom laughed and kissed him again. Kit hummed into Tom's lips, a hum that Tom escalated to a moan with a slow roll of his hips, but Kit couldn't bring himself to be embarrassed, or to spare a thought for the dormitory's paper-thin walls.

There was only this. Only them. This feeling, a low, warm expansion, relief at some great weight tumbling from his chest. Their bodies crushed together, lips and chest and hips and legs, a shameless tangle, impossibly close, impractically perfect. The trembling lightness of knowing that for once, doubt didn't matter. That nothing else would ever make as much sense.

Nothing more natural. Nothing more honest.

The peak of it, deep, shocking, rising, felt like Kit left his own body, like the ocean rippled in his veins, like he had swallowed the stars.

He collapsed back, breathless.

Tom wasn't long behind. He lay beside Kit, breathing hard, the shadow of a laugh in the exhale, the sweet mist of sweat dampening his skin. The candlelight and its shadows were wondrous, Kit thought. Tom's body looked like a statue, gilded in shifting bronze. To hell with any other muse. This would do. He could have gone on lying there forever, curled in the curve of Tom's side, feeling Tom's heartbeat against his own ear, pulsing with the life of him.

Several minutes passed before Tom spoke, voice dry with understatement. "Well. Here we are."

Kit laughed, unable to help it. Everything seemed funnier now. "Here we are indeed. Christ. I'll write sonnets in honor of your cock."

Tom made a derisive noise and shoved Kit off him. "Highest of all poets, you."

"It's not fair, keeping your talent a secret. All of England deserves to know." He adopted a grandiose tone and traced a one-armed arc before them, illustrating the title page of an imagined volume. "Watson and Marlowe, inheritors of the cult of Venus and Adonis, or, I mean, I suppose Adonis and Adonis, if you want to be anatomical—"

"Shut up, you." Tom kissed him to ensure it.

If every order to keep silent came with a kiss like that, Kit would happily never speak again.

"And you, my dear poet, were magical for a first time," Tom said, when they lay again side by side. He brushed one hand against Kit's forehead, sweeping away a renegade strand of hair. It had grown longer in the time Kit had been away. The tacked-on clause, that *for a first time*, snagged in Kit's ear, but the thrill of Tom's touch kept him from lingering on it.

"As I say," Kit said. "Anyone who doesn't love tobacco and boys is a fool."

"Do you say that?" Tom asked, eyebrows raised.

"I fully intend to start."

Tom laughed. "Mind who you say it to."

Kit felt the glow of his happiness flicker. "What do you mean?"

Tom sighed. "Kit, don't. You're misunderstanding me on purpose."

It was not on purpose. "But—"

"I'm not saying I'm ashamed." Tom propped himself up on an elbow. Kit forced himself to focus on Tom's words instead of the sweep of freckles along his chest, this lean bare body right next to him, touching him, his. It was so damned hard to focus. "God's death, I think I want this more than you do. I've been daring myself to ask you for almost a year."

"A year?"

God. More than three hundred days of heaven wasted. Kit could have wept.

"But you know we have to be careful."

Tom was right. The law was clear, though Kit couldn't remember an instance of its ever having been enforced. Sodomy was punishable by death, along with a whole brood of sins Saint Paul had sprinkled into his verbose letters to the Corinthians. In the rush of warmth still flooding his body, he'd forgotten what was now becoming inescapable—that speaking the truth about anything would undo him. Even something as beautiful as this.

"Don't worry," Kit said. "I can keep a secret." He could say the words, but could not keep the bitterness out of them.

Tom, sensing Kit's discomfort, lay back and wrapped one arm around Kit's shoulders. Kit nestled into the space with a sigh, taking comfort where it was offered. "Have you told Norgate you're back?" Tom asked.

A heavy-handed change of subject, but at this point, Kit would take it. "He did most of the talking," he said. "I'm held to the same requirements this term as everyone else, he said. So if you need me, I'll be neck-deep in last month's reading, trying not to kill myself."

Discussing his absence with the master without knowing how much Norgate knew had been like trying to embroider a tapestry with a broadsword. Frankly, Kit still didn't understand how he'd disappeared for almost two months and escaped without punishment. He supposed he had Walsingham's interference to thank. The average scholar couldn't pack his bags and vanish without consequences. More than that, he couldn't say.

"You're brilliant, Kit," Tom said, interrupting the memory. "Mad, yes. A complete idiot, absolutely. But brilliant. You'll be fine."

Kit felt his chest contract around his heart, making each beat twice as resonant. He'd seen that spark in Tom's eyes. In a life built on lies, he needed no more truth than this.

"I can help you study, if you like. And if you start to doze off . . ."

Tom shifted out from beneath Kit's back. Kit whined, resenting the distance, but not for long. Tom moved to lay a soft kiss in the curve where Kit's neck met his shoulder. And then another, lower, along his collarbone. And another, lower still.

"I know a few ways to keep you entertained," Tom murmured. Kit shivered. The brush of Tom's breath whispered along his belly, and then, lower, to—

"Plague on the fucking sacrament, Tom, *Jesus*—"

The vibration of Tom's laugh was almost too much for Kit to bear. "God, are you always this vocal?"

Twelve

K it flinched, barely preventing himself from falling asleep. Even with lit candles clustered on the long table in front of him, the small reading room off the main Cambridge library was dim. It was six in the morning and felt like three. Across the table, Master Seymour watched him without speaking. Judging from the expectant way he'd interlaced his long, tapered fingers, he must have asked a question, though Kit had no idea what it had been.

He looked at the poetics professor, wide-eyed and half asleep. "I'm sorry, sir. I . . . what?"

Seymour sighed. "Marlowe, have you always been unable to function before seven, or is this a new development?"

In response, Kit yawned.

Seymour shook his head and gestured at the book open on the table between them. The volume was massive, a thousand pages if anything, and in Kit's state the words bore no resemblance to English. "I asked you to translate this paragraph of Longinus, if you recall."

Kit squinted at the page, then winced. That was why it didn't look like English. It was Greek. He might be months away from a master of arts, but there was no way in hell he could manage Greek translation this morning. He could barely manage consciousness.

Any other Cambridge fellow would have abandoned Kit to his ruin after such an abysmal performance. But then, no other fellow would have been in the reading room at six in the morning, tutoring a student as far behind and ill regarded as Kit. Seymour had always been kinder to Kit than he deserved. He'd met with Kit after classes for hour-long far-ranging discussions of Ovid, recommended books of poetry and history that might interest him. He'd even read scenes of *Tamburlaine* in early drafts, an honor Kit had granted no one else, not even Tom. Kit suspected Seymour was the only reason he hadn't been expelled years ago. Without his help, Kit would never graduate, that was certain. But at the moment, he was too tired to muster any gratitude. Ten days had passed since his return to Cambridge, and he was no nearer to catching up than the night he'd stumbled in. He hadn't slept for more than thirty consecutive minutes in at least a week.

Of course, Tom was partly responsible for Kit's late nights. But he preferred to blame Norgate and the ancient Greeks.

"Marlowe?" Seymour prompted.

Kit stared at the impenetrable page of Longinus. Unless the Delphic oracle itself appeared in the library and intoned the answer unto him, there was no hope. He looked up at Seymour with helplessness so total the professor didn't need to ask again.

"Marlowe, you have to sleep," Seymour said. "I know you have reading to complete, but a degree isn't worth dying for."

Kit's laugh echoed off the dusty bookshelves. He arched his back, felt his vertebrae pop, and winced. "Would you mind letting Master Norgate know, sir?"

"Hang Norgate," Seymour said. Kit's eyes widened, surprised at the professor's vehemence. "I know you. You're one of the few students in this damned school who aspires to anything beyond running errands for the Privy Council." Seymour was too intent on his point to notice Kit color at this. If he'd only known about the errands the Privy Council already had Kit running. "But if you insist on working to the point of death, you'll ruin yourself before you get the chance."

For any other student, Seymour was right; a degree wasn't worth dying for. Tom had his parents' fortune in London. Nick had the family estate near Wentworth. If they failed, they'd survive. But if Kit slunk out of Cambridge with his tail between his legs, he'd die as he was born, the worthless son of an unlettered shoemaker. He'd seen that future too clearly in Canterbury to forget it. Employment from Walsingham or not, Kit needed this degree if he was ever to become anything. And he'd do whatever it took to get it.

He smiled at Seymour, acknowledging and dismissing the advice at once. "Doesn't Longinus say greatness comes on the back of suffering, sir?"

"So you *can* read Greek," Seymour said. "Still, even *On the Sublime* wouldn't condone two weeks without sleep."

"Forgive the interruption, Master," came a voice from beyond the door. "I need to borrow Marlowe a moment."

At these words, Kit was wide awake. Without turning, he could see the puritanical man who had spoken, that unreadable expression, that perfect posture. Kit felt Seymour's skeptical gaze over his shoulder but didn't dare meet it. He rose as Walsingham stepped into the room. In the hovering glow of candlelight, the secretary reminded him of a priest entering the nave of Canterbury's cathedral, back when Kit's mother had dragged him to services. He could only hope the mental comparison boded grace, rather than martyrdom.

"You know this man?" Seymour asked.

Kit nodded. For a moment, he toyed with telling Seymour the truth. *Sir, meet Sir Francis Walsingham, the queen's spymaster, here to kill me for disappearing to Canterbury without warning.* Instead, he tossed out the first lie that came to mind. "A solicitor, sir," he said. "He handled my father's affairs when I was home."

Walsingham inclined his head in wry concession. For a moment, Kit feared that Seymour saw through the lie—no man like Walsingham would take the case of an illiterate drunk. Then, with a sigh, Seymour stood. He said nothing as he left, but he gave Kit a lingering look, exhorting him to remember what he'd said about self-preservation.

Walsingham closed the door. As he turned again toward Kit, the candles caught the sharp planes of his face, casting gold light and deep shadow in turns. His footsteps made no sound against the wooden floor.

Kit took a step back. "Master Norgate didn't mention you were coming."

"I come and go as I wish," Walsingham said. The calm of his tone warred with the storm on his brow. "A privilege, I might add, that is not granted to you."

Walsingham stood a foot from Kit now. The room, once large enough, now felt as narrow as a coffin. At least that settled the question of grace or martyrdom. Kit took another step back—the last possible step, as the wall of books brushed against his shoulders. He looked to the floor, courage failing.

Walsingham gripped Kit by the chin and jerked his head up until their eyes met. His grasp remained there a long moment. Kit's jaw tightened. In Canterbury, in Cambridge taverns, he'd broken men's noses for less than that.

"Do you have any idea," Walsingham said, "how unpleasant it is to explain to Her Majesty that the spy I expected to find in Cambridge has vanished?" He did not release Kit so much as shove him away.

Kit did not break his gaze. Walsingham would soon learn that frightening Kit was harder than he thought. Even if the words *Her Majesty* had sent a thrill down Kit's spine. "Very unpleasant, I imagine," he said.

"You were to come directly to Cambridge," Walsingham said. "What part of that was unclear?"

Kit gritted his teeth. Don't stutter. Don't break. "My sister—"

"What about her?" It was barely a question.

"She died, sir."

Walsingham's laugh sounded like a gunshot. "I don't care if she became queen of Portugal. You had orders."

Kit's fingers, with more daring than his brain, curled into fists. Walsingham and Bradley merged into one co-extant source of hatred, a single sneering voice: *I don't care, not the husband's fault, should have kept her legs together.* That laugh. Kit had failed Jane in every way that mattered, but to endure that laugh in silence would be a new betrayal.

"Do you think as secretary I could afford to lose my head with self-pity every time I heard of a death?" Walsingham said.

"I doubt it, sir. That would require your knowing what pity meant."

The back of Walsingham's hand struck Kit across the jaw like the flat of a sword. Kit turned with the blow, his opposite cheek flush with the shelf of books behind his head. His gasp cut through the library's new stillness. He raised one hand to his jaw and ran one hand along the line of it, tender beneath his fingers. The humiliation was sharper than the pain. A blow for an unruly servant. No, even when he'd been a footman, no one had dared. Like kicking a dog.

Walsingham stepped away. "You are not important enough to be insolent, Marlowe," he said, turning his back.

Kit drew his fragmented dignity around him like a hawk settling its feathers. His shoulders would not relax, but there was nothing for that. Only so much calm could be expected. Walsingham had crossed back to the table, where he produced two pieces of paper from an inner pocket of his doublet. They landed on the reading table, folded in half and unsealed. Kit approached, curiosity cutting through the shame.

"We've managed to intercept some of the Scot's letters to Babington," Walsingham said, gesturing to the papers. "Poley, who it seems you met, had them copied out."

Kit did not reach to take them. "Why bring them here, sir?" he asked. "Shouldn't Whitehall—"

The remainder of the sentence died in the face of Walsingham's expression. He gestured at the pages, inviting Kit to read them. Not without reservations, Kit picked up the first sheet and unfolded it. Stunned, he let it fall from numb fingers.

This was the letter he'd sought at Sheffield. That he'd believed would reveal everything. It stared up from the table, its contents projecting between spy and spymaster. A full page of shapes, signs, symbols. Meticulously printed and meaningless. No alphabet Kit had ever seen. An impossible tangle of cipher, without a key.

Kit looked up from the table. He began to speak, then again abandoned his sentence midway through.

"You see the issue," Walsingham said. Spotting *On the Sublime* still open on the table, he nodded. "But you should make short work of this. Small step from Greek to cipher."

It wasn't so small a step as that, but nothing in Walsingham's manner suggested that contradiction would be welcome.

"For your work in Yorkshire," the spymaster added, and pressed a small purse into Kit's hand. "Somewhat in arrears, though I won't take the blame for that."

Kit stowed it in his pocket without looking at it. He'd done this for money, but it hardly felt like salary now. More like the bribe you passed a politician after threatening to cut out his tongue. And besides, he'd taken his payment into his own hands earlier, as Gregory had no doubt noticed by this point.

Walsingham turned. His movement cast a long, distorted shadow against the wall of books, darkening their spines. "Meet Gregory at ten o'clock on the first and fifteenth to report your progress toward breaking the cipher. The usual place."

"Yes, sir," Kit said, but by then, Walsingham had already gone.

Kit sank into the chair and slumped forward, head in his hands. The two worlds on either side of the door, Cambridge within and London without, had collided with the force of two continents, leaving the library's former peace in ruins. The book-covered desks of the Cambridge library, the faint trace of tobacco clinging to the clothes he hadn't changed from the night before, the philosophical wanderings of the ancient Greeks—what did any of that matter when Walsingham could shatter his world at any moment? How stupid he'd been, to think he could do this.

His head snapped up at the sound of the door opening. Christ. Could he not have a moment without—

"Tom," he said.

Tom smiled as he stepped into the library, a volume of Plato under one arm. Last-minute work to complete on his end as well, then. Kit shouldn't have been surprised. He had, so to speak, been monopolizing Tom's evenings lately. On any other morning, this unexpected arrival would have been perfection. Now, what could he say? Walsingham had bought his ability to speak.

"Wake me when you leave next time," Tom said. He glanced over his shoulder to ensure they were alone. "Gets cold, the bed all to myse—" He broke off, staring at the red sting rising along Kit's jaw.

"It's nothing," Kit said, turning away.

Tom sat beside Kit, inches between them, and set his book on the table. "Christ, clearly it's not nothing."

The breath caught in Kit's throat. But Tom had placed the book on top of the letters, its leather covers hiding Walsingham's prize. Tom hadn't seen. A stroke of luck. Well, he was overdue for one.

"It was an accident," Kit said. "I fell." Damnation, he could lie to anyone else, why couldn't he lie to Tom to save his life? What kind of fall would leave a mark like this?

Tom rested one hand on Kit's knee. The fingers of his other hand tapped against the table, counting out the rhythm of a question. "Tell me one thing?" He faltered. Tom, who was never at a loss. "It's not, you haven't been going to, to town, have you?"

Kit blinked. "Have I been to a whorehouse, do you mean?"

Now it was Tom's turn to flush and look elsewhere. "Tell me if you have," he said, addressing the floor. "You've been up late, gone early, and I know you used to like— What?"

Kit couldn't fault Tom for his irritation. He'd burst out laughing before the end of the question. As if his distraction and imminent bruise were the result of an overzealous city girl. Prostitutes? Jealousy? If it were only that. "Tom, now that you've shown me the light," he said, "most whores are missing a fairly important piece of anatomy."

"And that man leaving the library?" Tom asked, his irritation rising now—Kit had pushed him too far. "I suppose he's nothing too?"

God and Christ. Tom had seen Walsingham. Had the spy-master said anything? And if Tom guessed, what then? Not only would Kit be exposed, but Tom would be implicated. He'd have given anything to tell Tom the truth—surely he owed him that much. But for the sake of the hand now holding his, the body intertwined with his in the dark, this man he was discovering he would do anything for, he would lie, and lie, and lie.

"Tom," he said, "it's better if you don't ask."

Tom looked at Kit with the discernment of an aspiring lawyer. For a moment, Kit feared he would press the point. Fragile and startled as he was, Kit would say something he'd regret. But then Tom sighed and squeezed Kit's hand. "I've told you the most dangerous secret I have," he said. "I don't know what else you need before you trust me."

Kit would bear any danger. Put his own life at risk, fine. But to hear that betrayal in Tom's voice, know he was the cause, and have no power to change it stung with something sharper than guilt. If Walsingham knew what Kit's loyalty cost him. There was only one thing he could do. He took Tom's cheek in one hand and kissed him, open door be damned. Tom hesitated a moment, surprised, before returning it. It was the first time they'd ever kissed for any reason other than passion or affection. This kind of kiss was an apology, and it was a kind Kit wished he'd never had to learn.

"It's not my secret," Kit said, the words barely above a breath. "I'm sorry."

Tom's smile was resigned, not accepting. He brushed his lips against Kit's cheek, the tender skin that by the next day would spread into a shadowed bruise. "Don't apologize," he said. "It's not like you."

———

The candle guttered out with a smoky sigh. Kit groaned and slumped forward onto the desk, head resting on his forearms. Faint and indistinct, the bells tolled from the courtyard. Dreading the result, he counted.

One.

Two.

Surely not past two . . .

Three.

Damn.

He'd been at this for hours. Once Tom fell asleep, soon after midnight, Kit had disentangled himself from the sheets, moved to the desk, and taken up the letters. He'd burned through a full candle, worked himself into a splitting headache. And still he had accomplished nothing. His primary state of being these days, it seemed.

If only Greek were as useful as Walsingham believed. Years of translating Heraclitus came up useless against the monstrosity of these letters. Kit knew Mary was clever. He hadn't considered how that cleverness could mock him from a hundred miles away. He and Tom had built their own cipher years ago, to pass notes in Master Crawley's dullest mathematics courses. They'd thought it unbreakable, but all they'd done was shift the entire alphabet five letters sideways. The Gordian knot of Mary's system revealed how childish their attempt had been.

Kit leaned back in the chair and closed his eyes. Now the spitting candle had been silenced, he could hear Tom's soft breathing from where he slept, burrowed against the cold in Kit's bed. Remembering their careless caress of hours before, Kit felt his face flush in the darkness. It hadn't been luck their first time, that flash of euphoria. Lightning striking again and again, more intoxicating each time. He'd never known anything like it.

Not that it hadn't felt good with the girls at the White Stag, of course. Good enough, anyway. Fast. Mechanical. A lingering craving in the back of his mind that vanished the moment someone sated it. Maybe that was the way it was, he'd thought, physical and uncomplicated. I scratch your back, you scratch mine, and then we avoid each other for several days until we've both forgotten. What the poets found in the process to get worked up about, he'd never understood.

But that had been before Tom.

Beginning with perfection and rising higher every night, since Kit had begun to learn the tricks Tom had mastered from the start. He smiled remembering it, with more than a hint of bitterness. Who had taught Tom this dance, for that matter? How many times had Tom, embraced by tangled sheets, moaned a man's name that wasn't Kit's? *For a first time.*

As far as distractions went, jealousy was effective, but it burned out like the candle soon enough. He reached into a drawer for another. After a few minutes' hard effort—past three in the morning, the most menial tasks increased wildly in difficulty—a shifting light again illuminated the cipher's taunting strokes. Perhaps he was going about this the wrong way, he thought. There were only so many symbols. How had he taught Meg to read? Language was repetition and arrangement, a framework of sounds scaffolding rhythm and meaning. Each symbol corresponded to a sound. Isolate the letters, then look for patterns. Which behaved like vowels, which grouped like consonants.

It was a puzzle. A puzzle like Greek, like the Holy Trinity, like the human heart. And damn it all if he would quit before he found the key.

Thirteen

When Tom entered the White Stag with Kit and Nick, it was packed already with the evening crowd. Working people and students alike crowded the tavern's front room, toasting the Christmas season with cheap beer and irreverent conversation. Never mind what deals Mistress Howard's girls made in the back rooms—those activities stopped for no man, not even Christ. The roaring fire drained the chill of the walk and melted the snow from Tom's boots, leaving dirty puddles along the floor as they took their usual table in the corner. The tapster, knowing the trio well, had three pints on the table before Tom ordered. A group of five men near the door, thick beards and thicker tongues, culminated the final strains of a bawdy carol Christ would have blushed to hear his name inserted into. The cry for more drink followed like a coda.

It felt like London, Tom thought. Warm and close and harmlessly transgressive. It felt like home, in a way Cambridge never had.

Not that the college didn't have its bright spots, he thought, glancing at Kit sprawled in the chair beside him. Kit didn't notice. He was shouting good-natured blasphemies at Mistress Howard from across the taproom—their traditional form of seasonal greeting.

"Can the three magi expect nothing better from you than shit beer, mistress?" he called, gesturing with his pint at Tom and Nick.

Mistress Howard rolled her eyes. "It's a broad definition of wisdom, Marlowe, if they're calling you a wise man," she said, though not without affection.

"Wise enough to know piss when I taste it," Kit said, and drank. "Even Christ wouldn't forgive this sin against ale."

Tom shoved Kit in the shoulder. "Let her be."

Kit grinned, that wicked, untrustworthy smile that robbed Tom of his ability to think straight. "It could be worse," he said. "I could be telling her the truth about the Virgin Birth."

Tom and Nick groaned. They'd both heard that theory before. But surely even Kit wasn't stupid enough to shout in a crowded tavern that the Virgin Mary had fucked a Nazarene stable boy and paid the Archangel Gabriel to cover it up.

Surely.

The fellows of Corpus Christi would rail against their being in the tavern that evening at all, Tom knew, blasphemy or no. Cambridge approached the season the same way it approached everything: with sobriety and austerity. Services had been lengthened and sermons intensified until Tom was convinced he spent more time in church than out of it. But this was the only proper way to celebrate, he thought. Self-affliction and piety belonged to Good Friday or Lent. December belonged to the taverns.

And Tom hadn't seen Kit relax in ages. Not since that man visited him in the library—the one Kit wouldn't explain, the one Tom hadn't forgotten. Not since he'd started spending every waking moment studying, or whatever he did with the papers he whisked out of sight when Tom entered the room. But secrets, like prayer, could wait until after the holiday.

"Have you turned highwayman as well as blasphemer, Kit?" Nick asked. He leaned his chair on two legs, resting its back against the smoke-stained wall.

Kit blinked. "What do you mean?"

"Don't know how else you'd come into money, beyond robbery. I mean, look at you." Nick made an ornate gesture with his left hand, illustrating Kit's general presence. "Never known you to dress like a lord."

Kit took a terse sip of ale. "I have aspirations."

Tom picked at a hangnail, tearing thoughtless until the blood came. Nick always brought it back to money, though Tom bent over backward to avoid speaking of it. Their first week at Cambridge, he and Kit had each unintentionally scandalized the other with careless references to the homes they'd left. Tom mentioned his private fencing tutor; Kit alluded to going without food so his sisters could eat. After that, it seemed easier never to bring it up.

Still, Nick was right: Kit's shabbiness had faded. The change hadn't been ostentatious: a pair of boots without a hole in the heel, breeches that fit in all the places breeches were supposed to fit—though Tom would admit to no one why he'd noticed this. Yes, the cut of Kit's emerald linen shirt was fashionable enough to turn heads, but what of it? Who was he to grudge Kit's having something new for once, especially when he wore it so well?

"Nick, this coming year, I mean to find you a hobby," Tom said. "Anything to keep you out of other people's business."

Kit shot Tom a grateful smile, though he spoke to Nick. "I hear carpentry is rewarding," he said. "Christ wasn't much good, but if mankind is made in God's image surely you can manage a stool."

After years listening to Kit's ever-escalating dervish of blasphemy, Tom saw no reason to address this latest scandal. Not given Nick's inability to go an hour without being an ass. At least Kit kept his voice down.

"When do you leave for London, Tom?" Kit asked, before draining his pint.

Tom bit his lower lip to tamp down a smile. Kit, not on speaking terms with his father, would pass Christmas at Cambridge as always. Which was why Tom had written to his mother earlier that week, claiming he had too much work to countenance coming home. She might not speak to him for months, but it was worth it for the chance to tell Kit.

"I thought I'd stay here, actually," he said. He let his foot brush across Kit's under the table and hid his smile as Kit shivered. God. He'd stay at Cambridge for the rest of his life, if only for that shameless pleasure. He'd never met anyone as susceptible to flirtation as Kit—nor, for that matter, as good at giving it back.

"Madmen, the pair of you," Nick said. Tom only half listened. Kit's knee now rested against his thigh, as if by accident, making it damn hard to concentrate. "First light, I'm off to London, like any rational person."

"Well, of course," Kit said. He was a man with a hundred faces. Even as his knee pressed against Tom's thigh, steadily driving him mad, Kit's voice went cold. "Your father the alderman will have a rich Christmas. Paid for by the poor he's robbed."

Tom kicked Kit under the table. For God's sake, he thought, taking a long drink. Nick was an ass, and his father was worse. But if there was ever a time for goodwill and drink and not picking hopeless fights, it was now.

Nick, to Tom's surprise, ignored Kit. This likely wasn't a decision to turn the other cheek. His attention was occupied by one of the tavern's whores, a short blond woman who seemed underwhelmed by his attentions. Nick pressed a gold coin into her palm as she passed. "An angel for an angel, darling," he said with a wink. "Merry Christmas."

The line didn't impress Tom; it impressed the woman still less. But in her business as in most, an angel was nothing to sneeze at. She smiled and pocketed the coin, a silent promise to return when she could. Tom half hoped she'd bolt with it, to teach Nick a lesson.

Nick thumped his empty pint on the table and wiped his mouth with the back of his hand. The snow continued falling through the window behind him, a silent arabesque filtered and muted through the smudged glass. "God, the moment I get out of this backwater for good," he said to no one in particular.

Kit laughed. "Tired of being around people cleverer than you?"

Nick's glare wished Kit dead. They were exactly the same, in some ways. If a dog took a shit in the street, they'd both take it as a personal insult. It was like being surrounded by children.

"No," Nick said. "Tired of country beggars who fake blasphemy to shock their way into a whore's skirts."

The table's mood took a turn. Tom reached a hand to stop Kit, who had begun to stand. Don't you dare, he thought. Kit glanced over, then nodded. He coiled back into his chair, though his air of a snake about to strike didn't fade.

Nick's jaw tightened. He'd had his heart set on a fight, Tom could tell, and would get it one way or another. "Then again," he said, and he turned not just his eyes but his whole head to Tom. "Maybe you're not after the whores."

Tom's reflexes were excellent. He'd studied fencing for almost ten years—that had to be worth something. But he never had a devil's chance of stopping Kit. It took half a second. The chair fell to the floor as Kit shot to his feet, pulled back, and punched Nick in the face as hard as he could. Nick yelped and fell, landing on the ground with a thud that silenced the rest of the room. Blood seeped through his fingers from his shattered nose.

Tom stared at Kit, who stood with tense shoulders and clenched fists. Kit watched Nick with a coldness Tom had seen only once before, the first time he'd asked about Kit's father. Kit looked down at Nick like a high priest passing judgment, then turned and stalked out into the snow.

Tom's hands shook. Kit couldn't have made it clearer he was fucking Tom if he'd invited Nick to watch.

Mistress Howard pushed through the startled crowd toward them, men parting before her. Moses might have split the Red Sea, but a tavern keeper on the prowl required no divine intervention to carve a path. Behind her, Nick's whore poked her head out of the kitchen, a pint in one hand and the other over her mouth to hide her laughter.

The matron didn't wait to reach their table before unleashing her tirade. "I run a respectable house," she said. "I won't have any commotion. Do you hear me, Skeres?"

Nick rose to his knees, still holding a hand to his nose. His eyes watered, diluting the blood. "Not to worry," he said, his voice unsteady. "Our commotion's just left."

Tom had to hand it to him. Even bleeding from the face, Nick could still be an ass when it pleased him.

Mistress Howard swept away, muttering something about youths and deviants. As she left, a dull murmur of conversation trickled back into the room. Men were punched in the face every day in places like this. If the single blow wouldn't evolve into something more exciting, Cambridge's tavern crowd had more pressing business to attend to. Drink, for instance.

Nick sagged down into the chair, tilting his head back and pinching the bridge of his nose. Even from this angle, Tom could see it had begun to swell and jutted out awkwardly. Broken, for certain. He couldn't claim the emotion filling him was sympathy.

"Get that set," Tom said, turning toward the door.

"Oh, for God's sake, Tom, not you too."

Tom ignored him. He snatched up his cloak and pushed out of the tavern, letting the door bang in the wind. The snow had worsened while they'd been inside. He squinted, struggling to see, but there was no one there. Only a trail of fast-disappearing footprints that began in the warm circle of light spilling from the White Stag and continued into the shadows.

Damn him, Tom thought. He eased into a loping run, following the tracks. What had he been thinking?

But Kit hadn't been thinking, of course. And if he didn't start, he'd give them both away.

It was hard to remember, sometimes, that Kit had never done this before. His militant blasphemy and bitter wit were as London as they came, but he'd grown up in a small country town where the cathedral's rhythm directed life's movements. Not as many opportunities to experiment as in the city. True, most of Tom's liaisons had unfolded in London's seedier public houses, and cost him a fair amount of money in the bargain. But at least he'd learned when to keep a straight face and be silent.

Finally, Tom spotted him: a fast-walking figure at the corner of Magdalene Street, the light from a nearby brewer's catching the copper in his light brown hair. Tom lengthened his stride to catch up.

"Kit," he said, laying a hand on his shoulder.

Kit whirled around, and for a moment Tom thought he would end up with a broken nose of his own. There was a wild, unsettled panic in Kit, one that disappeared or was covered up as Tom raised his hands, palms spread wide. In the snow-thinned light, Kit looked very pale.

"I won't say I didn't enjoy that," Tom said, lowering his hands. "But you shouldn't have done it."

Kit sighed and looked down. "I know. But he . . ."

Tom glanced over his shoulder. In snow like this, the street was deserted. Good. With one hand, he raised Kit's chin to meet his eyes, letting his hand linger near the fading bruise on Kit's jaw. For a moment, Kit stopped breathing. The snow settled gently in his hair, dusting him with white. Tom's hand moved to Kit's shoulder, pulling him closer. It never failed to surprise him how confident he felt, touching Kit, being near him. Had he been this way with the others and noticed it only now? He doubted it.

"It's just an insult," Tom said. "He doesn't mean anything by it. But if you give him reason to believe it, he will."

Kit paused. Tom didn't trust that pause.

"Unless you have other things on your mind," Tom said.

"No," Kit said without blinking. "There's nothing else."

Tom sighed. This man. This handsome, clever man who made Tom's life worth living, and who couldn't tell him the truth if his life depended on it. "You're a terrible liar," he said.

Kit laughed. "The worst," he agreed. "It's a good thing I never lie."

Damn him. A moment before, Tom had been determined to make Kit see the importance of being subtle. All it took was one laugh, one flash of the smile that did the strangest things to Tom's self-control. And now, look. All he could think of was how much he'd rather see Kit's new clothes on his floor. He could press Kit for answers later. They had the whole week, from Christmas to the new year. For now . . .

"Tell you what," Tom said. Compensating for Kit's recklessness with added caution, he glanced back over his shoulder. The street remained deserted. Nothing but the swirling snow, shielding their conversation. "Why don't we go back to my room and prove Nick right?"

Kit started and stopped three separate sentences. Helpless, he grinned, which Tom chose to read as a yes.

Two people in Cambridge, at least, were entitled to a merry Christmas.

Fourteen

By Christmas Eve, most scholars had left Cambridge for home. The chapel stood nearly empty at vespers, the hollowed-out carcass of some leviathan with empty pews for ribs. The rector's voice echoed and multiplied into a resonant host of a hundred voices preaching the same gospel. The dusky light through the high windows bleached the pews as gray as the snow-covered grounds.

Kit slouched against the chapel's back pew with the other poor scholars who, whatever else they'd learned at Cambridge, had learned their place. Those with money sat closer to God, those without grasped what they could from the back. Blessed are the poor, for theirs is the Kingdom of Heaven. Just as well, Kit thought—theirs was decidedly not the Kingdom of Earth. But then, when Christ spoke of the poor, he hadn't meant people who coped with poverty like Kit did.

He heard every word of the sermon and listened to none of them. He knew their God too well for that. The God who watched, cleaning dirt from under his fingernails, as men and women spied and betrayed and planned assassinations in his name. The God who dug in his heels over the minutiae of centuries-old ritual while giving his benediction to murderers and zealots. A God who would damn men for how they prayed and loved but not how they cursed and killed.

"And all that had heard it wondered at the things which were told them of the shepherds," read the rector. "And the shepherds returned glorifying and praising God."

The Catholics had one thing right, he thought, ignoring the rector. Both sects were hypocritical asses, but at least Mary Stuart and her lot understood theater. A little sleight of hand, a little magic, and before you could say "Ave Maria," bread into flesh. Quite the trick. The Church of England was an aesthetic affront. Stilted and sober, down to the diction of its Gospels. "The things which were told them of the shepherds." If Kit met a living human who arranged his prepositions and verbs that way, he'd take pleasure beating some rhetoric into them. The New Testament was as filthily composed as a grammar-school Latin exercise. Any poet worth his salt could do better.

"Then the Lord rained upon Sodom and upon Gomorrah brimstone and fire from the Lord out of Heaven . . ."

Kit flinched. Surely they hadn't returned all the way to Genesis, he thought, forcing himself to genuinely listen. No. The rector painted the same scene of the Nativity, button-eyed livestock watching the wailing infant savior. Nothing to do with the way Kit's attention wandered to the third-row pew where Tom's head bowed in prayer. If God couldn't bestir himself over sectarian violence, surely he wouldn't berate Kit for whom he happened to fuck. In any case, the distance between them would have satisfied the most celibate Levite. But that wouldn't erase the warmth of their bare skin together, the sound of Tom's hoarse voice when he whispered Kit's name the night before, lips meeting, first soft, then with urgency—

"And looking toward Sodom and Gomorrah, behold, he saw the smoke of the land mounting up as the smoke of the furnace."

Go to hell, Kit thought, turning away from the rector. All this from a God whose idea of morality oscillated between drowning the world and turning the other cheek. Murdering for peace. Sinning for salvation. At least the devil was consistent. Consistent as the death of a thirteen-year-old girl. As a well-crafted lie. As symbols on the page, omnipresent and tauntingly opaque. As the slanted beam of light from the high windows that made

Tom's hair shine radiant across the church. Always present, never turning.

"The Gospel of the Lord," said the rector.

———

Christmas came and went, then the new year, and still Kit was no better off than when he'd started. Mary's ciphered letters haunted him, mocking him every waking moment, worming their way into his dreams. He fought for calm, confidence, stasis. Three things in short supply as he stared hour after hour at a cipher that would not come right, feeling time slipping away.

Tom, knowing the symptoms of Kit's disquiet but not the cause, did his best to distract him. Tonight, Kit sat cross-legged on the floor of his dormitory, leaning against the bed with Tom across from him, a chessboard between them. Kit was on the defensive, dancing away from Tom's imminent threats, but that was all right. Between the letters, the disaster of his trip home, and the prospect of defending his degree in less than six months, his mind swarmed with anxiety. It was almost a relief to play a game he was allowed to lose.

"Your move," Tom said. He'd been waiting for Kit to act for upwards of three minutes.

There was a move here that would lead to victory, if Kit could only find it. But his mind would not stick on the pieces. "You can't rush tactical genius," he said to the chessboard.

"Tactical genius?" Tom repeated. "God help the battalion under your command."

"I don't know," Kit said, still looking at the board. Every move he saw led to death, one way or another. "I've always thought of myself as a latter-day Achilles."

"Absolutely," Tom said. "Renowned for the powerful thrust of your spear."

Kit looked up to see Tom's grin and laughed. Six months ago, he'd have spent a week trying to decide what Tom meant by that.

"You're becoming more like me every day, Tom. Your mother will be thrilled."

"Play," Tom said, gesturing at the board. "Before I die of old age."

Kit ran his thumb along the rounded top of his pawn, considering. Tom had left his bishop exposed, opening an opportunity for Kit's pawn to surge forward and sacrifice itself so that the queen could slice in for the kill. It was a good strategic move, but he wouldn't make it. His patience was ground to dust. Easier to vent your irritation on a stone queen than a live one.

At least Walsingham had made himself scarce since December, he thought, considering a horizontal slash of his rook against Tom's pawn. As promised, Gregory appeared in the village twice monthly to receive underwhelming reports of Kit's progress. Their most recent meeting in the White Stag lasted all of ten minutes, enough time for Kit to explain he knew nothing and for Gregory to swear like Whitehall paid him to do it.

He nudged his knight forward and across, beginning an advance on Tom's bishop.

Tom moved his king to safety—a vulnerability Kit hadn't seen. "What are you thinking about?" he asked.

Kit looked up. "What?"

"You could've had me. What is it?"

Any lie would do, but Kit's mind came up blank. His heart quickened to a rabbit-like fluttering. Damn it. This kind of panic had been overtaking him on and off for weeks, but now was not the time.

Tom raked his hair off his forehead. "Kit. If you have something to say, say it."

Kit's dormitory, never spacious at the best of times, now felt like a prison. Tom watched him close, questioning. He had to say something. But his nerves were stretched so thin his tongue wouldn't form words. He coughed, forcing himself to speak. "Light a candle, would you? It's getting dark."

Right. As if that would convince him to drop the subject. But he needed Tom to step away. Turn his back. For a few seconds. Kit's mask could not be allowed to slip, not now, but it was dangerously close to falling.

Tom looked at him with something between exasperation and alarm. Kit cracked the knuckles of his left hand, then the right. After a moment, Tom sighed, then pushed himself off the floor, crossing to the desk. Tom's back now turned, Kit drew a deep breath. The exhale rattled in his throat. Don't say anything you'll regret, he thought. Tom doesn't know anything. Nobody does.

"What in God's name . . ."

Kit stood so quickly he kicked the chessboard. A small army of pawns skittered into the room's far corners. Tom stood at the desk, two papers in his hand. One covered in hieroglyphic symbols, the other Kit's scratched attempts at imposing logic. The drawer where he'd stowed the pages stood open at Tom's knee.

The letters. The one thing he had to keep secret. How could he have been so stupid?

"It's nothing," he said. "Here—"

Kit cut forward and grabbed for the letter, but Tom was faster. He pivoted to block Kit with his shoulder and turned his attention to the page. Idiot, Kit thought. Show him it's important, of course he'd hold on twice as close.

"Nothing?" Tom's voice rose. In a moment, he'd be shouting. "What's wrong with you? What is this? Some kind of, I don't know, some kind of code—"

Kit swore and lunged across the room. He slammed the door and, under Tom's dumbfounded watch, drew the bolt across. But it might already be too late. Anyone might have heard in passing. And Cambridge's population was well connected to a fault. Anyone might have overheard, and who knew who they might tell. One wrong word could get him killed.

Tom looked at Kit, then at the letter, then back. Kit could see him putting the pieces together. The cipher. The two-month disappearance. The terror of discovery. Walsingham in the library. "Kit," he said. "Tell me what's happening."

"I can't—"

"You will."

A lie. Any lie. Tell him anything.

Kit opened his mouth, but only the creaking beginnings of words emerged. Every explanation seemed more implausible and frenetic than the last. A rush of air rang in his ears, a wild energy driving him mad, surely he would go mad, because the answer to Tom's question, *Tell me what's happening,* he couldn't answer that question, the answer to that question was madness. What explanation could there be for an unreadable code? He deserved to hang for being so careless.

He leaned against the door, fighting down the light-headedness of panic. He had to say something. Tom turned to face him, urgency driving toward anger. Tell him, Kit thought. You have to tell him. Better he knows the truth, so he knows to keep quiet.

When he spoke, his voice sounded muted, as if underwater. "I'm a spy."

The paper fluttered out of Tom's hand to the desk. "You're a what?"

"You heard."

Tom narrowed his eyes. "Kit, if you won't tell me, fine, but don't lie to me."

"I'm trying to tell you the truth!"

Kit hadn't meant to scream.

Tom fell silent, staring. Kit's heart had been beating so fast for so long that the inside of his ribs felt bruised. He ran one shaking hand over his mouth. When he spoke, the words were as calm and measured as he could make them.

"I've been working for the queen's spymaster since October," he said under his breath. "He suspects Mary Stuart of trying to assassinate the queen. And if I don't break that cipher by about yesterday," he added, "she might well do it."

Tom sat at Kit's desk, picking up the letters again as if he might find answers there. "Who would hire you to spy for Her Majesty?"

Kit's laugh was more than halfway to hysterics. "Why would I make up a lie this ridiculous, Tom, unless it was the truth?"

"Because you're you," Tom said, still staring at the letters. "You once told Master Seymour you hadn't finished an essay because you'd been visited by the Holy Ghost."

As if that was remotely the same thing. Kit sank down to the floor, his back against the door, and took his head in his hands. His heart pounded in his ears until he thought his head would split. "You see how that letter's signed?" he said.

Tom glanced to the bottom of the page. Seeing, Kit knew, two narrow, spiky letters beneath the lines of shapes and symbols. The letters that had been taunting Kit for weeks, months. *M.R.*

"Mary Regina," Kit said. "She's signing letters to English subjects as 'Queen Mary.' Do you think there's a woman more likely to want the queen dead than Mary Stuart, Margaret Tudor's grand-daughter? And," he added, speaking faster than he meant to, "the legitimate heir to the throne, if you believe Anne Boleyn was a harlot and the queen, her daughter, a bastard?"

The color drained from Tom's face. "Do you need to shout these things, for God's sake?"

Kit's voice had almost been softer than his heartbeat, but now wasn't the time to argue. The fallen white queen had rolled near the door—Kit picked it up and held it between his spread knees, turning it over in his palm. It was easier to look at it than any-where else. How many times had he longed to share his secret with Tom? He'd thought it would bring relief. But in speaking the truth, he'd doubled the risk, not halved it.

"You have to be careful," he said to Tom. "If you—"

The sentence failed midway. He had no wish to explore that hypothetical. But Tom wasn't stupid. He watched Kit from across the room, head tilted to one side, silent. Thinking, no doubt, what Kit was: one wrong step, one instance of trust misplaced, and they could each get the other killed.

"Kit," Tom began, but didn't go on. The color hadn't returned to his face. Kit wondered if it ever would.

Kit stood. His body had been so tense that the movement sent an ache through his thighs. "I . . ." he began.

"I've told you," Tom said. He crossed the room and laid both hands on Kit's shoulders. "You can trust me. You tell me to keep a secret, even this secret"—his voice hitched, but he pressed on—"and I'll do it."

Words abandoned Kit. He pulled Tom into a tight embrace, as if his arms were enough to keep away danger, to preserve this moment from any outside force that threatened it. Tears nagged at the back of his panic, but with a deep breath he forced them down.

"I love you," he said. Nothing else seemed worth saying.

Tom gave a soft laugh and ran a hand through Kit's hair. "I love you too," he said. "Although this isn't how I imagined hearing you say it the first time."

They stood that way a long moment, bodies entwined, Kit using the rhythm of Tom's breath to stabilize his own. Behind them on the desk sat the ciphered letters, unbroken, ignored but not for a moment forgotten.

Fifteen

Master Haywood, gray-haired and sharp-nosed like a disagreeable owl, paced the front of Cambridge's recitation hall. With forty upper-form students arrayed before him on amphitheater-style benches, he let fly a formidable onslaught of Latin without pausing for breath. Haywood's monotone flowed with such determination that his students drowned in a dark sea of nominative and genitive terms. They scribbled down every word they could catch, paper and books balanced on small tables, knees, or opposite arms.

Kit's pen, on the other hand, stalled.

Seated to the left and four rows back, he glared at the page. Any more venom and he'd start shouting curses at it. He hadn't heard a sentence of the lecture since its first, regarding the Ptolemaic model of celestial organization, or something of the sort. What did it matter? The planets could circle the earth, or they could dance a pavane around the queen for all he cared. Nothing mattered but the letters.

It was a risk, bringing them where anyone could see, but stress made him reckless. He couldn't miss the lecture—though Norgate had excused Kit's absence the previous autumn, the fellows hadn't let it pass without comment. Haywood in particular seemed to spend every free moment searching for reasons to have him expelled. But February's snows had faded into March. Kit couldn't put off Walsingham much longer. And the cipher continued to thwart him.

Kit had tried everything he could think of. Searching out characters in Greek, Hebrew, and Arabic that resembled the symbols. Testing Mary's favored proverbs and psalms as keys. Calculating the prevalence of each symbol against the frequency of Latin letters in common English phrases, then formulating countless potential tables. Nothing. Not a word. The pages seemed to taunt him when he flung them aside. There had to be something else. Some pattern he'd overlooked.

He turned back to the scrap of paper he'd brought along with the letters. In an anxious fit of productivity the previous week, he'd sketched fifty potential keys to Mary's cipher based on alphabetic frequency. Forty-seven keys, applied to the first line of text, yielded nothing but a string of gibberish. If the final three proved worthless—and the odds were increasingly supportive of this— Kit would be out of tricks. And if he failed to uncover a conspiracy that cost the queen her life, he'd be pleading his excuses to Walsingham from the wrong end of a noose.

He was running out of time.

Again disregarding Haywood and choosing one of the remaining keys, he began. His eyes flicked between the letter and the chart, matching symbol to symbol, transcribing on a third scrap of paper.

My

His pen fell to the floor. He did not move to retrieve it.

God's fucking seat in the firmament. *My*. A beautiful, English pronoun. *My*. It worked. The key had worked.

No. He scooped up his pen, forbidding premature hope. Any number of nonsense phrases could begin with M-Y. He bent low over the page, matching letters with the fanaticism of the possessed. His mind racing, his pen sketching words, letters flowing in a cascade of urgency.

Mytrustedandwellbelov—

A light tap on his shoulder. Kit flinched like someone had screamed in his ear.

"What in hell is that?" Nick leaned forward from the row behind, peering over Kit's shoulder.

Kit shifted a blank sheet over the cipher. With success so close, his nerves transformed into shapeless anger that latched on to the nearest target. "Nothing," he said. "Keep your nose out."

Nick frowned. "Don't be stupid. You expect me to believe *you're* taking notes?"

"I said it's nothing," Kit said, twisting round to give Nick the full weight of his anger. In that moment, Kit could have stabbed him. He couldn't be interrupted now, not with the answer this close, not by Nick. "Nose out, I said, unless you want it broken again."

"Marlowe?"

Kit turned, horror buzzing in his ears. Haywood had ceased his lecture and stood directly in front of Kit. The professor looked more than ever like an owl on the hunt. The entire hall was watching Kit now.

"Yes, sir?" he said, shrinking down in his seat.

"Have you had an astronomical epiphany with which you care to enlighten me?" Haywood spoke English now, a sure sign of ferocious disapproval.

If Kit were discovered not by Catholic insurgents but by an irate Cambridge professor, Walsingham wouldn't need to bother having him executed. He would die of shame on his own. "No, sir," he said.

Haywood glared at him—and then his eyes darted to the page of half-translated cipher balanced on Kit's book.

Kit stopped breathing. His hands trembled. He tucked them under his thighs and looked at Haywood with as much boldness as he dared. Kit hadn't prayed with conviction in years, but he implored any god that might be listening to keep him from looking as suspicious as he felt.

"Given that your graduation seems exceptionally precarious at present," Haywood said, "perhaps you would do well, Marlowe, to pay attention."

With that, he turned back to the room at large, lapsing again into Latin. The class scrambled to keep pace, Nick included, having escaped public chastisement by a hair. Kit knew he should wait, should run the rest of the key that night in private. But this was too important, Haywood be damned. He slid out the letter, keeping the key shaded by his book. Thank God the morning lecture lasted three hours. He'd need every moment.

The words came with effort, then faster as Kit eased into his stride. He'd wrongly identified a handful of symbols, flipped the G's and K's, but with the skeleton of the message in place it was child's play to correct his errors. The sound of the lecture faded away as the letter took shape before him.

My trusted and well-beloved servant,

In order to ground our enterprise and ensure its success, you must plan carefully what forces you may raise among you, and what captains and generals you shall appoint for them. Take me out of England in advance, and be assured to set me in the midst of a good army where I may safely remain until our foreign forces are assembled on these shores.

Kit set down his pen. His breathing unsteady, he pressed two fingers to the bridge of his nose. Calm, he thought. Finish the work. But he couldn't stop his hands from shaking. He stared at the page, at the words *foreign forces, in the midst of an army.*

He'd underestimated Mary. So had Walsingham. This wasn't an assassin's dagger concealed in a shirtsleeve. This was the Spanish Armada on the banks of the Thames.

This was invasion.

Beware of spies and false brethren, and never keep a paper around you that may do harm if discovered. Such errors have led

*to the condemnation of many, whose intentions could not have
been proven otherwise.*

It was horrifying. Meant death, war, revolution. But the absurdity of it threatened to make him laugh. *Beware of spies.* If he'd written it in a play, it would have strained credulity.

*God Almighty have you in his protection. Burn this privately and
quickly.*

Your assured friend,
M.R.

Kit set down his pen. The words gazed up at him. Translated. Broken. Finished.

He looked up. The lecture hall had emptied. Two and a half hours must have passed, perhaps more. In his frenzy of productivity, no one—to his surprise, not even Haywood—had dared interrupt him at lecture's end. Privacy: one of the benefits of a reputation for poetic madness. Standing felt like surfacing from an extended period underwater, dark blue silence echoing in his ears.

He'd done it. The cipher was broken. No more flinching at shadows, no more Arthur Gregory breathing down his neck waiting for news. Walsingham had trusted him, and he had done it. If the country were to fall, it wouldn't be because of him. He imagined it, thrusting the broken cipher in front of Walsingham and the rest of the Council, accepting their praise as his due. The queen's finest spy, the only man they could trust. He held Mary's downfall in his hands, but in that moment, all he could see in her shattered code was his own future stretching unchallenged before him.

"Are you coming?"

Kit's head snapped toward the door. Tom watched him with exasperated indulgence from just inside, the sole of one foot propped against the wall. God knew how long he'd been waiting.

Tom wasn't even enrolled in Haywood's seminar. Kit swept up the letters and tore down the stairs to ground level. The spring in his step must have looked ridiculous.

"How long have you been an astronomical devotee?" Tom asked, rolling his back away from the wall.

"Hang the planets," Kit said. Something close to hysteria bubbled within him; he felt laughter stretching toward the surface. "I've done it. It's done."

Tom looked toward the door, but there was no one there. The next lecture wouldn't begin for another hour. "What's done?"

The question tore the laugh out of Kit. Success went to his head, more potent than any liquor. If he could have burst into song without the college having him chained up as a madman, he'd have done it. "The letters. Words. Words," he said, brandishing the pages. He was hardly mastering words himself at this point, but no matter.

"What do they say?"

"Everything," Kit said, beaming. "War. Regicide. Treason. It's wonderful."

Tom raised his eyebrows. "Wonderful?"

Strangely, in that moment, it was. "I can't send this by post," Kit said, working out the problem as he said it. Sketching plans as before he'd sketched words. "And Gregory won't be back for two weeks, there's no time for that."

"Go to town," Tom said. He looked again toward the door, more alert against discovery than Kit, who had more reason to be. "Find a messenger. I'll pay, if you need—"

"No," Kit said. As the words formed, they seemed the most natural thing in the world. "I'm going myself."

Tom looked at Kit like he'd taken leave of any scrap of rationality he'd ever possessed. It was a fair assessment, given everything, but Kit knew what he was doing. He'd survived six weeks in Yorkshire among people who would have killed him in an instant if they'd learned his true purpose. After that, London would be simple.

"At least let me come with you," Tom said. "I spent my whole life in the city, I can—"

"No," Kit said—God, it was so easy to make decisions in this warm wave of euphoria. "We can't both disappear, they're more likely to notice that way. I need you to stay here and make my excuses for me."

Tom swore. "What excuses?"

"That I'm ill. Dying. Getting betrothed to a duchess. Whatever you like. I'll barely be gone a week." Kit was halfway through the door by the time he'd finished the sentence. A long beat of silence followed.

"Jesus Christ, Kit," Tom said, running after him.

Kit grinned. Of course Tom had questions. But they'd have the night together, and Tom might ask anything he liked before sunrise. At that point, Kit would be on the road, toward London, Mary's secrets safe in his head.

God Almighty have you in his protection, Mary had written. It was time to see whose side God was on.

Sixteen

K it had never been to London before. Fifty miles from home, yet the capital seemed a world away. But though he'd never seen it, he understood—he was sure—its soul. Tom, when drunk, would rhapsodize at length on his youth in the city. The scent of the docks. Saint Paul's steeple at sunset, against the hawking cries of booksellers and churchyard prophets. The tangle of whores and players and moneylenders roving the south bank like sin incarnate. The stories, secondhand though they were, lent Kit confidence. A city was a city, and he knew the taverns, brothels, and churches of home as well as anyone. What could be different in London except scale?

A great deal, as it happened.

As Kit approached the city, the suburbs greeted him first. London hung over the belt of its walls like a man grown too stout for his clothes. He wove through Shoreditch, a sprawling, ill-constructed neighborhood backed up against the dusty expanse of Finsbury Fields. Disarray and disorder, reaching north of the wall to house the excess.

What came next, as London itself rose before him, was the smell.

It seeped out through Bishopsgate like a living thing, and Kit gagged, pressing a hand over his mouth and nose. London was a city. Cities stank. But God, not like this. Enough to knock you over, like week-old meat smeared with shit. Like—

Heads.

He looked up. Four scarlet-stumped heads, speared on pikes atop the peak of Bishopsgate's arch. Eyes long since food for birds, their empty sockets leered down at Kit, rimmed with the black of weathered blood. Traitors. An example. He thought of Babington's haughty smirk, Morgan's sneer, Mary's sharp dark eyes— pecked out by crows. Food for scavengers. Stomach turning, Kit pushed through the gate, out of sight of their blind skulls.

Within the walls, the narrow streets ran toward mud, sodden with melting snow and rutted from carts trundling toward the Royal Exchange at Cornhill. Everywhere the thick scent of mildew and burning wood and shit and piss and the blood, congealed and steaming, that ran in viscous pools from the butchers of Hog Lane nearby. So loud. So much. Everywhere men shouting, swearing. Somewhere the bellow of a bull as its throat was slit. The shriek of a man from the stone edifice of Bethlehem Hospital, just outside the city.

So many people, pressing close to Kit, from all directions. Begging for money with the same phrases they'd said to a hundred men before him and would say to a hundred more after he'd gone. Kit pressed his hands into his pockets, his gaze on the ground. If they'd known, these desperates, that only the chance interest of wealthy strangers separated his circumstances from theirs, would they still have swarmed him? Likely yes. Poverty was not rational, but sprawled outward, many-headed, amorphous, all-encompassing. Walsingham ought to have paid some of his blood money here, where it could be used.

Tom had grown up here. He knew this city, knew its horrors and its cruelty. And he'd never said a word about any of this. If Tom had come with him, he'd have navigated the streets with native ease, glossing over the beggars, passing from person to building without registering the difference. No thought spared for this hell of wandering spirits. If he were to see Kit's family, with their mended clothes and boarded-up window—which he couldn't do, which he could never do—what would he think? Kit didn't know, and feared what the answer might be.

Don't think about that, he told himself. He hadn't come to London to philosophize. He forced himself to focus on the imminent threat of Whitehall, which he would reach in a matter of minutes. His mental picture of the palace was inaccurate, no doubt, but he'd rectify it soon enough. Walsingham would receive him, bring him to the Privy Council, to give his direct report to—

The Council. And he'd thought Walsingham's visit to Cambridge was agony. What would those men think of him? Worse even than a beggar: a poor man who aspired above his station. His nausea had nothing to do with the scent of the Pissing Conduit running along the churchyard nearby.

To hell with it, he thought. They'd want to hear from him. He'd done what they asked, what they thought no one could do. He was arriving in triumph, even if the smell of severed heads still hung in the air.

Through Cheapside out to the Fleet, then along the river, to Whitehall's north entrance. He skirted its main door and the ostentatious gate overlooking the main road, but even from an awkward angle, the palace was arresting. Not one edifice but a compound, sprawling across both sides of a broad avenue and backed against the Thames. Whitehall reveled in its own eccentricity, its varied stones and scattered cupolas jutting piecemeal skyward. If someone told Kit as a child that at twenty-two he'd walk into this palace seeking a meeting with the queen's secretary, he'd have laughed himself sick. There was nothing amusing about it now.

A servant met him at the door, an older man with a severe beard and unwelcoming eyes. Kit stood up straighter and tried to look as reputable as he could, stinking of horse, the stiffness of travel in every article of clothing.

"I need an audience with Sir Francis Walsingham," Kit said.

The performance wasn't as impressive here as it had been at Westgate. The servant narrowed his eyes and did not move. "Is Sir Francis expecting you?"

Kit paused. "If I say yes, would you believe it?"

"I would not, no."

"All right, he isn't expecting me," Kit conceded. He craned his neck, trying to see around the servant. "But if you'd only tell him Kit Marlowe's come with news, I promise he'll want to speak with me."

From the servant's tight lips, he doubted this. But there must have been something to Kit's words that rang true. Most likely he wasn't the first rough-looking fellow to turn up at the back door asking for the spymaster. The servant sighed, then glanced over his shoulder.

"Wait here," he said, snapping the door shut.

It wasn't the first time Kit had a door slammed in his face, but it was the first time he'd been left waiting on the doorstep of a palace. He took a deep breath, trying to tamp down the vomit rising in his throat. He would be all right. He would tell them what they needed to know. All he had to do was remember the letters, and not think of severed heads, and hope that the queen took the announcement of her pending assassination as good news.

"Come on," said the servant, opening the door again. "Sir Francis is in council, but he will see you."

All of the terrors at once, then. Well, Walsingham had never been one to waste time.

The servant led Kit into the corridor and toward the chamber where the Privy Council was in session. It wasn't far—not nearly far enough for Kit to quell his rising panic. With those words, *in council*, the terror swelled to an almost-unbearable pitch. He looked down at his mud-caked boots, bought with Walsingham's pay—the first pair of shoes he'd ever owned that John Marlowe hadn't made and mended. Pathetic, to think he'd ever be welcome in a place like this. But he'd done what none of them could. And he'd be damned if he'd let nerves undo him now.

They paused before a closed oaken door, a lion's-head door-knocker standing sentinel in the center. Kit could hear the pitch of male voices within, though the door obscured the words. He strained to listen, but before he could translate the sound into sense, the servant let the knocker fall back against the wood. The voices stopped.

After a pause, a man spoke. "Enter."

Kit took a shaky inhale. From nothing and nowhere to the threshold of the Privy Council. Everything depended on this performance. The queen's life and England's survival. Nothing like pressure to force one's hand.

"Go on, then," the servant said.

Kit opened the door and stepped inside.

Long and dim, the room dripped gravitas from its wide-set walls. A long table and fourteen high-backed chairs dominated its center, and heavy scarlet curtains shielded the tall windows. No late-night walkers in the garden below would catch sight of these proceedings, backlit by the fire sparking in the hearth. Scattered lamps illuminated each face around the table, giving the gathering the feel of a secret cabal.

Kit shivered. The Privy Council. It was like sharing a room with the Knights of the Round Table. He sank into a mute bow. Neither Canterbury nor Cambridge had taught him the vocabulary for this.

Rising, he found his focus pulled to the elderly, frail man at the head of the table. To his right, a small foxlike man with a sandy beard and a slight hunch watched Kit with a sour, appraising gaze. Though younger and with a decidedly more pinched set to his narrow mouth, his resemblance to the older man was unmistakable. Lord Burghley, head of the Privy Council, and Sir Robert Cecil, his son. Had Kit faced Abraham and Isaac themselves across the table, the effect couldn't have been more startling.

Walsingham, seated silent at the opposite end of the table, seemed to enjoy Kit's sudden humility.

How many other giants of English politics would in a moment hold Kit's life in their hands? He coughed and tried to stop his face burning through force of will. A chair stood empty at the table, beside Walsingham, but Kit wouldn't have taken it for a hundred pounds.

"You're Walsingham's boy," said Cecil, cutting through the silence. "Marlin."

Kit turned. Cecil's gaze stripped all other thoughts from Kit's mind. *Marlin.* Like the fish. Christ's light. He'd thought Gregory's quick temper had been off-putting, but at least Walsingham's man had bothered to remember Kit's name. "Marlowe, sir," he said.

"The Cambridge wit," Cecil drawled, as if Kit hadn't spoken. "Sir Francis has lionized your talents to me on multiple occasions."

Kit swallowed. The possibilities of what Walsingham might have said were horrifying. "I'm sure he exaggerates, sir."

"Without a doubt," Cecil said, with a rather pointed sweep of his eyes along Kit's doublet. It had seemed well made in Cambridge; under Cecil's observation, Kit felt as if he'd transformed into a Bishopsgate beggar.

Walsingham's patience for men like Cecil spanned about thirty seconds. His patience with Kit, though slightly longer, did not exceed twice that. "I must admit, Marlowe, I'm surprised to see you," he said. "I thought the arrangement between you and Gregory was quite clear."

"I'm sorry, sir," Kit said. "It couldn't wait. It's the letters."

Walsingham leaned forward, and his irritation turned at once into interest. Kit had to stop himself from grinning. He'd been right to come: Walsingham had waited for this as desperately as he had. Even a moment's delay would have been too long. The Council's attention shifted as one to Kit, and Lord Burghley leaned forward in his chair to see him properly. The old man had a nation resting on his frail shoulders. Every danger his concern, every plot his responsibility. Everyone in the Council knew of the letters, but none so intimately as Burghley.

Walsingham nodded. "Marlowe, you can read them?"

"I can," Kit said.

The room, quiet before, was silent now. Walsingham's expression bordered on a smirk. If Kit didn't know better, he'd think the spymaster was proud. Or perhaps the reason was simpler. Relishing the irony that a simple country peasant had outsmarted these perfumed bureaucrats. Anticipating the victory of disarming the Stuart threat. It was as practical as that.

Cecil scowled at Kit from across the table, his face alive with disbelief. Well, life was an exercise in being proven wrong, wasn't it? It wasn't at all productive to develop a deep and burning dislike for a member of the Privy Council, but Kit found himself privately hoping Cecil would trip down a flight of stairs on his way out of the palace.

Kit glanced away to the lamp in the center of the table, trying to lose his fear in the shifting light. He knew the letters by heart. Any poet would remember a resonant phrase, and these carried more weight than most. But that didn't help the terror that had permeated his blood.

"You may begin, Marlowe," Burghley said. "Uninterrupted," he added, darting a sharp look at Cecil, who pretended not to notice.

Kit closed his eyes. He knew this cipher now. All he had to do was read it as he knew it. "The first letter," he began, "was from Babington to Mary Stuart."

Cecil's brow darkened. The waver in Kit's voice had done nothing to challenge his first impression. Damn it, Kit was twenty-two, not sixteen. Couldn't he keep his voice from cracking for three minutes when it mattered? But as he continued, his hesitation strengthened into confidence. It was drama. A performance. And he'd never get another audience as rapt as this.

He took Babington's letter from his pocket and read it from the cipher without stumbling. How Babington met with a Spaniard who swore that King Philip was sympathetic and prepared to invade. How Babington sent funds to Spain, colluding with foreign forces to rescue Mary and remove Elizabeth from the throne. How six unnamed gentlemen, all Babington's trusted friends, plotted to murder the queen, to smooth the way for Mary's ascension. An undertaking he swore would succeed, at the hazard of all their lives. An undertaking that cast a chill through the room.

"Babington will be eliminated," Cecil said with a wave of his hand, directing his words at Walsingham and not Kit. "But severing his head only achieves so much, with Spain involved. Did Stuart respond?"

"She did, sir," Kit said.

Without prelude, he read the letter deciphered during the lecture at Cambridge. The second delivery came off smooth as the first, though he heard Walsingham's dry laugh at Mary's mention of *spies and false brethren*.

Finished, he hung back. The fear drained from him, leaving his body hollow and useless. It was impossible to think. He shifted his weight, breathing easily for the first time in minutes. The room's focus was no longer on him. He'd done what he'd come to do, and in a moment, he'd be back on his way to Cambridge, basking in victory. He could bide his time for a few minutes more and see how those with power made decisions.

"Treason," said another of the councilors, with more passion than originality. "As if the papist whore has the right."

"Her Majesty ascended lawfully and legitimately through the Act of Succession," Cecil said curtly. "Of course this is treason."

Burghley ignored his son with a saint's patience. It was like watching a wolf try to hunt with its pup nipping at its tail. "We will double the men at Sir Philip's command at Zutphen, should the Spanish turn from the Low Countries toward us," he said. "But for Babington and Stuart—"

"We have practices for dealing with traitors," Cecil interrupted. "Tyburn is well equipped for a brace of them."

Walsingham shook his head. "I appreciate your zeal," he said, "but think practically."

Cecil scowled. "I seldom think otherwise."

"You suggest we wait?" said a second councilor.

The nobleman wasn't alone in his surprise. Hesitation made no sense to Kit, not with six armed assassins to contend with. But Kit had said the piece he'd come to say. It didn't matter what they decided to do now. Kit would return to Cambridge, spend the months before graduation properly preparing for his examinations, pass his free evenings in town with Tom, use the remainder of his pay to set up in London in just a few months. He took a long breath, rocking forward onto the balls of his feet.

"If Stuart is removed," Walsingham said, "the Armada will be on our shores by week's end to retaliate, an attack we are ill prepared to defend against. And any strike against Stuart will spur immediate reprisals from her conspirators."

"I understand that," Burghley said wearily, "but we can hardly afford to wait."

"I don't suggest we wait idly," Walsingham said. "We need information. Abroad and at home."

Information. Kit turned away from the table, avoiding the Council's eyes. He knew what Walsingham meant, even if the rest of the room didn't. An early, uninformed strike would be ruinous, that was true. This wasn't a war, it was a game, and they needed intelligence to stay a move ahead. So Walsingham's spies would penetrate deeper into Mary's confidence.

And there was one spy she already trusted.

Whatever understanding Kit fancied he'd seen in Walsingham's black eyes, whatever faint pride or petty kindness, it didn't change anything. The spymaster's machine would work its course regardless. And Kit was a part of that machine now. Perhaps someday he'd be left to chart his own course, but not now.

For now, they needed him. The thought filled him with pride and left him nauseated at the same time.

Burghley tapped his fingers against the bridge of his nose, an apparent attempt to nurse a headache. With his hawkish son and the queen's iron-willed secretary in the same room, this was likely a common affliction. "You think your spy can identify the conspirators expediently?"

Walsingham smiled, not looking at Kit. "Stuart trusts Marlowe. We can easily negotiate his return to her service. She is now in custody of Lord and Lady Rich at Chartley Manor, given the unreliable behavior of Thomas Morgan."

Burghley nodded at Kit—the only man in the room to acknowledge Kit's continued existence. "You will depart for Staffordshire at once, Marlowe," he said. "We will expect your first report a week from your arrival, barring earlier necessity."

Kit's mouth opened, but nothing came out beyond a gust of breath. At once. He'd asked Tom to make his excuses for a week at most, and even that had him running the risk of expulsion. It was selfish, mourning the loss of a university degree with the fate of a nation in his hands, but he'd worked his whole life for this, only to see Walsingham and the Council toss it aside without a second thought.

Walsingham glanced over to Kit, and the flame in his eyes dimmed to something softer. When he turned back to Burghley, his voice was conciliatory. "Perhaps a day's rest first. The fate of the nation doesn't rest on one night."

Burghley nodded. "Very well. I shall arrange for his lodgings at Whitehall this evening."

Kit bowed his head. No one else looked at him. Nations and monarchs hung in the balance within that room, fates and condemnations dancing in the flickering lamplight. The Council had more important concerns than a spy's personal ambitions.

The Council, finished with its business, rose in a scattered wave. With each moment, the terrible sense of import that filled the room dissipated, until it was nothing but a large room full of rich, well-dressed men, speaking in clusters of two and three, laughing at one another's jokes. Planning business for the remainder of the afternoon. Hawking, hunting, drafting bills to be sent to Parliament, epicurean meals with diplomats from Venice or Castile. The everyday business of court.

Only Walsingham, as he moved toward the door, spared a glance at Kit. He nodded, his stern expression softened by faint creases around his eyes. "Marlowe," he said, nodding curtly. "Good work. God be on your side when you go."

Kit watched him leave. It was not the moment to explain that he and God had never been on each other's sides.

Seventeen

Chartley Manor inspired a wave of antipathy in Kit the moment he saw it. It was a forbidding place: a squat, sharp-chimneyed house that almost faded into the woods and craggy fields of Staffordshire behind. It brooded in the hazy predawn light, ringed by a stream that billowed mist across the grounds. Kit longed to turn his back on the place, but as the Council had made clear, this job had never been about what he wanted. It hadn't been his choice to return to Mary's service, but he would do what had been asked of him, whatever the risk, and if this was the only path open for advancement, he'd follow it as far as it would take him.

He strode to the door and pulled.

Locked.

Kit groaned and tilted his head back, looking at the foggy sky above. Of course. It was five in the morning. And this time, no one expected his arrival. The cold mist seeped through his clothes into his bones.

He knocked. Then knocked again. Then, with increasing impatience, a third time.

The door flung open, and Kit danced back in alarm from Anne Cooper standing in the doorway. Her hair hung loose and messy to her shoulders, and a woolen shawl the size of a blanket was draped over her nightgown. He must have woken her, he supposed. But the violence in her glare was too fierce to have been caused only by frustrated sleep.

Kit raised his hands and drew back another step. "Jesus Christ, Anne, I'm not trying to rob the house."

"Where in hell did you go?" she snapped, shoving him hard in the chest. He stumbled back, overbalanced and taken by surprise. "You reckless piece of shit."

"What—"

Anne didn't look like someone in the mood to argue. She looked more in the mood to cut him a second mouth. But she hadn't sent him away, and nothing mattered but that. They stood alone now on a long stone path sweeping from the house to the stream. Anne shut the door behind them and deepened her glare. As she closed the distance between them, the tail of her shawl brushed his arm, though their proximity was not in the least intimate.

"I thought you were dead," she hissed.

Kit blinked. It was touching that she'd missed him, but this did seem like jumping to conclusions. "What?"

"You disappear, in the middle of the night, without a word," Anne said, her voice still deathly low. "And when Beton asks what's become of you, that snake Poley pipes up straightaway with some cock-and-bull nonsense about a family matter, looking proud of himself as anything. With who that man is, what am I meant to think except that he slit your throat in a ditch?"

Words failed Kit. What was he supposed to say to that? It was a quarter past five in the morning, he'd been riding almost nonstop since the day before, and Mary's maidservant seemed to know more about the members of Walsingham's spy network than he did. And if she knew so much, what was to say she didn't know about him? Why else pull him aside if she didn't already know he had Mary's worst interests at heart?

The idea appeared fully formed in Kit's head, like someone else had thought it. He could kill Anne right now. Easily. Didn't need weapons to do it. If Anne had found him out, if she knew he worked for Walsingham, there was no other way. She stood alone, unarmed, in front of a sleeping house. Nothing simpler.

One quick decision could save his life. How fragile the human body was. It could be done in seconds.

He closed his hands into slow fists, considering.

Kit blinked, nausea rising. Was this who he was now? The kind of man Walsingham made him? A man who would kill to save himself?

No. Kit's weapons were words. His mind frightened him, the ease with which it had leapt to violence, but he could still say no to himself, if to no one else. He could still spin this to his advantage. She hadn't said she knew. He could still play the idiot, act his heart out. It was all he'd ever done, and he'd done it well enough until now.

"What do you mean, who he is?" he said. He lowered his voice, as though the mist might contain any number of listening ears. "Anne, what do you know?"

Anne shoved him again, causing him to stumble farther back. The grass gave a damp sigh under his feet. "By the Virgin, Kit, open your eyes. Whitehall sent Poley here to report on the Lady Mary. You know as well as I do how much they hate people who believe like us."

Kit's lips parted slightly, letting out a small breath. It was the best he could do, with words out of reach. His mind had given up on speech, as it whirled to reconfigure thoughts and fears and memories to fit this new picture. *People who believe like us.* Anne wasn't involved in Walsingham's schemes. She was a Catholic. And, somehow, she thought Kit was, too.

How could she think that? He'd given her no reason to believe—

Oh.

He almost wanted to laugh, it was so stupid.

Oh, he had.

What had he said, trying to convince her he was there to serve Mary? *When saints aren't protected, you wouldn't believe the terrible ways they can die.* He'd praised Mary like a seminarian doing devotion. Laughed off any attempt to pray from an English Bible. Made—ah, Jesus, he really had, hadn't he—made stupid jokes about the Eucharist, tobacco, and transubstantiation. He couldn't have been a more convincing papist if he'd done it on purpose.

All right. This was a complication, but not one he couldn't handle. Kit had always needed to play fast and dangerous to win, and if Anne had latched on to a false idea of his religious sympathies that made her trust him, he saw no reason to disabuse her of it. Confidence and recklessness were two sides of the same coin. One only became the other if you failed.

"I understand," Kit said. "Anne, I'm sorry I didn't tell you myself. It truly was a family disaster. My sister . . . Her death was sudden, and I wasn't thinking clearly. I didn't mean to make you worry."

Anne bit her lip, then touched his shoulder with grim sympathy. The anger had faded, replaced now only by this soft, dark wariness. It was enough to make him hate himself. He'd used Jane as leverage. Wielding one death to bring about another. Now his damnation was complete, and yet no fire and brimstone rained from above. Christ, like the Florentines, must subscribe to the policy of the ends justifying the means.

"I'm sorry," she said. "I know what that's like. But you have to understand you can't take risks like that. Nothing's safe here."

"I know," Kit said. "Will Mary take me back?"

Anne glanced back toward the house. Its windows remained dark, its doorways silent. No one to overhear this conversation, two servants whispering in the morning mist. "I think so," she said. "The Council halved her staff again. If you're willing to serve, she can't send you away. But she was livid when you disappeared. You'll need to tell her why. And if you can mention you saw to it that your sister received a proper funeral mass, that will help you."

Kit nodded. "I can do that."

Anne turned back toward the door. "Just watch yourself, Kit."

He smiled. "I always do," he said, stepping out of the mist into the manor. He looked back just long enough to see the first splash of sunrise above the trees, scattering sparks along the river, before the door closed behind him.

Eighteen

Master Robert Norgate sat at the large oak table in one of the college's offices, fighting his irritation with deep, steadying breaths. Around him in varying degrees of intransigence sat the four Corpus Christi professors jointly in charge of the college's administrative affairs. Haywood, professor of sciences. Crawley, mathematics. Dryden, philosophy. And Seymour, poetics. Four messengers bearing calamity, Norgate mused, thinking wryly of Revelation.

Avoiding the fellows' eyes, he focused on the solemn portrait of Master Emeritus Thomas Aldrich on the opposite wall. Norgate's immediate predecessor, stately and untroubled, was flanked by another ancient master on the left, a silver crucifix on the right. A good man, Aldrich. Norgate wondered if he'd ever had to endure the likes of this. But of course he had. The portrait's unperturbed appearance was a trick of the gilt frame, the dark wood behind. Every master of Corpus Christi College had been dragged into meetings like this against his will. Though, Norgate consented, perhaps not exactly like this.

"Sir, I appreciate your position," Haywood said. "But I don't think we have any choice."

"Review Marlowe's record," Norgate said, still looking at Aldrich's portrait, "and you'll see we have a multitude of choices."

"Robert," Crawley said. Norgate looked to him with frank astonishment. God as his witness, he'd never given Crawley permission to use his Christian name. "You know I admire your commitment to the poor scholars."

Admiration was an odd way of putting it, Norgate thought, petitioning the Lord for strength. At every convocation of the head council for the past five years, Crawley had argued for Marlowe's expulsion, citing his "unjustifiable expense on the college." It was a wonder he hadn't had the boy assassinated by now, to prove a point about economics.

"But if now isn't the time to revisit his eligibility for funding," Crawley went on, "I can't fathom what is. You have no idea where the boy's gone, and it's the second time in recent months he's taken off into the night. He's missed examinations, he's a terror in the lecture hall, and the college is still responsible for financing his costs when he does deign to appear—"

"By which you mean," Norgate cut in, "that if Marlowe were to pay his own way, you'd overlook it. It certainly seems to have been your approach to truant behavior in the past."

Crawley took a breath, fueling what looked to be a righteous tirade. Norgate pressed his lips together. This might go on for hours. But to his surprise, Seymour cut Crawley off before he could begin.

"Gentlemen," the poetics fellow said with a faint smile. "I respect your ethical devotion, truly I do. But Marlowe's circumstances are, I think, somewhat unusual?"

Norgate glanced at Seymour, who interlaced his long fingers with the shadow of a smile. Nothing in his manner betrayed special knowledge, but Norgate couldn't help but suspect. Did Seymour know how unusual Marlowe's circumstances were? After all, Seymour seemed to make a business of knowing things he had no business knowing. Norgate sighed. Behind him, the oil-painted faces of past college masters drilled history's conservative gaze through the back of his head.

They would never listen to him otherwise. He had to tell them.

Norgate thought again of his first conference with the queen's secretary. How the man had leaned forward when Norgate mentioned a poor graduate student with an expansive wit and a poorly developed moral center. Norgate's business was with books, not with men of that nature. He'd sworn to carry the secret to the end. But he'd also sworn to obey the queen's orders. And he could not now do both.

Damn it, he thought, reaching into the pocket of his scholar's robe for the letter. He would force his colleagues to pass Marlowe and then never think of the reckless student or the imposing spymaster again. Marlowe could get himself stabbed in a back alley the next day for all Norgate cared. The portrait of Thomas Aldrich regarded him with some reproof at this, but he refused to take the bait.

"Gentlemen, I don't think you understand," he said. "This debate is useless. We will grant Marlowe his degree. Because of this."

The sound of the letter slapping against the table silenced the room. The fellows peered at the delicate seal, the Tudor rose broken now but unmistakable. Crawley looked to Dryden, who gave a bewildered shrug. Norgate exhaled a single laugh. The rest of the head council wanted more involvement in the college's higher functions. See how they liked this.

"Master Seymour, if you would read the letter aloud, please," he said.

Seymour displayed no surprise or confusion. His expression was rather one of academic curiosity, a logical conundrum he would see resolved. He took up the page with a wry look at the master—reinforcing Norgate's notion that Seymour knew more than he let on.

Half smile still firmly in place, Seymour read.

"Dear sir, let me first commend you for your devotion to the education of England, and assure you how little I desire to interfere with the success of your profession. I write regarding the scholar Christopher Marlowe and his pending graduation. In all Marlowe's actions outside the university, he has behaved well and discreetly—"

Haywood gave a soft hum at the word *discreetly*.

"Well and discreetly," Seymour repeated, louder. "He has done

Her Majesty some good service, and deserves to be rewarded for his faithful dealings. Therefore, I request that he should be granted the degree he was to take this year. It is not Her Majesty's will that anyone working for the benefit of his country, as Marlowe has been, should be defamed by those who are ignorant of his affairs. Yours respectfully—"

Seymour paused. He coughed, then read the letter's signature with deceptive calm.

"Sir William Cecil, Lord Burghley, lord president of the Privy Council and royal treasurer to Her Sovereign Majesty Elizabeth, Queen of England and Ireland."

The fellows stared, stunned out of speech. Yes, gentlemen, Norgate thought. The student you've loathed and tried to expel for years has been carrying out clandestine operations for the Privy Council. Tell me again what you would do in my position.

"Well, gentlemen," Norgate said. "I take it we are decided?"

Haywood was reduced to stammering. "Sir, we. I. My God—"

"You're suggesting that because Marlowe ran off in the night to play the hero in Rheims, we are obligated to—" Crawley began.

"Rheims?" Haywood repeated. "You think *Marlowe's* passing as a *priest?*"

"As likely that as the idea *Sir William Cecil* is involved—"

"It doesn't matter where he's gone or what he's done," Dryden said. "Academic integrity—"

Seymour regained his composure in moments. The madness of poets, Norgate supposed, to accept the impossible as perfectly credible. "Do you prefer treason over bending a few rules?" he asked.

Haywood froze at the word *treason.* Crawley and Dryden were engaged in a rapid, silent conversation across the table, each daring the other to do something to stop this affront to all they held dear. Norgate groaned, though he doubted anyone but Seymour heard. If God himself blasted the words *Let Christopher Marlowe Graduate* into a stone tablet, the fellows would still debate the matter for hours. But Norgate was master of Corpus Christi. That came with a thousand annoyances, an eternal nightmare of bureaucracy. It also, on occasion, came with authority.

He stood, leaning his palms on the table. "Gentlemen," he said, "Marlowe will receive his degree this year, as planned. If that concerns you, I suggest you take up the matter with Her Majesty."

As Norgate swept out of the room, hearing Crawley splutter over his shoulder, he finally understood the attraction of empire. The Old Testament might warn against Pharaoh's tyranny, but it was the only effective model for making decisions.

Nineteen

K it lay on his back in the servants' quarters and gazed up at the ceiling, somehow both exhausted and on edge. Silence hung around him complete as the darkness. It was early still—half past four, he guessed—and what remained of Mary's reduced staff was still dead asleep. The previous day's work had been no less exhausting than any of the others, but Kit had nevertheless lain awake from midnight on, thinking, counting the minutes. It had been that way for weeks. The idea of sleep taunted him, just out of reach.

He sat up and leaned sideways, reaching for his shoes. It was so early it was still late, but his body hummed with energy, urging him to get up, to move. He had nowhere to go—wouldn't learn anything in a sleeping house—but at this point his choices were walking or screaming from frustration, and one seemed decidedly wiser than the other.

Chartley felt like a tomb, he thought, as he left the room and descended the darkened stair. The manor's entrance hall yawned before him, low arched ceilings with long shadows that licked his heels, and the walls looked silver with moonlight. The urge to scream still itched the back of his throat. He almost wanted to give in. Make this house ring with his fear, if only for a moment.

Two months. Two months he'd been back. Two months dreaming of the Armada on England's shores, waiting for the sound of cannon thundering in the distance. In all that time, Kit had heard nothing. Not a whisper. Nothing of Mary's assassins. Not a word from Anne about her faith, which would at least have been leverage, would have been something. Only the voice in the back of his mind, hissing, *You're wasting time, you'll fail, the Armada will come, and thousands of people will die.*

Kit paused. Through the stillness, the smallest sounds carried. Someone was walking nearby, too fast for half past four. Without thinking, Kit set off toward the sound. It didn't matter what it was. He needed something, anything.

Turning the corner, he found Matthew starting up the stairs. Between his disheveled hair, muddy boots, and the strong scent of horse, the groom must have arrived minutes before. And in his hand—Kit felt his blurred brain narrow down on it—in his hand he held a letter.

"Matthew," he said.

Matthew flinched. "Kit? What in hell are you doing awake?"

Kit shrugged. "I couldn't sleep," he said, still watching the letter. "Let me take that to Mary. You go rest."

"Are you sure?"

Kit had never been more sure of anything. That letter—if it was what he suspected—could change everything. But only if he read it and sent what he found to London before the manor woke. He felt Walsingham's cold presence behind him, and the disdainful glare of Sir Robert Cecil through the dim light. *You should have known better, Sir Francis, than to trust something like this to a country fool. What did I tell you would happen?*

No. He couldn't fail.

"Here," Kit said, holding out his hand. "Just because I can't sleep doesn't mean you shouldn't."

Matthew smiled and pressed the letter into Kit's palm. He yawned, a little ostentatiously, made a quick sign of thanks, and climbed the stairs with carrying footsteps. Matthew, at least, had nothing to hide at this hour.

God bless sleepless nights. Kit itched to read the letter then and there, but eagerness couldn't be allowed to spill over into stupidity. Anyone might discover him here, just as he'd discovered Matthew. He took off down the corridor and ducked through the first door he found, without thinking about what lay beyond it. Anything for privacy. It had never been so important to be alone.

He eased the door shut, turning the handle as he did to make no sound. Then, feeling his blood rush with each breath, he looked around.

He laughed. Just once, but he couldn't hold it in.

The room was small and well lit despite the hour, with a handful of candles casting golden light across two wooden benches. In front of the benches stood a low table bearing a gold crucifix, an open psalter, and two framed paintings: one of the Virgin Mother, the other of Saint Catherine of Siena. Mary's private chamber, and her space for prayer. Well, Kit did require a miracle of sorts.

The Virgin's painted eyes watched Kit in reproach as he turned to the letter. Through the page's single fold, he saw a familiar tangle of symbols, and an instinctive smile crossed his face. Babington's cipher. The source of so much fear months before, now as easy to read as English, as welcome as a dear friend. Kit sank down onto the bench and lifted the wax seal from the letter the way Gregory had taught him at Cambridge, so no one would suspect it had been tampered with.

In the golden light of the candles, he read.

My lady,

I have done as you asked. Before the usurper fortifies her forces, my friends and I prepare to strike. You may rely on these men as you rely on me. Barnwell and Tilney you've met and, as I think, trust. Father John Ballard of the Jesuit order is a stranger to you, but be assured my confidence resides in him more than in any man living. My lady, now is the time. I wait only for your word.

AB

Kit pressed a hand over his mouth. He'd forgotten to breathe. Names. Only three of the six assassins Babington had spoken of in his previous letter, true, but he had names. Barnwell, Tilney,

John Ballard the Jesuit. It was what Walsingham had sent him for. Would it be enough? It had to be. He would damn these men, he'd do it today, and their deaths would thrust a stumbling block in the way of England's ruin. Three lives for a nation. Three lives to return to his own. The equation felt perfectly balanced.

He heard the door open behind him.

Kit thrust the paper into the inner pocket of his doublet. Thinking fast, he dropped to his knees in front of the bench and bowed his head, praying aloud. A scrap of doctrine, stored out of sight until needed, stepped forward for the occasion. The Latin came easily, from that rote space beyond thought. He hardly heard what he was saying. At least this was a lie he'd practiced. How many times had he broken into loud, inauthentic prayer while the Cambridge rector glared at him across the chapel?

As Mary knelt beside him, he wondered if his Latin sounded as much like amateur necromancy to her ears as it did to his.

Mary folded her hands in prayer, though she said nothing. Her gown, black with gold stitching, put Kit in mind of a funeral pall. Ignoring him, she looked at the Christ pinned to his golden cross on the table. Christ looked back with the heavy-eyed resentment of a whipped hound. She waited for Kit to finish the Latin cadence before she spoke.

"I confess, I did not expect piety from you," she said, to all appearances addressing Christ. "You pray for your sister?"

Jane. Again Jane, whispering answers in his ear. God was a fiction, but if angels existed, Jane was one of them. "Yes, madam," he said.

"And you use the prayers of the true faith," she said, smiling. "Daring, in these times."

Kit blinked. Had he? The words had jumped from the darkness of memory to save him, but sure enough, no orthodox Protestant would have spoken that prayer. *Hail, holy Queen, Mother of mercy, our life, our sweetness, and our hope.* A prayer Kit's mother would murmur, late at night, when she thought no one could hear. A hard habit to unlearn. Back when Katherine Marlowe had learned to pray, Protestants had been heretics, and Catholics the righteous.

Under other circumstances, Kit would have laughed to think he couldn't tell the difference.

Mary crossed herself and sat on the bench, smoothing her dark skirts. When Kit stood, he kept several delicate feet between them. "How old are you, Marlowe?" Mary asked.

Mary's interest meant one of two things. Either she trusted him enough to care, or she suspected him and wanted to keep him talking until he condemned himself. Either way, fear and shifty silence wouldn't help.

"Twenty-two," Kit said.

She nodded. "Close in age. I thought so."

"Close to—"

"My son," Mary said, smiling. "He may resemble you, for all I know. I have not seen him in twenty years." She paused. "When my cousin kills me, Marlowe, do you think my son will pray for me as you pray for your sister?"

Any servant with experience in humility would have deflected the question like a swordsman turning a blow. He knew what he ought to say: something anodyne and reassuring, *I'm sure you have many more years to live, my lady.* But Kit knew Mary better than that. She was a formidable woman, but she valued faith over flattery, and a bold statement spoken honestly over cringing evasions. He'd been watching her so long that certain parts of her mind were as familiar as his own.

"It doesn't matter whether he prays or not, madam," he said. "I haven't known you long, but I know you don't need help to reach God's grace."

For a long moment, Mary said nothing. Kit shifted his weight, watching her. Maybe he should have said the usual thing. Perhaps he'd offended her, and his gamble would be read as a wish for her murder. But when she turned to him at last, she wore the same expression as the dog-eyed Christ: mournful, but gentle. "Do you know, Marlowe," she said, "no one else has admitted to me that I may die. Even Thomas Morgan could not manage that."

Hands clasped in front of him, he ran his thumb along his

opposite knuckles, watching it instead of her. "Madam, you're kind, and wise, and pious. But you aren't God, so yes, I expect someday you'll die, the same as the rest of us."

Another gambit that paid off, as Mary laughed. "Honesty suits you, Marlowe," she said. "I commend it." She looked back to the crucifix, considering. "I should have died earlier, I think. It would have been neater that way."

Kit didn't know what to say to that, but it didn't matter. To Mary, Kit was nothing but an abstraction to test her thoughts against, someone who had no choice but to listen.

"Women martyrs are always young, beautiful virgins," she went on, looking at the painting of Saint Catherine with something approaching scorn. "When tragedy is not beautiful, we do not care enough to call it tragedy. I am too old for martyrdom now. A wasted chance. It would have meant more earlier."

Kit flexed his fingers, then relaxed them, scanning his mind for something to say. It was one thing to want a woman's death in the abstract. Quite another to hear her speak of it herself, with the fearless calm of a resigned tactician. Saints and martyrs and the terrible ways they can die. England's fate rested on destroying this woman, but even looking at the cracks in her composure made him want to be sick.

"Was your sister beautiful?" Mary asked.

The shift in tone left Kit disoriented. A glimpse into Mary's mind, maybe. When your own death hovered so close, it held no more weight than any other subject of conversation. Your servants' siblings. Your head on a spike. The weather. "I don't think so, madam. People said she looked like me."

Mary looked at him straight on. Intent. Considering him. Kit remembered the sketch Gregory had shown him months ago, that same gaze interrogating him from the page. He wanted to crumble under it. "I see tragedy in you," she said. "I am sure I would have seen it in her as well."

It might have been a threat. It might have been a compliment. It felt like neither.

"I do not think the world has been kind to you, Marlowe," Mary said. "And I do not expect it will be kind to me." She sighed again, turned away. "I must be patient, as Christ was patient. I must endure."

Endure until Kit and Walsingham decided she couldn't any longer. Until Kit wrote to Whitehall and the dogs slipped their leashes, aimed their teeth at her throat. Mary trusted him. Her greatest mistake, and, if he succeeded, her last. The letter weighted down his pocket. He wanted to run. He wanted to tell her everything. He wanted to drive a knife through her heart, or his, and either way put an end to it.

Both Kit and Mary looked toward the Christ on the table, static and glittering like a pinned beetle. His arms stretched in both directions at once, pointing out no path.

"I will add your sister to my prayers, Marlowe," Mary said without looking at him.

It was the most backward dismissal he'd ever heard. Mary devoted her attention to the makeshift altar, Christ and the Virgin Mother, Saint Catherine beautiful and ignored to the side. She might not have seen Kit leave.

———

The letter's seal was cheaply made, easy to manipulate. In Chartley's small dining room, Kit softened the wax over a candle flame before pressing it back with the flat of a knife. He laid the letter near Mary's place at the breakfast table, then paused.

Three men would die because of that letter. Likely more. And Mary, contemplating martyrdom, praying for Kit, for Jane, while he prayed for her death. So four, at least, would die.

He couldn't afford to think that way. Twenty minutes ago, the letter had hung brilliant in his hand, the answer he'd needed. It was that still. This was what he'd come to do. Lie, and betray, and kill, and not question.

He turned away from the table and left the room. He had a message to get to Whitehall before dawn.

Twenty

Mary rested her forearms on the windowsill in her bedchamber. Breathing deep, she leaned out to survey Chartley's grounds, the trees, the river. The faint breeze toyed with the sleeves of her pale blue gown, sending the fabric rippling toward the horizon. She'd seen the pose in a painting somewhere, as a child: the besieged queen of the Chanson de Roland, or some other maudlin lady in a tower. Two weeks ago, she'd have dismissed the comparison as self-indulgent. Two weeks ago, she'd paced this room for nights on end, anxious and wild. Two weeks ago, she'd felt like cut crystal, sharp and ready to shatter.

Now, her confinement almost felt romantic. Anything would, so close to the end.

It wouldn't be long now. Anthony had left Cresswell three weeks ago for a rented house in Lichfield, a spit of a village fifteen miles away. She had arranged to meet his man Poley on the edge of the woods this afternoon, to pass off a letter. Short and to the point—at this stage, no call to waste words.

Do it, said the letter, behind the screen of cipher. *Tell your men to begin.*

It would be over soon.

And she could endure in the meantime. She could fill a week or two pretending Elizabeth's men had thwarted her, passing the time somehow, watching the idle dramas that occupied her staff. They thought she didn't notice, but Mary noticed everything. Noticed how Marlowe's grief over his sister had faded—not long after Anthony had written of the impending strike. Noticed the way he looked at Anne Cooper with more than an observer's interest, as if trying to see something essential about her. The young thought they invented these things, but Mary knew their game. Indulging the mood, she thought back to her decades-old wedding night with the dauphin, both of them children still. Sitting beside her in that grand carved bed, both trying not to think about the members of the French court arrayed at the foot of it, waiting to pay witness to consummation. François had looked down at his knees under the bedclothes and asked shyly to kiss her, and without speaking she ran one hand along his cheek and kissed him first. François had smiled then just as Marlowe smiled now. The smile of an anxious lover getting good news.

Mary stepped back from the window, though she left it open. A sweet boy, François. She'd been ill-starred in husbands since, but at least her first had meant well. And if Marlowe was clever enough to keep pace with Cooper, more happiness to him. The girl was smart, and kind, and easy to talk to: rare qualities in this household. Surrounded by such bores and bureaucrats, Mary even found herself missing Anthony Babington's inane flattery. At least insulting him gave her something to do.

Soon enough. When Anthony turned up at Chartley's door with an army, Mary could insult him with every breath in her body. She pressed one hand against the waist of her skirt, feeling the letter safely folded in the fabric. Then, decided, she swept down the stairs and into Lord Rich's study. The lord of the manor was under royal command to approve or deny all unplanned excursions, but that didn't mean she needed to ask politely.

"I will take a walk on the grounds," she said, instead of hello. She didn't sit. Sitting would signal she meant to discuss the matter, which she didn't.

Sir Robert Rich looked up from the manor's account books, spread across the desk in his study. He scowled, round eyes suspicious behind a fussy pair of spectacles. No wonder Lady Rich spent little time with him. A dull businessman, spending his life indoors totaling up ledgers. Not exactly the gallant knight of a woman's dreams. "Do you think that's wise, madam?" Rich said.

"That is not your concern," Mary said.

As her jailer, it was in fact his concern, which she expected him to point out. Technically, she was permitted to walk the grounds as well as the manor, but Rich followed rules beyond the letter of the law.

Rich removed his spectacles and pressed his thumb and middle finger to his closed eyes, circling away a headache. Mary smirked. Sir Robert Rich was the kind of man who inspired headaches in others. Only fair he should take his turn. "You are not to leave the grounds," he said. "And you will bring Cooper with you, for supervision. No untoward behavior will be tolerated."

Mary's smirk widened. "Untoward behavior? With Cooper? Sir, you mistake my intentions."

Rich colored, to her satisfaction. He waved a hand toward the door, intending to get Mary—and the headache she brought into his life—out of his study. "Go, then. Be back within the hour, or I will send the dogs after you."

Fair enough, Mary thought. She wouldn't need the hour. And Cooper could keep a secret.

Walking the sweep of the grounds, Mary felt the glow of a laugh rise from the base of her ribs. She heard the song of a skylark nesting in the woods, somewhere past the narrow stream. It was beautiful, she thought. The world was beautiful. Made that way by the letter stowed in her skirt, a simple note that would set everything in motion. Reckless, perhaps, to deliver it herself, but Mary was through waiting for others to act. Now, at the end, she would be where she belonged, at the center of it all.

"You seem happy, madam," Cooper said, walking beside her.

Mary laughed. "I am. The strangest feeling in the world."

"Good news?" From another person, the question might have been dangerous, a sign of discovery. But Mary trusted Anne Cooper with her life. She'd heard the maid pray, more than once, and watched her make the sign of the cross without pause. Once you'd heard how someone prayed, knowing whether to trust them was easy.

"The best," Mary said. "Change is coming soon, my friend. I promise you that."

Mary crossed the narrow bridge to the edge of the woods, Cooper close behind. She looked through the trees, whose thin branches and dry leaves had withered in the scorching summer. One note, passed from hand to hand, and in a few weeks, it would be done. She would be free. She would be out.

She would be queen.

Poley would come soon, Mary knew. Anthony was an idiot, and his opportunistic man no better, but she trusted them to keep their promises. She walked the length of the woods, listening to the sound of the skylark, to the ripple of the stream.

To footsteps against the crumbling leaves.

Mary saw them at once. The uniformed men, emerging from the yellow scrub and brittle trees. Eight? Ten? She didn't count. It didn't matter. Each with the same embroidered scarlet-and-gold rose on their lapel. The Tudor rose. Elizabeth's rose.

Mary's hand rose to her throat. She forced herself to lower it.

The suave, slightly hunched man at the head of the company looked as surprised to see Mary as she to see him. Regaining his composure, he smiled, then extended a hand. Mary stared down at the man like he'd vomited at her feet. Through her alarm, she was glad the diminutive Sir Robert Cecil stood nine inches shorter than she did. There was a petty pleasure to be had in that.

Cecil's smile did not dip. "Mary, my dear," he said, retracting the hand. "How thoughtful. You've saved us the trouble of coming all the way to the house."

"Sir Robert," Mary said. Her heart trembled, but her voice held steady. "What a pleasant surprise."

It was a marvel Cecil found a way to speak around his smile. "I doubt that very much."

"What is the meaning of this?" she said. "We are still on the grounds, as my cousin instructed."

"We?"

Mary looked back. She stood alone. Cooper must have bolted at the first sound of the guards. She'd been right, then, about the maid's beliefs. Perhaps she'd done more than follow the true faith privately, if Cooper felt the need to flee at the first sign of danger. Every woman for herself, then. Mary had been surrounded by advisors and conspirators and idiot husbands all her life, but one by one they had left her, and in truth, she had always been alone. It seemed fitting, to face this man one to one.

"I have done nothing to offend," Mary said.

"Mary, my dear," Cecil said. "The time for that game is up."

A soldier stepped forward, drawing his blade. "Mary Stuart, we arrest you on charges of treason, heresy, conspiracy, and intended regicide."

If Mary had one asset to her name, it was stoicism. She stood still, the blue of her summer gown fluttering behind like the trappings of some fairy queen. The soldier's naked sword hovered against her heart. She raised her chin and looked down at Cecil as if the blade weren't there.

"A convincing performance," Cecil said. "I almost want to believe it."

Mary didn't want to lie to Cecil. She wanted to tell him everything. Yes, she hated Elizabeth. Yes, she wanted her cousin dead; her cousin deserved it. Yes, she would put herself on the throne in a heartbeat, and do whatever it took to get there, because it was her throne, her right, her country. Yes, a hundred times yes, to all of it.

But Mary was righteous, not stupid. She smiled, cold enough to freeze a man's heart. "You will kill me if I resist."

"I expect so, yes," Cecil said.

Mary drew herself up to her full height. "Lead on, then," she said, "where you will."

Twenty-One

Sir Francis Walsingham stood in front of Chartley's door, watching. He wouldn't have left this task to Cecil if he'd had any choice: Sir Robert's enthusiasm for justice made him tend toward unnecessary cruelty in its execution. But there were limits, now, to what Walsingham could do. That summer had been difficult. Though the sickness had struck hardest in London's piss-stinking alleys and brothels, Walsingham's habits left him vulnerable. He'd paced Whitehall's corridors one too many nights, forgotten to eat for one too many days, and illness, sensing an opening, had pounced. He resented the silver-topped cane he relied on now, resented having to delegate the arrest to Cecil, but with God's grace he would be well again soon. He didn't have time for illness. Not with so much in motion.

Mary stood near the woods, surrounded by eight soldiers and Cecil, a naked sword at her breast. Yet she did not flinch. Walsingham respected that. He hated that he respected it.

Beside him, Marlowe had folded his arms and curled his fingers around his elbows as if to keep warm. He seemed thinner now, the shadows in his face deeper. For the first time, the boy's reckless confidence had shrunk into something quieter, something afraid and uncertain. Something terribly far from how he'd appeared in Whitehall, delivering the broken cipher with the glint of triumph in his eye. Perhaps he understood, now, what it was for actions to have consequences. None of Walsingham's agents understood that from the beginning—if they did, they would never sign on.

But they all realized, sooner or later, what victory felt like. Hazy and sour, like a half-remembered dream.

"You've done well," Walsingham said. He didn't look away from the woods. It was true, what he said, but he wasn't in the habit of saying it. "Better than anyone expected."

Marlowe didn't blink at the praise, backhanded though it was. "What happens now?"

The next move on the chessboard. Much as Marlowe might try to deny it, he and Walsingham were just the same. Give him thirty years and the last traces of the boy's idealism would wash away, leaving him with the same focused efficiency Walsingham wielded at fifty. At Marlowe's pace, he might not even need that long.

"The trial will be held at Fotheringhay Castle in Northampton. We will retire there at once to arrange the details."

Walsingham heard Marlowe laugh under his breath at the word *details*. Irony: another indulgence that would erode with time. Mary Stuart was a heretic and a traitor, and she would receive the punishment reserved for heretics and traitors. Any other concerns were details.

"Sir," Marlowe said.

The wind sent a chill through Walsingham, which turned to a stab of pain shooting up his left leg to his hip. He hissed through his teeth and gripped his cane. Marlowe glanced over with something slightly too hard for pity. Walsingham did not look at him, grounding himself instead through the cool metal in his palm. He would be well soon. He had to be.

"What?"

"Will you promise me something, sir?" Marlowe said. He turned back to the woods, where two of the soldiers manacled Mary's wrists behind her back.

"What is that?"

"After the trial," Marlowe said, "I'm finished. The Council sends me on my way. You gave me a job, sir, and I've done it. Promise me that's enough."

He'd developed a conscience, then. Walsingham had been right: it was guilt he'd spotted, newly born. The spymaster felt an uncomfortable stab of remorse, which he refused to tolerate. What the boy asked was impossible. Even if Walsingham had sworn on the cross to end Marlowe's commission after the trial, he'd perjure himself without pause. Marlowe was exceptional. He'd succeeded where every other man in Walsingham's arsenal had failed, and had done it in time to save a nation. Marlowe could be trusted. And in these times, a trustworthy man was a rare commodity. He couldn't allow the boy to walk, not with what he'd proven he could do.

It was a heavy price Walsingham asked of him. Surrendering a corner of your soul. No one knew that better than Walsingham, who'd barely seen his wife in six months, who'd once ducked out of a Privy Council meeting ten minutes early to bury two sons, whose granddaughter wouldn't have recognized him in a crowd. A heavy price, but a man of talent had no choice but to pay it. Intelligence had always come with a cost.

Walsingham turned away, toward the manor. The twinge between his ribs had nothing to do with his illness.

Ten years ago, he'd have felt nothing. Would have lied to the boy through his teeth, then dispatched him overseas the moment the axe fell. By the cross, he'd sent Gregory to Douai the day before the man was to bury his mother, and he'd slept soundly after, too. Perhaps he'd outlived his own nerve. Gone from the queen's most steadfast advisor to a tired, overworked man past fifty. Graying at the temples, creased between the brows, crumbling from within. Weak. Old. Sentimental.

"We leave in three hours for Northampton," Walsingham said, without looking back. "Gather your things."

———

Fotheringhay Castle looked as though it had stood abandoned for decades. Tall grass ranged through the courtyard, unchallenged and unkempt. The lilac-shaped heads atop the boldest stalks bowed in the wind like a priest before an altar. Indoors, statesmen and courtiers had held hushed debates over heresy and treason for weeks, the air heavy and still, close as a confessional. It was almost a relief for Walsingham to stand here in the September chill, watching the wind race across the scaffold. His leg trembled, an overreaction to the cold, but the pain seemed worth it. Mind over matter. There were more important things.

Things like the two men on the scaffold, hands bound with a rough length of cord, silent as their spectators.

At first, Lord Chancellor Bromley hadn't wanted to waste a trial on Anthony Babington and Thomas Morgan. Skip the speeches, straight to the denouement, which after all they had known from the start. It had fallen to Walsingham to explain the value of setting an example, for dissuading tomorrow's would-be assassins. Never underestimate the power of theatrics. Perhaps Marlowe was rubbing off on him, Walsingham mused. In any case, it hadn't taken long. There had never been any question what the sentence would be, there in Fotheringhay's high-ceilinged hall. Babington's letters—signed in his own hand, the stupid child, he hadn't even thought to cipher his name—had damned him from the beginning. And Morgan, his accomplice, shared the guilt. The comfort of certainty was worth the delay.

Walsingham watched as Morgan looked down the scaffold, toward where Babington stood. The rope collared the young gentleman's neck already. Babington's knees trembled; Walsingham could see it from here. He wanted to take the fool by the throat and shake him. Babington would die, fear or no fear. After what he'd done, the least he owed the queen was to die with dignity.

The hangman draped the noose around Morgan's neck and slipped the knot tight. The sound that escaped Morgan sounded like an injured bird—soft, yet carrying. Perhaps there was no dignity among traitors.

Babington looked up from his feet, across the crowd. He'd been crying, it seemed. His wide black eyes were rimmed with red, and splotches of color disfigured his cheeks and nose. But he did not cry now. He stood tall, squaring his shoulders against the noose. He spotted Walsingham, one face among many, and smiled, insolent, peacocking for the crowd. A dandy's dignity, then, or something close.

Anthony Babington was young. Walsingham had forgotten that. Twenty-four. Barely older than Marlowe.

Walsingham glanced over his shoulder, where Marlowe stood near Fotheringhay's eastern wall, as far as he could get from the scaffold without leaving the courtyard altogether. They were old enough, Walsingham thought, turning back. Old enough to commit treason, attempt regicide. Old enough to unravel a plot across two countries, stabilize a throne. Both men had chosen their sides. And neither youth nor age mattered to the hangman.

First the platform would fall, and then the rope would tighten. Then the gasp, the snap, the twitch. After that, their living bodies would be cut down and thrown to the grass, where they would be torn open, their insides unlaced from their ribs. They would be cut into four pieces, quartered down the middle, and then their heads removed, which Walsingham supposed, arithmetically, made five. Not that it mattered. Whether it took ten minutes or an hour, both traitors would be dead by sundown. Long before, ideally. Something to be said for theatrics, but Walsingham had work to do, and time was scarce.

"Confess your treasons," said the priest from behind Morgan. "Confess and repent, and go to your graves fearing God."

Repent or don't, Walsingham thought. It didn't matter now. The platform would fall either way.

Morgan spat on the scaffold. Babington flinched. Over his shoulder, Walsingham felt rather than saw Marlowe do the same.

"I have nothing to repent," Morgan said. "God save Queen Mary."

"God save Queen Mary," Babington said. His voice held steady, with strength Walsingham hadn't expected. Neither had Morgan, from his owlish stare. Babington smiled, giving the older traitor a soft nod. "God save Queen Mary," he repeated, louder.

"And death to all tyrants," Morgan finished.

Death to all tyrants.

Death to rebels first.

The wind tore through the courtyard, the tall grass and the priest bent their heads as one, and the ropes jerked as Morgan and Babington fell.

Twenty-Two

Mary had been arrested in August and brought to Northampton to stand trial, but October arrived without any move to summon the court. The Privy Council and the lord chancellor locked themselves in the castle's library and argued legal precedent long into the night. They claimed these meetings were essential to prepare an effective case, but Kit, who'd been tasked with transcribing them for the queen's benefit, knew this was a lie. After the first meeting, the argument was so straightforward that a first-year Cambridge undergraduate could have made it. They needed the queen's permission to begin, that was all. Until they got it, they would wait. And Kit would remain here, crafting memoranda to Whitehall, encoding his transcriptions using a cipher he'd been tasked to devise for the occasion, scribbling notes with a shaking hand.

Kit slept worse with each passing week. Soon, he stayed awake until three or four in the morning, pacing the castle's halls in endless, anxious circles to outrun the ghosts of Morgan and Babington. His nerves gnawed at him like acid through iron. He'd thought he'd understood the consequences of what he'd been told to do, but it was different writing it out in his own hand. Hearing it. Dreaming it night after night, the tortured screams of two men, and knowing that once their wracked bodies finally found their graves, he was the one who'd sent them there.

Robert Poley, on the other hand, seemed untroubled by his role in the matter. He arrived at Fotheringhay three days after Kit and Walsingham, striding about with a careless bounce in his step. He haunted Kit's pacing, attempting to trade stories as if he and Kit had always been friends.

"I wish you'd seen Babington's face, Marlowe," Poley said. Kit feigned interest in a tapestry hanging in the west corridor, hoping Poley would take the hint. "When the soldiers came. His eyes got wide as gold sovereigns. God's teeth, I thought the man would cry."

Kit felt the retch rise in his throat. That stupid peacock Babington. Heads spiked atop Bishopsgate. The snap of the rope, and the half-choked scream when the rope was exchanged for the blade. He turned his back on Poley and bolted into the privy, where he vomited for a full minute. He shook his head as he rose, knees weak. He couldn't crumble now. This wasn't the end. Not by half.

It was almost a relief when Walsingham announced the trial would begin on the fourteenth of October. Anything was preferable to waiting.

The tribunal met in Fotheringhay's great hall, a cavernous space with a vaulted ceiling like an ancient mead hall. Two long rows of benches had been pushed along either wall for the nobles. A table for the notaries stood in the center, behind which sat a row of chairs for the lord chancellor and the lord chief justice. A bar had been raised at the back of the room, cordoning off a space for men without pedigree to watch. Windows in the room were scarce, and already the thick panes were fogged against the chill outside. A short autumn, then, and a hard winter on its heels.

Kit entered as late as he could, when the room already teemed with noblemen. He felt them turn to look at him. Not seeing him but measuring him, and not liking what they found. He shrank into himself and stood behind the bar, resting his hands on the wood. Running suddenly seemed more attractive than ever.

"Didn't think you were coming," Robert Poley said, from Kit's left.

Kit jumped. He scowled at Poley, his anxiety funneling into rage. Of all the people he could have stood beside.

"Bromley sent the summons half an hour ago." Poley nodded toward the back of the lord chancellor's head in front of them. "Your Scottish heretic is taking her time. She must like an entrance."

Would Poley have answered Bromley's summons sooner, in Mary's place? Would he have sauntered into a room of men determined to condemn him any way they could? Kit's fingernails bit into his palms. He turned the pain over in his head, using it as a center of gravity. He could pretend none of this was real, nothing but the sharp bite in his hands.

The door opened, and two guards entered, flanking Mary between them. Kit's chest tightened around his lungs.

She looked like a queen still. Dressed simply, in a black gown with a white lace veil over her hair, she stood straight, towering. Her eyes flicked across the assembled noblemen—not like a hunted deer, but a snake preparing to strike. Her guards led her to the front of the room, but she ignored the chair set before the table. Tall and confident, she looked at the impatient Lord Chancellor Bromley, at the fragile Lord Burghley, at the imperturbable Sir Francis Walsingham.

At the common men standing behind the bar.

At Kit.

There was no question. She recognized him at once.

Poley scowled at Kit, then thumped him on the back hard enough to jar him. "You're a damned hero, Marlowe," he muttered. "At least pretend like you're enjoying it."

Kit closed his eyes. The trembling in his head was easier to manage in darkness. When he looked again, Mary had sat down. The lord chancellor rose and paced to the front of the room, displaying a pathological need to command a crowd's attention. Well, let him, then. The sooner Bromley began, the sooner this would finish.

"Madam," Bromley said. His voice was too high to perform his office with dignity, but no one dared laugh. "We are gathered to

166 + A TIP FOR THE HANGMAN

examine serious charges against you, to secure the safety of Her Majesty's person by reaching a just verdict."

Mary smiled. Kit had seen her mock Anthony Babington with that same smile. "I am familiar with the idea of a trial, Lord Chancellor," she said.

Poley snorted. Kit could have killed him.

Bromley's eyes narrowed. "In that case," he said, "you will also be familiar with the terms of the Act of Association."

"I am."

Every soul in that room was. No paragraph had been read, repeated, and debated more in the previous weeks. The Act of Association, to protect the life of Queen Elizabeth at whatever cost. Any conspirator who attempted, intended, or considered a plot against Her Majesty would be executed for treason. And if a conspiracy was discovered to place someone else on the throne, that person would be executed as well—whether they knew of the conspiracy or not. A crafty piece of legislation, and a new one. Walsingham had written it himself, scant months before recruiting Kit. Too neat for coincidence. Walsingham had set the legal precedent to condemn Mary for his suspicions, then found an agent to confirm them.

"Then you understand the charges against you?" Bromley asked.

Mary's smirk had not faded. "Have you charged me with anything, Lord Chancellor? I thought you were providing a dramatic monologue."

"She's stalling," Poley said under his breath.

"Stop it," Kit hissed. This was agonizing enough without Poley treating it like a spectacle in need of commentary.

Bromley's words came fast and clipped. Under less formal circumstances, he would have shouted. "Mary Stuart, you are charged with treacherous violation of the Act of Association. You are charged with plotting against the life of Her Majesty Queen Elizabeth. Of conspiring with traitors. Of instigating plots against England from the moment you entered this country."

Mary's lips twitched with a smile at this. She bowed her head to

Bromley, like a musician accepting applause. Did she want to die? In a room like this, where every word and every gesture meant life or death, she had no room for carelessness. And that bow was a deadly mistake.

But then, nothing would change the court's mind. She had dignity, this way. Perhaps that was the point.

"Madam," Bromley said, "tell the court of your association with Anthony Babington."

"I apologize, sir," Mary said. "I do not know the gentleman."

Bromley scowled. "Sir Robert Cecil," he said.

Cecil stood from the right-hand bench, a paper in his hand. He'd been waiting for his cue like an overeager player.

"If you would read Babington's confession for the court, Sir Robert," Bromley said.

Cecil began to read, but Kit wasn't listening. He'd already heard Babington confess, voice wavering, edging toward tears, pleading without shame. Not the kind of confession he would forget. Instead, he watched Mary. Though she didn't move, her face paled as Cecil spoke. Kit could see her putting together the pieces.

Anthony Babington was dead. Mary, confined and isolated, must have suspected, but she hadn't known until this moment. Now Mary could imagine what Kit had witnessed. Dying screams. Flesh burning in the courtyard. Perhaps she'd heard it, from whatever corner of the castle they'd imprisoned her in, but dismissed it as the product of an overstrained imagination. Would the memory, even diluted by distance, linger for her the same way it did for him?

"Anthony Babington and Thomas Morgan have been justly punished for their treasons," Cecil said. "Their brood of assassins will follow. And all swear they acted in your name."

Mary made the sign of the cross, then let out her breath slowly. When she spoke again, her voice was level. "I will pray for their souls as I pray for all Christians," she said. "But beyond Morgan, who managed my household for a time, I do not know them."

"You corresponded with Babington," Cecil pressed. "You wrote your intent to practice against the queen's life. You cannot deny that."

Mary sat up straighter. Her dignity flashed like a comet, screaming fire at the end of the world. "I can and I will. Show me one letter in which I said I would harm my cousin. Show me one."

Cecil's smile was inhuman. A hunting dog's smile. Kit could almost see blood on his lips. "With pleasure," he said. "Perhaps this will look familiar."

A sergeant handed a paper to Cecil, who extended it with a cruel flourish of his wrist. The familiar lines of the cipher stared up at Mary. Her hand traveled to her throat before she could stop it. Kit forced himself to look away from the letters. Each even breath had become a question of will.

"I see no treason in this," Mary said. Her voice sounded very small, and very far away. "I see no meaning there."

The lord chancellor smirked. "Oh, I think you do. Permit me to refresh your memory."

Kit couldn't have been farther from Bromley if he'd tried, but even from this distance, he could see the second piece of paper Bromley thrust in front of Mary. Another copy of the letter, this one annotated with Kit's own script. Her treasons laid out for the whole world to see. Bromley read them aloud: the generals, the foreign forces, the invasions. And the final note, the one Kit had deciphered here at Fotheringhay, the one in her possession at her arrest: *Do it. Tell your men to begin.*

"Madam," Bromley said coldly, recitation done, "do you deny you set these words down and signed them with your name?"

Mary's voice faltered, for the first time, as she replied. Her hand was still at her throat. "I am queen of Scotland still," she said. "If there is justice in this court, you will not convict a queen."

"Madam," Bromley said. "You neglect my question. Did you sign these words with your name?"

Mary laughed, softly, a quiet rumble between weeping and shouting. "Sir," she said, "you are my enemy."

"No, madam," Bromley said. "I am the enemy of the queen's enemies."

Mary's eyes swept across the bench. Burghley would not help her, nor would Cecil, or anyone. Mary had played Whitehall's game, and played it well, but they had played one step ahead.

Then, maddeningly, she turned to Walsingham and smiled. Kit wanted to scream at her to stop. That smile would earn her nothing.

"Sir Francis," she said. "I know you have no love for me, or my religion. I do not ask you to deny this. But you are an honest man. You will not let this continue. You will see reason."

Walsingham didn't blink. It was as if Mary spoke a language he didn't understand. "Madam," he said, "you mistake me. I do not consort with traitors."

Mary laughed like cannon fire. "No?" she said, locking eyes with Kit at the back of the room.

Mary had known Kit as her servant. She'd spoken to him, prayed for his sister, trusted him with her fears. And now she would kill him if she could. Kit no longer cared what the tribunal thought of him. Let them stare. He couldn't endure the accusation in that look another moment.

Walsingham looked at Kit, nodded, then turned to Mary with a smile. You thought that man was yours, the smile said, but he is mine. He has always been mine. He owes you nothing. And you will get what you deserve.

"Mary Stuart." Bromley's voice came from a great distance. "This court finds you guilty of practices against the life of Her Majesty Queen Elizabeth. The penalty for such treason, as established by the Act of Association, is death. Your sentence shall be conveyed to Her Majesty, to be enacted at her pleasure."

Mary's expression did not change. "Very well," she said. "But grant me one thing."

"Madam?" Bromley said.

"Let me spend my final days away from devils like you."

She swept past Bromley, who made no move to stop her. The tribunal watched her go in silence, followed close by her guards.

At Babington's execution, Kit thought he knew the sensation of blood on his hands. Now, he truly understood what it was to be a murderer.

Twenty-Three

Kit pressed his forehead to the window overlooking the courtyard. The icy glass felt both brutal and soothing against his burning skin. Winter had buried Northampton in snow, and icicles hung like dragons' teeth from the bare trees. Their branches were the only gallows remaining, though even now Kit could see the swinging silhouette of Anthony Babington, suspended by a frozen rope. That had been early autumn. It was now February. How could it possibly still feel so warm?

Against the window, he waited for the vertigo to pass. He'd spent five months in this manor, taking down encoded messages from the tribunal to dispatch to Whitehall, deciphering the replies. It was the most pressing crisis in England—if their correspondence fell into the wrong hands, there was no telling what might happen. Kit knew what he was doing mattered, but that didn't erase the strain of five months surrounded by these cold, cruel men, hardly sleeping, going days without anyone addressing him by name.

The verdict had been sent to the queen at once, but what followed was an agonizing exercise in equivocation. The messages Kit deciphered from Whitehall were circuitous, stating no opinion and agreeing to nothing. A bit late for a stab of conscience, Kit thought. The queen should have had her second thoughts before backing her prey into a corner and giving her hounds the taste of blood.

"There you are." Walsingham's voice, behind Kit, seemed filtered through several feet of water. "What are you doing?"

"Casting my horoscope," Kit said, without looking. "Scorpio seems to be ascending."

Walsingham took Kit by the shoulder. His grip was firm, some-where between a father to a wayward son and a jailer to a con-demned man. Kit flinched. He'd never seen Walsingham look at him quite like this before.

"Come with me," Walsingham said. "It's beginning."

The dizziness rushed back, blurring Kit's vision. He pressed one hand against the window, to transfer its chill to his burning blood.

"Marlowe. Come."

Did Walsingham give the same command to his dogs?

"The sentence will pass at ten o'clock in the hall. Five minutes."

The hall. Kit's mind stuck on the words. An indoor execution. It felt ludicrous. A masque, a spectacle, theater. Five minutes? He hadn't seen a new message from London in days. "Has the queen ordered—"

Walsingham shook his head. "The queen's advisors act in Her Majesty's best interest."

She didn't know, then. The Council had grown tired of waiting. If they could see what Kit saw, hollowed-out bodies hanging from a frozen tree, would they be so impatient to act?

He felt his stomach turn and swallowed. Walsingham tightened his grip on Kit's shoulder—reassurance or the tug of a noose? In what world was it so hard to tell? Then Walsingham let go, turned his back on Kit, and set off down the corridor. Kit had no choice but to follow.

He'd walked these passages hundreds of times, but through the fog of his whirling mind, they felt skewed, dreamlike. Their two-minute journey seemed to take hours. At last, they reached the hall, where the tribunal already waited within. Kit could hear nothing through the door. The silence terrified him.

He knew what he would see inside. He hadn't stopped seeing it since Mary's arrest. He didn't want to see it now. Kit turned back—to hell with consequences, he would not sit in that room and wait for the axe to fall, he couldn't. But Walsingham stood behind him, between Kit and freedom.

"Only cowards close their eyes at the last stroke," he said. "You're many things, Marlowe, but not a coward." He waited, severe as iron, blocking Kit's retreat.

Better a coward than a murderer. But then, Kit was one of those already.

He turned away from the spymaster and opened the door.

The hall was full. Well-dressed and impatient noblemen crowded the makeshift scaffold at the head of the room. No one looked at Kit. He looked only at the scaffold. Two feet high, twelve feet broad, draped with black. The priest, hands folded as if this were any Sunday mass. The executioner, standing beside the wooden block, with its notch for the neck. Kit's breath roared in his ears.

The door opened again.

Mary did not look at anyone. Certainly not at Kit. A pale specter dressed in black, her eyes hollow, her bearing proud. She was attended by one of her ladies, likewise clad in mourning.

Mary is a traitor, Kit told himself. She deserves this.

When Mary reached the scaffold, she stopped a foot from the platform. Paused, but unwavering. The woman took Mary's hand and gripped it tight. Differences in rank collapsed in the hour of death.

The priest, looming above Mary on the scaffold, spoke in a piping, reedy voice. "Madam, confess your sins and repent. Accept God's forgiveness for your—"

"Save your breath," Mary said. The priest blinked, startled. Likely no one had ever interrupted him before. No one had ever been eager for him to finish. "Your faith has nothing to do with me, and mine has nothing to do with you. I shall die a Catholic, whatever you say."

With a nod at her maid, she raised her arms. The woman helped Mary remove the black shell of her gown. Beneath, Mary wore a scarlet chemise, which flashed through the room like flayed skin.

"Thank you," Mary said. She began to turn, toward the scaffold, but then turned back. "Send word to my son. Tell him I send my love, and to be strong in his faith."

"Yes, my lady," the woman said, curtsying.

As if the maid could send word to Scotland. As if she could have said no.

The climb. Only three steps. Mary started to speak at the top of the third.

"Hail Mary, full of grace, the Lord is with thee. Blessed art thou among women . . ."

Kit felt his vision narrow. Beside him, Walsingham never turned away from the scaffold as Mary knelt before the block. She clasped a rosary to her chest, bone-white against blood-red. Kit had never heard a woman pray so loudly.

"And blessed is the fruit of thy womb, Jesus. Holy Mary, Mother of God, pray for us sinners . . ."

"Madam, I implore you," began the priest.

"Now, and at the hour of our death. Amen."

Mary picked up the thread of another prayer immediately, loud as the first. The executioner stood behind her, waiting. Could they kill a woman in the middle of prayer? Even a Catholic prayer? The room hummed. No one seemed to know.

"In thee, O Lord, have I hoped. Let me not be confounded, and deliver me in thy justice."

Kit heard her voice catch as the executioner's footsteps approached, but the prayer would not die. Kit couldn't see Walsingham beside him. He could see nothing but the red-clad figure kneeling on the scaffold, praying to the rafters, as the axe neared.

The blade arced upward and hung a moment there, suspended. Mary spread her arms, neck resting on the block. The rosary still dangled from her right hand.

"Into thy hands, O Lord, I commend my—"

The axe fell.

Mary screamed.

Kit's courage shattered like a thousand panes of stained glass.

The crunch of steel striking bone.

A pause, as the axe was wrenched from Mary's neck. Kit saw her twitch. He saw her lips move, as if she would continue to pray.

The axe fell again.

The silence was louder than the scream.

The axe fell a third time.

Mary's rosary landed against the scaffold. The skittering ivory sounded like a gold coin dropped on a desk.

The hum in Kit's ears was deafening. He couldn't concentrate on the room. It kept slipping out of focus, blood-slick around the edges. He was breathing too fast. There wasn't enough air.

"Marlowe," he heard Walsingham say. "Marlowe, breathe. Look at me."

The weight of a hand on his shoulder. Kit pushed it off and bolted.

It seemed impossible his legs could carry him so fast, or so far. With every step, around every corner, the bloodied wreck of Mary Stuart, hanging like a scrim before his eyes. He shouldered open the door and burst into the snow-blasted courtyard. A shallow breath of bitter cold knifed through him. More air, all the air in the world, and it still wasn't enough. Ghosts here, too. Even pure white snow could not hide so much blood.

Kit sank to a crouch, head in his hands, and screamed, screamed until something between his ribs shattered, something that could not be put back together.

Twenty-Four

The execution's aftermath passed in a gray haze. It took Kit from Northampton to London, and then to Whitehall's back rooms, where terse politicians debated the state of the Scots and the Spanish. Everyone knew Mary's death would not go unavenged, though no one took the threat more seriously than Cecil. He raged at the Council, urging preemptive action: naval escalation, scouting parties into Scotland, domestic raids. His reaction was zealous and bloody, but not irrational. The English navy couldn't fend off the Spanish Armada without fortifications. And with hives of English Catholics hungry for vengeance, Cecil feared attack from land and sea. From the righteous pitch of his belligerence, it was hard to remember that England had, in fact, struck first.

It was hard to remember they'd won.

Kit heard all this, but vaguely. The threat of insurrection paled against the memory of the axe, that scream. He couldn't keep down food, slept little. When he did, the dreams woke him gasping for breath more nights than not. He felt transparent, brittle, as if too-sharp thought would snap him.

His first day back in London, Lord Burghley shook his hand in congratulation—an action that would have caused John Marlowe, had he known, to die of shock. But no one else in Whitehall seemed even to see Kit. The Council treated him just as the tribunal had in Northampton: a penniless scribe to take dictation and be silent. Even Walsingham became colder. Some divine edict seemed to forbid him to look at Kit directly, or spend a moment longer than necessary in his company. He left Council sessions the moment Burghley stopped speaking, vanishing into the recesses of the palace, saying nothing.

Kit should have been stronger, so that something so trivial wouldn't have troubled him. He should have been like Sir Francis, like Gregory, like Poley. Detached. Cold as steel and as hard to damage. So that nothing frightened him or kept him awake with regret because no one had a hold on him. But as much as he'd learned in recent months, he still hadn't mastered that trick.

In this time of crisis, the Privy Council met twice daily, near daybreak and just after sunset. The time between sessions Kit had to himself, for better or for worse. The councilors filled the interim with business: ambassadors to flatter, letters to write, vast estates to manage by proxy. Kit had nothing but his own mind and the ghosts that occupied it, which proved abysmal company. He'd found a small sanctuary in which to kill the long hours: a window seat in an out-of-the-way corridor, safe from the politics swirling through the palace. A quiet corner where he could write, or try to.

He'd swiped a leather-bound ledger from one of the palace's lesser-used studies—with what he'd sacrificed for the crown, this felt like reparations, not theft. Intended for bookkeeping, the grid across the pages slashed his line in blatant disregard for the poetic foot. But that didn't matter. Nothing he'd composed since Mary's arrest had been worth the ink it took to write. He looked down at his latest line, the product of a good half hour, and scowled. Thirteen syllables, God help him. Surely he hadn't come within spitting distance of a master's degree from Cambridge only to forget how to count to ten.

"Marlowe. A word?"

Kit turned from the page. Walsingham stood ten feet away, arms folded across his black linen doublet. Typical that after treating Kit like a ghost for two weeks, he'd haunt the only place Kit tried to find peace.

"Sir," he said, closing the book. The ink would smear, but that was only a tragedy when it ruined something worth reading. He nearly asked how Walsingham had found him, but then, the queen's spymaster always knew where his agents were.

Walsingham nodded toward an open door, half revealing a sparse parlor with two couches, a low credenza, and little else. Kit followed, sitting opposite him. The scene had the unpleasant feeling of a trial. He clasped his hands between his knees and tried not to look guilty.

"Now that your initial commission has been fulfilled," Walsingham said, without a breath of preamble, "I'd like to politely suggest that you remain here, in London. Having you nearby would be of great use to me, depending on how the issue of the Armada resolves itself."

Resolves itself. A curious choice of words for a foreign force that might still obliterate the country Kit called home. And the phrase *of great use* had an echo to it that Kit didn't like. He was hesitant to speak his mind with the stakes so high, but Walsingham had asked for this conversation. It was worth trying now, if ever.

"I understand, sir," Kit said. "It's only that . . ."

"It's what?" Walsingham prompted.

Kit sighed. "It's not that I'm not grateful for what you've given me, sir," he said. "But I worked five years toward a degree, and now I've had to throw that away. Without that, I . . . well. I don't have many prospects without it, and I don't expect I can afford to stay here long."

It sounded as petty as he'd feared. Between saving the life of the queen and sitting a handful of master's-level examinations, only a fool would have voiced regret at not having chosen the latter. But it was true, what he'd said. A degree meant London, meant money, meant proving to the pack of them that he could be more than they'd imagined. The idea of it had sustained him through nights listening to his father shout at the constable in the street below, days enduring the sneers of Cambridge's better-off pupils. If Kit was to spend the rest of his life haunted by Mary Stuart's final scream, at least he might have had something to show for it.

Walsingham smiled at this, as Kit had half expected him to. But he'd anticipated cruel mockery, and what he received was not that. There was no motive behind this smile. "I meant to tell you," Walsingham said. "I've dealt with that."

Kit started. "Excuse me?"

"I had a word with Lord Burghley. He recommended the Cambridge fellows consider your . . . additional employment a sort of academic equivalency. They've already granted your degree. You may call yourself Christopher Marlowe, master of arts, until your voice gives out."

He must have misheard. Sir Francis Walsingham, royal secretary to the queen, the man with the nation's safety resting on his back, pulling strings to ensure that the scholarship of a shoemaker's son didn't go to waste. Because of Walsingham, Kit would never have to endure the jeers of men like Nick Skeres, men like his father, about how ill-suited he'd been for a university education. Because of Walsingham, Kit would be somebody—in this role and out of it.

"Thank you, sir," he said quietly.

"Lord Burghley was perfectly willing," Walsingham said. "He spoke quite favorably of you that first evening he met you. Naturally, I told him your acquaintance was like a strong Scotch whiskey."

Kit frowned. "Sir?"

"One only needs a little."

Kit laughed, startled into it. He couldn't recall Walsingham ever doing anything as frivolous as joking. Victory would do strange things to a man. Or threat of defeat. Or simply knowing that whatever nightmares haunted his sleep, at least one man, one other in a city of thousands, might share them.

Perhaps Walsingham even liked him. Mad as the idea seemed.

"You're all right, Marlowe?" Walsingham said, somewhat gruffly. "After it all?"

Kit pressed his lips together. If Walsingham had to ask, he must not have hidden his strain as well as he'd hoped. Though the thought of concealing anything from the spymaster was ridiculous, least of all this feeling.

"When does it get easier?" Kit said quietly.

A slight softness came to Walsingham's stone eyes. That sympathy frightened Kit to his bones. "It doesn't," Walsingham said. "But you learn to bear it."

He'd known that before he asked. What they'd done, what they'd seen—it wasn't the sort of memory that could ever be dismissed. But it was different hearing Walsingham admit it. Walsingham, who had never shown Kit fear even for a moment.

"The Armada, then," Walsingham said. "Did Stuart ever speak of it?"

Kit cleared his throat, shaking himself back into the present. If he had no choice, he would learn to bear it, and do what was needed of him in the meantime. "Occasionally. Not as much as we'd hope."

They spoke for an hour, reviewing Kit's report, sketching possible threats and analyzing potential dangers from the king of Spain. Perhaps Walsingham had the right of it after all. It was a relief, to think of nothing but the work, traitorous plots spinning out like Ariadne's thread.

The bells outside tolled the hour, jarring Kit's nerves. The break in Walsingham's dark mood had eased Kit's anxiety, not cured it. As if cued by the time, Walsingham glanced at the window, though the curtains were drawn. When he turned to Kit—impossible though it seemed—his eyes were smiling.

"Marlowe, you're dismissed," Walsingham said. "I expect the Council to complete its business by the end of this week, at which point you'll be free to go. But I'll expect you at this evening's session."

"I burn with anticipation, sir," Kit said, earning himself an exasperated sigh from the spymaster. He didn't bow, but then Walsingham knew better than to expect that.

Kit ducked into the corridor. It was late afternoon, but the days had begun to lengthen again, and the last dregs of sunlight still streamed through Whitehall's leaded windows. Perhaps he might be able to write something worthwhile today after all. In the light of the dying afternoon, he thought he could hear the poetic line again in the soft footsteps down the corridor, quick iambs, one-two, one-two.

He looked up and saw something that couldn't possibly be real.

A man had stopped at the far end of the corridor, catching sight of Kit in return. A handsome man of medium height, broad shouldered and blond, wearing a forest-green linen shirt and tan breeches Kit remembered as well as if they were his own. When the faint smile broke across the man's face, it felt like home.

It was impossible that he should be here. It was equally impossible to deny that he was.

It was a stupid risk, with Walsingham on the other side of the door and the entire Privy Council mere steps away, but Kit had been taking risks for so long that he felt entitled to a frivolous one. He took the corridor at a run and threw his arms around Tom with such force that he knocked him backward, into the nearest wall. Tom laughed, and the sound was so brilliant that for the first time in weeks, Kit felt the shadows drop from his mind. The world was light again. The world had color.

"Hello, you," Tom said, his voice muffled by Kit's enthusiastic greeting.

Tom was here. Holding him, being held by him, in the queen's palace. It seemed impossible, but if it was a dream, Kit was content to sleep forever.

"Hello," he said, grinning like an idiot, and pulled Tom close and kissed him. Tom's arms felt so familiar. Stronger than Kit's, and warmer. He could lose himself in those arms. Tom's lips parted, and Kit sighed, feeling stronger than he'd felt in months, and more helpless too. He breathed in Tom's scent, its undertones of cedar, and smiled through the kiss. *Home at last*, he thought, like the sentimental idiot he knew himself to be.

They stood there, nose to nose, close enough to kiss again.

"They let you in," Kit said.

"There's no need to sound so surprised," Tom said. "They let *you* in, and you look like you walked here from Cornwall."

"All right," Kit said, pushing Tom away, "if that's what I get for sincerity . . ."

Tom laughed. "I've been in London for a few weeks now, since Cambridge. Sir Francis Walsingham sent a man by my rooms yesterday. Must have heard I'd been asking Norgate about you. He said I might come today at five and find you here."

There were only two reasons Walsingham would go to Tom. Either this was a strategic play—give Kit what he wanted to heal the wounds left from Northampton, to keep hold of a spy who had proven himself. Or it was meant as a warning. *I know about the two of you, I know what he is to you. Don't ever think you're a step ahead of me.* Well, of course Walsingham knew. If it was a fact in the known universe, Sir Francis Walsingham was aware of it. But whether the spymaster's motives were strategic or manipulative, it didn't matter. Tom was here. It was impossible to care about anything beyond that.

"I love you," Kit said, without thinking.

Tom ran a hand through Kit's hair. Kit pressed his cheek to Tom's shoulder and sighed, with a smile he couldn't help. "You did it, love," Tom said. "You've won."

The door opened, and Walsingham stepped out into the hall, a sheaf of papers under his arm. Tom froze and started to step back, but Kit didn't move, or take his arms from around Tom. He'd waited too long to let Tom go now. Walsingham watched them silently, Kit and Tom pressed close as the sea to the sand.

"Thank you, sir," Kit said quietly.

"For what?" Walsingham asked. "It can't be for teaching you subtlety," he added over his shoulder, heading down the corridor, "as that seems to have been a profligate waste of time."

Perhaps, Kit thought, watching him go. But then, what good was being careful if you weren't sometimes allowed not to be?

They stood like that together, bodies entwined, until Kit could feel the rhythm of Tom's heart fall in time with his own. The sun, flashing from behind a cloud, spilled across them, preserving the moment in gold, whispering of time drawing to a close.

"So what happens now?" Tom said quietly.

Kit grinned and kissed Tom once more, simply because he could. "Now," he said, "we go home."

PART II

Prince of Darkness

SEPTEMBER 1592–MAY 1593

MEPHISTOPHELES: Hell hath no limits, nor is
  circumscribed
  In one self place, for where we are is hell,
  And where hell is must we ever be.
  And, to conclude, when all the world dissolves,
  And every creature shall be purified,
  All places shall be hell that is not heaven.
FAUSTUS: Come, I think hell's a fable.
MEPHISTOPHELES: Ay, think so still, till
  experience change thy mind.

Doctor Faustus, 2.1.122–29

Twenty-Five

Five years, seven months, and eight days after he left Whitehall and the ghost of Mary Stuart behind, Kit passed through the gates of Canterbury in high style, on the back of a horse he'd paid two shillings to borrow for the day. It had been an extravagant expense, and he was quite sure the carrier had fleeced him, taking him—correctly—for a Londoner who wouldn't know a fair price if he saw one. Still, as he watched the children playing near Saint Peter's Well drop their ball and crane their necks up at him in amazement, he felt that every penny had been well spent. He nodded at the children, who retreated into a tangle of whispers and youthful excitement Kit remembered from his own younger days. Who was that well-dressed man on the fine horse, riding through these streets as if he owned them? A visiting lord? A foreign ambassador?

Not quite, he wanted to tell them. Only Kit Marlowe, the most famous poet in all of London.

He dismounted near his father's shop and tied the horse at the post outside, paying a passing youth a penny to supply the beast with water. That done, he leaned against the post himself, looking up at the house with some satisfaction. There were ancillary benefits to literary fame, which the Marlowes realized each time Kit sent them a cut of his profits from a play he'd staged. *Tamburlaine*—finished, revised, and onstage at last—had replaced the shop's long-broken window. Then the sequel to *Tamburlaine*, dashed off as a stopgap to sate the crowds while he scrambled for something original; not his best work, but it had permitted the

Marlowes to own the shop outright. Then a bloody tale of deception in Malta, so wildly irreligious that Ned Alleyn, the company's lead actor, had jokingly offered to perform a ritual cleansing of the stage. Katherine would have denounced the play's themes if she'd known them, but all she knew were the fine feather bed and three sets of winter clothes *The Jew of Malta* had paid for.

You built this, he thought as he surveyed the shop, stronger and more solid with each passing year. You and your words, you built this.

Meg and her husband had a home of their own, and his father made a point of being away each time Kit paid a visit, but the rest of the family greeted him eagerly as he entered their lodgings. Anne and Dorothy had been not quite ten when Kit left for Cambridge; now they were bright, ambitious girls of about twenty, with a renewed interest in their extravagant elder brother now that London's crowds knew his name. Little Thomas—not so little anymore, as the youngest Marlowe stood three inches taller than Kit—shook his hand with a man's grip, then sat beside him at the table and peppered him with a child's profusion of questions.

"Is it true they played *Malta* in front of the queen?" Thomas said. "What did she say? Will she give you a knighthood for it?"

The notion was enough to make Kit laugh. "People like us don't get knighted, little brother. But Ned told me she didn't fall asleep, which means she liked it well enough."

"But you were introduced at court, surely?" Dorothy asked.

"The *actors* went to court. I've only ever met the queen's secretary, and I doubt you'd like him."

"Dora, your brother won't get you a place at court, so don't ask him," Katherine said from near the fire, where she sat working the heel of a stocking and watching her children like they themselves were a stage production. "Christopher's already given us more than he can afford to, I'm sure."

Dorothy blushed, but Kit shoved her playfully in the shoulder. He was awful with finances, as Tom never tired of reminding him—*money isn't inexhaustible, love, someday the play won't land, there's a thing called "economizing"*—but after more than two decades of thrift, the luster of spending shone bright. How could anyone expect him to be responsible with money when irresponsibility was so satisfying?

"Don't worry about that," Kit said. "There's more to come, which is what I came to tell you. I have a patron now, you see."

Anne received this as if Kit had come into possession of the Holy Grail. "How?"

"Surely you know your brother's a genius," Kit said, then at Anne's exasperated expression, amended. "In all honesty, I hardly know myself."

Kit might be the brilliant star of London's theaters now, but he hadn't had an auspicious beginning. Securing an introduction to Philip Henslowe, impresario at the Rose theater, had taken a week of cajoling and shameless flattery, and even then he'd only earned a probationary place among the company's stable of poets. But Kit knew *Tamburlaine* was good, and London saw it for what it was worth. Packed houses week after week, until Kit started to see members of the audience, groundlings and galleries alike, murmuring the words along with the actors. And now, after *The Jew of Malta* had played its turn at court, the impossible had happened: Lord Strange, the company's patron, had written to Henslowe, offering to fund Kit's future works personally. Even after five years earning a living with his pen, it all felt like a dream that might be snatched away at any time.

"A patron is quite something," Katherine said, with her usual equanimity. He could have said he'd conquered all of Greece, or that he'd finally learned to make a proper buttonhole, and in either case Katherine would reply, *That's quite something.* "You'll stay for supper tonight? Nothing grand, but—"

"If it's with you, it's grand enough," he said. It never failed to stun him how much easier it was to be with his family when another, more comfortable world waited to welcome him back afterward. "And Meg?"

Katherine hesitated, and Kit didn't ask why. He scarcely saw his oldest sister now, their communication dwindling as his financial means increased. Privately, he believed Meg's husband was to blame. William Bradley wasn't the type to accept help from a man he deemed beneath him, and Meg had little choice but to avoid the people he told her to avoid. Kit knew he should write to her, and promised himself he would the moment he returned to London, as he had promised himself many times, to no effect.

"Never mind," he said, waving off an explanation. "I'm as happy to spend an evening with the four of you."

"You'll take me back with you one day, won't you, Kit?" Thomas asked eagerly. "To the city?" In his brother's eyes, Kit could see the glimmer of court masques, royal favor, all the gold-edged parts of London life.

Kit smiled and clapped Thomas on the back. "London's a den of iniquity, my boy," he said. "Best keep your tender soul far away."

"*You're* going back," Thomas muttered.

"Naturally. It's too late for me."

———

He returned to London shortly before curfew, stopping only to return the horse to the untrustworthy carrier before setting off for home. Not exactly high living: he and his co-boarder, an actor and poet named Thomas Kyd, split a single room in Shoreditch, near the sprawl of Moorfields and Bethlehem Hospital. The first six weeks after Whitehall, shrieks from the hospital had infiltrated his dreams, blending with the echo of Mary's scream to form something horrible, half nightmare and half memory. But as time went on, the dreams faded, and so did his awareness of the madmen outside the door. Proof, he supposed, that a man could get used to anything.

Thomas Kyd was lying across his bed when Kit entered, staring at the ceiling with a stymied expression. Faintly amused, Kit shrugged off his cloak and dropped down on the bed beside his co-boarder, earning himself an irritated noise in return.

"Trouble with act three still, Hieronimo?" he asked.

Kyd groaned and turned his face to the wall. "Don't."

"Don't what? Sympathize?"

"Don't be successful around me. The play's a disaster and I can't bear it."

Kit shrugged, then stood and crossed to the desk where Kyd had left the abandoned wreckage of an incomplete third act. "If it soothes your pride any, I just spent an evening with my mother, who three times asked me if I'd invited my parish priest to see my plays."

At this, Kyd sat up, shaken out of his own self-pity. "I assume you didn't mention the priests you strangled in *Malta*."

"Or the holy books we burned in *Tamburlaine*. Sometimes it's best to eat quietly and say nothing."

"For you, maybe," Kyd said. He gestured at the pages in Kit's hand. "Give that back. I won't have the king of Bankside crowing over my failure."

"I wasn't crowing," Kit said indignantly, but he did return the pages to the desk.

Turning away, he leaned absently against the windowsill, watching as candles illuminated the covered windows in the building opposite, one by one like a sky dotted with stars. The sprawling countryside of Kent he'd traversed that day had been beautiful, all vast fields and endless sky. But it inspired nothing in him compared to this dingy little street in north London that turned to impassable mud each time it rained, where screams were so common they faded to nothing in time.

Five years of London living had changed everything. Ciphered letters and rising armies had become an unpleasant dream that could be dismissed with the morning light, the Armada nothing but splintered wreckage at the bottom of the sea. The world wasn't shadows and secrets anymore—it was roaring crowds, thrilling words, coin in his purse, and no one to answer to but himself. It crossed his mind, not for the first time, how little the city resembled the London he'd first entered as a student, that grim place where each street seemed to wish him gone.

Somehow, that forbidding city had become home.

Twenty-Six

If there was one thing Kit liked about Lord Strange's Men, it was that these actors could always be counted on for a drink when a man needed one. The raucous crowd from the Rose had spread across two tables at the Mermaid Tavern as late afternoon deepened into evening. A handful of actors, some with faces still half painted from the production, plus their fearless playwright, plus one guest—a Fleet Street lawyer permitted by express invitation of said playwright. Something about it was reminiscent of the White Stag in Cambridge, those long-ago evenings that bled into mornings. That same sense of buzzing triumph, that sense of having pulled off some grand heist to spite a doubting universe. And yet, the Mermaid felt like the jurisdiction of a different world, one a shoemaker's son turned poor scholar would invent in the throes of some fever dream. It never became less thrilling, no matter how many times he came here on the heels of a fresh conquest.

This most recent production had been a daring one, one whose reception Kit had spent a week of sleepless nights worrying over. *Edward II* had no shortage of ways to distress the common spectator: royal corruption, a treasonous queen, regicide, the lovingly rendered intimacy between the king and his handsome favorite. Apparently, however, London was hungrier for scandal than its priests and Puritans gave it credit for.

Kit raised his pint for a toast, and his companions followed suit without waiting for the prompt. Anything he meant to toast, they would drink to, fellow professionals, theater haunters, dregs of society, friends and sinners all. Thomas Kyd, a little lopsided from liquor, a few flecks of pig's blood still discoloring his hair from his role as Mortimer. Ned Alleyn, a glittering comet both onstage and in the tavern, whose Edward had brought the audience to its knees. Will Shakespeare, a new fellow in from the country who'd given a promising performance as the bloodthirsty assassin Lightborn. And Tom—always Tom, so close his knee rested against Kit's thigh. Tom, who blended with this crowd of theatrical misfits as if he'd been born to join them. Tom, whose rented rooms near his law offices in the Fleet had housed them through God knew how many afternoon trysts and lazy late mornings. Tom, who loved him. Kit looked at them all, and he thought he might die that very minute and regret none of it.

"To the theater," Kit said, earning an echo from the rest of the group. He drained his pint and slammed it back onto the table. His arm moved faster than his brain, and he swayed a little before Will reached out to steady him. Will upheld easily the soberest edge of the quintet, but though Kit's own world tilted slightly to the left, he didn't mind.

"The church says actors are sinners," Kit said, leaning back, "but Christ was the best player of all. Rising from the dead? Now that's theater."

Thomas Kyd rolled his eyes and drank. "If you're hanged for blasphemy, find me another renter? I can't afford living alone."

"Certainly," Kit said, slinging an arm around his shoulders. "I'll put out an advertisement from hell."

Ned toasted Kit with his now-empty pint, the movement of his wrist looser than sobriety would permit. "Edward's the best part you've ever written me," he said.

"That's what you said about Tamburlaine," Kit said with a smirk.

"Ah, but did a woman in the pit ever faint during *Tamburlaine?*" Ned countered.

Kit stared. "Did she really?"

"On my honor," Will said—the only one among them with any honor left to swear on. "Right when Ned caught the poker up his ass."

"A death," Ned said archly, "for which I shall never forgive you, as it happens."

"Pathos," Kit said. He reached across the table for Tom's half-finished beer, draining that too. Tom scowled but didn't argue the point—after all, Kit had bought the round. "The key to greatness. I'll explain it later."

A small cough came from behind them.

Kit turned. Behind him, as he'd known from the moment he heard that cough, sat Robert Greene.

The poet and critic leaned forward, his hands laced around a drink. Red haired and red bearded, Greene towered six inches above Kit when standing, and even bent over a tavern table he seemed built for two pastimes: drinking and throwing other men through windows. Perhaps not the best man to antagonize, but Kit's ratio of cups full to cups empty had put caution out of arm's reach. And in any case, the premiere had been a triumph. If he wasn't allowed to needle an old enemy in the lingering halo of glory, when would he be?

"Anything to add, Robert?" Kit asked.

"Only that the keys to greatness seem out of your sphere," Greene said.

Kit straddled his chair backward to face Greene, draping both arms over the back. "Forgive me," he said. "I shouldn't dare claim greatness in front of the bard who wrote *Friar Bacon and Friar Bungay*."

Greene's jaw twitched, but he merely made a practiced gesture with one hand, calling for more stout. "Your plays, Marlowe," he said, "are a swamp of vice and immorality. Limping rhythm and melodrama. From a university man, I expected better. And your actors? Christ's death. Dick Burbage puts your preening sodomites to shame."

Tom glanced at Ned, imploring him to stop Kit from beating Greene's face in, but there was no need to worry. Ned had seen Kit tear critics to pieces before. There was no need to turn to fists, not when Kit was ready and willing to attack with words. Kit smiled and rose from the chair. The rest of the table followed suit, Will to Kit's left and Thomas Kyd to his right.

"Your thimbleful of wit is appreciated," Kit said. "When London stops paying money for vice and immorality, you'll be the first to know. Until then, I'd suggest not giving artistic advice to a writer who outsells you seven to one." He glanced back at his friends. "Shall we go, boys?"

"Let's," Ned said grandly. "The company in this establishment has taken a sad turn for the worse."

Together, they spilled through the door into the street beyond, leaving Greene to stew in his own outrage.

The sun sank beyond the city's tangle of low-hanging roofs. Above them, the pastel sky wrapped the filthy streets in pink and blue-green, and feathered clouds brushed like paint strokes across the sky. Saint Paul's steeple loomed in disapprobation as they walked, but Kit barely noticed it. Let the church judge as it liked. A different deity governed men of the theater.

"You had me worried, Kit," Will said. "But then, I suppose tavern fights aren't your style."

"You'd be surprised to learn what Kit's style is," Tom said wryly. "If I had to count the times I've seen Kit punch a man in a tavern—"

"You'd count exactly once," Kit snapped.

Tom raised his eyebrows. "I'm sorry, was that not you in Eastcheap last winter?"

"All right. Twice."

"Greene has a point about Burbage, though," Will said idly. "He's good, Kit. You know that."

"I'd sooner string myself up at Tyburn"—Kit flung an arm wide, nearly overbalanced, righted himself with a hand from Tom and a laugh—"than take a word of advice from Robert Greene. You take Burbage, Will. Ned reads my lines better than any man alive."

Ned, despite the playful tone, colored. "You flatter me, Kit."

"Absolutely," Kit said. "My plays come out best when I flatter you to death."

"Speaking of plays," Tom said, glancing at Kyd. "Anything new from you, after your *Spanish Tragedy*? It's been ages since we've been blessed with a Thomas Kyd production."

"Blessed?" Ned repeated, eyebrows dubiously aloft.

"Oh, you were happy enough to play my Hieronimo," Kyd snapped.

The conversation drifted easily, as easy as the possessive slide of Tom's hand along Kit's hip. Kit leaned into it, body humming with Tom's nearness. Six years since they'd admitted to loving each other, and it still felt as mad and wonderful and improbable as ever. He would never know anyone, want anyone, feel so much himself with anyone as Tom.

"Don't talk to me about writing," Kyd muttered. "My mind's a blank. I've stared at half a line for six months. 'Hamlet, revenge!'" He raised a dramatic hand to the sky, then let it fall. "And that's where I end."

"You need six more syllables," Will said.

"Thank you, Master of Verse," Kyd said. "You know so much, you write it."

Leaving the Mermaid, they took the long way, skirting around Cheapside. Not for them, tonight, that crowded market, where men and women hawked bolts of cloth and joints of meat at prices no one among them could hope to pay. Instead, they angled away from the cathedral along Thames Street, keeping the distance between themselves and Bankside as slim as they could. When Tom took Kit by the arm and stopped him, no one protested. Walking farther meant returning to the everyday world, where respectable people went about respectable business.

Kit must have had more to drink than he thought. One moment he was watching Tom, brilliant and beautiful in the sunset, and the next his back was pushed hard against the wall of a nearby cobbler's shop, and there was no space between him and Tom, none at all. Tom kept him there with a hand on each shoulder, Kit's spine flush against the stone.

Tom's thigh pressed between Kit's legs, firm and perfectly aimed,

and Kit felt his own breath shudder on the exhale. They were cel-
ebrating. They were drunk. They were young still, mostly, twenty-
eight was almost young, and stupid enough to make up for it. Kit
had just watched his words captivate the better part of London
for two hours. This was freedom. This was what it meant to live.

"You ass," Tom said. Kit shivered with the pressure of Tom's
thigh, just exactly in the right place, and Tom's breath close against
his throat. "You didn't tell me *Edward* was going to be like *that*.
My God, why does Henslowe put up with you?"

Kit smiled. "My unparalleled genius, I expect."

"I thought I'd read the worst," Tom said, soft and low and far
too close to Kit's ear for him to focus. "That damned poem you
showed me last Christmas, your lecherous Poseidon leaping out
of the sea to fuck Leander."

Kit laughed. He'd forgotten that.

"But this, could you have bothered to pretend? You'll get yourself killed. Even if you did . . ."

Tom made no attempt to describe the death Kit had written
for Edward, but the scene needed no reprise. A searing white-
hot poker slicing through the king's rectum, impaling his guts,
the imagined scent of charred flesh filling the theater. That image
stuck with a person. A feint, of course, and an obvious one. Pun-
ish sodomy with enough allegorical verve in the fifth act and the
master of revels let you do anything you liked during the first four.
But still . . .

Kit smiled. It was the same smile he'd worn at Cambridge before
explaining in exacting detail why a drunken orgy would bring
Protestant priests closer to God. Or when he'd told Thomas Kyd
his commission for a poem on Saint Paul was like writing an epic
about a charlatan pushing pigs' bones as saints' relics. The smile
of a man who knew a comfortable death alone was worse than a
hot and passionate damnation.

"I couldn't have done it without you," he said. "'London harbors
my lord, on whose bosom let me lie—'"

"Don't quote yourself at me." Tom's hand grew bolder, leaving his shoulder, sneaking between the fabric of Kit's breeches and his bare skin. Kit tensed, barely breathing, shivering at the warmth of Tom's breath, the slow—so slow—movement of his fingers. "If you're going to write a play about us, love, give it a happy ending."

Kit's yelp came out much louder than he meant it to.

But what did it matter? He ached with wanting Tom, would take him in the middle of the street if there was time enough. Tom pressed close, and Kit closed his eyes, soaring. God above, if they could manage this much in the open street, think of the promise of privacy.

"Steady on, boys," Ned said.

Kit glanced over Tom's shoulder. Right. They did still have an audience.

He and Tom stepped apart, not quite looking at anyone. Tom elbowed Kit in the ribs, and Kit, glancing down, hastily turned away. Their knowing laughter at his back, he walked ahead of them toward the river, steadfastly focused on the least arousing subjects he could conjure. Trade embargoes. The election of the new lord mayor. The Lord's Prayer, backward.

Ned might have thought Kit and Tom's behavior stemmed from drink, or he might have suspected something deeper. Kit neither knew nor cared. The church and the crown would have them strung up by their bowels for it, but the theater didn't give a damn where men's pricks pointed them. Men proclaimed undying love to other men every afternoon on the Rose's stage. And it took a great deal to shock an actor.

"This is why the Puritans want to shut us down," Will said, gesturing toward Tom.

"Vulgar crowd of miscreants, the lot of us," Thomas Kyd agreed.

"Master Marlowe, sir, wait please!"

"Speak *miscreant* and messengers come running," Will said under his breath.

Kit glanced down Cannon Street. A boy raced toward him,

shabbily dressed, with a cap pulled low over limp brown hair. Kit had never seen him before, but that was no surprise. London was full of them, these young messengers prized for their quick legs and their inability to read the messages they were delivering.

The boy skidded to a stop in front of the group, then glanced between them. At last, he craned his neck up at Ned. "A message for you, Master Marlowe," he said tentatively.

Kit cleared his throat and stepped forward, ignoring the snort of laughter from Thomas Kyd. He could sense the boy's disappointment: it would have taken a Kit and a half to form someone of Ned's stature. But then, he hadn't been crowned king of Bankside on looks alone. "Me, I'm afraid," he said. "Who sent you? If it's my landlady," he added on reflection, "tell her I'll pay the moment the profits come in from this play. You may give her my word as a poet."

"And as for the word of a poet," Kyd muttered, no doubt thinking of the nine weeks he'd spent haranguing Kit for his half of the rent, "at least it sounds sterling."

The boy shook his head and thrust the letter forward. "I was told not to tell you who sent me. He said you'd know."

The street, London, all the world narrowed down to the page in the boy's hand, and a wash of panic sent Kit shivering.

He extended a hand, and the boy pressed the page into his palm. He'd known even before he looked what he would see, but it was different, holding it in his hand. The page marked with that scarlet seal, the rounded petals of a rose embedded in its wax. He would recognize that seal anywhere.

Beside him, Tom cursed under his breath. So would he.

He should have known it wouldn't last. Five years of freedom, of earning a living with his words as he'd always said he would. Give it another year and he might have been able to sleep in peace, without dreams of shrieking women and armed rebels, not waking with a raw scream when Tom's hand shook him out of the nightmare. But of course a life like that didn't come free. He thought he'd paid his due by watching the axe sever the neck of a woman who had trusted him, but the devil didn't make a bargain without coming round to collect.

"Thank you," Kit said quietly. All the warmth of drunkenness had drained from him; he was now sober as a sermon. "Did he want a reply?"

"No, sir," the boy said. He didn't move—waiting for a tip, Kit realized. How odd, still, to be standing on this side of the divide, the one with the purse. He tossed a penny to the messenger, who took off like a shot.

Ned and Will exchanged skeptical looks, no doubt wondering what kind of legal trouble Kit had tangled himself in this time. Thomas Kyd, though, was attuned enough to Kit's moods, and had suffered through enough of Kit's nightmares, to know a private moment when he saw one. He glanced at his fellow actors, then at Tom, who nodded.

"There's hours yet until curfew," Kyd said casually. "And I know of a house in Southwark that's more than happy to have us stay the night, if you lot are interested in that sort of thing."

"What, my company isn't enough for you, Hieronimo?" Ned teased.

"Not unless playing Edward has changed your tastes," Kyd shot back.

They were actors—fresh voices and new preoccupations were their business. Whether they cared enough to give Kit privacy or they couldn't be bothered to think about something that didn't concern them, it didn't matter. Before long, the three men had taken their leave, wandering toward Southwark where the radiant Mistress Hopewell and her band of girls would, apparently, ensure a pleasant evening. Tom and Kit stood alone. The air felt colder now, the last dregs of summer gone in a moment.

Tom sighed and rested one hand on Kit's shoulder. It was all Kit could do not to flinch. The surprise had left him jumpy, like a rabbit after the first bay of hounds.

"I thought you were finished," Tom said quietly.

"I thought so too," Kit said, unfolding the paper.

It was a simple letter, written in a fine hand and unsigned. As if the letter writer had taken pains to include the least amount of information possible.

W requests a meeting at ten o'clock on the seventeenth of September. Come promptly. Use the west entrance. Keep unnecessary theatrics to a minimum.

If there had been any doubt of the sender before, the last sentence settled the matter. At ten o'clock the next day, he would be back in Whitehall, across a desk from Sir Francis Walsingham. The man who'd sent him into the lion's den all those years before, the puppet master who steered Kit's movements until the show was over and the axe had fallen. How many nights had he lain awake, listening to the shrieks from Bedlam and imagining Mary's eyes staring from her neckless head? How many dreams of the axe, of Babington's swinging corpse, of Robert Poley's smooth, satisfied smile across a makeshift courtroom?

How had he been so stupid, to think Walsingham would let him leave that life behind? What a fool he'd been, to believe his new life didn't rest on a foundation of bones.

"You're going, then," Tom said flatly, reading over Kit's shoulder.

Kit crumpled the page in his fist. "I can't very well say no. But I'll be careful."

Tom sighed again, then kissed Kit lightly on the cheek. "You've said that before."

Behind them, the sun settled behind Saint Paul's steeple, shadows leaning forward to lick Kit's heels. While Tom watched, he tore the message into strips, until his fist teemed with stray letters. Then he opened his palm and let them fall into the Thames. The paper and ink hovered there a moment, until water soaked the weave and they sank, feather-like, to the silt-choked bottom below.

Twenty-Seven

When Kit arrived at Whitehall the next day, the servant who opened the side door barely blinked at his request to meet with the royal secretary. Perhaps Kit had finally managed the right mix of respectability and menace after all this time. Despite the dread rising in the back of his throat, he couldn't help but appreciate the quiet deference as the servant led him to Walsingham's study. Apparently all it took to earn the world's respect was a confident voice and the swaggering stride of a highwayman.

Walsingham glanced up at Kit's unheralded entrance. He sat at his desk with three stacks of paper spread before him in disarray. Many of them, Kit saw upside down, bore an alphabet he couldn't read. More cipher? Or something else—Turkish? Close to Greek, but not that. Between Gregory and Master Dryden, he could have read Greek upside down and backward. It was easier to look at the pages, puzzle through their meanings, than to look the spymaster in the face after so long away.

"When a door is closed," Walsingham said, setting a paper aside, "the implication is for you to knock on it."

"It's a pleasure to see you too, sir," Kit said—bravado was not quite confidence, but with luck Walsingham wouldn't tell the difference. The spymaster made a curt gesture toward the chair, and Kit sat with his forearms leaning on his spread knees like a sailor at an Eastcheap tavern about to cast a pair of dice. "Although I'd started to hope you'd forgotten me."

Walsingham leaned back, and now that the first rush had faded, Kit realized with a jolt that the passage of nearly six years had more than taken its toll on the spymaster. Those bottomless eyes, the stern brow, the perfectly starched and pressed clothes that made him look like the strictest Puritan, none of that had changed. But Kit lingered on the deep shadows under Walsingham's eyes, the fresh gauntness to his face, the way his doublet hung awkwardly off narrower shoulders. The silver-topped walking stick leaned on the desk—new just before Northampton, its head now tarnished from heavy use. Something had happened, warping something essential about the spymaster. Kit's fear of what was to come faded, replaced by sudden terror of what had happened to Walsingham, and the absolute knowledge that he could never ask what it was.

"I couldn't forget you, Marlowe," Walsingham said, perfectly deadpan. "The nightmares won't permit it."

Kit laughed, and the worst of the shock quieted. Nothing serious would happen to Walsingham. The terror of the world, the man with a hundred faces. Near sixty years old, yes, but Walsingham had always seemed like Enoch and Noah, great patriarchs destined to live nine hundred years. It seemed inevitable that Walsingham would carry on so long as the sun went on rising— because without him, surely, England itself would grind to a halt.

"Delightful as this is," Kit said, "I doubt you called me here for social reasons."

Walsingham nodded. "Give him a moment first. He's late."

"Who's—"

The door behind him flung open. The man who entered, as he strode into the study and took the chair next to Kit, was unshakably aware of his own importance. He was dressed as if for an audience with the queen, though his exquisitely tailored doublet did not quite mask his slight hunch. What had once been apprehension turned to dread in Kit's stomach. The man looked only at Walsingham, as if Kit were a pile of clothes that needed washing. If Kit didn't know better, he'd have sworn he saw a twitch of irritation flash across Walsingham's face. But that was his imagination getting the better of him. Just because Kit had nothing but bitter memories of Sir Robert Cecil didn't mean Walsingham would be reckless enough to show he agreed.

"I hope I haven't kept you waiting," Cecil said.

"Not at all," Walsingham said. "You remember Christopher Marlowe, I presume."

"Your gutter scholar from the Yorkshire business. Of course."

Sir Robert Cecil wasn't a large or imposing man. Had he been anybody but who he was, a man of his stature would have found the world an inhospitable place. But he had a kind of cruel power about him, one that stripped away years of Kit's life and left him as self-conscious and exposed as he'd been at twenty-one. No matter how many of his plays took the stage, no matter what success he'd earned in Walsingham's service, Kit would never be anything but a shoemaker's son to Cecil, a Canterbury grifter who'd aspired above his station.

"My lord," he said with a curt nod. "Did you call for me, or did Sir Francis?"

Walsingham paused. "It might serve you better," he said, "to think of Sir Robert and myself, in this business at least, as interchangeable."

Kit would rather have thrown himself into the Thames. "What do you—"

"I've asked Sir Robert to assist me in overseeing you and your fellow associates," Walsingham said, in a voice that expressly forbade questions. "He has been invaluable over the past few months in recruiting new spies, and I expect no disruption of the intelligence flow between his circles and mine."

Kit sank back into his chair with a soft breath. The words were innocent, or would have been if anyone but Walsingham had said them. Assistance? The Walsingham Kit knew would rather have swallowed hot pitch than ask for help, least of all from someone like Cecil. The more people who knew the crown's secret machinations, the more avenues for betrayal. If Walsingham had reached out to Cecil—and judging from the smirk painting Cecil's face, he had—it could only be for one reason. Kit gritted his teeth and tried not to think about the walking stick, or Walsingham's artificially stiff posture. There was, after all, another part of the sentence to address.

"My fellow associates," he repeated. "Sir, I'm finished. Spying, code breaking, that isn't me anymore. It's been years, I have a life—"

"A life you're prepared to devote to the service of Her Majesty, like any loyal subject, I'm sure," Cecil said coldly.

Walsingham had said he wanted to keep Kit close at hand in London, but as the years went on, it had only been too easy to forget, to assume the spymaster would never call on him to make good on that insinuation. Kit drove one fist into his thigh, hating himself more as the truth became inescapable. "Why did you give me five years, then? If you always meant to bring me back?"

"It certainly wasn't the plan," Cecil said tersely, though Kit hadn't been speaking to him. "But the moment Sir Francis let you out of his sight, you immediately set about becoming the best-known poet in Bankside. Staying discreet is something of a challenge when the better part of London knows your name."

Despite himself, Kit inclined his head. "You flatter me, my lord."

"I certainly don't mean to."

"Believe me, Marlowe," Walsingham said, his weary voice severing the fight brewing between Kit and Cecil. "If there were a way for us to let you carry on as you were, we'd have taken it."

It might have sounded like an insult, but somehow it didn't. There was something odd in Walsingham's voice, something almost approaching fondness. As if Walsingham had followed Kit's rise from afar with satisfaction, enjoying the notion that at least one man had disentangled himself from the queen's intelligence service. Far from reassured, Kit felt his shoulders tense. If Walsingham was bringing Kit back in against his will, it was because there was no other way, and nothing he could say would stop it.

"We need you," Walsingham said simply. "You're the best code breaker we have. No one else comes close."

Cecil cleared his throat as if sincerely doubting this. Kit clenched his hands until the joints of his fingers ached.

"What's the job?" he said coldly.

Walsingham sighed. If he could not have courtesy, it seemed, he would settle for obedience. "It has to do with your new patron," he said. "Lord Strange."

He had to bite his lip to keep from swearing. His patron, the sign that Kit had talent worth rewarding, Lord Strange was tied to Walsingham. The news seeped through Kit's memories like a pestilence, coloring everything he'd experienced anew. All of it, all his successes one long strand of a silken web, with Walsingham and Cecil as twin spiders at the center.

"It won't surprise you to learn," Walsingham said, shooting Cecil a sharp look imploring silence, "that the death of Mary Stuart left a void in the Catholic hopes for succession, and the rebels have dug up a number of other claimants to fill that space."

Of course there were other claimants. From what Kit had heard, Mary's son, James, was out of contention. Too selfish, too flighty, too much a reckless man of twenty-six. And having your mother executed for treason was, likely, something of a deterrent against trying it yourself. Still, there were others beyond James. The Stuart line went deep, with distant cousins and great-great-grandchildren scattered from Scotland to Venice. It startled him, briefly, that he was already thinking this way—mentally running through the list of potential usurpers across Europe, evaluating their threats to the crown. As if he'd been quietly monitoring England's political threats in the back of his mind all this time.

As if some part of him, some small, reckless, irrepressible part, had hoped this meeting would come.

"You expect me to believe Lord Strange is choosing the Catholic rebellion's next messiah?" Kit said.

"No," Walsingham said. "I have reason to believe they've chosen him."

"His mother, Lady Clifford, was named heir presumptive to Her Majesty by the late King Henry," Cecil said, before Kit could voice a word of surprise. "Lady Clifford is a hellion of a woman, but she has little by way of subtlety, and Her Majesty has her under constant surveillance. Her son, your Lord Strange, is a different matter. A slippery devil, with more connections to suspected papists than an innocent man can be expected to have."

"Our spies," Walsingham added, "have also intercepted these coming to and from his estate."

Kit said nothing as Walsingham gathered a selection of papers from across his desk and pushed them forward. He didn't mean to look, but his traitorous eyes raked across the ciphered page, looking for patterns among the symbols. Already, he saw resemblances to two alphabets—Greek letters blended with stylized Latin ones, a starting point if nothing else. Not like Mary's long-gone cipher: this one looked seductive, wide open, welcoming him in.

No.

He turned the topmost page over, glaring at the verso. He'd been used. All this time he'd thought he was building a life for himself, scraping his way up with nothing but determination and talent, Walsingham had been two steps ahead, smoothing his way. All this time he'd thought himself a free man, he'd still been at the end of Walsingham's leash—imprisonment, still, however long the tether.

"Take those with you," Walsingham said, as if Kit had already agreed. "Keep us informed as you progress. And in the meantime, work your way into Strange's confidence."

"I imagine most of your work might be done from London, but some excursions to Strange's estate in Derbyshire will be necessary," Cecil said. "You can control those movements as you see fit, but come to the palace the moment you have something worth reporting. Either Sir Francis or I will receive you."

Kit wouldn't let anything shake him, not in front of Cecil. He would be stone, unmoved, unmovable. His nod was as curt as a soldier accepting orders. "Understood, sir."

"If there are other questions," Cecil said, rising, "Sir Francis can address them. I am needed at present with the Privy Council. Go out the way you came when you're finished, Marlowe." The unspoken *Don't touch anything* was clear.

The air in the room seemed instantly lighter the moment Cecil left. Walsingham let out a sigh that, if Kit didn't know him to be the apotheosis of proper conduct, might have been irritation.

"Close the door, Marlowe," Walsingham said.

When Kit had done so, Walsingham gave a small grunt as his back touched the chair. He winced slightly, but if he didn't intend to acknowledge his pain, neither did Kit. "I can't fault Sir Robert's skill or his thoroughness," Walsingham muttered, "but God knows I can fault his personality. Now. You look like you have something to ask me."

Kit paused, then sank into the chair in front of Walsingham's desk, gripping the arms until his palms ached. The prime thing he wanted to ask was foolish, and he knew Walsingham would only think less of him if he asked it. But the question raged so loudly in his ears that he couldn't pay attention to anything else unless he asked.

"I . . . My patronage, sir. From Lord Strange. Did he give it willingly, or was that you?"

Walsingham laughed, surprised. "I've just told you your patron may be plotting a revolution, and that's what concerns you?"

Kit raised his chin and looked Walsingham dead in the eye. "It is, sir, and I think I deserve an answer."

Walsingham sighed, his left hand toying with his walking stick. "I may have placed a word somewhere I knew it would travel. An endorsement from the right person can encourage a man to consider an investment he'd previously overlooked."

So he was right. Kit pressed one hand to his mouth, feeling sharply ill. Was that all he'd ever been? A pawn stupid enough to briefly think itself a king? As if he could have earned what he'd achieved on merit. The world hadn't changed so much as that.

Walsingham must have seen Kit's hurt. He sighed and leaned

forward, resting both elbows on the desk. "What does it matter? I placed your work in front of Strange, but I didn't force him to take it. And I didn't bribe all of London to praise you. Your pride is admirable, in a foolish sort of way, but surely even you must see the past five years of work are yours. *Tamburlaine, Malta,* the rest of it."

"I didn't know I had an admirer in you, sir," he said coldly.

Walsingham scoffed. "You don't. I find the theater ridiculous. But my daughter is a devotee. I fear someday she may ask me to facilitate an introduction."

Maybe it was all part of Walsingham's game. Flattery, kindness, subtle bribes to keep Kit under his thumb where he was most useful. But flattery had never been the spymaster's game before, and he'd have known better than to think Kit could be bought off so easily. The compliment was genuine, then. It didn't matter, not in the face of Kit's life crumbling to dust around him—but that didn't mean Kit didn't like to hear it.

"Write to me next week and tell me how you get on with the letters," Walsingham said. "If you get somewhere sooner, come in person."

"Assuming I agree," Kit said. "Assuming I'm willing to go through with this. Which I don't recall saying I am."

Walsingham began to rise, a serpent unfolding to its full terrifying length. But halfway up, he broke off with a hiss and a curse, sinking back to the chair. Kit saw the spasm shivering through Walsingham's thigh, the muscle shaking, strained and unsteady. Walsingham's hand convulsed, gripping his leg with crooked fingers. His mouth tightened to a pained slash. Kit jumped up, but Walsingham waved him off. He hung back as Walsingham pressed his eyes shut, breathing sharply.

The shadows under his eyes. The thinness across his shoulders. Walsingham could not be ill, and yet here they stood. Kit found himself unable to look at the spymaster, focusing instead on Sir Robert Cecil's empty chair.

"If I am indisposed," Walsingham said, "give your report to Sir

Robert. I do not have time to argue with you, Marlowe. I need you on my side."

Kit paused. Walsingham's breathing was not quite even. The hand on his thigh trembled.

"Yes, sir," Kit said.

————

Kit arrived at Tom's lodgings shortly before sunset—too close to city curfew to pretend he meant to return to his own bed that night. They rarely risked this so blatantly: living on opposite sides of the city was an inconvenience, but it was also plausible deniability against a curious landlady or other prying eyes. But tonight, Kit couldn't bear to be alone. Besides, Tom knew the appointment had been set for ten in the morning. No use pretending Walsingham had forgotten, or that the letter hadn't meant what they both knew it did.

Tom opened the door the moment Kit knocked. The room behind him was poorly lit, which made him look sallow, almost unhealthy. He said nothing, and Kit said nothing either, for as long as they could let the silence stretch. Then, sitting together on the bed with a terrible, empty space between them, Kit told him everything.

The silence that followed was worse than the one that had come before. It seemed to stretch from each shadow, cold fingers reaching for both of them.

"I'm sorry," Kit said quietly.

He reached for Tom's hand, but Tom brushed him aside with a brusque laugh. "No, you're not."

"What do you—"

"You love this, Kit. I know you do."

He pulled back from Tom, chest tightening. "How can you say that? How can you think I want more blood on my hands? Don't you think I have ghosts enough?"

Tom's face was blank as glass. "Of course I think so. But you don't."

Did he?

He'd rebelled at the very idea of it, terrified into silence by the apparition of yesterday's messenger. It had all come back to him, the drudgery of intelligence work, the constant fear of discovery, the ever-present threat of war and destruction that could be sparked by the slightest mistake. It had almost broken him in Yorkshire. When he'd turned his attention to poetry, he'd sworn he'd never go back to that life. And here he was, entering upon it again.

Worse still, Tom was right.

There was a thrill to it, one that rang even louder than the fear. Walsingham trusted him. Walsingham needed him. Once again, Kit would be part of these men, these powerful anonymous men whose intelligence and audacity shaped England's future. With Walsingham, he had the means to rise. To matter. To be the agent no man could replace. Plays were one thing, but this was another sort of immortality.

Kit pinched the bridge of his nose, refusing to look at Tom. He couldn't bear to see himself in Tom's eyes, see the selfish liar he knew he'd find there. "It's different this time," he said. "I'll work from London, at night; you'll hardly notice. I have the theater, I have my friends, I have you. Nothing needs to change."

Tom looked at him in silence. Even after Kit looked away, he could feel Tom's gaze bearing down on him, anatomizing every lie, every unspoken thought. Tom knew Kit better than Kit knew himself. There was no hiding anything from him.

"Just don't talk about it any more tonight," Tom said. "I can't stand to hear it."

It was easier said than done. Kit tried to oblige, to talk about nothing, about the daily business of London living. But underneath every word, he heard a silent scream, a reminder: this is a lie, this life is not your life, this may never be you again.

They went to bed early, the darkness new enough to feel tenuous. Kit ran one hand along Tom's shoulder in a gentle invitation to intimacy, but Tom shrugged him off and edged to the far side of the bed, his shoulders hunched. Kit sighed and lay on his back, staring up at the ceiling. He could still feel Tom's warmth beneath the blankets. He could sense the familiar rhythm of Tom's breathing. And yet all the while, they were in different worlds. Tom dreaming of the terror, the risk of discovery, the months of panic and sleepless nights and lies. Kit wide awake, thinking of the letters he'd tucked into the interior pocket of his doublet, both doublet and letters across the room in a pool of moonlight.

Sleep wouldn't come, no matter how much he wished it would. Not with this new task hovering before him, the letters whispering through the silent room.

Kit crept out of bed and removed the letters from his pocket, squinting at the topmost one in the dim glow. Some of it was Greek, certainly, but too much to hope that each letter had simply replaced its Latin counterpart. The Greek and Latin letters alternated in what looked to be a semi-regular pattern—perhaps there was a clue in that?

"Kit," Tom said quietly from the bed.

Kit let out a long breath, but he didn't put the letters away. "Go back to sleep," he said, bending over the page.

Twenty-Eight

Edward went on the way it had begun, as raucous a success as ever, but it scarcely mattered to Kit anymore. He hadn't felt this nervous—or smoked this heavily—since the first production of *Tamburlaine*. Then the nerves had been from standing on the brink of a new life, waiting to see what would emerge when the play stood on its own legs. This time, the fear was of his old life rising back up, and whether he'd be clever enough to live through what followed.

After each performance, he broke away from the players early and retired to his Shoreditch room, puzzling over the letters by candlelight. Thomas Kyd, interpreting this as evidence that the muse struck at all hours, said nothing at all about it. Each night, Kit worked until he couldn't keep his eyes open another moment. Each night, he felt the weave of the cipher loosening, more entry points unfurling to meet him. The work was thrilling, in a way he'd only ever felt after the close of a new play. The thrill of doing something he was good at, of transforming chaos into narrative.

Lord Strange clearly thought himself clever, but he was nowhere near as shrewd as Mary had been. It took slightly more than two weeks before Kit, hunched over his candle sometime past midnight, felt the intoxicating current of a freshly broken code. The letter before him was a short one, and it took almost no time at all to match each ciphered letter to its equivalent, the revealed message spilling forward at his command.

*Ask de Vries to approximate how much he'll need for the task,
using the figures provided in your last letter. Impress upon him
that time is of the essence.*

Kit scowled at the paper. Strange's cipher might be easily broken, but at least when Kit had untangled Mary's, he'd known at
once what sort of crisis he and Walsingham faced. All Strange
had given Kit was the name of a Dutchman and a need for haste.
It might have been anything: typical business, a trade deal Strange
wanted to follow personally.

It might have been, but it wasn't. Innocent men didn't cipher
their business communications. There was more to this, but Kit
wouldn't find out what through Sir Robert Cecil's sanctioned
channels. No, when he returned to Whitehall with news, he'd
have something more to show for it than this.

———

The following week, Kit watched the afternoon's performance of
Edward II from his usual haunt in the second gallery, doing his best
not to let his anxiety show. It became increasingly difficult as the play
neared its climax, and when Henslowe appeared beside him at last,
the theater manager's appearance startled him as if he'd been slapped.
He jerked away, attracting annoyed glances from the spectators, who
had paid for a seat precisely so people like Kit wouldn't disturb them.

"He's here," Henslowe said simply.

"Where?" They both kept their voices low—the audience had
turned back to the stage, more interested in the drama in front of
them than the one behind.

"Outside," Henslowe said. "First rule of theater: Don't antagonize the money."

Kit gave him the ghost of a smile. "I thought the first rule of
theater was 'Don't antagonize Philip Henslowe.'"

"For you, Marlowe," Henslowe said gravely, "I've had to write a
great many new rules."

As he followed Henslowe down the rickety stairs to street level, he tried to siphon confidence out of the man's terse remarks. Kit had the talent and the social cachet to needle the owner of the city's most celebrated theater and get away with it. He wasn't a nobody anymore—he knew how to get what he came for. They left the Rose and stepped into the muddy Bankside street, and Kit stood as tall as he could. He kept his expression as mild as a tractable servant. Someone with nothing to hide.

"My lord," Henslowe said.

A man standing alone in the street turned to face them, and Kit laid eyes on Lord Strange for the first time.

By now, Kit had lived in London for a quarter of his life. He'd shared rooms and streets with powerful men of all kinds: men who pretended to gentility, who expected a full theater to fall silent and gape as they entered. Kit had always enjoyed a private laugh at these people's expense—given what it had cost him to make London know his name, the idea that anyone owed you respect was laughable. You receive the respect you earn.

Or so Kit thought, until he first saw Lord Strange.

The man's charisma was undeniable; even Kit, who would have dearly liked to deny it, couldn't do it. Elegant, graceful, a native Englishman with the hooded eyes and dark flowing hair of a foreigner, Strange commanded attention. He looked nothing like Anthony Babington, except in one respect: though Kit had expected him to be older, he couldn't be far beyond thirty. His doublet nearly blinded Kit—a rich purple no flower would have dared to sport—but he wore flashiness well.

Kit sank into an elegant bow, a far cry from his awkward attempts at Cambridge. This was the bow of a man who spent his time among people in power. One harder than most to scare. Lord Strange's Men weren't the only people who knew how to act, after all.

"Marlowe," Strange said, and there was something energizing about it, to hear his own name spoken to him in that way.

"At your service, sir," Kit said.

To his surprise, this made Lord Strange smile. "Believe it or not, Marlowe, today it isn't your service I'm after. I've wanted to speak with you for some time, so I was happy to receive your request to meet. You're at liberty for supper?"

As Kit's usual dining plans involved a meat pie in one hand and a bedraggled copy of Ovid in the other, *at liberty* was putting the matter somewhat grandly. "Of course, sir."

"Good," Strange said. "If a conversation can ever be had over food, it should be. I know a place not far from here. Good day, Master Henslowe," he added pointedly.

Henslowe's mouth narrowed. "Good day, my lord," he said. As he turned, he shot back a sharp glance that detailed how deep and protracted Kit's suffering would be if his misbehavior caused Lord Strange to withdraw his patronage. Kit didn't have the heart to tell him that if this meeting went as he hoped, Lord Strange would soon lose a great deal more than a theater company.

As it transpired, Strange's destination was the George Inn, a Southwark tavern that, while by no means seedy, was nonetheless several notches below the sort of place Kit imagined a member of the peerage spending his time. He watched in surprise as his patron greeted the tapsters and drawers by name without pause, before commandeering a table set slightly off from the main room by a wooden partition. Two pints of ale appeared before them almost before Kit had fully sat down.

"Yes, Robin, the usual will do nicely, thank you," Strange said to the boy who had appeared over Kit's shoulder. The boy bobbed his head and ducked away without a word, and Strange arched his back before taking a drink with relish Kit associated more with an apprentice than a nobleman. "It's a relief to get away from the estate, frankly. So thank you for that, as well as for making my players the most successful in London."

"I don't take credit for that, sir," Kit said, with his best approximation of modesty.

Strange laughed. "That's not what Henslowe tells me."

Until now, Kit had been aligning his behavior with the sub-servient, respectful persona he'd adopted in Mary Stuart's ser-vice. Henslowe's voice in the back of his head, murmuring, *Don't antagonize the money*, was just as strong as Walsingham's orders to probe the depths of Strange's secrets. But with this remark, he felt the last of his reserve drift away. Not enough to indict him-self with a thoughtless phrase—the task at hand still came before anything. But enough to imagine that, if Kit himself had come into wealth, he'd behave with it more or less like this. At least, it was pleasant to imagine he might.

"I hope you don't pay too much mind to Henslowe," Kit said. "The portrait you'll get of me might be accurate, but it won't be flattering."

Strange shrugged and leaned back in his chair. The whole atmo-sphere was so reminiscent of the White Stag that Kit almost checked over his shoulder to see whether Mistress Howard wasn't surveilling their conversation. "I pay you to butcher people onstage in verse, Marlowe," Strange said, "not to make friends with Philip Henslowe. If that were the task, I'd have to pay you double."

"Let me know if there's too much butchering, sir," Kit said. "I'm afraid pastoral comedy has never been my strong suit." Walsing-ham would have been bursting with impatience if he could see Kit's tactics—to say nothing of how Cecil would have responded—but with this man, Kit was certain, the indirect and convivial route would be by far the more effective. Besides, what he said was true: the only shepherd he'd ever written about had killed a dozen kings.

"Too much?" Strange repeated. "Don't be absurd. It's what the people want, any fool can see that. That's the trick to getting ahead, Marlowe. Listen to the people and give them what they want."

He glanced at Robin with an appreciative smile as the boy returned with a roast capon, browned skin steaming over a bed of roasted root vegetables. The boy glowed with pleasure at the acknowledgment before skittering back into the kitchen at a shout from the cook. Strange took up the knife and carved the capon expertly, transferring a piece to Kit's plate before taking his own. It was, frankly, remarkable. Kit had expected Strange to be another Babington. He'd never met a nobleman like this, who served poets before serving himself.

"What do you think they want, then, sir?" Kit asked, stabbing at a quartered parsnip as casually as though Strange were Ned Alleyn, and the George Inn the Mermaid Tavern.

Strange glanced over his shoulder, though with the partition and the ambient noise of the front room there was precious little risk of their being overheard. Perhaps that wasn't the point at all—rather, to signal to Kit that what was said next would be worth listening to. "Tell me something," he said. "I've seen your plays, and there's something in them I've never seen from another poet. Are you angry, Marlowe?"

Kit wrapped both hands around his pint, appetite suddenly gone. Was he?

If Strange had asked the question while Kit was writing *Edward II*, he'd have said no, not in the slightest. He'd have said London was everything he'd dreamed, that he was free and successful and exactly where he wanted to be. But in this Southwark tavern, plagued by the memory of Sir Robert Cecil's terse orders, he knew the truth, and the truth was that he'd been angry every day of his life for seven years. Ever since Arthur Gregory first showed him the sketch of the woman he was meant to betray to her death. His hands the ones covered in blood, so that a queen who would never even speak to him might wield power beyond imagination. Might conquer the world while Kit fought for a cut of his own profits, to spend an uninterrupted hour with the man he loved, to stay alive in a world where he could trust no one.

Yes, Kit was angry. And there was something intoxicating about admitting it.

"It's hard not to be," Kit said. "If the world gave me a reason not to be angry, I'd happily take it."

Strange nodded, seemingly pleased with Kit's answer. "That's all the people want, in my experience," he said. "A reason not to be angry. Or, failing that, a sense that their anger can have some effect. That it matters."

Priests strangled by freed slaves. Twenty young women beheaded and spiked on the gates of a besieged city. The king's triumphant procession into his sacred city, drawn not by an ass but by six bridled captives, each man burning with shame, frothing at the mouth with pride. Anger that achieved something more than a scream in the middle of the night, more than a gesture into the dark. Kit imagined Mary Stuart sitting in the empty chair beside him, the black-marble eyes of Catherine of Siena gazing through the back of his head. Strange couldn't have given Kit a better explanation of his own plays if he'd tried.

"Surely it's not our place to be angry, sir," Kit said. He methodically drained away the honest emotion he'd allowed himself to feel, mentally chastising himself for it. He was a spy. A spy could not allow himself to be seen so clearly, not by a man like this. "Or it's not *my* place. It's the way the world is. Men like me, we don't change that."

Strange looked at him searchingly. From the other side of the partition, the sound of men in warm conversation, the clink of knives against plates, a call for more ale. The sounds of men like Kit, men beneath notice, without influence. Men who, perhaps, harbored unspoken anger in their breasts too.

"The world is one thing," Strange murmured. "But surely every man has the right to look after his own soul?"

And there it was. A backward way of expressing the creed— Luther himself couldn't have put it better. Strange could have passed the sentiment off as pure Protestantism, if anyone in the George Inn was listening with an ear to theological orthodoxy. But Kit knew what his patron meant. Look after his own soul by turning to the doctrine that would send it closest to heaven, its incense and holy relics and feast days of saints. Kit should have felt triumph. He'd guided Strange around every conversational bend until they arrived here, the one place Walsingham and Cecil needed him to be. From here, the task was simple. Why, then, the rancid taste rising in his mouth, as though the words he was about to speak next had spoiled?

Perhaps, he thought, it was because the crown's justifications had never touched his heart quite the way Strange's had.

"Would to God every man did," Kit said, steadying himself with a long drink of ale. "You wouldn't think that would be a radical proposition."

Strange nodded. He didn't take his eyes off the capon, but Kit felt the man's energy shift. Had he pushed it too far? Had that word, *radical*, had that been too obvious? It had been years since Kit had tried to extract information like this, and while the theater had been its own sort of practice, he felt the pit of his stomach drop at the thought that he couldn't play the part anymore, that years of London living had robbed him of his touch.

Then Strange looked up, and Kit caught the tail end of the emotion his patron had been trying to hide. It wasn't distrust.

It was hope.

"True enough," Strange said, "and all the more reason not to say too much here. Privacy is one thing, but it's not the same as solitude. If you were to come by my estate, perhaps next week, we might discuss further."

Kit's mouth tasted metallic now, as if he had swallowed gunpowder. He clenched one fist until the nails carved into his palm, but when he spoke, his voice was clear. "I'd like that very much, sir. I think we might have a great deal to talk about."

Strange smiled. "I think we might. Now, enough of this. We have business to discuss."

As though a spell had been lifted, Kit felt the noise of the tavern crash over him, the usual melodies of Southwark. Shouts, curses, laughter, rage. Not far off, Ned Alleyn, rising from the dead to take his bows as Edward. The city hadn't felt so vast or so loud since his first day in London, when every voice called its own damnation, when every hand grasped for his throat.

"Do we, sir?"

"Of course." Strange raised his pint in a toast that seemed only half ironic. "This play, Marlowe. My God. After *Malta*, I thought you couldn't startle me more, but clearly your well of ways to kill people never runs dry."

Twenty-Nine

The entrance of Strange's manor felt like a cloister, with its vaulted ceilings and symmetrical lines of arched windows. The agonizing quiet strengthened the impression, broken only by the muted drumming of raindrops outside. Kit's boots left tiny mirrors of water along the stone floor. The invitation from Lord Strange's man had been precise: Strange's Derbyshire estate, three o'clock. And yet Kit had been alone in this hall for upward of fifteen minutes, waiting to be seen. He clasped his hands behind his back and tilted his head to the ceiling, feigning interest in the rafters. A good spy was never bored. Never agitated. Nerves and impatience were for the theater, not this.

There were a hundred reasons Strange might be late. Perhaps he'd gotten waylaid by business, whatever sort of affairs went into running an estate of this size. Perhaps it entertained him to have his social inferiors cool their heels in the entrance hall, regardless of the affability he'd shown at the George Inn. Perhaps he'd brought Kit here to ambush him, suspecting his game, and an assassin stood just around the corner, waiting for Kit to venture in undefended—

"Marlowe," said Strange, striding down the hall. "Excellent."

No more thinking like that. There was a thin line between caution and delusion, and it wouldn't do to cross it. Kit intended to bow, but Strange extended a hand instead, and Kit shook it as though they were business partners on equal footing. "Good afternoon, sir," he said. "I hope I'm not interrupting."

"You can't interrupt if I invited you," Strange said. "This way."

Bracing himself for the worst, Kit followed.

It wasn't Kit's first time in an aristocrat's home, but those manors had all doubled as prisons. Mary's decor had been muted as a nunnery, but Strange clearly found himself under no such compunction. Each room they passed seemed as grand as Whitehall, gold-threaded carpets and priceless portraits adorning even the plainest surfaces. Kit saw his patron's touch on every inch of it, that natural gravitation toward the bright and gaudy. At last, Strange led Kit into a room on the left—his private library.

Kit let out a long, low whistle. The room was a treasure trove. Shelves packed full lined each wall, the spines of Tacitus and Cicero and Montaigne crammed shoulder to shoulder, even stacked atop one another when shelf space ran thin. The fellows of Cambridge would have sold their souls for such a library, Kit thought; he himself would certainly have bent a few laws to get one. Clustered candles glowed on low tables between the room's armchairs, giving the dark wood a warm golden undertone. Against the windows—the only break in the shelves—raindrops left comet-like tails down the glass.

"Do you like it?" Strange said, smiling.

Kit laughed. "My God. It's incredible. I hope it's all right if I quit London and live here instead."

Strange's smile held steady, but there was something more to it now, something Kit couldn't quite follow. "You're more than welcome to use it anytime you like," he said. "But the books aren't what I wanted to show you."

He crouched to the floor, where a corner of the bearskin rug had been flipped askew. Strange slipped two fingers into a crack between the boards and lifted. A full square of floor rose on a hinge, revealing a black hole in which Kit could make out the top of a ladder.

God's death. A priest hole. This was the fanciful nonsense he'd imagined when Walsingham recruited him at Cambridge. Secret rooms for Catholics to hide in when the queen's soldiers led raids.

And here one was, in this ludicrously respectable Derbyshire library. He'd known, before, what he was getting into. And yet it had never felt so real, so potentially deadly, as it did now, staring into that gaping hole in the floor, close and cold and forbidding as the mouth of a grave. Innocent men didn't need places to hide.

"You'll forgive the inconvenience," Strange said, gesturing toward the priest hole as if it were a stack of unwashed dishes. "My guests and I err on the side of caution."

Kit cleared his throat. "Very wise," he said. "You want me to—"

"If you don't mind. You can close the door behind you."

Strange climbed down the ladder, disappearing into the dark as easily as slipping into a bath. Kit was left alone, staring down after him.

This was what Walsingham and Cecil wanted. Sending Kit into this lion's mouth, and God only knew if the teeth would close over him. Kit's palms itched with sweat; he wiped them on the thighs of his breeches. He could still turn back to London, back to his cut-rate lodgings in Shoreditch and his half-finished play about the Saint Bartholomew's Day massacre. He could present the broken cipher to Walsingham and remove himself from the rest of the work, and let Lord Strange make what he would of Kit's sudden cowardice.

He could, but he wouldn't. Everything Walsingham needed rose from this secret room, and no one but Kit could get it. Ignoring the tightness in his chest, Kit stepped down the ladder, then turned the door on its hinge above him. The wood settled into place, and so did the darkness.

Kit's heart echoed in the thick silence. It reminded him of the dream that had haunted him since Northampton, not the sound of Mary's scream but the other one, of being buried alive, the dark funereal and final. Too disoriented to climb, he hung there at the top, feeling his breath quicken. He forced it to slow, counting each inhale for four and each exhale for six. After a moment, he heard the hiss of flame catching. A faint glow rose five feet below.

He dropped down into a stone room, eight feet square. Its ceiling was low—Kit was short, but he still felt the stone close above his head. Poorly lit, only a flickering circle from the stubs of two candles in sconces in the wall. Strange was there, of course, but he wasn't alone. A woman stood next to him, though Kit could barely make out her face in the poor light. Heart pounding, he took a step forward, the beginning of a greeting on his tongue.

Then he felt a hand grip his hair, jerking his head back. The cold flash of a knife pressed against his exposed throat.

He hadn't seen or heard the man behind him. Still couldn't, didn't dare to turn his head. Whoever it was, his knife hand was perfectly steady. Kit bit his lip, feeling his rapid pulse against the blade. So this was how he died. Surrounded by rebels, in the dark, under the earth, alone. How long would it take them, in London, to notice?

"My apologies, Marlowe," Strange said. His posture was casual, leaning against the opposite wall with his arms crossed, but he did genuinely look sorry. "But we can't afford to take risks."

"Be careful with him, Evan," said the woman to the man with the knife. "I have a few questions I want to ask this one."

Kit's breath hitched, this time for a reason that had nothing to do with the steel against his throat. He knew that voice. And as his vision adjusted, he knew that face as well. Those sharp eyes, that long copper hair.

"Anne," he whispered.

Anne Cooper said nothing, but the man behind Kit—Evan, she'd called him—dug his fingers into his hair until the back of Kit's head nearly touched his shoulders. The knife would draw blood soon.

"When Lord Strange told me you were writing plays in London, I hardly believed it," Anne said. "But where else would you go, after you betrayed Mary to Cecil? Stay close to the crown, so you can see us all hanged, one by one."

Cecil. Had she seen him all those years ago at Chartley, standing beside Walsingham while Cecil made his arrest? Or had she bolted by then, heard his name mentioned secondhand? It was impossible to know how much she knew or how she knew it, but her knowing anything was too much. How had she even come here? He'd thought Anne's loyalty was to Mary alone, but he'd been wrong—it had been to the faith more than to the person. An opportunist as well as a militant Catholic, then. Following the winds and offering her service to the current favorite, swapping Mary for Strange after the axe fell. Kit needed to think, but his mind was jolted loose and useless. He felt vacant, as if the knife had pierced the back of his skull and let the stagnant air empty him from within.

"You've made your point, Master Lloyd," Strange said, gesturing in Kit's direction. "Don't get carried away."

The blade twitched against Kit's throat. He swallowed and felt a drop of blood glide along the cutting edge. The moment seemed to stretch a hundred years. Then, at last, Evan Lloyd removed the knife from Kit's throat, shoving him forward into freedom.

Kit stumbled, dropping to one knee, and took a rattling inhale. *Alive,* his heartbeat said in his ears. *Alive.* Without thinking, he brought a hand to his throat. His fingertips came away wet with blood.

"Get up," Anne said coldly.

Kit didn't move. He no longer felt part of his body, only a thick cloud of fear above a man that had once been him. He knelt where he was, trying to think of nothing but his own breathing. To his surprise, a hand reached into view, palm up. A hand that, ten seconds ago, had held a knife at Kit's neck.

Evan Lloyd was tall and blond, with a wispy mustache and eyes that, despite the knife in his left hand, looked kind. His grip was firm, and when Kit had staggered to his feet again, Evan gave him a sharp clap on the shoulder. It wasn't much to go on, when his remaining life seemed to be measured in seconds rather than years, but Kit would take what he could get. He gave Evan a grim nod, then turned back to Anne. The thrill of the blade had silenced him at first, but now his fear had pushed over into focus. His head hummed with the clarity that came after cannon fire.

All right, he thought. You're a liar and a talker. So talk. And lie. Act, because your life depends on it.

"So you were part of this," he said to Anne. "All that time. And you never told me." He pressed one hand to his mouth, as though trying to hold himself together. "My God, Anne. I could have helped you, if I'd known."

Clearly Anne had expected panic, fumbling attempts to defend himself. She hadn't expected him to turn the accusation back on her. It was one of the oldest tricks in Kit's arsenal: flipping the argument upside down, catching his opponent on the defensive. Let her prove her dedication to him, and she'd have no thought left for his own.

"Don't act surprised," Kit said. He pitched his words higher, looser, aiming his tone like a bowshot toward indignation. He'd always been a capable liar, but this, this was virtuosity. No place like knifepoint to hit your stride. "You knew what I believe, and you still think I want that heretic bitch on the throne? After everything I gave for Mary, you think I'd turn my back on that now? I won't be lectured for my faith, Cooper, not by you. Not until you've risked everything I have."

"And what is that, precisely?" Strange said softly.

Given three minutes to concoct a more prudent answer, Kit wouldn't have said what he did. But he didn't have three minutes. He had this moment, right now. The key to a convincing lie was confidence, and the last thing he could afford was a stuttered excuse. He had to explain why he—a Catholic—had been seen with Sir Robert Cecil, why he'd come to live in London. And the answer came to him, not through divine inspiration but in Arthur Gregory's voice, drifting across the years from the back room of the White Stag: *Walsingham and I both knew you wouldn't have lasted a day with the priests.*

This was the biggest gamble he'd ever taken, but there was no reward without risk. And if anyone could do it successfully, Kit could.

He paused, as though weighing the risk of revealing a long-held secret. Then he sighed, closed his eyes briefly, and spoke. "Anne knows I'm a true Catholic, sir. What she doesn't know is that I studied at the English College in Rheims."

Strange raised his eyebrows. "You were a seminarian," he said. "You."

"*Testor Deum*," Kit said. His proficiency in Latin was thanks to the bawdier passages of Ovid rather than Catholic scripture, but there was no reason for Strange to know that. "I didn't study long enough to reach the priesthood—"

"Really," Anne interrupted.

"Because I found another way to serve the cause," Kit continued, as though she hadn't spoken. "The English College is crawling with the queen's spies; everyone knows it. One of them, he went by the name of Father Gregory, he took a liking to me. I nurtured that friendship, made him believe we wanted the same things. And then, after a time, he introduced me to his master, Sir Francis Walsingham."

"The queen's spymaster," Strange said. It was impossible to read his voice. "You're working for Walsingham."

"He thinks so," Kit said. "And if he finds out I'm undermining his plans from the inside, it'll be my head on London Bridge. That's why I couldn't tell you, Anne," he said, turning to her. "I wanted to. But with Poley there, and then Lord Rich, I couldn't risk it, do you understand? I did everything I could. It wasn't enough, but I tried."

He let out a long breath and waited. The room seemed to grow smaller by the minute, the ceiling unbearably low overhead. He'd laid the lie down, for them to do with what they would. One more life to live alongside the others: a Catholic double agent, a seminarian turned rogue. He'd play the part as he'd played all the others, doubling roles and swapping masks to get what he needed. If it worked, if the rebels trusted Kit enough to confide in him, he'd be the greatest spy England ever had.

And if it failed, he would be dead, and none of it would matter anyway.

"When exactly were you in Rheims?" Evan said. His pale blue eyes were weak compared to Strange's charismatic gaze, but they still kept Kit frozen where he was.

"I went when I was sixteen," Kit said. "I met a Huguenot pilgrim in Canterbury who helped pay for passage. When I left, I went straight to Sheffield, where I met Anne." It was true enough that Canterbury had crawled with Huguenots during Kit's childhood— it was why he'd begun to write *The Massacre at Paris* in the first place, and, God willing, the research he'd done for that play would carry him through any questions of doctrine.

"And before that?" Strange said. "Were you raised Catholic?"

The absurdity of the question made Kit want to laugh. Bless their papist hearts, they were making this easy. "I believed many stupid things as a child because I'd been taught to. But I know better now. The queen's church is a joke, created so her impotent old father could fuck whoever he liked. And their Bible is a travesty. England's poets should have hanged Tyndale for crimes against metaphor."

Strange laughed, and for the first time in minutes Kit allowed himself to breathe easy. That was the same laugh Kit had heard at the George Inn, the laugh of a man amused by someone he considered an equal. There was a world of hope in that laugh. Never let it be said a little well-timed blasphemy couldn't serve the purpose.

"And what will you give for the true faith, Marlowe?" Evan said.

It was an olive branch, of sorts, and Kit knew how to take it. "My life," he said. "I thought I'd made that clear."

Strange pushed himself up off the wall at last. At his full height, his head brushed the low ceiling. Kit felt profoundly small, like an insect waiting to be crushed. Then, Strange extended a hand. Kit shook it, and he took his deepest breath yet. The ache in his breastbone sharpened, as if his lungs had forgotten how to expand. If Evan had slit Kit's throat, would Strange have looked on with that same smile? It was impossible to say.

"I meant what I said to you in Southwark, Marlowe," Strange said. "The people are angry. With the crown, with the church, with all of it. They want that anger to matter. They want to be led by someone who listens to them."

There it was. The plot coalescing, just out of reach. If Strange wanted to frame his quest for power as a populist uprising, let him. Walsingham could use that. Silencing a threat of this nature was as much a question of mastering public opinion as it was of direct action. They'd have to work fast, if the queen didn't want a second iteration of the Pilgrimage of Grace from her father's reign.

"I know that," Kit said. "That's why I've been doing this for so long. I want to help you, if I can."

Strange nodded. "Anne?"

Anne scoffed, but Kit could bear any skepticism so long as it wasn't accompanied by a blade. "I still don't trust him."

"I wouldn't respect you if you did," he said.

"Did you stay?" she said. "Until the end?"

It didn't matter whether or not he had. Mary was dead and buried. Even if her ghost haunted Kit's dreams, the next move on the chessboard was Strange, and Strange alone. But if it took a show of solidarity for Anne to trust him, he could spin a tale of remorse to convince any audience. Like all of his lies to these people, they rested on a foundation unsettlingly close to truth.

"I did," he said. "For the trial, and after."

Anne's face had lost its soldier's hardness. He wondered, absently, if she would cry. "How was she? At the end."

Dead, Kit thought. "Like a queen," he said.

Evan crossed himself, but Strange didn't react. Mary was nothing to him. Putting a Scottish-born, French-raised queen on the throne of England would have done nothing to advance his dream, this vision of an England brought forward by the voice of the people. If Mary was gone, so be it.

"Walsingham suspects you," Kit said to Strange. "That's why he wanted me to earn your patronage. But I can keep him misinformed for as long as necessary. And anything you need to know from inside Whitehall, I'm your man."

Strange hummed softly. "Feeding lies to the wolf. There's an irony to it. I have to admit, Marlowe, if I needed an unscrupulous liar, you'd be my first choice."

"My mother would be proud to hear it, sir," Kit said, earning himself a short laugh from Evan and no reaction at all from Anne.

"If you can really do this, Marlowe," Strange said, and Kit could see him thrill with the thought of it, "find out when Walsingham's men are planning their next raid on the estate, and report that back to me. If your information is reliable, we can move from there."

Kit nodded. "I can do that."

"Where do you live now?" Evan said.

Christ. This kind of lying was dangerous enough without the risk of suspicious Catholics visiting in the middle of the night and stabbing him in his sleep. But they'd need to find him, to trust him. Keeping idle information secret would win him no friends. "Shoreditch," he said. "Across from the church. Ask for Sarah Talbot's house."

"I'll come to you next week," Evan said, "and pass your news to the rest."

Kit swallowed a curse. That wasn't enough, for everything he'd just risked. If Strange met with Kit directly, Kit could learn the whole of their plans, not just what Evan Lloyd thought he could be trusted to know. Walsingham could arrest him, then. Strange would be trapped, like Kit was now, a rabbit in this stone warren.

"You can trust me to—" he began.

"We know Whitehall's methods of questioning," Evan said with a grim smile. "The less you know, the better."

It would never happen, Evan had the wrong end of it entirely, but Kit couldn't help following the insinuation to the end, to himself broken on the rack, each finger crushed, his breath the hitching whimper of a dying dog, and through the darkness of

Whitehall's subterranean passages, Strange's handsome face, and that grim smile.

"We'll send for you soon," Strange said, nodding toward the ladder. "Don't let us down, Marlowe."

Kit hesitated, then nodded curtly. "You know where to find me," he said.

As he turned his back on them, he could feel them watching. Evan, bright-eyed with hope that they'd found a supporter. Anne, alive to any suggestion of betrayal. And Lord Strange, turning this small room into the center of a people's revolution.

Kit pushed the trapdoor and emerged into the library, into the light.

Thirty

Two days later, Kit knocked on the door to Walsingham's office. The swaggering confidence of his earlier visit had vanished; now, he waited on edge for an invitation. His dreams, these last two nights, had worsened. Now, along with Mary's endless shrieks and the depth of a grave, Kit dreamed of his own body thrown into a stone pit, throat slit and bloody, Strange's laugh in his ears.

The door opened a moment after his knock, revealing a face Kit hadn't expected. A tall man dressed plainly, hard face weathered from rough living and light sleep. When he saw Kit on the threshold, he let out a small laugh.

"If it isn't the king of Bankside," Arthur Gregory said, not unkindly.

Kit hadn't realized how desperately he wanted a familiar face until the cool wave of relief that came from seeing Gregory. They'd never been friends—grudging acquaintances if anything—but they understood each other, and there was a comfort to that. "Good to hear you've missed me," Kit said.

"Do you know the maddest thing about it, I have," Gregory said, leaning against the doorway. "Cecil's bringing in his own men now, but Christ knows none of them have your flair for wild heroics."

"God broke the mold after making me," Kit said, with a facetious half bow.

Gregory scoffed. "Or while he was doing it. Come in, then."

He stepped aside, gesturing toward one of the chairs in front of Walsingham's desk. Walsingham himself sat behind it, stiff-backed and edgy. It hadn't been long since their last meeting, but the spymaster's health had deteriorated faster than Kit had expected. He had lost weight, and his face shone paler than ever against his black doublet. Walsingham noted Kit's alarm at once—and the hairline cut, still healing, along his throat—but said nothing about either. Ignoring the chair Gregory indicated, Kit sat on the edge of the desk, angled sideways to face Walsingham. After the ambush of two days before, turning his back to doors sent his pulse racing.

"Were you followed?" Walsingham asked.

Practicalities first. Always. "No," Kit said. "I made sure of it."

"Good." Walsingham held up a hand, bidding Kit wait. He opened a drawer, then procured a small bottle, which he passed to Kit with a knowing look. "Pull yourself together, then tell me everything."

Kit laughed and took it. The whiskey was excellent and burned his throat like holy fire. "You have this just in case?"

"I work with Sir Robert Cecil now," Walsingham said. "There is no 'in case.'"

Kit drank again, longer this time, then passed the bottle to Gregory. "I have to admit," he said, "I'm glad it's the two of you here, not him."

"Told you you'd warm to me," Gregory said.

"You never."

"You came here with news, I assume," Walsingham said sharply. "Regarding the cipher?"

Kit flushed. Comforting as their presence felt, Gregory and Walsingham were not his friends, and he had a job to do. "Yes, sir," he said. "I've solved it, and more than that."

The words poured out of him, detached and foreign as if channeled from a far-off spirit. Thank God his voice didn't waver. He drifted above his body, describing a nightmare that had happened to somebody else. He'd never admit how deeply it rattled him, the chill of the knife against his throat, not in front of the queen's spies. But of course, Walsingham and Gregory both knew what a brush with death did to a man.

Walsingham listened in silence. The only way for Kit to gauge his reaction was the tightness of his mouth, which thinned until he seemed to have swallowed his lips. But when he learned about the gamble Kit had made, what he'd claimed about the English College, the spymaster's iron restraint gave way. Gregory's shocked oath was nothing compared to Walsingham's anger, so fierce Kit's voice died in the face of it.

"How dare you," Walsingham said. Kit drew back, standing now with the desk between them. Five years ago, Walsingham would have taken Kit by the collar and thrown him to the ground, would have backed him against the wall until he stammered a desperate apology. Even ill as Walsingham was, that cloud of power had not left him. "I brought you in as a code breaker, Marlowe, not as an ungovernable madman who follows whatever foolish scheme comes to mind. You've tipped our hand to a band of Catholic murderers, so you can—"

"So they'll trust me," Kit said. His nerve had quailed, but he screwed it into place again and stood his ground. Walsingham had changed since Kit had been out of service, but so had he. No matter what Walsingham thought of Kit's methods, they'd worked, and whatever worked was right. "They think I'm a double agent, sir. One of their soldiers."

"And the moment they doubt you, they'll undo everything we've—"

"Sir," Gregory said carefully. Both Kit and Walsingham looked at him in surprise—interrupting Walsingham was a risk for only the direst of circumstances. "It's madness, I'll be the first to admit it. But it isn't a bad plan. If they trust him, if it works, they'll tell him everything."

Walsingham's stormy brow remained unmoved. For a moment, Kit thought Walsingham might dismiss Gregory on the spot, or worse. Then—like a beam of light through the dark—Walsingham extended a hand to Gregory, who grinned and placed the bottle in it. Walsingham drank deep, with a wince at the burn.

"Then they have to trust you," he said grimly, replacing the bottle in the drawer.

Kit let out his breath at last and sank into the chair beside Gregory. "They will," he said. "When are you planning to raid his estate next?"

Walsingham blinked. "I wasn't," he said waspishly. "Placing you in his employ was meant to relieve the need for that."

"I need you to," Kit said. "Within two weeks. He's testing me by asking for a warning."

Walsingham was no longer looking at Kit but somewhere over his shoulder, lost in the web of connections only he could see. "The twenty-first," he said, after a moment. "Two o'clock. I'll see to it. Marlowe, be careful. I need you where you are."

Emotions were Kit's stock in trade. He catalogued them for a living, for the stage or for the palace. But the one that surged through him at those words, *I need you where you are,* that one he'd never felt before. Terror, certainly. The thought of the knife against his throat would not leave him, and if this gambit failed, he risked worse than that. But at the same time, he'd have accepted no other answer. Walsingham needed him to stay, and Kit needed it too. Risk aside, death aside. This was his plan, and he had to see it through.

"We'll need to work on the opposite end of this as well," Walsingham said. "If Strange is depending on popular support, he'll have men he trusts to muster it. Any names, any correspondences, you are to pass those directly to me, or to Gregory if I am indisposed."

Kit nodded. Whatever Strange was planning, the net would have been cast wide, and each contingency would have its own contingency. If his time in Mary's service had taught him one thing, it was that a rebel's partners mattered as much as the rebel. "I understand, sir."

Walsingham palmed the top of his cane, regarding Kit at a soft angle. "Do you know, Marlowe, I think you finally do."

No one could best the spymaster in the art of the backhanded compliment. Kit defied any man in the nation to try.

"You're still safe among them?"

Kit shrugged. "I'll have to be."

Walsingham nodded. "You will. Now, if you'll excuse me. Gregory. Marlowe."

Gregory had risen straightaway, as if the half-formed request had been gospel. Kit followed suit a moment later, looking back at the spymaster. Walsingham hadn't moved, but there was a faint twitch in his jaw that hadn't been there before. Just before Gregory closed the door behind him, Kit heard a small gasp, the faintest grunt of pain. The sound of an ill man's mask shattering.

Gregory and Kit stood in silence outside the closed door. Neither of them dared to look at it, as though casting their eyes on the handle was an unforgivable invasion of privacy. Further down the corridor, Kit heard the murmur of voices, the familiar ripple of royal business.

"He'll recover," Gregory said.

"I know," Kit said.

He meant it, despite the tightness in his chest. Sir Francis Walsingham couldn't die. Or, if he did, he wouldn't die from illness. He would go out with fire and sword, not with the quiet whisper of sickness in the dark.

The voice in Kit's head knew better. He thought of the final scene to *Tamburlaine*'s sequel, the one he'd scribbled down with his back against a deadline. His cruel, conquering hero, the fierce Scythian warlord, laid into a grave by pestilence. An unsatisfying ending, but an honest one. *Shall sickness prove me now to be a man, that have been termed the terror of the world?* Kit had written it himself.

"I know he will," Kit said again.

———

He should have told Tom right away. It would have been the honest thing to do. The fair thing. Brave. But Kit hadn't felt fair or honest since Walsingham's messenger had cornered him on the banks of the Thames, and it took every scrap of bravery to live with the memory of Evan Lloyd's knife against his throat. Something had to give. Something had to remain simple, comforting, safe. And that something, he'd decided, was Tom.

Cruel as it was, there was also kindness to it. Tom's relief when Kit lied—when he said he'd broken the cipher, that his task now was to observe Strange and nothing more—that relief justified everything. How could anything be wrong that made Tom pull Kit into his arms and kiss him until Kit's body felt sanctified, every inch of him made holy? The truth would only have left Tom as hollow and nervous as Kit was, flinching at every shadow. There was no way for Kit to escape it, but that didn't mean Tom had to live that way.

"Thank God," Tom murmured. Kit laid his head on Tom's shoulder, losing himself in the gentle circles Tom traced along his back. Outside, rain beat against the windows facing Fleet Street, turning the roads outside to an impassable tangle of mud. "Christ, love, I'm so glad. You'll be safe."

"I will," Kit said, listening to the rain.

The tip about the raid was handed off without incident, and when Evan Lloyd returned on the twenty-second, it was clear that Kit had proved his worth to Strange, at least temporarily. What followed was a balancing act that pushed Kit to the very limit of his skill. Kit and Gregory kept in regular contact, meeting at taverns north or east of the city where prying eyes and curious ears were unlikely to follow. Kit asked Gregory the questions he'd been set by Strange through Evan—particulars of the Royal Navy, Walsingham's suspicions of other members of the Stuart line, Lord Burghley's designs on Douai—and Gregory gave him bits of information in return. Not lies, which would cost Kit the trust he'd so carefully built, but half-truths and insinuations, ones Kit embellished and packaged to prove his value to the rebels without putting Walsingham's plans in too great jeopardy. Kit seldom met with Strange directly, but every so often Evan brought along a note in his patron's broad, flowing hand, accompanied by a small purse as a token of gratitude. It was tainted money, but a bloody shilling went as far as a clean one in London.

In the meantime, there was more to be done. Walsingham retained his avenue into Strange's correspondence, and Gregory continued to pass Kit intercepted letters in groups of three and four. Strange seemed to rotate between ciphers, one designated for each recipient—smarter than Kit had originally given him credit for—but with enough late nights and stolen minutes, Kit forced the ciphers to crack one by one. Messages to Strange's supporters in the country, just as Walsingham had suspected. Not every note contained a name, but every one that did went straight to Whitehall, and a fresh agent was dispatched in the direction of the suspect.

And then there was the theater: rehearsals to haunt, actors to shout at for wrongly emphasizing a line, an irritated theater owner to mollify after the fact. To think that at one point in his life, writing plays had been Kit's way to relax.

"You're coming at it too strong, love," Tom said, as they cut from the Rose to Kit's Shoreditch lodgings. Tom had stopped by that day's rehearsal on a rare afternoon off. It was the first time in ages he'd seen Kit at work, and Kit's anxious style of artistic management had only gotten worse as the stress of intelligence work grew. "It's already brilliant. You don't need to work yourself to death fiddling with it."

Kit didn't meet Tom's eye. They kept their heads low as they passed through Bishopsgate, both refusing to see what sort of trophies were spiked above them. "I'm not fiddling. I'm improving."

This was a lie: he was fiddling. There were a hundred details he wanted fixed, angles adjusted, tones shifted, but none of it mattered, really. Kit knew he was hiding in work, tweaking minutiae to avoid thinking about his visits with Gregory, Walsingham's gaunt face, the flash of a knife in the darkness. Cowardice, maybe, but there was no shame in self-deception. Not if it worked.

Kit knew something was wrong from the moment he and Tom stepped inside the boardinghouse. He knew it from the knit of Mistress Talbot's brows as she pointedly turned her back, resuming her conversation with another lodger. That was the look reserved for someone already on her mind. Someone who'd recently been asked for.

Kit swallowed hard. There was no graceful way out of it now. He climbed the stairs, Tom behind him, each step like the ascent to the scaffold.

When he stepped into his room, Thomas Kyd stood awkwardly near the window, arms folded as if warding off a worse chill than October had to offer. And there, leaning easily against the ladder that led up to the loft, stood Evan Lloyd.

He smiled when he caught sight of Kit and pushed himself upright, unfolding his grasshopper-like limbs. Kit felt Tom's eyes narrow, heard the beginning of a question, and for a moment he thought his own panic might overwhelm him. But the most important thing now was the work. He couldn't let Evan see that he'd been startled. He needed to maintain cover, work through the interaction without giving himself away. After that, he could pick up the pieces of his life. But not until this was dealt with.

"Good afternoon," Kit said. "You might have sent word you were coming."

"I was in the neighborhood," Evan said. "And Master Kyd has been very accommodating. I really am sorry about disturbing you."

"Quite all right," Thomas Kyd said stiffly. He exchanged a panicked glance with Tom, and Kit turned his back on both of them. Every moment he thought about what his co-boarder and Tom might be thinking was a moment of inattention that might cost him everything.

"Take a walk with me?" he said to Evan.

Evan's smile seemed genuine. "By all means."

"I won't be long," Kit said to Tom.

"Don't be," Tom said. His voice landed like a hammer against an anvil, tossing out sparks. Kit led Evan downstairs without looking back.

They walked side by side through the still-muddy expanse of Shoreditch, heading gradually north. The suburbs were unruly up here, tavern brawls and family disagreements drifting through open windows, the flap of clothes drying on Finsbury Fields between grazing livestock. It felt like home now—a hundred years away from the terrifying crush that had greeted his first steps into London. Now, walking with Evan Lloyd beside him, that old unease had returned. The notion that every bowed head or grasping hand wanted something, and would do whatever it took to secure it.

"Apologies for that," Evan said. "There's never been anyone by when I've come before, so I assumed you lived alone."

"You don't know the price of London lodgings then," Kit said. "Watch your step." He guided Evan around a fresh clump of manure, barely distinguishable from the surrounding mud. "You have news for me?"

"Do you?"

It was a fair question, and in Evan's amiable tone it didn't sound like an accusation. Still, it was hard not to hear it as one: if you don't, what good are you to us? Fortunately, Gregory had made sure Kit was prepared.

"Lady Arbella Stuart is their concern now," Kit said, his voice carrying only to Evan and no farther. "Mary Stuart's niece. She's barely out of the schoolroom, but Cecil has it in his head that she or her guardians have their eyes on the throne. Naturally, I've done my best to encourage the idea."

True enough, as far as it went. Gregory had told him as much: the Stuart girl had as good a claim on the throne as her aunt had, if not the unscrupulousness or the pride. She was worth keeping an eye on, and Whitehall was doing so. If she wasn't their primary focus—if that focus was reserved for the charismatic nobleman and his populist leanings—there was no cause for Evan Lloyd to know that.

"Will Cecil send you off to the Stuart girl, do you think?" Evan said.

Kit laughed. "I doubt it. He's sent one of his more reliable agents to be her tutor. Can you imagine? I'd raise that girl into a hellion."

"So much the better," Evan said with a grin. "I'd hate for you to miss the fun."

Kit held his breath. He doubted that Evan Lloyd shared his definition of "fun."

"You know the mistake Mary Stuart made," Evan said. Kit could think of a few—treason, trusting an idiot like Anthony Babington, opening her doors and letting Kit in out of the rain—but Evan didn't leave much time to wonder. "The Armada was always a risk. Relying on foreign forces. A stiff gust of wind blows in the wrong direction, and suddenly all your hopes are at the bottom of the ocean."

Kit bit his lip, refusing to let his unease show. There was no time for fear. This was what Strange had always hinted at. Armies raised from native soil. The anger of the people had always been theoretical, but it seemed that Strange was moving swiftly toward the concrete.

"Taking a different approach isn't easy," Kit said, keeping his eyes on the muddy road ahead of him.

"No," Evan agreed. "It's not. And it's expensive. Costs more than even Lord Strange can manage."

It seemed as if Evan had slipped into a language Kit spoke only haltingly. "If you're asking for a contribution to the cause," Kit said carefully, "I regret to inform you that I'm renting one half of one room, and these boots are three years old."

Evan laughed. "No," he said, "trust me, no thinking man would ask you to finance anything. Here's the business. I know a man in Flushing, as staunch a believer as any of us. And the best goldsmith north of Florence. A forge that turns out more than jewelry, if you follow."

Kit couldn't help himself. Between the nerves and the sheer madness of the suggestion, it was too much. He laughed, the sound bubbling up, uncalled-for. Church-sanctioned counterfeiters. Moneylenders in the Temple. If he put it in a play, Henslowe would accuse him of heavy-handedness. Well, God had always been an opportunist. Proclaim the gospel with whatever tools came to hand.

"So you want me to go to Flushing," Kit said.

"You and me. I've asked Lord Strange his opinion, and he agrees."

The boldness of the plan drew Kit in. Too risky to coin in England, under the nose of the queen's justice, and too dangerous to travel alone. The opportunity was more than Kit had dared to hope for when he'd donned the mask of the double agent and prayed it would hold. And now that mask would need to hold with double strength. He'd need protection on every front as he played both sides of a civil war, where either commander might slide a knife between his ribs to keep him from talking.

Once in the Low Countries, Kit and Evan would meet with the goldsmith and arrange for the production of a sizable sum of money. Then, as Evan explained it, they'd work with a local fence—de Vries, perhaps, from the first letter?—to secure the arms England's papists would need. The rest of the funds would be funneled back to Derbyshire by sea, under the pretense of a merchant outfit investing in one of Strange's business ventures. That was as much as Evan knew. When they needed more details, Strange would provide them, and not a moment before.

"You should get back," Evan said. Without saying anything, they'd reversed their path, tracing the muddy road back toward the bells of Shoreditch Church, the shrieks of Bedlam. They were only a few minutes' walk from home, but Kit felt as though he'd slipped into a separate country, one connected to the London he'd known by the most delicate of threads. "Your friend doesn't know my business, but he'll ask more questions the longer you're away."

It was a thoughtful consideration from Evan, smoothing Kit's path into his other life. But it wasn't Thomas Kyd that worried him. After the third night Kit stayed awake until sunrise reading the prologue of *The Jew of Malta* aloud with varying inflections until the verse lay flat, a less-than-forthcoming visitor would be a minor annoyance to him at most.

No, it was Tom's reaction that troubled him.

"You're right," Kit said. "When do we leave?"

"Few weeks," Evan said with a shrug. "Enough time to set your affairs in order, if you have affairs to set. I'll come by once Strange decides which ship will carry us."

Reasoning that if he had to play the role, he might as well do it properly, Kit clapped one hand on Evan's shoulder, sending him off like a brother in arms. "Tell Strange, when you see him, that we won't fail."

"We won't," Evan agreed.

It was almost frightening, Evan Lloyd's facility at disappearing. He had only taken a few steps north, the back of his blond head catching a fragment of sunlight. And then he had disappeared, lost among the shifting bodies around them, and Kit hadn't seen where he'd gone.

He blew out a long breath. Follow the money, he could hear Walsingham telling him. Follow the money, and you'll find the conspirators, find the armies, find the threat. Counterfeiting coin was treason, but it was also the perfect way to lay a trap. Follow the trail, and track the wolf back to his den. The notion of leaving England left a chill in his stomach, but there was no time to consider that, not yet.

"Kit," said Tom, from the front door of the boardinghouse. He hadn't waited for Kit inside—and Kit had counted on the time scaling the stairs to pull himself together, to come up with whatever in God's name he was supposed to say. That time was gone, and there Tom was, flinty eyes sharp, more anger coursing through him than Kit had seen in years.

"Tom, I can explain," he began.

"Come with me," Tom said, grabbing him by the arm and leading him back down the street. "We're going to have a talk, you and I."

Thirty-One

Tom clearly had a destination in mind, but Kit didn't dare ask what it was. As Tom led him south, nearer the city proper, all he could think was that Tom was taking him to the constabulary, that he'd been exposed and was about to be arrested. The image overwhelmed him—a dark windowless cell, the moans of men bound for the scaffold—until he thought he might retch. Then Tom tugged him into Hog Lane, a scrap of rutted dirt along Spital Field that had all but been turned into a bog by the rain. It was a dirty, ill-reputed corner of the suburbs, one even Kit usually kept his distance from. And Tom's tolerance for filthy living had always been lower than Kit's.

Kit tugged his arm free, and Tom stopped walking at once, a darkness settling over his brows. They earned a few curses from the crowd for blocking the middle of the road, but neither of them moved.

"What is this?" Kit said.

"You're one to ask," Tom snarled. "I want you to tell me the truth, Kit. And I want you to tell me in public, because evidently you're being followed at all hours and if I speak to you somewhere unprotected we'll both most likely be killed."

He turned his back and pushed into a tavern, a rundown public house in Hog Lane with an emblem reading "The Star and Spur" above the door. Kit hung back, alone in the dirty street. Surely Tom knew that being with Kit had never been safe. Not that first night in Tom's Cambridge dormitory, and certainly not now.

Finally, Kit sighed and followed after. There wasn't enough

drink in the world to make this conversation bearable, but a pint couldn't make matters worse.

Kit had never been in the Star and Spur before, but he'd been in a dozen taverns identical to it. No matter the city, Cambridge or London or Constantinople, a man could always find a drinking hole like this. The same smoking fire; the same overpriced, watered-down ale; the same thick-paned window sturdy enough to stop men from being thrown through it. Tom hadn't chosen it for Kit's comfort, but it gave him something to cling to nevertheless. Here, at least, he knew the rules.

The drawer, a nervous boy whose stammer was as evident in his manner as his voice, dropped two pints on the table at Tom's order. He was called away almost at once, summoned by a raucous group of men whose faces were indistinguishable through the strained light.

Tom drank deeply and avoided Kit's eyes; Kit did the same. The beer soothed the tattered edges of his nerves, not enough to calm him, but enough to help him think. At times like this, he could almost see what his father saw in drinking. He wiped his mouth and closed his eyes. Yes, he'd performed well for Evan, but if he couldn't talk his way out of this, if Walsingham and Cecil's machinations cost him Tom's trust, then none of it was worth anything.

"You lied to me," Tom said.

Kit drank again, as if he could ease his guilt by drowning it.

"You're going to tell me who that man was," Tom said. "Why he knows where you live. And then you'll tell me why you went behind my back, when you promised you would never. After that, I'll decide if I can forgive you."

"Tom, I—"

"Did I ask for excuses?"

Tom's words were low under the rumbling voices throughout the Star and Spur. It was a good place for secrets that way. Three dozen lives rattling back and forth in the room, the lines separating them faded by drink. Hiding in plain sight. Maybe Walsingham had recruited the wrong man, all those years ago in Cambridge. If

Tom had been in Kit's position, perhaps he would have thought of a better way to keep all of his masks separate.

"Walsingham's having me do more than watch Strange from the theater," Kit said.

Tom did not blink. "I gathered."

"He . . ." There was no good way to say this, but he had to try. Reticence now would only make matters worse. "Strange has friends. You've just met one of them. Friends with a plan Walsingham doesn't like."

A plan for civil war. Burning cities, raiding Protestant estates, breaking down the gates of Whitehall, and leaving the queen's head on a spike for London to admire. There were some things Kit couldn't bring himself to speak aloud lest he summon them into existence, like a magician pronouncing a demon's name.

"And why are those . . . those friends coming to Shoreditch?" Tom murmured.

He had to say it. He had to grit his teeth and say it, and deal with the consequences as they arose.

"Because they think I'm one of them."

Kit watched as the pieces slipped together into the mad, complete picture. Tom's hands clenched so tightly around his beer that Kit saw the veins rise around his knuckles. It was anyone's guess whether Tom would rather have been throttling Kit than a watered-down drink in that moment.

"That's your game?" Tom said. Kit could hear it now, the battle it took to keep his voice low. If they'd been alone—and thank God they weren't—Tom would have been shouting. "Play both sides of the field. Christ's bones, Kit, do you wake up every morning and *decide* to put yourself in danger? At what point did you plan to tell me?"

Tom's anger was fully justified. But it was asking a great deal to accept this kind of indignant lecture, as if he'd hammered on the doors of Whitehall and begged Sir Robert Cecil to put him back out in the field. He leaned forward until his ribs brushed the table, bracing for a fight.

"None of this was my idea," Kit hissed. "I'm trying to stay alive. And I'm trying to keep you alive too. What part of that don't you understand?"

"Don't." Tom pushed his chair back—perhaps a fistfight in a public house wasn't out of the cards after all. "Don't pretend this is for me, when this is all you've ever wanted, to be London's hero, darting around in disguise like the Christ-damned Robin Hood of Bankside, and what did you think I was meant to do?"

"It isn't about you," Kit said—his ordinary speaking voice now, which given their previous circumspection felt like a full-throated yell. "If you don't understand that, Tom, I don't know what to tell you."

"Kit, people will hear you," Tom hissed.

Kit began to stand, but Tom reached across the table and gripped his shoulder, trying to force him back into the chair. Kit shook him off.

"People always hear me," he said. "You think a day goes by I'm not being listened to? Think about what that's like, and then realize why I might want to keep a few secrets."

Tom remained seated, his face closed. Kit so rarely saw Tom angry, he barely recognized it. Kit grew angry the way he always did, hot and wild and reckless, but Tom retreated into himself, a man chipped out of steel, every edge meant to cut.

"This isn't what I agreed to," Tom said.

"It is," Kit said, and he was yelling now, he couldn't keep the anger out of his voice. "Every minute you've known who I am and you haven't turned tail and run, this is what you agreed to. Every bit of it."

More than a few heads in the tavern turned in their direction, no doubt trying to guess what the tall man in the forest-green doublet had done to make Kit Marlowe the poet nearly upend a table to get away from him.

"All right now," a man said, standing up from a table near the back of the room. "Hard as it is for you, try not to make a scene."

Kit stared, anger momentarily frozen into shock. He hadn't

seen this man in years. Not since he was a student, thrown back into the town he'd been born in, aching with guilt from his sister's death. But one glance from those narrowed, watery blue eyes, and Kit was back in the doorway of a Canterbury shoemaker's house, with the possessive lean of a shoulder barring his entry. Meg had told him William Bradley came to London often on business. And London was large, but it wasn't a world to itself. Kit knew more of its haunts than he was proud of, the dimly lit shabby places a cruel man in need of a drink might go. It had only been a matter of time before he and his sister's husband crossed paths.

Bradley wove through the tables toward Kit, one large hand taking him by the shoulder. Kit shrugged him roughly off. He felt his anger growing, uncomplicated now, eager to settle on this welcome new target.

"Don't touch me."

"I forgot, you don't condescend to the likes of us," Bradley said. "You'll get the watch called on you, if you're not careful." He tried again to steer Kit out of the tavern, and again Kit threw off his grip. Kit wouldn't be moved and directed and told what he could say and what he couldn't. These people—Tom, Bradley, any of them—couldn't understand what it meant to live as he had to. They never would.

"I don't want trouble," Kit said coldly. "Go your way, and I'll go mine."

"If only you would," Bradley said. Kit had forgotten until that moment how tall Bradley was. "You know what lies they're spreading now? That Will Bradley can't do a damn thing without the king of Bankside's say-so, that it's your money that buys my bread. When I'm the only one who's ever worked an honest day. You want to bring down the watch, carry on, then. Carry on to hell, and I'll be glad to see the last of you."

It was the last thing Kit's already-frantic heart could take quietly. The panic of roiling civil war and Evan Lloyd's shadow on the floor of his lodgings, of Walsingham's muffled cry of pain, of

Tom's frozen anger, and then the broad hand closing on his shoulder, a third time trying to shove Kit out the door. Tom reached out, hoping to steer them both away from what looked increasingly like a fight. But Kit took another step forward. He wasn't the boy he'd been the last time he'd met Bradley. He was one of Walsingham's men. He'd watched the axe slice a woman's neck, glittering comet-bright as it fell. He couldn't fight Tom, couldn't fight Cecil, couldn't fight nameless Catholic rebels. But he could fight William Bradley. And he'd never wanted to see something break so badly.

Kit shot an arm forward and sent the nearest pint skittering across the ground. Beer spilled in a slow-moving pool around their feet. The tavern was dead silent now. Kit never turned away from Bradley, who stood there with drops of beer pattering from the soaked hem of his doublet to the floor.

"You haven't changed, have you?" Bradley said, his voice low and cold. "Still no idea what rules apply to you. Margaret's the same way. Stands up for you, doesn't she? Hasn't learned her lesson yet, but it's one I enjoy teaching."

"Jesus Christ, Kit, don't—" Tom began.

But Kit's self-control had fled the scene, leaving only the echo of Bradley's voice and the yearning to take something between his hands and break it. Meg. Meg, with this man. And he, fifty miles away, letting this man do what he liked. And then it wasn't Meg's face before him anymore but Mary's, severed head lying in a pool of blood and still screaming because that was what happened, you screamed and you screamed and nobody listened to anything but the silence after the screaming stopped, once the war had ended and there was nothing but your wide-eyed staring body in the grass, crumpled and bloodstained like the used sheets on a wedding bed . . .

Kit threw himself at Bradley, sending him sprawling to the ground.

His fist shattered Bradley's smile. Teeth bit against his knuckles, blood and spit swimming against a background of darkness. Tom lunged to pull Kit back, but a man grabbed his arm and held him away, trapped in the crowd hungering for a fight.

Bradley wasn't fit to live. A rat. Something to target, something to break. Kit felt the slick of blood against his knuckles and smelled the hall of Fotheringhay Castle, heard the creak of hanged corpses and the crunch of bone. If the rest of Walsingham's men could kill without compunction, then he could get rid of this creature, this nothing.

The fist hit his temple before Kit saw it coming. His vision exploded into specks of gold, a shimmer of pain, and he gasped and stumbled, a fraction from falling. He'd been wrong. Bradley was larger than Kit, but that didn't make him slower.

"I'll send for the constable!" shouted the tavern keeper, but the crowd pushed him back. Kit had dug his own grave when he opened his mouth. It was for him to get out as he could.

Bradley caught Kit by the collar and flipped him, his back landing with a thud on the floor. His head cracked against the boards. His ears rang. Bradley was twice his size. Dizzy, he scrambled away, landing an elbow to Bradley's face before a series of blows to his stomach doubled him over, breathless. He retched. Bradley had him flat, his fists, his boot falling, endless, he cringed and shielded his head with his hands, something exploded into his ribs and he screamed with the last of his breath. His vision pinholed down, black around the rim.

This wasn't a fight. This was a murder.

Thirty-Two

Tom's sightline shifted through a lattice of arms and shoulders. Kit was hidden by bodies, but Tom heard him cry out, heard the thud of blow after blow. Heard his own heart roaring in his ears. He should have known. Hadn't he said it himself, that nowhere was safe? The entire city was a trap now, dangers around every corner. It didn't matter who this man was, whether he was one of Lord Strange's men who'd found out Kit's true allegiance or one of the queen's spies who thought Kit had gone turncoat. Both sides were deadly now, and a single mistake could spell death.

There was no time to think that through. No time for anything. Five minutes ago he'd have punched Kit in the throat himself, but the sound of Kit's whimper from within the tangle of bodies shut everything else out.

Kit was right. By loving him, Tom had chosen this. He hadn't known he was choosing it, but he had. And once Tom Watson chose something, he saw it through.

His mind was blank, his body decisive. He shoved through the crowd to the open air at the center. The blade of his knife, long enough for a sword, shone through the half-light.

Bradley paused. Beside him, Kit lay crumpled on the floor, head cradled in his arms. Each breath caught with a whimper, loud against the silence, like a gutted dog. Conscious, if barely. Bradley's knuckles glistened with blood. Kit's blood. Tom had never wanted to hurt someone so deeply in his life.

"If you fight him," Tom said, "you fight me." Though his chest tightened, his hand did not shake. The gift of a swordsman. Eternal balance.

Bradley scoffed. "You think I give a fuck about you? Go your way, boy."

Action erased Tom's fear. The confidence of doing what he had to, of knowing there was nothing else he could have done. "Unless you're afraid, sir?" he said. The taunt of that *sir*, cold and sharp as the knife.

Bradley looked Tom over. Sizing him up, Tom knew, and not liking what he found. Tom was taller than Kit, and stronger, knife aside. But a man with blood on his hands couldn't choose his enemies. The tavern blurred, Tom's vision sharpening on his opponent as Bradley drew his own knife from his belt. The shimmering, white-hot silence between the challenge and the lunge.

Bradley hesitated.

Tom struck.

The room's silence broke into panic. Someone screamed. Tom couldn't understand the words. Wasn't listening. His tutor had taught him to fight like a gentleman, but hate made him forget all of it. This wasn't swordplay, this was knife work, the hot-blooded challenge of back alleys where death, not honor, was the final prize. Bradley leapt back from Tom's first thrust, slashed out in an unplanned, unpracticed flail. Tom felt mad energy rising in him and shifted his grip. Played it loose. Danced back, letting Bradley exhaust himself. Bradley was all blunt force and determination, but Tom was quicksilver fast.

Watch the knife, he thought, cycling the words over and again. Never take your eye off the knife.

He'd forgotten Bradley's feet.

A kick swept Tom's legs from under him. He stumbled, catching himself against the circle of men. Unbalanced, but keeping his grip tight on the hilt. Bradley didn't waste his advantage. He caught Tom by the collar. Close enough to see the blood cracking on his knuckles. Bradley pulled back, blade flashing in the low light.

That was his mistake.

Tom cut forward and up, slicing the knife between Bradley's ribs.

Easy as goring a rabbit. Steel cut so well through flesh. It should have been more difficult than that.

Blood stained Bradley's shirt, spreading outward in scarlet ripples. His knife fell from nerveless fingers to the floor. Steel echoed loud against wood. Tom could hear Bradley's breathing, thick and filtered through blood bubbling in his throat.

Tom's father had told him once that the dying were thought to see the future. Through the scrim between this world and the next, they could prophesy the ends of the living and see the realm of the dead. But Bradley didn't look wise. He didn't look inspired. More than anything, as he sank back onto the floor, his blood staining Tom's blade, he looked surprised.

And then if he'd seen anything to tell, it was too late.

Tom wiped his bloodied hands across his breeches. The energy drained from him in a single breath. All he wanted was to wash his hands. The smell of blood was intolerable. He'd killed a man, yes, but protecting Kit was protecting the crown. No one would have expected him to do less.

An innocent man, he thought dully, wouldn't spend so much energy counting the reasons he was innocent.

He sat on his heels beside Kit, who began to sit up, slowly and not well. Tom brushed the blood from Kit's brow with his thumb and ignored the forty men watching them. The unevenness of Kit's breath. The hand Kit pressed to his side as though holding his ribs together. All Tom could see was Kit's blood on his own hands, and Bradley's. But Kit was alive. Bloodied and panting and pathetic, but alive.

"Stand down, in the name of Her Majesty the Queen."

Tom looked over his shoulder. The voices sounded distant, vacant. Three uniformed men ringed him and Kit, their swords turned on his chest. Behind them, nearly eclipsed by their broad shoulders, the young drawer stuttered out his statement to a fourth man. Of course. He'd run for the watch the moment fists turned to blades. No doubt the tavern keeper sent him.

A temporary inconvenience, Tom told himself, willing down the panic that had begun to butt up against the numbness. Of course the watch wouldn't know Kit had only fought on the crown's business. They wouldn't know the difference between a street fight and an act of political violence. Tom's heart flailed against his ribs, but he stood, relieved his legs could hold him. Prison, but only temporarily. Until Kit got word to Walsingham. Until they explained.

"What man is this?" The nearest watchman tipped his sword at the body.

"One who deserved what he got," Tom said.

The man stared. "You confess?"

Tom raised his bloodstained hands, fingers wide. No need to say anything else.

He didn't resist as the men grabbed him and wrenched both arms behind his back. Beside him, they yanked Kit upright onto legs that barely supported him. Kit almost lost his footing in the slick of blood but kept his balance, face pale and jaw set tight. The crowd parted to let them pass.

The watchman who had spoken jerked his head toward the door. "Take them away."

Thirty-Three

Kit awoke in darkness. He lay curled on his side, left arm pressed hard to his ribs. The ground beneath him was cold, slick, rough. Stone, he thought. Blood had pooled beneath his head and dried there. He felt the stain crack as he winced. Everything hurt. His ribs most of all. He took an experimental breath—it hitched, but he'd expected worse. Perhaps not broken, then. Though all but. With a small moan, he opened his eyes. It was so dark he might as well have left them closed.

"Welcome to Newgate, Lazarus," said Tom from somewhere nearby.

Kit tried to sit. The pain made him retch; the pervasive scent of shit did nothing to help. Resigned, he lay back again. "I am risen," he said, leaning on irony as he might a crutch. His voice sounded awful and felt worse against his throat. He'd have given anything for a drink.

"I assume you have a plan." From Tom's voice, he assumed nothing of the sort.

Kit didn't respond. He lay flat, looking at the ceiling. From here, their prison seemed vast, twice the size of the Rose's stage. High walls stretched like the sides of a pit, punctuated at the top by narrow barred windows. Tendrils of moonlight drifted above, casting a hovering glow that failed to reach the floor. Around him, Kit heard the indistinct shadow of men's voices.

He remembered all of it now. Evan's proposition, Tom in the tavern, the fight with Bradley. He searched within himself for guilt at having incited his lover to kill his sister's husband, but

258 + A TIP FOR THE HANGMAN

found nothing. Meg would be better off without that man. Meg would be free to accept help now, and he'd send her his full cut from this latest play. She'd marry again, and happier this time. She would be better than she'd been before. At present, the only futures that alarmed him were Tom's and his own.

With great care, he tried again to sit. The room blurred again, but he put his head between his knees until the wave passed. "How long?"

"Two days. As best I can tell." He could see Tom now, sitting beside him. Legs folded, back straight. A crust of dried blood slashed across his brow. Kit wondered whose it was.

Tom had been conscious for two days. Consumed by the stab of hunger and the stench of shit, both worsening every hour. Feeling dried blood crack and peel on his hands. Listening to the murmurs and labored breathing of unseen men in the darkness, the occasional curses and fights as fear spilled into rage. Anger was understandable.

"I've been waiting for you to come round." Tom's voice sounded terribly distant through the dark. "No one's asked about that man, so I have to assume he was one of Strange's people. If you'd attacked someone on Cecil's pay, they'd have had something to say about it."

Kit pressed his eyes closed. His brain was still loose in his skull, but even if it wasn't, he wouldn't have had a way to explain this. Tom thought—

Of course Tom thought. Only an idiot would risk his life over anything less than the life of the queen, especially when he had so many other opportunities to get himself killed.

"So what happens next?" Tom said. "After Walsingham manages this. You can't go back in with Strange, not after you've—"

"Tom," Kit said wearily. "That man wasn't with Strange."

"Then who was he with?"

"He was my sister's husband."

Tom fell so silent Kit could almost hear him blink. Kit didn't need to ask what he was thinking. Tom was a lawyer—he knew what would happen next. Murder in defense of the queen would have been ill-advised but defensible. Walsingham and Cecil could smooth that over with a few coins and a promise to look the other way. Tom might even be commended for it: extraordinary acts of heroism. But this? Murder in a public house, unprovoked? Men were killed like animals for that.

"I see," Tom said slowly. "So the danger here isn't that Lord Strange might have you murdered. It's that you are, without a doubt, the stupidest person I've ever met."

"I—"

"You almost got both of us killed," Tom said over him, voice rising, "in a fistfight with your drunk brother-in-law. And because you wouldn't know self-restraint if it shook you by the hand, we're both set to be hanged. Whatever connections you think you have, they won't save your neck from this. Or mine. Christ, Kit," he shouted, his voice breaking, "you've made me a murderer, did you ever think about what that might mean?"

Kit took his head in his hands. He couldn't think fast enough to argue. Tom was right. If Kit hadn't lied, Evan's appearance wouldn't have sent Tom into a panic. If Kit hadn't been reckless enough to pick a fight, Tom wouldn't be here. If Tom hadn't become a murderer, Kit would be lying in a back alley, a broken corpse for rats to pick at. If not for Tom, knife dripping scarlet in his hand, death dispensed with a flick of the wrist. Tom had driven a knife through a man's ribs, to save him.

"They won't hang us," Kit said. It took no effort to keep his voice down. His lungs could only pull enough air for a murmur. "They need me. What I found out, what Evan told me, it changes everything."

"It's been two days," Tom said. Kit had never heard his voice so cold, not even with a knife in his hand. "If they were coming for you, they'd have done it by now."

Kit's vision still blurred when he turned his head too quickly, but he reached to put one hand on Tom's knee. "Thank you," he said, "for—"

Tom twitched away. "Don't touch me."

Kit opened his mouth, but speech wouldn't come. Only words precisely chosen could bridge this gap, and at the moment, even coherence felt ambitious. He shifted gingerly to lean his back against the wall. The cool stone against his spine was both painful and soothing. He tilted his head back and closed his eyes. His stomach chose that moment to let out a loud moan. Kit winced again. He hadn't been this hungry in years.

"Damn it to hell," he muttered.

Tom's laugh reminded him of a bloody cough. "Honestly, Kit. Where do you think this is?"

———

How Tom had measured time in Newgate, Kit had no idea. Minutes, hours, weeks, all felt the same, undercut by the low breathing and rough voices of strangers. Tom didn't speak to Kit again, and Kit didn't expect him to. He drifted in and out of consciousness, between the fear of sleep and the pain of waking. And all the while, his mind clung to Evan's words like a conjuration, turning them over and back in his head.

A goldsmith in the Low Countries. An army raised on English soil. Walsingham and Cecil would find value in that. They had to. Everything depended on it.

When he heard the noise, he thought it had been the stray invention of a rattled brain. But then he saw the other prisoners turn to the door. A few feet away, Tom stood, as if his nerves were wound too tight for his legs to stay bent. No hallucination, then. The footsteps were real. The rattle of iron keys, that was real, too.

The door opened, admitting an influx of light from a torch, and a man holding it. The light would have been too dim to see by under ordinary circumstances, but in the gloom it made Kit squint.

"Marlowe, God damn you, get up," said a man's voice. "You've been sent for."

Kit had never been so happy to hear a stranger curse him to hell.

Ignoring the prisoners staring, the man crossed the pit toward them. In the wavering illumination of the torch, he drifted, pale-faced, phantasmic. His long hair and spotty beard, in the poor light, seemed colorless. An unremarkable man, dressed plainly but well, and yet there was something about him Kit disliked immediately. Walsingham could have commanded the prison with a word, but this man looked as though he feared catching plague from breathing Newgate's air. The stinking bowels of the city's underbelly were no place for a man dressed in pressed linen. He didn't belong here. People with Kit's clothes, Kit's habits, Kit's lack of aversion to sitting on a floor reeking of shit—they did.

"Standing isn't in the cards at the moment," Kit said. "My apologies."

The man loomed over him, the torch painting his broad face in shifting light. He looked down at the bloodied patchwork of bruises rising on Kit's face and made no effort to hide the curl in his lip. Kit did not stand—both from the bravado that came with a severe head injury and lack of confidence in his legs to support him.

"Christ's mercy, Marlowe, what in hell did you do?"

"Christ's mercy had very little to do with it," Kit said. Time had not improved the strength of his voice.

The man grabbed Kit by the collar and jerked him to his feet. The pain was unreal. As if this stranger had shattered Kit's rib with a blacksmith's hammer. Kit cried out before he could swallow it and steadied himself by leaning heavily on the wall.

If this troubled the man, it didn't show. "Pull yourself together, Marlowe. We haven't got time for theatrics."

"Who are you?" Kit managed.

"Richard Baines," the man said coldly. "Cecil sent me. What's your crime? He didn't say."

Breathing hard, Kit looked over Baines's shoulder toward Tom. Tom's jaw twitched—weighing anger against self-preservation. At last, Tom took a long breath, then moved to stand beside Kit. Without speaking, he offered Kit a hand and pulled him up off the wall. Tom dropped Kit's hand again at once, but it was a start. United, at least for the moment.

"Murder," Kit said, adding a "sir" dripping with insincerity.

Baines blinked. Evidently he had expected a smaller infraction. Blasphemy. Burglary. A drunken brawl with an alderman. "Murder," he repeated. "Christ. Cecil left out the part where he ordered you to become an assassin."

"It wasn't him," Tom said. His voice was quiet but firm. Shoulders set, back tensed, fists clenched.

Kit could read Tom's thoughts in the shifting torchlight. Blood between fingers, knife between ribs, the smell of a butcher, the last gasp of a man. Sliding to the floor like a gutted fish, leaking blood. Kit reached over for Tom's hand, intending to reassure him, but Tom brushed him off like an irritated cat and folded his hands behind his back.

Baines watched them coolly. The movement of Kit's hand, the shift of Tom's shoulders, the way the space between them felt different, smaller and wider at once. Baines's eyes were always narrow, but they became even thinner, until his pale eyelashes nearly obscured his vision. If Baines was one of Cecil's men, he made his living in observation. Surely he noticed. Perhaps he knew. Well, and if he did? Cecil's spies had better things to do with their time than wonder whether Kit spent his nights with Tom or some Southwark whore.

"A fight got out of hand," Kit said. "Tom killed a man to save me. You should be thanking him. Without him, I wouldn't be here, and you'd never know what I know."

Baines frowned. "And what do you know, exactly?"

It wasn't quite the upper hand, not when standing upright still felt like a desperate gamble, but it was close enough. "That's safe in my head, my friend." He let the remainder of the thought hang unspoken: that if Baines wanted Cecil to hear it, that head needed to remain attached to Kit's shoulders.

Baines swore and stepped forward. "Cecil said you were an arrogant fool," he muttered. "But I didn't think he meant *this*. Come on."

"Kit," Tom said, grasping the situation a moment before Kit did.

Baines shifted his grip, taking Kit again by the collar. The torch in Baines's other hand sent warm light licking his face, split between brightness and shadow, expectant like Charon awaiting payment. Kit twisted round, caught in Baines's grip. Tom looked back like a dead man and said nothing. He knew. He'd known from the beginning.

"Tom—"

Baines jerked Kit forward, the movement sending wild pain through his bruised ribs. He stumbled but didn't fall. He lacked the breath to scream, brain reeling, vision filled with golden specks and the warning fog of vertigo, and he retched, tasting vomit. He could make no sense of it. It couldn't be happening like this.

It couldn't have happened any other way.

If Whitehall lost Kit, they lost their connection to Lord Strange and his Catholic militants. He was useful, but Tom was no one, a Fleet Street lawyer who'd been dragged in over his head. Kit was the one they needed.

"Come," Baines said, and he propelled Kit toward the door. Kit felt Tom's eyes on his back—desperate, angry, betrayed, alone—before the door shut behind him.

The hall whipped past, half shadowed in torchlight. He could hardly stand, see, think. He had no sense of distance or direction. When Whitehall finished with Kit, what would stop the Privy Council from getting rid of him, now they knew he couldn't be trusted? What good was a spy who brought the watch down on him for nothing more than a personal grudge? And Tom was part of all of it now. Tom had held the knife. All Kit could think of was the silhouette of the scaffold, and Tom's neck, ringed by the rope, and the half-choked scream of Anthony Babington echoing across the years.

A man emerged from a small office along the hall, dressed in black and wearing a stunned expression. The provost, most likely. "Sir," he said, "this prisoner is under my jurisdiction, you cannot—"

"Watch," Baines said, without turning. He flung open the door at the end of the hall—a blast of cool air curled through Kit's lungs—and shoved him hard in the small of his back. Kit flung out his hands to catch himself as he fell.

A fetid wetness soaked through his knees, reached past his wrists. Hands stinging, he looked up. Clear water pattered against his face. Dried blood began to flow down his brow, coaxed into motion by the rain. He stood, up to his ankles in mud. It was early evening, though the persistent rain made it hard to tell. And he was outside. Kit stood with Richard Baines in the middle of a filthy, deserted alley outside the city walls, frightened and aching and confused, but in the open air.

"This way," Baines said. He turned away, with total certainty Kit would follow.

Kit remained where he stood. The gray stone of Newgate gazed down from behind him. Accusing him. He was guilty of everything.

Baines turned back. "You can't be that much of an idiot," he said. "We have rules in our business, Marlowe. That's how things get done."

"What about—" Kit began.

"Your boy whore? Not my remit. Take it up with Cecil."

Kit was breathing too fast. The light-headed panic rushed back, threatening recklessness or tears. He bit his tongue hard. Everything depended on his control. "I will," he said. "Bring me to him."

Baines scowled and spat against the ground, sending ripples through an inch-deep puddle in the rutted road. "What the devil do you think I've been trying to do?"

Baines set off again, and this time Kit had no choice but to follow. The rain coursed down his cheeks, dripping from his hair. He was crying. He had no idea how long that had been happening. Newgate watched him go, growing smaller with every step until they turned a corner and its stone walls disappeared completely.

Thirty-Four

Once inside Whitehall, Kit and Baines followed a long
tiled corridor in which servants appeared as if by conjuration. Baines ignored them, a practice Kit strove
to mimic despite the staff's brazen stares. He'd never belonged
here, but it had never been so obvious as now, with the fumes of
Newgate still clinging to his heels. At last, Baines paused before a
closed door and gestured curtly.

"He'll see you now," Baines said.

Before Kit could form even the briefest terse remark, Baines
shoved him forward. The door slammed shut behind him with
unsettling finality.

Kit had grown used to the spartan decor of Walsingham's study,
which made Cecil's opulent tastes feel ridiculous. Oil portraits on
the walls of ancestors long past. A blade mounted on the mantel
above the empty hearth—twice as long as anything Cecil could
have lifted. A setter lay on the rug in front of the desk, speckled
white and black, its head resting on its paws. The dog watched
Kit's entrance with a slow swish of its tail. Kit kept his distance.
He braced himself with one hand on the back of a chair, intensely
aware of the filth coating his palms. His body felt like a joint of
meat in a butcher's window, bloody and tender. He wondered
what it smelled like to the dog.

From behind his desk, Cecil watched him as warily as the
dog did. "My God," Cecil said. "You look like you've come from
Bedlam."

Kit's jaw twitched. "Bedlam, Newgate," he said with a shrug that ached the muscles all down his back. "Details."

Cecil leaned back, either to convey boredom or to edge farther from the reek of sewer spilling from Kit. "I would give a good deal to learn what went on in Walsingham's head when he recruited his agents. Common brawlers and cutthroats, all of them. Lacking a gentleman's understanding of circumspection. How much time he must have wasted, dragging his men out of prison and sending them back on their way."

Kit had forgotten since Cambridge how deep that sneered *common* could cut. To hell with prudence. Nerves, fear, and a strong, persistent loathing formed a kind of madness that scorned caution. "I'd rather speak with Sir Francis, if it's all the same to you," he said.

Cecil frowned. "Ah," he said. "You don't know. I suppose in Newgate you wouldn't."

Kit hadn't thought his stomach could drop further. "Know what?" The setter, as if sensing the turn in Kit's mood, raised its head to watch.

Cecil stood. A mistake, Kit thought, from a great distance. He couldn't remember the last time he'd been taller than someone. Walsingham loomed over his agents like the statue of a saint, but Cecil ought to know he was more impressive seated than standing. It was easier to think this than to imagine what Cecil might say next, what exactly it was that Kit didn't know.

"Sir Francis Walsingham passed away three days ago," Cecil said. "From a long illness. Full management of Her Majesty's intelligence forces has descended onto me."

Kit said nothing. There was nothing to say. He tilted his head back and closed his eyes. He was purged clean, an empty shell where Cecil's words could rebound and echo.

Dead.

It had never occurred to him, somehow, that he might outlive the spymaster.

They drifted back to him, an unbidden memory. Walsingham's glittering black eyes, drilling through him, trusting him, choosing him.

What the devil does your father have to do with it? My concern is with you.

The ache in Kit's chest sharpened. Piercing, silencing. He let his head fall forward and gripped the back of the chair as tightly as he could, lingering drops of rainwater falling from his hair to the wood. It hurt. It almost bent him double, this mad, irrational grief. It hurt, and it made no sense, and he didn't ask it to.

Walsingham. The man who had seen him at Cambridge. Who had used him and exploited him, yes, but who had seen him. Who believed Kit could be more than he was, more than a poor boy with wild dreams and a deviant reputation. Who believed in his capabilities when no one else did. Who gave him freedom, gave him theater, gave him all of this.

Sir Francis Walsingham was dead. Kit had never felt more betrayed.

And Robert Cecil. His destiny rested in the hands of this petty little man who looked at Kit like horseshit in a public lane, who'd leaned forward to watch the axe cut Mary Stuart's neck like an apprentice at a bearbaiting. His destiny and Tom's. Kit's head felt thick and blurry, but he forced himself to ignore the erratic thud of his heart. Sorrow was for men who didn't still have a job to do. He could mourn once Tom was safe.

Cecil paced to the fireplace, looking at the ash-strewn stones. The setter shambled out of the way, nosing at the hearth as it went. A small line of soot smeared across its nose. "So if you have news," Cecil said, as though he'd remarked on the weather, "you might deliver that to me."

He could hate Cecil all he liked, but not until he'd gotten what he needed. Kit inclined his head and took another moment to steady himself. Then he spoke, as coldly and quickly as he could, telling Cecil everything Evan Lloyd had shared in Shoreditch.

Once Kit finished, Cecil remained gazing into the unlit hearth. He laced his fingers behind him, resting his knuckles on the small of his back. Though Cecil—the spymaster, now—said nothing, Kit could see his jaw working, as though testing out words before speaking them.

"It's clever, I'll grant you that," he said finally. "You find yourself in Newgate on track for the hangman, and suddenly the papists have invited you to flee the country."

Flee? As if Kit had invented the threat of revolution for his own benefit. Walsingham would have trusted Kit implicitly, but if Cecil didn't find his report credible, he'd be staring down his own death. "Sir," he said—it bordered on pleading, but honor was hardly the primary objective now. "I'm not lying. The names I've given you, Strange's contacts in the country, that proves it, it's all true. If they're trying to buy an army in the Low Countries, you want me there."

It felt like the end of the world, waiting for Cecil to speak. His face was unreadable. Even in the earliest days of Kit's service, when Walsingham had seemed to be an unknowable, omnipotent force, he had never been like this.

At last, Cecil turned to look at Kit properly. "When the rebels send for you, you will go," he said. "You will join them in Flushing. I will expect written, ciphered reports, twice monthly or the moment you learn anything of value. Be detailed. And Baines will accompany you."

The words landed in Kit's ear like a death sentence. Strange and his people trusted Kit—as much as they ever trusted anyone— but he was already on delicate footing. If he turned up in Flushing with Richard Baines at his elbow, what would they think? That they'd been betrayed. Only an idiot would think anything else. Cecil would get Kit killed this way.

Seeing the coldness in Cecil's eyes, Kit wondered whether that wasn't the point.

"Sir Francis may have entertained your unorthodox methods,"

Cecil said with a visible sniff at Kit's doublet, split up the shoulder at the seam, the shirt beneath stained copper with blood, "but I am not Sir Francis." The dog watched Cecil pace away with something that Kit, in a sudden wash of empathy for the animal, interpreted as relief. "Baines will provide his opinion of your behavior and your information upon his return. I will not allow your poor judgment to jeopardize England."

No, Kit thought. Cecil's poor judgment would take care of that.

Probation. Suspicion. To believe he intended to cross sides and join the rebels, with the stakes this high. Walsingham would have shouted at Cecil until his voice gave out if he'd heard about this. Walsingham would have trusted Kit. He always did.

But Walsingham was dead, and Kit had to keep living, however he could.

Cecil sat, reaching for his papers. The dog sat in front of the desk, ears pricked at attention. "You may go," Cecil said. His focus was elsewhere, as if Kit had metamorphosed into a piece of furniture before his eyes.

Kit stood his ground. "Sir," he said. "There's something else."

"Is there," Cecil said without looking up.

It felt like asking a favor of the executioner, but Kit didn't have a choice. He could see Tom in his mind again, the dead-eyed expression of a man who had seen this coming before the thought even dawned on Kit. *I know,* Kit thought. *I know, it's my fault. And I'm trying.*

"My friend," Kit began, and the evasion tasted sour on his tongue, as if he'd betrayed Tom all over again by speaking it. "Tom Watson. We were both arrested, but none of it was his fault. He was only involved in this because of me."

"Yes," Cecil said. "I keep myself informed."

Now or never. If he had to get on his knees and grovel, he'd cut out his own pride with a knife and do it. "Sir, please. Send him a pardon. Anything you want from me in return, you'll have it, just, please. This one thing."

The silence that followed was as charged as a lifted axe, one that might be tossed aside or slice through bone. Kit was no longer breathing. The back of the chair dug into his hands.

Then Cecil frowned. "That would hardly be in my best interest, would it?"

Kit's knees buckled. If not for the chair, he'd have fallen. "Sir?"

"You're a risk, Marlowe," Cecil said. He made a note on one of the papers, as though Kit's rising panic wasn't worth his attention. "Walsingham may have found your recklessness attractive, but I don't endure risks without surety. Your friend will live in Newgate under my protection while you are in the Low Countries, to hang or be freed at my word. So I suggest, in future, you behave rather more carefully than you're used to."

Kit's mind burned. The flames crept bolder, slowly at first, then all at once. His panic crumbled under the heat of his anger, into moth-gray cinders and curling smoke. When he spoke, his voice was low, hoarse as a curse.

"You can't do this."

Cecil made a dismissive noise and gestured toward the door, but Kit had the audacity of a man with nothing to lose. Ignoring his own pain, he leaned over the desk and shoved Cecil's papers aside, scattering them like leaves in the wind. Beside him, the setter gave an alarmed bark, then retreated to the corner—clearly no guard dog, as Kit would throttle Cecil if he could manage it.

"Lord Strange trusts me," Kit said. "He wants the queen dead. I know his contacts across the country. He's building an *army*. Do you know what I could do with that, if you test me?"

"So you'll turn traitor?" Cecil said. "Run off and join the Catholics? How Walsingham got anything useful out of an idiot like you is beyond me. Betray us and you'd be at Tyburn by sundown, hanged by your own bowels."

The threat breezed past Kit. He had never cared less for his own life. Even the sound of Walsingham's name in Cecil's mouth was a desecration. "You'll release Tom," he said. "And you'll do it now."

Cecil's laugh was like bellows to the flame of Kit's anger. "I offered you his life," he said. "Without me, he'll swing by week's end. You won't get a better bargain."

One man was dead already. What was another? The devil himself couldn't have played Kit so expertly as Cecil had. Kit was unarmed—Newgate had seen to that—but he'd never needed a knife to make a man bleed.

But what good would that do? None, but to cost him his head. And Tom's.

So he would remain silent. Humble. Servile. Quiet, obedient, with no protests and no questions. Under observation, watched like a criminal. Controlled by a man who didn't care if he walked or hanged. Until Tom was free. After that, he would make Cecil pay, whatever the cost.

"I'll go," Kit said, his voice a hard-edged murmur. "But when you wake in the night with my knife at your throat, I want you to know why."

Cecil shook his head. "You think you're the first man to threaten me with a knife? Again, you are dismissed."

Kit stood one moment more and thought of his fist shattering Cecil's satisfied smirk, taking that expensive pen from his desk and stabbing it through the spymaster's neck. The blood would spurt up like a fountain. It might even be worth the hanging that would follow, for the chance to see it.

As he opened the door, he heard Cecil's voice call one last time.

"And for God's sake, Marlowe, have a wash. You smell like you've slept in shit for a month."

———

He considered returning home from Whitehall. Wash the blood from his hands, burn his clothes in his landlady's hearth, and drink until it was possible to fall asleep again. But Kit was no longer inside himself, a body piloted without an animating spirit. He couldn't go to that building in the shadow of Bedlam, where the tiny room would make him think of Walsingham's grave, and the screams that had become routine would now forever remind

272 ♦ A TIP FOR THE HANGMAN

him of Tom, sitting alone in the darkness, waiting for the shadows to swallow him.

Kit went, instead, to the only place in London that still felt safe.

It was nearly sundown, and the Rose was long empty of the crowds that had flocked to see that afternoon's production—judging from the bills nailed up outside, Robert Greene's *Orlando Furioso*. The season was nearly over, moving rapidly toward winter, but the air still hummed with the snap of late autumn.

He sat on the edge of the stage, legs dangling several feet above the ground, and looked out into the empty pit. In war, he thought, they buried men in mass graves about this size. Sir Francis Walsingham would be buried at Saint Paul's, with as little ceremony as his surviving relations could manage. Walsingham would rather have died a second time than have London's essential operations disrupted on his account. Kit would visit his grave when he returned. If he returned.

He would be in the Low Countries by week's end, with a sea between him and Tom, and nothing he could do but pray that Cecil was a man of his word. But that didn't mean he couldn't leave something of himself behind.

The tiring-house was cluttered with props and prompt books and other detritus actors had left behind—a thief's paradise, if any of it held the slightest value. Still, what Kit needed was priceless beyond measure, and the theater had always been one place he could count on getting it.

Sure enough, it was the work of a few minutes to dig out two pieces of paper that were blank on the verso, along with a cracked pen and the bare minimum of ink. He sank onto the stage floor, muscles aching, and wrote until the light disappeared entirely. He'd have Gregory see to both matters in the morning.

———

Evan Lloyd was as good as his word. When Kit returned home that night, sunset sending its last flaming fingers between Shoreditch's cramped buildings, a piece of paper waited for him on the threshold. He bent to snatch it up—no doubt Thomas Kyd had walked past it half a dozen times already, refusing even to touch anything associated with Kit and his friends. Leaning against the door for support, he unfolded the note.

Friday. First light. Burn this.

That night, he did, watching the flames curl and char the page.

The next day, he sent word to Cecil telling Richard Baines to prepare for departure. Thursday, he paid Thomas Kyd the following month's rent and moved out, leaving his scant possessions in the Rose's attic space for the time being. Who knew how long he'd be gone? Just before curfew, he met with Arthur Gregory, handing him two papers. One with simple instructions on where to send Kit's pay in the time he was abroad—a Mistress Margaret Bradley in Canterbury. The other a letter, carefully sealed, with curt instructions on where to deliver it.

Then, once the city streets were quiet and the only eyes to avoid those of the watch, Kit crossed south of the river to the George Inn, where he knew full well he was expected.

The door was unlocked despite the late hour, which Kit had anticipated. The front room was dim, most chairs flipped upside down onto their tables to bare the floor for cleaning. The only light came from the moon through the window, and from a tiny flickering light, its source concealed behind the wooden partition. Kit moved toward it like a bewitched man.

At the same table he'd taken before, Lord Strange took a deep pull on his pipe before exhaling a lungful of smoke into the room. The light in the bowl was strengthened by a single candle on the table, both of which gave Strange's face a darkened cast, like a statue carved into a deep alcove. He nodded toward the empty chair across from him, and Kit sat without protesting.

The moment Kit was properly in view, Strange inhaled sharply and leaned across the table. "By the Virgin, Marlowe," he said, the oath escaping in a breath of smoke, "are you all right?"

Kit unconsciously brought one hand to his left eye, where he knew the bruises were at their most lurid. It didn't escape him that Cecil hadn't asked anything of the sort. "It's nothing," he said. "A stupid mistake. I'm ready for tomorrow."

Strange nodded, though Kit's half-hearted reassurance evidently hadn't convinced him. He extended the pipe stem first, and Kit took it gratefully, inhaling deeply before passing it back. The inn felt doubly silent this late at night, every whistle of the wind loud enough to startle.

"I've arranged your passage on the *Mercury*," Strange said, settling back into the chair. "From Gravesend. Ask for Anders; he'll be expecting you. Evan will travel separately, for caution's sake, but you're to meet him at Saint Jacob's when you arrive."

Kit nodded. The facts etched themselves into his memory, sounds without feeling attached. *Mercury*. Gravesend. Anders. Saint Jacob's. A series of steps between him and his return to London, when he could take Tom's hand in his again and see him safely in the light. Gravesend. Saint Jacob's. Tasks to complete one by one until nothing more remained.

"I wanted to tell you, Marlowe," Strange said, after a moment's pause. "I know what you're risking, in a role like yours. I know what I'm asking isn't easy. But we *will* succeed. And when we do, no king will ever do more by a subject than I will by you. I promise you that."

King. It was the first time Kit had heard Strange say the word aloud. Unable to think of more, Kit added it to the list, another task. *Mercury.* Anders. Saint Jacob's. King.

"Good luck," Strange said quietly.

Kit bowed his head. "Thank you, sir."

Thirty-Five

Robert Poley slouched in an armchair in Cecil's study, forcing himself to listen to the spymaster without bitterness. The conversation had begun as a discussion of Poley's new rank and responsibilities as Cecil reassigned Walsingham's former agents to suit his needs: the most interesting subject, in Poley's opinion, that the spymaster could have chosen. Arthur Gregory had been Walsingham's right-hand man, but it was as clear as watered-down ale that Cecil wouldn't keep him in the role. Cecil operated differently. He needed someone who understood the way he thought. And while the conversation had tended in that direction, Poley had been only too happy to listen. No decisions made at present, but he'd take progress as it came.

But now, Cecil's original brief had turned into something of a monologue about the Catholics' plot to crown Lord Strange, a turn of events that somehow required paying attention to the Low Countries. The change of subject was deeply irritating. Strange was Marlowe's division, and the last thing Poley wanted to discuss with the spymaster's mind on promotions was the exploits of another spy. Still, Poley's primary objective was to be as useful to Cecil as possible. Only a fool wouldn't give the new spymaster what he wanted, whether that was a listening ear or someone to blame. Advancement came from nurturing the right friendships, thinking three moves ahead. And knowing more about the competition could only be to his good, however unpleasant it was to hear.

A knock at the door. Poley sat up and cocked his head at Cecil like a curious hound. "Expecting company?"

Cecil didn't dignify this with a response. "Come in."

The man who entered was one of Cecil's newer recruits. Poley had met him a handful of times and hadn't remotely enjoyed any of those meetings. Though Richard Baines's clothes were impeccably tailored and his shoes clear of mud, there was something about his mane of hair and patchy beard that always made him look unpardonably dirty. At least there was no cause to worry about this interruption. Baines was useful the way a jar of leeches was useful, but there was no risk of Poley losing out to this man.

"You called for me, sir?" Baines said.

"Mm," Cecil said. It was hard to imagine a sound containing less enthusiasm. "I have your orders. Gravesend, tomorrow morning, first light. The *Mercury*. You have everything you need?"

Baines nodded. If the idea of leaving the country in less than twenty-four hours alarmed him, his servile nature kept him from showing it. "Yes, sir."

"Remember what I've told you, Baines," Cecil said. "Do what you must. You may both go."

Baines bowed; Poley sighed and stretched out of the chair. He could feel the irritation spilling from Baines as he left the room, and he couldn't deny the reciprocal pleasure the feeling gave him. Richard Baines—useless, pedantic Richard Baines—would be an ocean away this time tomorrow, forced to play nursemaid to a spy Cecil clearly considered to be more important. Meanwhile, Poley would be here, at the spymaster's elbow. Not quite the right hand, but such things played out in stages, and he was willing to wait.

The hall outside Cecil's office was deserted, awash with the warmth of afternoon sun. Autumn moved slowly that year, taking its time departing, but the season might turn at any time. All for the best, then, that Baines take the crossing. He tried not to smile at the thought of Richard Baines huddled in a sodden cloak, lank hair spilling water down his forehead, scowling like a drowned polecat. No, he would enjoy that image later, in private.

"God give you a good journey, my friend," Poley said, his jauntiness insincere enough to be offensive. And good riddance. He turned to go, but Baines stopped him, a deep furrow between his brows.

"Robert." Baines darted a glance at the door to Cecil's study, the worry etching deeper. "Do you trust him?"

"Cecil? It's treason not to, Richard."

"No. Marlowe, I mean."

Poley laughed. Idiot fellow. There was only one rule to this business, and that was to assume every person you couldn't control might be an enemy. "I don't trust anybody. You don't want a knife in your back, I suggest you start thinking the same."

"You know that's not what I mean," Baines snapped. "Do you *trust* him? Or should I . . . well."

Poley took a step back and looked at Baines as if seeing him for the first time. He'd be lying to say he hadn't thought the same thing, but he'd never imagined someone who cared for protocol and procedure as much as Baines did would have the foresight to think strategically. It wasn't respect, exactly, what this development engendered in him. But he took a sort of condescending pride in seeing that Baines had very nearly reached Poley's own conclusion.

Sir Robert Cecil was in charge of the queen's intelligence. Cecil decided who fell and who thrived, who held the kind of power ordinary men only dreamed of. And Cecil didn't trust Marlowe. For good reason—Marlowe was Walsingham's golden boy, and anyone could see his loyalty had been sworn to the man and not to the office. Cecil wanted proof his suspicions of Marlowe were well founded. And a man who pointed out a Judas before he could do damage could count on a reward beyond measure.

"Keep an eye on him," Poley said. "Don't do anything rash, but see what you can learn. And send it on to me with Cecil's reports."

Baines nodded. "Anything we can use, I'll share it."

"Good man," Poley said. He extended a hand, and Baines shook it, then vanished down the long corridor to prepare for his journey across the sea.

It was almost a shame, Poley thought. He arched his back, taking pleasure in the way his vertebrae popped and released the tension from an afternoon of sitting. Marlowe was an idiot, yes, and twice as arrogant as any living man had the right to be, but if Poley were forced to choose Marlowe or Baines to pass an evening at a tavern with, well, Baines would spend the night alone and sober. But that, of course, was beside the point. Poley's opinions were malleable, easily adjusted for the right price. No one rose in this world without stepping on the back of another.

He strolled toward the outer courtyard, humming the snatch of a tune he'd picked up in a Whitefriars tavern the evening before. Times were changing, and by God, he'd see that they changed in his favor.

Thirty-Six

The *Mercury* drifted toward Flushing's docks just as the sun sank from sight. Over the rail of the ship, the waves glittered a slick, sealskin purple, the sharp red of approaching sunset flaring at the horizon. Kit's stomach turned with the remnants of seasickness. Lips pressed together, he gripped the ship's rail until splinters sliced his palms. Before this, he'd never left England, never set foot on a ship, never braved water wider than the Thames. Nauseated and fighting a splitting headache, he began to understand why.

He watched the city rise into focus as dockhands rushed to prepare their arrival. From afar, Flushing had been a dark smudge on the horizon. From here, their ship swaying at the docks, it exuded a slanted, rickety dignity. Kit felt most at home these days among close buildings and briny streets, but London always seemed to have sprung up overnight, houses rising in a panic to cope with a sudden onslaught of men. Flushing laid claim to the land and water as twin birthrights. Its two long, narrow docks jutted out into the North Sea, which penetrated the land in a thousand places, canals and inlets and waterways slipping narrow fingers through the city's brick and stone walls. From the center of town, a sharp steeple stretched toward the heavens. Sea and land and sky and God, cutting against one another until their borders blended.

Kit felt a firm hand on his shoulder. He turned, irritation rising with the bile in his throat. Richard Baines stood behind him, expression sour, pale skin slightly pink from the sun.

"Keep your head down, when you go," Baines said.

Kit shrugged his hand off. "I have someone to meet," he said in Dutch—rusty but passable, dredged up from Cambridge lessons he'd never expected to use. "I'll find you when you're needed."

He felt Baines tense, but he didn't care. Kit had a job to do, and he meant to do it fast. Yorkshire, Staffordshire, Northampton—those had been easy compared to this. Yes, the stakes had been high, a nation's safety depending on his quick thinking. But it was different now, the consequences more immediate. Any mistake could be the one to get Tom killed. It had never dawned on him until now how much he suddenly had to lose.

If only there had been someone else he knew he could trust. But the only man who had ever been able to help him in this business was Walsingham, by now entombed in marble. Walsingham would never pull him aside again to propose a solution, to reveal the next step, to lend him the warm glow of confidence, of faith. Kit was on his own.

The moment Kit's boots hit the dock, a rush of relief spilled through the nausea. A voyage spent vomiting had left his head pounding and his stomach weak. He longed for a few restorative hours of darkness and silence, but that would have to wait. He wandered along the inner harbor, going slow while his legs remembered the feel of land.

London fancied itself cosmopolitan, but its fear of immigrants, sects, and difference permeated every wall and cobblestone. Kit hadn't realized the extent of that fear until now, when he saw its absence. Stepping into Flushing was like tumbling into a kaleidoscope. Kit had never seen a patchwork of humanity like this. People everywhere, weaving across the cobbled streets, pouring out of buildings timbered like matchsticks, shouting at one another from the rigging of bobbing ships flying flags of a dozen nations. He heard five languages without trying, though the throaty, lilting voices of Dutchmen seemed to carry the loudest.

An ideal city for a man to disappear in. So much the better.

A broad canal split Flushing in half, narrowing as he plunged deeper into the city. Gradually, he reached the square at the center of town, where a market would spring up the next morning. Nearby, a stone bridge spanned the canal, now only ten feet wide, too narrow for ships. Kit saw his destination on the opposite bank: the steps of Saint Jacob's, the tall-spired church that spiked upward like the Tower of Babel.

He settled in to wait as Flushing's inhabitants milled around him. He sat midway up the stairs, leaned back on his forearms, and stretched out his legs. The welcome of dry land nursed his headache. The sun had dipped behind the buildings, eliminating the stabbing pain of reflected sunlight. Sparks like will-o'-the-wisps danced along the waters of the canal. It might have been beautiful, if he'd been in the mood to find it so. But all he could see were the lengthening shadows, spreading like the dark double images of gravestones at sunset.

Distraction would only open him to mistakes, and he couldn't afford to be careless. He'd think of Tom when he was alone, once the day was finished and he'd chased down a flea-bitten bed somewhere in this rickety city to call his own. Then he could hate himself as long as he cared to. Now he would do what he'd trained to do.

Walsingham would never have believed it, but years of intelligence work had taught Kit patience. It took half an hour before he saw two men cross the bridge toward him, but the time hardly troubled him. He unfurled from the steps, nodding as they approached. Evan, looking fresh and unbothered by the sea crossing—more happiness to him, if he'd been born with sea legs. And a second man, short and ginger haired, dressed in rough wool. The man took in Kit's appearance in one sweep of his eyes, evaluating him as a potential threat. Kit couldn't see where he concealed his weapon, but surely this man never went anywhere unarmed.

"Marlowe," Evan said, beaming. "Pleasant journey?"

Kit thought of the hundred and fifty miles he'd spent vomiting into the sea, Richard Baines over his shoulder looking for reasons to have him hanged. "We didn't sink," he said fairly.

"Although it looks like you've suffered everything else," Evan said, taking a step nearer. "Mary and Jesus, what happened?"

"This?" Kit gestured vaguely at the bruises across his face.

Evan sighed. "No. Your charming personality."

"It's nothing," Kit said with a shrug. "You ought to see the other fellow."

"Something tells me I don't want to." When Kit didn't contradict him, Evan—perhaps wisely—elected to change the subject. "Apologies for the wait. I had a friend to collect. Gifford Gilbert, goldsmith extraordinaire," he said, indicating the ginger-haired man.

"I've heard reports of you, Marlowe," Gilbert said. His voice took Kit by surprise: higher than he'd expected, and rougher, as if he spoke only when necessary. "Lord Strange says you're quite the poet."

International celebrity, or something close. "I try to be," Kit said, with unconvincing modesty. "But that's not why I'm here."

Gilbert smiled. Kit thought of a lizard sunning on a rock, lipless mouth curved. "No," Gilbert said, "it isn't. Unless you need to rest?"

Kit shook his head. He hadn't had a proper night's sleep in weeks. No reason to begin now. "Lead the way," he said.

Evan clapped Kit on the shoulder as they left the church, his smile warm beneath his weak mustache. Kit suspected Evan was new to Lord Strange's ranks. Perhaps this was his first official task, to accompany Kit across the sea. It seemed the only way to explain his enthusiasm. Evan was thirty if a day, but Kit felt like a jaded old man beside him, wary and bitter.

Gilbert guided them off the main thoroughfare, into the heart of the city. Even as they left the canal, Kit could still hear the soft lap of water. Perhaps there was another conduit nearby. Land threaded through with sea, like blue veins on the back of an old man's hand. They passed into the southern quarter, where Kit could see the city walls in the chinks between buildings, each brick slick and almost green with the sea air. As in London, the build-ings grew shabbier the farther they passed from the city center. Not quite Bankside's orgy of immorality, but all the same, these were the sorts of alleys mothers warned their children to avoid.

The shop, when they entered it, reminded Kit at once of his father's. The tools were different: harsh iron shears, a battered mallet, delicate knives for etching, the forge reeking of smoke. But the feel of it, everyday objects broken down and made strange, came too close to childhood for comfort. Gilbert looked at home here, as he lit a lamp and bathed the shop in amber light. Kit could picture him working contented for hours, shaping and bending ribbons of gold. He shivered, though the room was warm.

Gilbert bent to a cabinet along the wall and pulled a small key from his pocket. As he spoke, he pulled the door open, then rifled through the detritus inside. "The funny thing about gold," he said, "is how little you need. So long as the outer layer looks good, no one cares what happens inside. Like a courtier, hmm? Loyal on the outside, rotted black within."

He stood with a grunt, holding two small circular pieces of metal in his hand. Kit stepped forward, squinting at them. It was as if someone had split a shilling in half. The queen's portrait, etched in perfect sunken reverse on one side, and the crown embedded into the other. A mold, Kit realized, picking it up to examine it. An impeccable piece of work.

"Dip a circle of pewter in gold," Gilbert said, "close it in this, strike it hard enough, and not a man alive will know you're pass-ing it off."

Kit grinned and handed the mold back. "An artist," he said. "Christ. Where were you five years ago, when I was walking around with holes in my shoes?"

Gilbert warmed at Kit's appreciation. He removed a box from the cabinet, in which Kit could see a collection of molds in varied sizes and denominations. "It's slow going. A one-at-a-time busi-ness. But if you want something done right, you don't rush."

This wasn't what Kit wanted to hear. The longer they took, the more chances for Kit to fail, to let something slip, to get himself caught. The longer Tom would be at risk.

"We'll begin in the morning," Evan said, with a soft yawn. "You've found lodgings, Marlowe?"

Kit nodded. He hadn't, but he didn't want a place at Evan's recommendation. Not when Richard Baines might appear around any corner expecting a report. He had two masters as long as he was here, and the only way he'd stay alive was if the one never met the other. "I'll be back first thing tomorrow," he said.

"Good," Evan said. "Rest well. God help you, but you look as if you need it."

Outside, night had fallen, and the cobblestones seemed coated in silver, counterfeiting as pearls. He took a deep breath of briny air, then let it out. Maybe it was the stress of the journey, maybe something else, but he couldn't stop thinking of strangers watching him in the dark.

"It went well, I take it?" said Richard Baines, leaning against the building opposite.

Kit swore. His hand jerked toward his knife without thinking. Baines's unfriendly smile looked alien in the moonlight.

"You followed me?" Kit said.

Baines shrugged. "Of course. That's why I'm here."

"Don't let them see you with me," Kit snapped. "They'll have me killed." He started to walk toward a public house he'd spotted on the way to the church, one that looked dirty enough to offer cheap rooms. Baines followed on his heels. "Christ, are you planning to lodge with me?"

Kit said this without the slightest hint of an invitation. If he found anything less appealing than sleeping on the street, it was the notion of Richard Baines as his bedfellow. But Baines looked at Kit with too much disgust for an ordinary insult.

"Not on your life." Baines slowed his pace, widening the distance between them. "You think I don't know what you are?"

Kit blinked. "And what am I?" he said coldly.

"Kit Marlowe, king of New Sodom," Baines said, spitting against the street. "I swear to the living God, if you think I'll make a fair substitute for your Newgate whore, I will—"

It would have been so desperately easy to knife Richard Baines between the ribs and leave him to bleed out in this Flushing back alley. It wasn't as if he'd have people home in London to miss him. How was Kit meant to bear it, this man who could think of Tom in the shadow of the hangman and see only something perverse? If it had been Kit's life alone at stake, he'd have done it, and to hell with the consequences. Instead, he turned away.

"My dear man," he said, heading back in his original direction, "I would rather fuck the devil himself than attempt to seduce you. Rest easy."

Baines's rough hands moved faster than Kit expected. They shot out, gripping Kit by the collar, and pinned him hard against the nearest building.

The wall thudded against the ridge of his spine, jarring his bruised ribs. Kit stifled everything but a small whimper. It hurt, but the anger was stronger. His childhood instincts flooded back, sparked by his racing pulse. He could have freed himself and given Baines a black eye to remember this bad decision by, but he remained still. Caution. Quiet. Keep his head down.

"Watch yourself." Baines spoke low but close. Kit could see every one of his teeth. "Your life is in my hands. Your whore's too."

Kit narrowed his eyes. "I'll remember that."

Baines pushed Kit away. The back of Kit's head cracked against the wall, stinging hard to the roots of his teeth. He winced and put a hand to his hair, feeling for blood, but said nothing. If this idiot thought Kit was a risk and a traitor and a sodomite, so be it. At the moment, Kit had broader concerns than what Richard Baines believed.

"Good night," he said coldly, turning his back.

Thirty-Seven

The door groaned open, and a guard's torch glared through the dark. Tom winced, his pupils contracting against the influx of light. He sat in the corner of the pit and hugged his knees close. The walls pressed against both his shoulders. His breathing rasped loud in his ears and ached his chest. God willing, the guard would be gone in a moment. The light made Tom want to vomit.

"Which one of you is Watson?" the guard said, sweeping the torch in a slow circle.

Tom shivered. Cleared his throat. The fever had begun about a week ago and had dug in its heels. Since then, he didn't trust himself to stand. "Me," he said.

His voice sounded awful. He hadn't spoken in three weeks, not since Richard Baines had come and taken Kit away, leaving him alone here in the dark.

The guard turned to Tom, then strode across the pit. The light stabbed Tom's eyes with each step. Tom knew he ought to be nervous but couldn't dredge up the energy. After enough time waiting for death to catch up with him, it no longer seemed like the worst thing that could happen.

Keeping the torch aloft, the guard crouched beside Tom, there on the shit-reeking floor. Tom fought down a wave of nausea to look at him. No. This wasn't a guard. Newgate's jailers would never dare get so close to the prisoners they kept. The man's face was rough and tanned even in the torchlight, and though he didn't look disposed toward smiling, Tom didn't sense cruelty in him either. Even so, Tom edged away, though his sore muscles ached from it.

"Thomas Watson?" the man said.

Tom nodded and said nothing. Newgate had robbed him of speech, of vision, of fight.

"Arthur Gregory," the man said. "I've been sent by a friend to give you this."

In his free hand, Gregory held a folded paper, like a cat suspending a mouse by the tail. Tom stared. Who would write to him here? What idiot would think a letter could solve anything? Torn between resentment and desperation, he took the page. Surrounded by the dark, the smell, the rats chattering in the corners, it was too easy to forget the man he'd been when free. A man someone would write to.

"'Thank you,'" Gregory said, after a pause. "That's your line, isn't it?"

Maybe. Not until Tom knew what he'd be thanking this man for. He unfolded the letter and smoothed it against his thigh. One glance at the handwriting—urgent, slanted, as if its owner's pen couldn't keep up with his thoughts—and his heart shuddered, in both anticipation and anger. Even in the poor torchlight, he knew. No one else wrote like this.

I'm sorry. As if that does you any good. I've petitioned Cecil on your behalf. By "petitioned," I mean "threatened with a knife to the throat." You'll be freed when my job is finished, he says. I will kill him for this, but not yet. Not until you're safe.

   I have no right to ask you to forgive me, and so I won't. I won't fall back on the old lines either, that God purifies through suffering. Even if I believed in God, which I don't, he'd burn us as sinners if he could. Job is the rich man's way to avoid thinking of the poor man's pain. We suffer because the world is full of suffering. Nothing metaphysical to that.

*This is cruel, and you deserve to hate me, and all of it is my
fault, and I will fix this. I promise.*

I love you.

Tom laid the letter back against his thigh but did not stop looking at it. Damn him. That was his solution? Keep working and
hope Cecil decided a promise to a penniless spy was worth something? He looked at the last, scribbled line, *I love you*, and winced.
Whether the fever or the words made his stomach turn was anyone's guess.

"Where did you get this?" he said.

Gregory paused, silent but intent. "You sound like death."

"Give it time. Where did you get it?"

"I work with Marlowe. He gave it to me before he left. I haven't
a damn what it says."

Before Kit left. He could have screamed or wept or raged, but
instead Tom felt a mad laugh rising, and he made no effort to stop
it. The laugh bounced and multiplied against the walls, a horde
of madmen laughing with him. It spilled over into a dry, hacking
cough that bent him double. "Left?" he managed finally. "What do
you mean, left?"

"Cecil sent him off," Gregory said. "I don't know more than that."

Of course he didn't. Kit was never one to tell a person what he
was doing. Wasn't Tom living proof?

"You want to deliver a useful message?" he said hoarsely. "In
three weeks, visit my parents near Charing Cross and tell them
to claim my body."

"No need to snap," Gregory said. Tough as he seemed, Tom's
words had rattled him. "You have enemies, but I'm not one of
them."

Tom set the letter aside and took his head in his hands. He
hadn't spoken this much in three weeks. Alone, he'd forgotten
how to speak. How to think. "Why are you doing this? Your master doesn't care if I die. Kit said as much."

Gregory cocked his head to the side. "You call him Kit?"

Tom nodded, though this hadn't answered his question. He suspected Gregory's mind circled the image of Tom's body being dragged out of Newgate, smelling of shit and death, limbs twisted, lungs sunken with fever. It should have unnerved Tom, how easy he found it to conjure up that picture. He felt nothing, thinking of it.

"I do," he said. "I don't suppose your friends call you Gregory."

The torch crackled through the silence.

"No," Gregory said. "They don't." He bit the inside of his lower lip. When Gregory spoke again, he spoke with the voice of a man who had surprised himself into honesty. "I don't turn my back on my partners. You matter to him, so you matter to me. Next time you see your Kit, you remind him of it."

Gregory didn't turn his back on his partners. That made one man in this world. The next time Tom saw Kit, he'd kill him. This was Kit's fault. All of it.

"Will you be back?" Tom said.

With a small grunt of effort, Gregory pushed himself to his feet. "I'll speak to my master for you," he said, looking down at Tom. "Do what I can."

"Charing Cross," Tom said, hugging his knees again. "Remember."

Gregory paused. Then, without speaking, he turned. The torch hissed and flickered with his movement as he vanished into the hall.

Tom looked at the letter on the filthy ground beside him. Through the dark, he heard the sound of a rat skittering somewhere nearby. Searching for food, for company, for freedom. A man with less to live for than a rat. The drip of a leak high overhead. The snap and flicker of a torch in the corridor. The murmur of men's voices, speaking to one another, to themselves, to no one.

Tom took his head in his hands again. Caring nothing for the prisoners around him, he screamed. He screamed until his throat scratched raw and his voice faltered. He screamed until he felt light-headed, until the dizziness spun into nausea and he pressed his forehead to his knees. The scream became a sob. The sob became silence.

I love you.

The rat's claws scratched again through the darkness, nearer.

Thirty-Eight

In some ways, Kit's work at Gilbert's shop was ideal. It was mechanical, mindless, yet artistic. Every day, until the shrinking window of sunlight made detailed work impossible, he shaved and shaped rounds of raw pewter to roughly the weight and thickness of a shilling, then watched Gilbert's crucible bathe the gray lump in shimmering gold. With so much at stake, it was exactly the kind of work he needed, the kind that left his mind blank and malleable as the pewter in his hands. There was calm in manual work, the same meditative state he'd entered when scrubbing floors at Sheffield. It was enough to make him wonder if he'd had the wrong end of it after all, if he weren't better suited to life in a workshop than with a pen.

The work and the idle chatter that bounced between himself and his two companions, the hiss of the crucible and the wisps of tobacco smoke shrouding the workbench—it might all have been pleasant. God help him, but he liked Evan and Gilbert. They were the kind of people he'd always longed for in Cambridge, the kind who made Bankside feel like home. Quick, irreverent working men, always ready with a joke, who judged you on what you could do and left your family's money out of it. Put sunny-mannered Evan Lloyd up against Richard Baines's unveiled disdain, and it was almost enough to make a man wonder.

But Kit knew their game. The money they forged would go to pay weapons dealers, purveyors of guns and powder outside the eyes of the law. The Spanish Armada of years ago had sunk into the sea without firing so much as a shot on English soldiers, and the money they coined here was resurrecting its bones, animating its soldiers, placing weapons in their hands, and shoving them toward London. He couldn't afford to forget that. Walsingham would never have forgotten it for a second. Richard Baines never let him forget it either, catching Kit midstride and leading him into taverns and alleys and abandoned churches to wheedle reports from him. In a blink, Kit would put on the mask of a staunch Protestant soldier again, the relaxed counterfeiter left outside. Neither face quite true, neither quite a lie.

And beneath it all, the inescapable reminder that Tom was still buried underground, waiting for the noose, because of Kit.

The coining moved as slowly as Gilbert had predicted, and winter came and settled in for a long stay. Though the canal didn't entirely freeze over, chunks of ice drifted through its ripples, and the icicles dangling from the eaves chimed like the most delicate church bells. They passed a quiet Christmas alone in Gilbert's forge, working their way through more wine than Kit had thought possible. Darkness fell early now, until it seemed as though it had been weeks since Kit had seen the sun.

A week after Candlemas, Kit and his companions worked by candlelight in the pitch-black late afternoon, an arrangement that left Kit squinting until his head ached. It was in this hushed atmosphere—dim, intimate, faint streaks of fresh-falling snow reflected through the window—that a messenger arrived.

Kit didn't rise to hear what the boy said. He left that to Gilbert, who conducted the exchange in rapid Dutch that even Kit, after nearly three months in Flushing, still struggled to parse. A few terse words, a slammed door, and then Gilbert was among them again, his rough features uncharacteristically alight, a long leather-wrapped package under his arm. Kit stood up, hoping his energy looked like enthusiasm and not alarm.

Evan pushed his work aside. "Good news?"

"See for yourself." Gilbert set the package on the workbench and uncovered it, his usually stoic face triumphant.

Kit, Evan, and Gilbert looked down at the musket lying on the table, resting on its leather wrappings like a crown on a pillow. Kit's stomach roiled, and he gripped the table to steady himself. Sharp movement felt dangerous, as if every breath might be his last.

"I sent off a purse of our first batch a few weeks back," Gilbert said. "Our fellow from Antwerp sent this ahead as a check for quality. No one trusts anyone in this business."

"Wise," Evan said with a small laugh, "seeing as we're cheating them." He reached out one hand to stroke the barrel of the gun.

"All as planned, God be praised," Gilbert said. He settled back into a chair, where he filled a pipe and lit it from the embers in the crucible. "Marlowe, write to Strange and let him know we're under way. Assuming a favorable wind, what, first shipment by Ascension Day, would you say?"

"Or sooner," Evan said. He took the musket and weighed it in his hands, testing the heft. He knew enough not to point the barrel at anyone, but it was the only thing Kit could see, that endless darkness down the mouth of the gun, shrouded in smoke from Gilbert's pipe.

The first weapon of hundreds. Thousands. God alone knew how many. Enough to man an army, to break down London's walls and send mercenaries streaming into the streets of Bankside by Ascension Day. Shoreditch burning, the screams from Bethlehem Hospital reaching a fever pitch, mirrored by the death cries of strangers in the street. Ned, Will, Kyd, Henslowe, the lot of them, tattered and broken corpses in a pile along the river, nosed at by dogs while behind them the Rose burned.

And Tom. The doors of Newgate flung open, insurgents releasing their own and taking to the streets, guns shoved into the arms of the faithful. Tom, turning to run. Tom, bleeding out in a narrow alley, his face pale beneath dirt and grime, a thin trail of blood slicing from his hairline like a scar down his cheek. Better to hang than to die that way. Better the scaffold take them both.

"Marlowe?" Gilbert said, the question drifting through a haze of pipe smoke. "What in hell's come over you?"

"Kit?" Evan set the gun aside. The sound of metal against wood grated Kit's nerves beyond bearing.

"I'm sorry," he said, backing toward the door. "I need some air."

The night was cold, the streets dark, the stars pale and far away. Kit tilted his head back and let the sharp air shock him, his breath escaping in a fog. It had snowed again that afternoon, and a fresh crust of powder brushed the streets. Breathe, he told himself. Just breathe, and think about the rest when you can bear it. You've done what you're meant to. All these weeks, this was what you wanted. Antwerp, Ascension Day. Send word back, and you can—

"A graceful exit," said Richard Baines from across the street. "You plan to tell me what that was about? Or do you mean to stand there all night?"

Damn everything. Not right now. Kit couldn't bear it right now. "Please," he said. "I need time to . . . to think."

"I'm sure you do," Baines said, taking Kit by the arm. "If you were the kind of person I could let out of my sight, I'd let you have it. Now come on."

Baines guided Kit down the street, toward a shuttered church they'd commandeered for hasty conversations like this one. Kit, mute and rattled, followed. It was too much to think about evading Baines. Inside, moonlight shed a silver glow through the dirty windows. A simple maritime church, wooden pews and raftered ceiling, smelling of salt, and crypt silent. Baines sat in the back pew. Kit stood in the aisle, hugging his ribs, not looking at Baines. His fingers kept picking at the fabric of his doublet. He couldn't seem to make them stop.

"Clearly you've seen something," Baines said, stretching out his legs. "I saw the boy with the package come and go. So you'd best tell me what was in it."

"Weapons," Kit snapped, the word like shattering glass. "What in hell did you think it would be?"

Baines frowned and sat up. "What's wrong with you?"

What was wrong with him? Tom was waiting for the noose and Gilbert had begun importing guns from Antwerp, that was what was wrong with him. Why was he *here*, when everyone who needed him was in London, everything he'd ever cared enough to protect was across the sea and under threat from the very rebels he was arming? Kit wiped his hand down his face, grasping for calm.

"If you've lost your nerve—" Baines began.

"I haven't *lost my nerve*," Kit snarled. Anxiety had flashed hot into rage, and in that moment he'd have given anything for Baines to throw a punch, just to have an excuse. "I'm tired, can you understand that? Everything depends on me and I'm stretched thin and I'm tired and my friends might be dead and it's more than I can *bear* sometimes—"

Baines stood up. He towered over Kit, blocking the door. "Marlowe," he said. "Take a deep breath."

But Kit would be damned if Richard Baines told him what to do tonight. He shouldered Baines out of the way. Baines, too surprised to resist, stood unanchored in the center of the church, like a saint struck dumb by the divine. Kit would regret that flash of temper in the morning, he knew, but for tonight the only thing he could do was to get away.

The winter air outside slapped Kit's burning face. His lungs ached with the biting wind, but the cold was healing, purifying. He walked in the direction of the boardinghouse, but once he came to the door he kept going, following the length of the canal until he'd walked all the way to the harbor. Cold wavelets rippled in the wind, which tossed Kit's hair like a battered flag. Across this sea, England. Across this sea, Strange and Cecil, Whitehall and rebellion.

Across this sea, home, if only he could get there.

Thirty-Nine

Kit woke early the next morning, but it took ages to drag himself from bed. There was nothing to induce him to leave the warm nest of blankets for the frozen city and its thousand dangers, not when all that awaited him was the promise of imported arms and an increasingly mistrustful Richard Baines. Still, he couldn't delay forever. After his abrupt departure the night before, Evan and Gilbert would need reassuring. He had to be there.

When he stumbled into the shop at last, just past ten, Evan and Gilbert were already deep in the day's work, materials spread across the bench, heat emanating from the crucible. They looked up as he entered, then glanced at each other. Kit saw Evan's silent burning desire to ask what was wrong. And he could see just as clearly Gilbert shutting down any questions. They hadn't written him off, or they'd have barred the door against him. But even so, he would have to answer for last night.

"Good morning," Kit said carefully. He received no response.

Ignoring them, Kit sank down at the workbench and set to his task. His hands moved without thought, and the repetitive gestures soon replaced his sharp awareness of their stares. He'd played the part perfectly for months, never let the mask slip for a moment. They would forgive one night of odd behavior—easy to explain by overwork, by exhaustion, by the fumes of molten metal soaring to his head. They'd have to.

Morning wore into afternoon, as did the silence. He heard nothing but their breathing, the lap of the canal outside, the forge's gentle thrum. It was enough to make him feel mad, as though he'd slipped into the crack between two worlds and no one could see him clearly in either. It seemed as though the quiet might go on forever.

Until there came a thundering pound on the door.

Evan froze. Kit and Gilbert both leapt up and kept their weight low, ready either to attack or defend. Kit reached for the knife he kept at his belt. Gilbert had no weapon, but Kit doubted he'd be at a disadvantage fist to fist, if it came to that. Which it might not, still. The door shuddered again, and Kit knew he was only deceiving himself. They knew no one else in Flushing, no one who needed to knock. Evan, mastering himself at last, swept the coins they'd minted that morning into his palm and flung them into the open cabinet, which he shut and locked.

"Open the door, by order of the governor!" came a voice, followed by another knock that made the hinges flinch.

Gilbert whirled round to face Kit, his anger incandescent. "Did you—"

"Never," Kit said. "You—"

The door gave way, sagging on knocked-loose hinges. Six soldiers stormed the room, Dutch guards armed to the teeth. They fanned out, taking in the evidence. The forge, the shaved pewter counters, the half-filled molds. The single counterfeit coin that had slipped from Evan's hands and now lay with the queen's head facing the ceiling. A soldier picked it up and turned it in his palm. It was a failed attempt, one they'd have melted down at the end of the day to try again. The gold didn't quite cover the surface. A scratch of ungilded pewter ridged its rim.

"Bring them in," the soldier said, nodding to his fellows.

Kit tried to make a run for the dangling door, but it was six men to three, and all six outweighed him. A soldier grabbed him by the back of his collar and shoved his chest against the wall with enough force to rattle his teeth. His head was pushed sideways, cheek pressed to cold stone. The soldier wrenched Kit's arms behind his back and tightened manacles on his wrists until his shoulders screamed with the stretch. Another soldier's hands went to Kit's belt, relieving him of his knife. In seconds, they found the smaller blade tucked into his boot and removed that too.

The soldier dragged him forward, through the door behind Gilbert and Evan, both similarly bound. Kit craned his neck, gazing back at the shop.

There, watching the proceedings with unshakable calm, stood Richard Baines.

Baines. Of course it was Baines. Betrayed by the only person in this God-cursed city who knew what Kit was attempting to do, and how much it cost him. Kit swore and strained against the soldiers' grip, but they dragged him forward, and he could do nothing but keep his feet and be moved. Baines caught Kit's eye and smirked before falling back into conversation with the soldiers, trailing a few feet behind.

The guards led them to an outpost of the law near the harbor, where the three men were thrown together into a holding cell. Kit staggered at the shove from a guard and fell hard on his knees, wincing as the floor jarred his bones. The door slammed behind them, the key grating in the lock. Six feet by six, the cell barely had room for all three to sit. A chink of a window, about the size of two fists, let a beam of light strike the stone floor. Kit shivered. The window had no glass, and winter air poured inside. He could see his breath. He hunched his shoulders against the cold, taking up as little space as possible.

Prison. Trapped here in another cell, waiting for another sentence to fall. He thought of the sick overconfidence that had plagued him in Newgate and wanted to retch. In the terrible silence of the tiny room, he imagined Tom whispering to him from the shadows, his voice barely audible. *It's over. You've lost. You've damned both of us.*

Evan sat silent in the corner, his lips tracing the outlines of words. His face was deathly pale, even in the poor light. He continued his prayer, eyes shut, ignoring both of them for a world beyond this one. Gilbert, for his part, left God alone. Seconds of silence became minutes.

"Who did you tell?" Gilbert said at last.

"No one," Kit said. "I swear."

Gilbert cursed, and the manacles around his wrists rattled as though he'd forgotten about them and tried to lunge at Kit. "Don't lie to me. You think I'm a fool? You panicked last night, then you ran out and gave us up."

"I didn't," Kit said, though it wasn't worth arguing. Counterfeiting was a hanging offense under English law, which was why they hadn't done it in London. But if Baines made a London court take interest, they'd all be dead in the morning, whatever Gilbert thought Kit had or hadn't done. "Believe me, I would never—"

"I believe you're a faithless, vile little—"

The door opened, and both Gilbert and Kit fell silent. Evan still had not opened his eyes; it was doubtful whether he even knew they'd been interrupted. The soldier who had opened the door collared Kit and dragged him to his feet with a sharp jerk. Kit stumbled, off-balance without the use of his hands. The memory of Newgate sharpened, along with a rising swell of fear.

"What are you—"

Without a word, the soldier pulled Kit from the cell and locked the door behind him. Again, Kit found himself marched forward, through the long hall of the outpost. A door hung open at the end, and the soldier made directly for it.

Inside, the room was spare. Nothing but a desk, two chairs on either side, candles burning at the center, a few maritime maps nailed to the walls. It might have been midday or midnight in the windowless room. The soldier unlocked the cuff on Kit's left wrist and closed it on the right arm of the nearest chair, forcing Kit down with one hand on his shoulder. Kit, rattled, didn't fight it. He didn't speak, barely thought.

A well-dressed man with a sweeping mustache entered and sat opposite Kit, his expression grave and his posture unimpeachable.

The magistrate, Kit assumed. There was a sorrow in the man's eyes, as if he regretted whatever sentence he was about to pass. A moment later, Richard Baines followed and stood beside the magistrate, his expression impossible to read. In that moment, Kit came to a decision. He would not be hanged. Not for this crime. No, if he were put to death, it would be because he'd stabbed Richard Baines through his lying throat.

The magistrate pulled a writing tablet and pen toward him across the desk, before placing a pair of spectacles on his long nose. As he did so, Baines caught Kit's eye. *Lie,* said his gaze. *Keep your cover.* As if Baines needed to tell Kit that. He'd lie with the best of them to save his own life, without prompting from Richard Baines.

"Name?" the magistrate said, without looking up from the tablet.

Kit swallowed. "Christopher Marlowe, sir."

"Profession?"

"Scholar and poet, sir. From London."

The magistrate held up the coin between two fingers. Its pewter stain looked like a gaping mouth, obvious even in the poor light. "And what, pray tell," he said, "is a London scholar doing in the company of a pair of counterfeiters?"

Kit's wrist ached against the tight ring of metal. He focused on the pain, letting it ground him through the lie. "I met those men last night, sir," he said. "The goldsmith bragged he could coin as well as the queen with common pewter, and his friend challenged him to prove it. I wanted to see. It was a stupid thing to do, but we'd had too much to drink, and I thought it would pass the time. I meant nothing more by it than that."

The magistrate slapped the coin on the desk. Kit flinched at the sound.

"It hardly matters at this stage what you meant," the magistrate said. "You are aware, Marley, that coining is punishable by hanging in England?"

Kit said nothing about his name. All he heard was the word *hanging*. His blood flashed cold as the manacles. He looked at Baines, swallowing his pride, pleading silently. There had to be something Baines could do to nudge this conversation toward safety. A few words, a few coins in the right hand, and Kit would go free as a bystander, someone caught in the wrong place at the wrong time. Real gold could sway justice in any nation on earth, and Baines was hardly too scrupulous to stoop to a bribe.

Baines looked away. Kit had never hated anyone so much in his life.

"I promise, sir," Kit said, "I only wanted to see his cunning in his trade. That's all."

Baines turned to the magistrate. "Surely you don't believe such an obvious lie, sir."

The words punched a hole in Kit's lungs. He'd always known Baines hated him. But enough to kill him?

The magistrate frowned. "His story is plausible," he said, as if Kit weren't there. "After all, he hardly seems a competent criminal."

"The worst ones often look that way, sir," Baines said, gesturing vaguely. "For all you know, this flea-bitten pup could be a rebel, using these false coins to fund the Catholic threat facing London."

Kit choked on a curse. That snake, that rat, that wretch. "Rebel?" He leapt to his feet, though the chain still kept his wrist anchored tight to the chair. In his anger, he thought he could break it, could leap the desk and rip the life from Baines. "What's to say you aren't the traitor, accusing me to save yourself?"

"You've some nerve," Baines cut in, glowering.

"Have I? With what you've—"

Baines slammed his hands on the desk, leaning forward, toward Kit. "Go to hell, you piece of filth—"

"Anywhere you are is hell, you toad, you pox-ridden son of a whore—"

"All right," said the magistrate, holding up a single, weary hand. "That will be quite enough."

Kit fell silent, breathing hard, and sank back into the chair. His wrist had chafed against the metal cuff, and he felt the skin blister. A drop of blood trailed between his thumb and forefinger.

"You are an English subject, Marley," the magistrate said, making a note in his tablet. "And you've counterfeited English coin. You and your companions will be shipped to London in three days, to be tried before an English court."

"By the royal secretary," Baines said. "Sir Robert Cecil." He glared at Kit across the table, as if to say, *There now, you see what I'm trying to do?*

It was as if Baines had removed an iron ring around Kit's lungs. He couldn't afford to show relief in front of the magistrate, but he felt it like a cool current through his blood. This was what he'd wanted. The work was over. He was going home, to London, away from this winding city where criminals and arms traders slipped like devils through the shadows. Cecil knew his loyalties and would release him. Kit had done what he'd said, and in a matter of days, he would see Tom again.

If Cecil kept his word. The new hope sank as quickly as it had risen. And why would he?

Baines had pulled Kit out too soon, shattering the trust he'd built with Evan and Gilbert, eroding Kit's carefully laid plans. If everyone but Kit was hanged, Strange would know him for a traitor. And on the other side of the game, in Whitehall, Baines thought Kit was compromised—a fact he would certainly pass on to Cecil.

"Come, Master Baines," the magistrate said, rising from the desk. "I will write to the secretary and explain the business. Your testimony will assist me in producing an accurate report."

"Yes, sir," Baines said. "I'm at your disposal." He left Kit with a sideways smile.

The door closed, and Kit was alone, chained to the chair, watching the flickering candlelight. He leaned his head into the palm of his free hand, his elbow on the arm of the chair. His breathing sounded like cannon fire through the quiet. The ripple of relief hadn't left him entirely, but it was ebbing with each heartbeat. With Baines's testimony, Cecil would see Kit's weakness laid bare. He would be a liability. An error in need of correction.

And to think that only a day ago he'd been longing to return to London.

Forty

It was early, not yet seven, and weak winter light strained through the narrow windows of Westminster Palace. Kit's shoulders and wrists ached from the manacles still keeping his hands pinned behind his back. They'd docked only an hour before, the Dutch prison ship coasting into the Thames shortly before sunrise. From there, Baines dragged Kit to shore, leaving Gilbert and Evan aboard, and led him here, to the central hall of justice in London.

Baines opened a door and shoved Kit forward without releasing his hold on Kit's shoulder. Kit stumbled, then looked up.

He stood in a moderately sized wood-paneled room, lined with tall leaded windows on both sides, a fire roaring in the hearth at the back. After the dim corridor, this room shone with light, a pale glow falling cold and silver against the floor. Kit's focus drifted to the ceiling, painted deep blue and dotted with golden stars that formed true constellations. The Star Chamber: where the queen dispensed justice. A man might try to read his fate in those stars, but Kit had no faith in astrology. If he lived through this, it wouldn't be because some heavenly farce had saved him, celestial or divine.

At the center of the room stood a table. Behind the table stood a chair. In the chair sat Sir Robert Cecil.

Cecil leaned forward, resting both elbows on the table. Kit wished he could be surprised that Cecil sat where the queen should have presided. A blazing flash of ego, one that would cost most men their heads. If Cecil could sit there without fear, that gave Kit a sign of how the new spymaster had flourished in his absence.

Baines shoved Kit forward, but Kit shrugged out of his grip. Yes, his hands were chained, he smelled like a Dutch holding cell, he was filthy and hungry, his clothes stiff from brine and over-wear. He might be walking to his death, but he'd walk there on his own. He stepped forward to stand before Cecil, Baines still at his shoulder.

Just like the stage, he thought. Hit your mark and tell him what he wants to hear. Easy as lying.

Cecil balanced his chin on his fist. His narrowed eyes never left Kit's face. "And so the great Christopher Marlowe returns to England," he said. "In chains, charged with treason for false coining. Somehow, you look even worse than when I saw you last."

At this point, Kit's best weapon was silence. He would stand here like an actor center stage and say nothing, not until Cecil pinned him with a direct question. He could feel Baines's breath behind him, like a wolf at his throat.

"What happened?" Cecil asked.

Richard Baines happened, that was the truest answer, but this was no time to develop a reputation for honesty. Kit clasped his hands behind his back, running his thumb along the blisters on his wrist where the iron had shifted. It hurt, but he needed it to. Without the pain to focus on, he would panic, and the devil only knew what he would say then.

"I told you the plan," he said. "I was after their connections in the Low Countries, the conspirators selling weapons to England's Catholics."

"And being thrown in prison, that was part of the plan as well?"

"No," Kit said, his voice tight as the manacles. "That was a com-plication." He craned his neck to scowl at Baines. Baines replied with an infuriating smile.

Kit knew Cecil didn't miss a drop of the antipathy sparking between him and Baines. Cecil was narrow-minded, not stupid. But Kit had spent four days being dragged from holding cell to prison ship to courtroom, underfed and anxious and chained. The anger had to go somewhere, and Baines was a safer receptacle than the spymaster.

"You bid me watch the boy, my lord," Baines said to Cecil.

Kit clenched his fists. The chains jangled like the tolling of a bell. He would be twenty-nine in a matter of days. Christ above.

"And your opinion?" Cecil said.

"Mixed," Baines said. "To put it mildly."

"You're a shit-crusted toad, is putting it mildly," Kit said, head twisted over his shoulder to address Baines. "You called the law yourself, you—"

Baines gripped the back of Kit's neck in one hand and shoved him forward. Kit flinched, from shame as much as pain, and fell silent.

"Yes, I called the law, sir," Baines said, releasing his hold on Kit's neck as though relinquishing a pleasure. "With reason."

Without emotion, Baines recounted the night before Kit's arrest. His outburst had felt harmless, honest when he made it, but repeated with Baines's inflection the words sounded like nothing less than an admission of betrayal. Kit watched Cecil's narrowing gaze watch him, until—he didn't know when it happened, only that it did—his eyes dropped to the floor. The air felt spun out and clouded, filling his lungs with dust.

When Baines finished, Cecil folded his hands on the table. Kit could feel the blood rushing through his body.

"Your work wasn't entirely useless," Cecil said. "It's confirmed the story you told before you left. And I imagine this interruption will slow Strange's preparations for war. Evan Lloyd and Gifford Gilbert will be held at the Tower, where I will personally ensure their sentences are carried out within the fortnight."

Kit kept his eyes on his boots. He thought of Gilbert's skilled hands and brusque pride in his work, Evan's easy smile. The three of them in Gilbert's workshop late at night, savoring the taste of wine and the sound of their own laughter. Yes, they'd been preparing an army, weapons enough to raze a city. But Evan Lloyd, that kind man with his warm handshake and calloused palms . . .

The man who would let London's streets run with blood. Who'd caressed the barrel of a musket as if it had been a gift from kings.

The frightened man praying in a prison cell.

The silence stretched endlessly. Kit knew this was a test. Cecil wanted a reaction, a traitor's desperate plea to save his Catholic friends from the rope. Kit raised his head, chin tilted boldly up, and said nothing. It had always been his job to ensure that Gifford Gilbert and Evan Lloyd would die. All he could do was try not to join them.

At last, Cecil flicked an unconcerned hand in Kit's direction, as if clearing a cloud of smoke. "Baines, release him."

Baines spluttered an incoherent protest. "Sir—"

Cecil silenced him with a sharp raise of his eyebrows. Scowling, Baines wrenched Kit's wrists toward him, nearly tearing Kit's right shoulder from its joint. Kit yelped, unable to stifle it. Baines snapped open the cuffs, and Kit's arms floated to his sides, as if they belonged to someone else. He rubbed one wrist with the opposite hand and winced. Thick rings of blisters had risen where the iron chafed against his skin.

"Marlowe, you will maintain your position," Cecil said. "I cannot risk replacing you with another agent at this stage in the proceedings. But from this moment, consider yourself warned."

He bit his lip and said nothing.

"You will report to the Privy Council at eight o'clock Thursday," Cecil said, "and each Thursday following, until you are informed to the contrary. I will expect detailed reports of your actions and your findings. You are expected to follow orders to the letter. No improvisation, no initiative. Behaving otherwise will be taken as proof of your disloyalty and will result in immediate consequences. Am I quite understood?"

More surveillance. More men around every corner, Catholics and Protestants both. Cecil hadn't dismissed the hangman. He'd told him to wait. And he still hadn't answered the only question Kit cared about.

"Yes, sir," Kit said. "But you gave your word."

Cecil's expression did not change, and Kit's body flashed cold. That was it, then. Cecil had gone back on his promise. Idle words, tossed off to make sure Kit followed orders. And the moment he was across the sea, a quick note to the provost of Newgate, *Get on with it then*, and the scaffold would be readied for the next morning. Kit found himself praying from pure reflex, needing someone to beg favor of. *Please. Let me be wrong. Let him have remembered his promise.*

Then Cecil nodded. "Thomas Watson was released from Newgate three days ago, when I received confirmation from the magistrate of Flushing of your return. You might lie as you breathe, Marlowe, but I, at least, keep my word when I give it."

Kit's knees buckled. The news, after months of living with the knife to his throat, was too much to bear. He sank to one knee, bracing himself on the floor. His breath came tight, but every lungful tasted like heaven. Tom was alive. Nothing mattered beyond that. Not the way Baines looked down on him like an insect that had crawled into Westminster, not Cecil's barely concealed sneer, nothing.

"Thank you, sir," Kit said quietly.

"Thursday," Cecil said. "Eight o'clock. Until then, you are dismissed."

Kit forced himself to stand. The walk out of the sun-flooded room, Cecil and Baines watching every step, seemed to stretch for miles, but he bore it with as much dignity as he could.

The moment he passed through the door, he broke into a run toward Fleet Street.

———

Out of breath and faintly light-headed, Kit stood outside Tom's Fleet Street rooms. The run had been ambitious, given that he hadn't slept or eaten anything worth speaking of since well before the prison ship departed. But now that he found himself here, he wasn't certain that exertion was entirely to blame for the light-headedness. He could see a sliver of light under the door, but he heard no movement from within. Perhaps the room was empty. But after so long in Newgate, where else would Tom long to go but home?

Please, he thought, reverting to the eerie practice of praying to no one. Please. Help me do this.

With the awful sensation of shouting into a grave, he knocked.

A moment of silence, and then Tom opened the door.

It was all Kit could do not to gasp. Tom looked terrible. He had lost an alarming amount of weight, leaving him swimming in a soft linen shirt that had once fit him perfectly. Deep shadows played beneath his eyes. His hair was poorly cut, and specks of blood flecked his cheek, as if he'd sat down his first day out of prison with a razor and sliced off his hair and beard with trembling hands. But least familiar of all was the set of Tom's mouth, lips pressed tight, and the half step he drew back when he saw Kit outside his door.

Kit felt the screws tighten in his chest. He wanted to hold Tom close and absorb his pain. Wanted to apologize for a week, a year, ten years, whatever it took to erase what had been done. Wanted to scream so the whole street would hear, *Stop looking at me like that, do you think I did it on purpose, do you think I wanted this?* Instead, he wrapped his arms around his chest and waited. Tom's silence reminded Kit of churchyards.

"You're back," Tom said. His voice, like the rest of him, was colder now.

Kit nodded. "Less than an hour. I came from Westminster." Not that Tom cared, but if Kit didn't speak, he'd be left with nothing but the shame, and that was abject enough already. Tom should have flayed Kit's skin from his bones with a penknife, and it would be just punishment for what he'd done.

Tom approached until they were an arm's length apart. It was beautifully close, and yet farther apart than they ever would have stopped before. Kit felt Tom take him in: the open sores on his wrists, the smell that had woven into his clothes after two holding cells and a prison ship. Flushing had worn him down in other ways as well, ways most men wouldn't be able to see—but Tom had never been like most men.

"You look like hell," Tom said finally.

It was so blunt, coming from this haunted, reduced version of Tom, that Kit found himself wanting to laugh and cry at the same time. Instead, he took a step nearer. Tom watched him, hesitant. It was like trying not to spook a deer.

"Can I come in?" Kit asked.

Tom's time in prison had left his emotions close to the surface. Kit watched the anger pass through him, leaving its traces on every muscle. And behind the anger, something Kit couldn't name, but that he found himself staking all his hopes on. Something that came after the anger, and stayed longer.

"This was your fault," Tom said. "Everything that happened to me. It was all your fault."

Kit nodded. "Yes."

"I should hate you."

"You should."

Tom's brow lowered. "Stop agreeing with me."

"All right."

"Damn it, Kit—"

It was stupid. He should have waited. Let Tom work out his anger, his blame, all of it justified, Kit deserved it all. But he couldn't help himself. Months since he'd seen this man. Months of waking in the middle of the night, cold and panting, having dreamed him dead. And now Kit was in London, standing outside these sparsely furnished Fleet Street lodgings, and here Tom was. Alive. Breathing. Kit rested his hands on Tom's waist and pulled him close.

Tom froze. Stunned that Kit had dared. Then Kit felt his bitterness melt, and he rested one hand on the small of Kit's back.

"Can I?" Kit asked.

Tom hesitated. His lips parted, choosing between responses. To forgive, or not to. Then Tom let out a small breath, and Kit heard it in his voice, the ghost of a smile, the memory of something beautiful raised from the dead.

"You're impossible," Tom murmured. And he embraced Kit, and led him inside.

Under any other circumstances, this would have been cause for a grand reunion. Affection and lust tangled together, each hungering for the other's body after so long away that nothing could keep them from making love, not even if the queen herself were in the next room. But it wasn't like that now. Tom held Kit close and kissed him, slowly, gently. Then without either saying a word to the other, Kit slipped off his boots, and they climbed into Tom's bed, still dressed, and nestled together beneath the blankets.

For the first time in months, Kit felt the muscles in his back unwind. He unclenched his jaw and sighed into the pillow, while Tom settled in with his chest against Kit's spine. He could feel Tom's breath, feel the stubborn pound of Tom's heart against his own back, sense the slight pressure from each of Tom's ribs. Tom lay one hand over Kit's stomach, and Kit held it close, briefly raising it to press a kiss against Tom's knuckles.

"I shouldn't forgive you," Tom whispered in his ear.

"I know."

"But I've missed you," Tom said. His voice, soft as it was, broke over the last words. "So much. Even when I thought I might kill you, this was all I ever wanted."

"I love you," Kit said, because it was the only true thing he could say.

Tom sighed and held Kit closer, and the world shrank until it contained only this bed and the warmth of Tom's arms. "I love you too. Don't ever leave me again."

Kit smiled and closed his eyes. For the first time in God knew how long, he slept easily, and dreamed of nothing.

Forty-One

The trials of Evan Lloyd and Gifford Gilbert were swift, efficient, and unsurprising. Twin guilty verdicts, released promptly on each other's heels, executions proclaimed for subsequent days within the second week of March. London greeted the news with its usual cruel joy. Hangings were a de facto public holiday. Half the city would take off work and turn out to Tyburn to watch two Catholic conspirators jerk and twitch.

The morning of the hanging, Kit and Tom lay in bed together in Tom's rooms near the Fleet, where Kit had moved after his return. He'd intended it to be a temporary solution until he found a place of his own, but after a week of living with Tom he couldn't bring himself to leave. To hell with the danger. If Cecil had him executed, it wouldn't be for this. And with dreams of Tom's gutted corpse drifting back more nights than not, he couldn't bear to have the length of a city between them.

Besides, he wasn't the only one with trouble sleeping now. Though they never spoke of it, he suspected Tom needed him close as much as he needed Tom. What had happened to them, in Flushing or in Newgate, laid a weight over their silences that was impossible to escape.

The same weight that forced Kit to attend this hanging, when he would rather have been the one sentenced.

Kit was still curled up with his head on Tom's collarbone, nestled against his side. Tom had wrapped one arm around Kit's shoulders. His other hand gently traced the ring of scars around Kit's wrist: healing well, but still tender. Beneath the blanket, Tom's newly angular body was warm against the wind outside, freezing even as spring drew nearer. Hard enough to leave this for any reason. If he could have shut out the world and existed only in this bed, he'd have done it.

"Are you sure?" Tom asked.

"I owe him that," Kit said. "He's going to hang because of me."

"He's going to hang because he's a traitor. That's not because of you."

Kit shook his head. "You don't know him. I have to go."

Tom sighed, then shifted to kiss the top of Kit's head. "All right. But I'm coming with you."

God forbid. Tom, standing there at Tyburn, looking up at the scaffold that, if anything had gone wrong, would have been the last thing he ever saw. He couldn't bear to imagine Tom anywhere near that Golgotha, the bloody boards and well-serviced ropes. "Tom, you don't have to—"

"I know I don't have to," Tom said.

He sat up, and Kit saw the determination on Tom's still-hollow face. Some of the color had returned to his cheeks, and Kit had seen to it that he was eating well, though his appetite had shrunk almost to nothing. He was getting better, and would be better still, given time. But being reckless, moving too fast would help no one.

Still, Tom's resolve didn't waver. "You don't have to do everything alone, Kit. Not this. I wouldn't offer to come unless I meant it."

I don't want you there, Kit tried to say. *Please don't.*

But lying to Tom had gotten them here to begin with. And he did want Tom beside him, selfish and troubling though it was. For that long, slow walk to the gallows, if nothing else.

"All right," Kit said. "Come on, then."

———

London had three primary sources of entertainment: Bankside's theaters, Southwark's stews, and Tyburn's executions. Kit had so far avoided the last. He dreamed of enough disemboweled men, enough women's heads on spikes without needing to see them in daylight. He and Tom kept to the edge of the crowd, a writhing mass spilling around the scaffold, north and west of the city walls.

The crowd. He'd spent so much time fearing the hanging that he'd never stopped to think of the people surrounding it. But Kit had seen crowds like this before—recognized some of the faces from it, calling to one another, laughing as though it were any public holiday. He knew these people: the same people he saw five afternoons a week at the Rose. There, they'd flocked to Bankside and spent their meager pay to see Tamburlaine slaughter Saracens and women and Moors, Barabas the Jew boiled alive, Lightborn the assassin leaving Edward and his lover writhing in blood and smoke.

Was this any different? He'd always thought it was. *The people want to believe their anger is worth something,* Strange had said. But did they? Kit wrote death to purge it from his mind; London watched death for the theater of it. They'd revel in real death like poetry, and when they left, life would wash the blood from them like rain, and they would return to their work, to peace.

He would never see these people the same way again. He should have known this about them long ago. He might have done everything differently if he had.

Tom glanced at Kit, then, without speaking, took his hand, pressing it tight. In a crowd like this, no one cared anything for them. They could risk it. Tom's skeletal hand was warm and steady, slowing Kit's trembling.

When a pair of guards brought Evan Lloyd to the scaffold, Kit gripped Tom's hand so hard he saw Tom wince.

After weeks in English custody, Evan barely resembled himself. Tall as a free man, he had shrunk in prison, bent and battered, moving so gingerly it made Kit nauseated to think about it. His fair hair was lank and dirty, and the shadow of a beard discolored his hollow cheek. He looked down at his feet. Kit couldn't see his eyes. Wide and innocent, those warm eyes, those easy jests, that kind laughter. The extended hand in the underground chamber in Strange's library, helping Kit to his feet. The country boy and his calloused hands.

They stood far enough away that Kit couldn't hear the executioner, which was only half a blessing. Kit already knew the accusations. He knew the sentence. He knew everything.

The hangman circled Evan's neck with the noose, and only then did Evan look up. Kit's heart shuddered. Evan's eyes flashed, bright and daring, with a fanaticism Kit knew. The same swirling danger that had flamed through Mary Stuart. The ferocity of a man who had seen death and no longer cared. It would have been easier, Kit thought, if prison had broken Evan. If Kit hadn't seen the saint trapped within him break free in fire. He hardly recognized this man. Cecil had turned a man Kit knew—a workingman, a friend—into something frightening.

"Hail Mary, full of grace, the Lord is with thee," Evan said, chin up and bold. His voice was not loud, but it carried straight across the years, to Mary in the shadow of the axe.

Kit swayed, an inch from fainting. Tom took him by the shoulder, keeping him steady. "Kit, let's go," he said. "You don't have to—"

Kit shook his head, and his vision cleared. His jaw ached from clenching. "Not yet," he said.

Mary Stuart, Queen of Scots, had been allowed to finish the prayer. Evan Lloyd, nobody from nowhere, was not extended the courtesy. The noose tightened on the word *sinners,* and the platform dropped, and the body shuddered, a wild macabre dance, a trembling.

Kit, damned forever as a coward, could not look. He turned away, Tom's hand on his shoulder, to the crowd.

He saw the man at once, as if he'd been meant to. The usual florid doublets and cloaks were gone—out of place for the occasion— but even in muted black he was a man who would draw Kit's eye anywhere. He looked up at the scaffold, his sensitive lips moving in the clear cadence of prayer. Eyes locked on the body, which would still be twitching from the rope, some minutes yet in dying.

Of course. Lord Strange wouldn't abandon his followers without the last rites of their faith. In his mind, his revolution was for men like Lloyd as much as for his own gain. If it had been Kit hanged in Strange's service, his patron would have stood here just the same, speaking the same prayer for Kit's soul.

As the body on the scaffold stilled to a shiver, then to a slow revolving sway, Strange turned away, and his eyes locked on Kit's. It wasn't hate, what Kit saw in those eyes. But it was an order, one he didn't dare countermand. He had to speak to Strange. Had to explain, or try to. If Cecil and Baines thought he'd betrayed their cause, Strange had twice as much reason to think so.

Gradually, the crowd began to disperse. Not back to work, not yet—the holiday atmosphere would last all day, long after the criminal had been cut down. But they would move their revels somewhere else, away from the body, which no longer offered any entertainment, and would begin to smell.

"Kit," Tom said. "It's finished. Come on."

"You go," Kit said. "There's something I have to do."

"Kit, please."

Kit turned to look at him. Tom held both Kit's hands in his. Kit could read his thoughts as if they were his own. Please don't do this. Stop taking risks, stop planning, just stop. For once in your life, put this aside and come home with me, like any normal person would do.

This kind, handsome, clever man, brave and loyal and charming, who loved him. Who had suffered for him and still stood by his side, wanting nothing more than a breath of quiet in repayment. What wouldn't Kit have given to leave this behind, turn his back on the gallows, and give Tom the peace he'd always wanted?

"I'm sorry," Kit said, kissing Tom on the cheek. Willing to risk anything, to make him understand. I know I'm hurting you, the kiss said. But I'm doing it so I won't hurt you more. So nothing else will hurt you. "He's here."

Tom glanced into the crowd—as if he'd have known whom to look for. His entire body tensed, leaving him looking vulnerable and barely healed despite the swordsman's stance. Finally, he nodded. He held Kit's hands another moment, then brought them to his mouth and pressed a soft kiss on the inside of Kit's wrist, right at the line of his pulse, gentle against the scars. He let go and turned, disappearing into the crowd.

When Tom was safely gone, Kit pushed against the retreating tide of bodies, toward Lord Strange.

Strange stood tall and impassive, looking intently at the body. He didn't so much as glance at Kit. Deep shadows circled his eyes, as though he hadn't slept well since the announcement of Lloyd's sentence. Kit had no doubt he looked much the same.

"A question for you, Marlowe," Strange said softly, his breath fogging in the cold. "Is it coincidence that every person of faith who works alongside you ends up dead? First Mary Stuart, now this. It's enough to make me wonder. Will it be me next, do you think?"

"I didn't—"

"No," Strange interrupted, "don't answer. I already know what you'll say. You were all caught together, but you pled your case in front of Cecil. You claimed you'd planned this all along. Is that it?"

Kit lowered his head. "The job was a risk," he said. "We all knew that. Evan is a good man." His voice cracked as he realized what he'd said. "He was a good man," he corrected quietly, swallowing hard. Tears, though honest, would ring false to Strange. He had to be who Strange thought he was: a man willing to sacrifice, dedicated to the cause, and strong enough to bear it.

"He was," Strange said. "See that you remember it. Every day, if you can."

He looked over his shoulder at the clearing crowd. Few people remained in the square now, only the dregs. Pickpockets, beggars, a woman wailing to herself in a language Kit did not know. Not much time left—Strange couldn't be the last person in the crowd, not when the body of his fellow believer still hung from a rope over their heads.

"I'm not accusing you of anything, Marlowe," Strange said. He still hadn't looked at Kit. "Men want to live. It's only natural. But I need to know you're willing to do what it takes, if the moment demands of you what it demanded of Evan. I'll let you decide how you intend to prove it to me."

Without giving him a chance to respond, Strange joined the sweep of people streaming south toward the city. In a moment, his distinctive stride disappeared into the crush of fabric and footsteps and voices, vanished with the skill of ghosts and hunted men.

Kit turned back to the scaffold. The motionless body of Evan Lloyd still dangled from its dirty rope in front of him, its staring eyes wide. Kit stood there, staring back.

Forty-Two

Across the square at Tyburn, wrapped in a fox-fur cloak against the cold, Robert Poley leaned against an overturned cart beside Richard Baines. Together, they watched Marlowe stare up at the traitor's slowly revolving body. He stood alone, long after the man in the black cloak left him. He said nothing, did not move. Poley hadn't seen Marlowe look like that since Northampton, when he'd fled Mary Stuart's execution. Like a sleepwalker, or a mourner at a funeral.

It was suspicious.

Moreover, it was an opportunity.

Poley glanced to Baines and cocked an eyebrow. "What do you make of that?"

Baines spat against the dirty ground; it smoked in the cold like hot piss. "I don't trust it."

That was hardly a resounding endorsement of Poley's opinion. Richard Baines would suspect his own mother if he could benefit from it. But Cecil didn't trust Marlowe either, and in Poley's current profession Cecil's opinion was the only one that mattered.

At last, Marlowe turned away from the body and left the square, back toward the city.

"Follow him," Poley said, nodding after Marlowe. "Today, tomorrow, whenever you can. See what you can find. Cecil will want to know."

Baines nodded grimly. "I'll find enough," he said, setting off.

———

320 + A TIP FOR THE HANGMAN

Weeks later, Poley made his way to Whitehall after dark, in blatant disregard of the city curfew. Most men would be nervous, receiving a summons from Sir Robert Cecil at this hour, but Poley had worked hard to be sent for like this. If Cecil needed him, it was because Poley had gone out of his way to be needed. Flattering Cecil at every turn, even before Walsingham died, the moment he saw how the wind was blowing. He'd never once strayed from his devotion to the work, volunteering his services while Kit Marlowe—once Walsingham's shining star—faded into a life of taverns and playhouses. Marlowe's return to intelligence work had been a complication, and for a short time Poley had feared Marlowe would usurp his place as the spymaster's right-hand man. But after the Low Countries—ages ago now, with the last of winter's snows gone and the bodies of the two counterfeiting traitors long since food for crows—Marlowe's star had plummeted, and Poley could feel his own soaring like a comet.

Two men already occupied the office when he entered. Cecil, of course, at his desk as always. He'd pulled the curtains over the window, keeping out the night, and sat surrounded by papers: ledgers and trade maps and a thick manuscript, written in verse. The furrow in his brow seemed deeper now. Clearly no one had warned Cecil that the corollary of absolute authority was paperwork. Richard Baines sat in a wooden chair near the hearth, expression sour as ever. He and Poley nodded at each other, the easy familiarity of partners but not friends. A man couldn't choose his allies, nor expect them to be especially charming in conversation. Poley had no particular love for Baines as a person; truth be told, he'd cut Baines's throat in a heartbeat if it served his purpose. Still, for the moment, Baines made Poley look valuable in Cecil's eyes, and that was enough to go on with.

Cecil cleared a space on the desk to rest his elbows. "Thank you, Poley, for deigning to join us."

"What's the business, sir?" Poley said, choosing to ignore the tone.

"Of all my agents," Cecil said, "you and Baines are most familiar with the matter of Christopher Marlowe. I wanted your opinions, before I decide."

Decide. Well, that didn't bode well for Marlowe.

Since his exoneration, Marlowe had presented himself weekly before the Council as commanded, making up in punctuality what he sorely lacked in manners. But his reports, though honest, lacked detail. Critical details that Poley and Baines, who had tailed Marlowe since his release, made certain Cecil knew. Those second thoughts at the execution. Multiple meetings with untrustworthy strangers, including a copper-haired woman Poley had vague memories of from his days in Sheffield. Marlowe's well of information dried to a trickle. April was halfway gone, and Marlowe had little to show for his months of work other than an ever-bolder Catholic threat.

Poley reported it all, week after week, faithfully. Cecil listened with rapt attention, his reliance on Poley's judgment rising day by day.

"For someone meant to keep a low profile," Baines said, "Marlowe seems to enjoy his celebrity, doesn't he?"

It was an anodyne place to start, but not an incorrect one, as it drew a laugh from Cecil. "His plays make him the most infamous man in London," the spymaster said. "The commoners at the theater call him everything. Marlowe the Heretic. Marlowe the Atheist. Marlowe the Sorcerer. And then, there's this."

Cecil tapped the side of his hand against the manuscript. Poley frowned and leaned forward, elbows on his knees. Cecil would never have read Marlowe's plays of his own volition. Perhaps Edmund Tilney had sent it over. The master of revels must have his work cut out trying to censor the barrage of scandal Marlowe brought to the stage.

Cecil lifted the pages, letting them hang meaningfully in his hand. Despite his manifest distaste for the theater, his dramatic timing was faultless. "A draft of his latest," he said. "Untouched, as yet, by the censors. The hero is a necromancer. Conjuring the devil."

Baines choked on nothing. "Conjuring the what?"

"The devil," Cecil repeated. "Onstage. Latin incantations, the whole production."

Poley rubbed his beard, considering. Surely the boy couldn't be as stupid as that. Although if he was, it would certainly make Poley's task easier.

"I mistrust him," Cecil said, leaning back. "Deeply."

Baines's eyes lit up like a child's. Christ, Poley thought. The queen's finest, this, and he couldn't hide his petty hatred of the man for thirty seconds. Poley's own face, he knew, was smooth as glass. It helped to feel nothing. Attach yourself to nothing. Marlowe meant nothing to him, no more than Baines or Gregory or Babington or any of the others had meant anything. Men were only chess pieces, there to be moved for the greatest advantage. When your only ally was yourself, you could never be betrayed.

"Before any action is taken," Cecil said, "we need to be quite certain. He's been valuable in the past. But if you can secure proof— incontrovertible proof—that he poses a danger, well, then."

"Then, sir?" Baines said.

Cecil didn't blink. "Then I will give Poley permission to take whatever course he thinks prudent."

Poley made no attempt to hide his smile. Ends and means, he thought as he stood up. Ends and means. He'd worked to hear those words for years. Whatever he thought best. Free rein, and trust, and no questions. It was only a step toward the final goal, but it was a momentous step, and he intended to savor it.

"Baines and I will set to work," he said with a bow. "We'll keep you informed."

"Do so," Cecil said to Poley. He gestured toward the door, scorning subtlety for effectiveness.

Poley went, Baines trailing.

The corridor outside was nearly empty. A lone servant passed, light-footed against the stone. At this late hour, candles lit the space at intervals, sending dim light dancing across their bodies. Baines and Poley shared a glance, then ducked into a small alcove near the door to Cecil's office. They both knew enough to prevent being overheard. Men had died for smaller acts of carelessness.

"We'll need to do this by the book," Baines said.

Poley sighed. "Richard, has anyone told you you're terribly tiresome?" He saw Baines narrow his eyes but didn't give a damn about it. He'd just been promoted to second-in-command. Surely that allowed him a few liberties.

"You heard His Grace. No questions, no doubts. That means the aboveboard way."

Aboveboard. Well. More *en règle* than a knife through the ribs in a dark alley, perhaps. "First things first, then," Poley said. "You'll need to compile—"

"A deposition," said Baines. "I'll handle the formalities. The rest I leave to you."

Poley shook his head. This was cowardice on Baines's part, handling the paperwork and skirting the physical responsibility, but Poley didn't mind it. In fact, if Cecil saw Poley doing the lion's share of the work, so much the better. A task such as this was unpleasant, but Cecil could only ask it of someone he trusted without reservation. Once he'd followed this order to its inevitable conclusion, it would be clear there was nothing Robert Poley wouldn't do for the security of the crown. He'd prove himself devoted enough to put personal feelings aside, demonstrate his command of every covert stream of information in London. The kind of man who, years in the future, might become spymaster himself.

Or, if he could prove his value to Cecil, perhaps sooner than that. The great man had never particularly wanted the job of spymaster—one more responsibility on his already sagging shoulders. If Poley proved he could take the whole affair in hand, what then?

"Productive meeting, gentlemen?"

Poley flinched. Arthur Gregory leaned against the far wall, in the fog of shadows between two candles. He pressed the sole of one foot against the stone, looking as if he'd stood there all night.

Only a man without a heartbeat could have remained that silent so long. Poley narrowed his eyes, irritably bringing his pulse back down.

"Productive enough," Baines said.

The unreliable illumination did nothing to make Gregory's glare less dark. Idiot, Poley thought. Walsingham's man through and through, he hadn't made the slightest effort to adapt to the changing of the guard. Showed what you stood to gain, staying loyal to a ghost.

"Eavesdropping is beneath you, Arthur," Poley said coldly.

"Eavesdropping is my job," Gregory said. Poley had forgotten how tall Gregory was. Extended conferences with Cecil had lulled him into a false sense of security in his own height. "You planned this all along, didn't you?"

Poley looked at Gregory like a horsefly buzzing in his face. "Not in the slightest."

"Don't lie to me. You've been tailing Marlowe for weeks."

"I've been following orders for weeks. You might try it sometime, Arthur."

"It's betrayal, is what it is," Gregory snapped.

Poley shook his head. Arthur Gregory's fatal mistake: loyalty. Make as many friends as you like, but don't cling to them when they're drowning, or they'll pull you down, too. It would be a lie to say he didn't take some pleasure in watching the man's prospects dissolve around him. "You needn't worry about a thing, if you're possessed of so tender a conscience. Cecil's made up his mind, and I've taken the matter in hand. I have people all over London willing to help me. In fact . . ."

He turned his back on the pair of them. The candles stretched his shadow along the wall as he passed.

"I think I know the perfect man."

Forty-Three

K it," Ned Alleyn said, and then again, louder: "Kit. The line."

Kit's eyes snapped back into focus. He stood to the side of the stage while rehearsals unfurled in front of him, until now without his paying attention. What was the last speech they'd practiced? Had it been Wagner's? Either way, they were well past that now. Ned was looking to him for a prompt, and Kit had been thinking of knives, of nooses, of the awful silence of a deserted church, and nothing of poetry.

It had been hell enough trying to navigate his weekly probationary meetings with Cecil. He pushed Anne Cooper as far as he dared for information, well aware that her distrust in the wake of Evan's execution was monumental. Strange was regrouping, reaching out to his contacts in the country to strategize after the disaster in the Low Countries. Kit continued deciphering the intercepted letters, but they only reiterated what Anne told him in their terse meetings: that plans would need to change, that they needed to develop a more careful approach. More now than ever, Kit needed a breakthrough, a shining gem of intelligence. Without one, God knew how long Cecil would give him the benefit of the doubt.

He and Anne met weekly in Saint Saviour Church in Bankside, an arrangement they'd begun in the aftermath of Evan Lloyd's execution. Each meeting lasted only a few minutes, clipped questions and shorter answers. And then, last week, she hadn't come. Kit had waited for hours, sitting in the back pew as the church gradually filled for afternoon services. It was easier that way, to let the world wash around him, as if he were only as much a part of it as the wooden pews, as the stone under his feet. In Anne's absence, each prayer from the priest sounded like a condemnation.

Onstage at the Rose, Ned sighed. "Figures of every adjunct to the heavens . . ." he repeated, beginning again the half-forgotten line.

"And characters of signs and erring stars," Kit said mechanically, without checking the prompt book.

"By which the spirits are enforced to rise," Ned said, snapping his fingers in satisfaction. He was off from there, charging forward through the scene. "Then fear not, Faustus, but be resolute . . ."

Kit let his attention drift away again, to the terrible silence of Saint Saviour. It was meant to be today, his and Anne's next rendezvous. A prophetic feeling in the pit of his stomach whispered that she wouldn't be there, but he couldn't go on like this, or his blood would burst his veins. He couldn't think about poetry if there was the slightest chance she might be waiting. Not if there was anything left for him to try.

He turned to Will, watching the scene with the rest of the actors not involved in it. Without explaining, he pushed the prompt book into Will's surprised hands.

"Take my place for a minute," he said. "I'll be back as soon as I can."

He hopped down off the stage and jogged across the pit, ignoring Will's protests that he couldn't manage the prompts, he didn't know the lines, he wasn't the one who'd written the bloody thing.

Saint Saviour's was nearly visible from the Rose, its four-peaked tower clear against the gray sky of a damp afternoon. The church had once been splendid, though nothing but a shadow of that remained. It looked half naked as he entered, stripped of its finery with only whitewash and plain stone to hide behind. High windows arched over the nave, but the glass was so clouded with dirt and grime that the light spilled through in beams as if at the floor of some great sea. A lone priest stood near the altar, his bald head catching the light, though the crucifix in front of him had fallen into shadow. Each of Kit's footsteps rang terribly through the vaulted space. Other than the priest, only a few people sat in the dim pews of the main nave, each of their heads bent in prayer.

And one of them, he saw at the front of the church, was Anne.

Kit felt his lungs fill with the first clear gulp of air in days. He rushed down the aisle toward her, already framing each movement as part of the story he would tell Cecil. *I came down the center aisle,* he'd say, *I genuflected at her pew and knelt beside her, and when she broke off from her prayer, she—*

When Anne looked up, Kit drew back as if he'd sat beside a monster and not a woman. Anne's face was narrower, her eyes rimmed with red. She looked at him like Christ on the cross, a silent dead-eyed gaze that looked down on sinners and let them assign the blame themselves. The silence seemed to last a lifetime.

"You didn't come last week," he said finally.

Her laugh made Kit think of the wind between gravestones. "No. I think you know why."

"Please. Tell me what's going on. I have to know."

Anne looked at him one moment more, then spoke without inflection, without anger, without anything at all. "Lord Strange is dead."

The words didn't make sense. They were simple enough, but they couldn't mean what he thought they did. It wasn't possible.

Lord Strange was dead.

That careless familiarity at the George Inn. The concerned frown behind a cloud of pipe smoke and shadow. Lips outlining silent prayer at a man's death. *Are you angry, Marlowe?* This had always been the intention; it was always meant to end this way. But Kit felt as though Anne's words had severed the muscles in his knees. He thought of the beads of Mary Stuart's rosary, skittering against the floor, dropped by a nerveless hand. Another tick on the list. Another man killed because of him. *Will it be me next?*

It had been. But not because of Kit.

"How?" he breathed.

"How?" she repeated. Her voice never rose above a murmur, but it didn't need to. No one needed to hear her but Kit, and he could hear nothing else. She turned in the pew, her knees pointed toward him. "Poison, as you know full well."

Poison. Kit felt the bile rise in his throat.

"He was at supper in Derbyshire a week past when he excused himself from table, claiming he felt ill," Anne went on, taking savage pleasure in the way the details struck him. "Thirty minutes later, he was vomiting blood. By morning, they'd called for the undertaker. But you know how poisons are. The expensive ones work fast. And no one even notices a drop in a glass of wine. Helps to have the well-connected on your side, to get the good-quality sort."

Kit sat still, feeling desperately exposed, like a heretic at the stake. Strange was dead. Strange, the people's man. Poisoned. Poison that turned breath to blood, that ate the body away from the inside. Kit's own insides roiled with acid. His own shame might eat him alive.

"How—"

"What do you mean, how? You told them to do it, didn't you?" It was the closest she'd come to raising her voice, and the vehemence didn't last. She turned away, red-rimmed eyes trained on the cross at the head of the church.

This was Cecil's work; Kit knew it as surely as Anne did. Cecil had given up on Kit's increasingly scant reports and taken matters into his own hands. He'd had Lord Strange poisoned, no doubt by an agent he'd placed within the Derbyshire household. An agent who wasn't Kit.

He clasped his hands until the web of his fingers ached. "I didn't know," he said. "They didn't tell me anything."

It didn't sound like an excuse, not to his ears and not to Anne's. It sounded instead like a magistrate passing sentence. If Cecil could do this without telling him, if he could sit stoic behind that grand desk of his and take Kit's reports while he held a stoppered bottle of hemlock in one hand and said nothing about it, then Kit was nothing to him.

Three weeks ago, he'd have spun any excuse that could save his skin, and he wouldn't have stopped building his wall of words until he was sure Anne believed him. But now, he had no words left. Words only did any good if someone was listening. Where before he'd been standing in a glass cage, his every action on display for both sides to scrutinize, now he stood in a windowless hallway full of locked doors, shouting in the dark to no one.

"They didn't tell me," he said once more, then let the silence rush through him like fire.

Anne still didn't look at him. Her face might have been carved from granite. "I don't care what they told you," she said. "I don't care if it was you who killed him, or who you work for, or what you are. You deserve to die, but I won't be the one to do it. Your life isn't worth the weight on my soul."

"Anne—" he began.

"Get out of here," Anne said, in that same low voice. "I don't ever want to see you cross my path again. And if you come back, it will be the last thing you ever do. Make no mistake."

Shut out. Turned away. Pound his open palm against every locked door and no one would come to answer him. He could scream as long as his voice held, and no one would come. There was only one thing he could do, one choice that was not a choice at all.

Without a word, Kit rose from the pew and ran.

Forty-Four

S ir, don't worry," Ingram Frizer said, grinning from ear to ear. "Do we look like two men who would steer you wrong?"

Based on Andrew Woodleff's expression, Frizer knew the man would have answered yes if he'd dared. Of course, the fool was too deep in debt to risk insulting anyone. That was how you made money as a bondsman, wielding both honey and the knife. Bring debtors in with your charm, then close the door behind. Fleecing a few idiots a week in the Bull and Boar's second-floor parlor wasn't as lucrative as it might have been, but he was good at this, and being good at something offered its own pleasure. The right slouch, the right angle to your smile, and gamblers like this thought you could move the moon and stars. It was steady going, if slow. Find a rich mark who'd pay up, and Ingram Frizer would be made for life.

He leaned forward, resting both elbows on the table. "Fifty pounds is no small sum, my friend," he said. "But it's nothing we can't manage."

Beside him, Frizer's partner Nick took copious, silent notes. An idiot and an ass, Nick was, but Frizer needed him. He himself had no head for numbers, and Nick had studied far beyond grammar school. A gentleman's son, fallen on hard times and then fallen into Frizer's path like a gift from God. Besides, Nick looked respectable. Barely thirty and almost handsome, with reddish-brown hair, a patchy beard, and a nose only slightly crooked. People trusted a face like that. Frizer himself, nearly six feet tall with a mane of golden hair and a flashy manner of dress that would have been flashier if not for his poverty, was all too aware of what he brought to the partnership. Nick brought a public face and an aptitude for calculation; Frizer the skill, brains, and charm.

Frizer glanced at the figures Nick scrawled in his ledger, feigning comprehension for Woodleff's sake, then resumed ignoring the whole affair. "We can lend you the fifty pounds, in sterling and commodity," he said, "to get you through the worst of it. All we ask in return"—he nodded to Nick, who took a swift note—"is something for our effort."

Frizer saw a smirk cross Nick's face, identical to the smirk currently adorning his own.

Woodleff shifted in his chair. "What do you mean?"

Frizer shooed away his concern. "Nothing to worry about. But my partner and I need to make a living, same as any man."

"That's to say," Nick said, "that if you fail to repay your loan by the stated date, the principal will accrue interest at a rate of—"

"Mathematics," Frizer interrupted, with a careless wave of his hand. "A dull business. Don't spare it a thought. I don't."

Woodleff, broke and desperate, had no choice, and Frizer knew it. He could almost taste success as Woodleff took the pen Nick offered, peering at the contract. Fifty pounds. And Lucifer himself couldn't keep up with the diabolical schedule of interest Nick calculated, the little Cambridge devil. Those fifty pounds would swell to sixty, eighty, a hundred. Frizer could live like a king on that. He closed his eyes, imagining it.

The door opened, and Woodleff dropped the pen like a poisonous snake. Frizer jumped up, hand traveling to the knife at his hip. Leaning against the doorjamb, Robert Poley regarded the trio with the barest hint of a smile.

Frizer's hand did not leave his hip. He might still stab this man before the day was out.

It had been nearly a decade since Robert Poley first crossed his path, back when Frizer made his living in the illegal boxing matches that kept money flowing in Southwark. He'd been a sure bet back then, penniless and twenty-two and happy enough to adjust the shape of another man's nose if it put food in his belly another night. He'd made Poley a comfortable sum the night they'd met, knocking out a fellow against five-to-one odds, and since then they'd struck up an occasional partnership. Frizer knew Poley's business. From time to time, he'd delivered messages and carefully balanced threats to one of Poley's enemies: a skill he'd honed over the years, and one he was well paid for. But that didn't mean he was happy to see the man, or that satisfied smirk, or the panic in Andrew Woodleff's eyes.

"Apologies, Ingram," Poley drawled. "I didn't realize you had company."

"What are you doing here?" Frizer said.

Woodleff glanced from Frizer to Poley, then back to Frizer. "Gentlemen," he stammered. "I've just remembered an appointment I need to keep."

In his haste to descend the stairs, he knocked against the scullery maid, who stood out of breath on the landing.

"I told him, Master Frizer, I said you weren't to be disturbed, but he wouldn't—"

Frizer's chest flamed with anger. He flung one arm wide, finger quivering toward the door. "Out."

The maid dropped a curtsey and beat a hasty retreat. Frizer slammed the door behind her. Poley stood not two feet away, that half smile firmly in place.

"God's death, Poley," Frizer said. He shoved Poley in the chest with both hands, to insult rather than injure. "We had him for fifty pounds. Fifty pounds and half his estate. You couldn't have waited ten minutes?"

"Ingram, don't think I'm not sympathetic," Poley said. "It's just that, speaking as your friend, I don't care."

"We aren't friends, Poley." Frizer flung himself back into the chair, still seething. Fifty pounds. Christ on high. No matter what Poley wanted, it wouldn't pay fifty pounds. "You don't have friends."

"No," Poley said. "That's true, I don't."

This preening peacock. The audacity of him. "Can't you take care of yourself for an hour at a go?" Frizer snarled. "You need a whipping boy for a scrape you got yourself in, look somewhere else. I'm not yours to come when you call."

"Don't flatter yourself, Ingram," Poley said. "I'm not here for you." And to Frizer's total shock, Poley shifted in his chair to face Nick.

Nick gaped. It was the second time in recent memory his expression had mirrored Frizer's exactly. "Me?" Nick said.

"You," Poley said smoothly. "Robert Poley, by the by. An occasional associate of your partner here, though it seems he hasn't mentioned me."

Nick stared. It reinforced Frizer's belief that his partner, though excellent with compound interest, was not terribly bright. "How did you know my—"

Poley swept over and sat in Woodleff's recently abandoned chair. "Knowing things is my profession. And it's not every day we find a genuine Cambridge graduate in our midst," he added, taking a savage sort of pleasure in Nick's shock. "Not your lot's usual social sphere. I understand it was the gambling debts that ruined you?"

Nick flushed to his hairline and said nothing.

Poley smirked. "I thought as much. I think the Cambridge term for your new profession is 'cruel irony.'"

Frizer pressed a fist to his mouth, folding the other arm across his chest. It was Poley all over, this playing with men's fears, but that didn't make it less irritating. Nick quaked to the worn soles of his boots. He wasn't cut out for this. Frizer was. He felt at home with the criminals and mountebanks roaming Bankside and the Strand, men who had killed and would kill again. It felt more honest than working for Cecil. Cruel as cats, the queen's agents, toying with their prey before they broke its neck. It had never been Frizer's way. Say what you wanted, take it with your fists, and be done.

"What do you want?" Nick asked. It came out like a whine, which caused him to flush deeper.

"Information," Poley said simply, folding one leg over the other.

"What kind of information?" Frizer said, trying to take charge before this turned sour. Nick couldn't tell a matter of royal intelligence from a Bankside bearbaiting. God's bones, Frizer barely trusted Nick to speak to marks, let alone this.

But Nick silenced Frizer with a curt gesture. He looked braver than Frizer had ever seen him, though admittedly the bar wasn't high. "You'll pay for that information?"

Poley grinned. "Of course."

"Then ask away."

Anxiety did not make Frizer agreeable. "You'll pay us fifty pounds, will you, for what you've—"

"Ingram," Poley said, "for once in your life, be quiet and listen." He slouched in his chair, one arm draped over the back. "Right, Nick. To it, then. Do you know a man named Christopher Marlowe?"

Frizer frowned. Marlowe? Christ. So Poley was running after poets now. From the queen of Scotland to the prince of Bankside. How the mighty fall.

Nick laughed, half surprise and half amusement. "Kit? Hell. Yes, I knew him."

"You do?" Frizer said, rounding to stare at Nick.

Nick pursed his lips. "I know people who aren't you, Ingram."

Irritated, Frizer waved a hand, gesturing for Poley to continue. What did it matter, if Nick knew more about the world than Frizer thought? He could hardly have known less.

"I wonder if you know how Marlowe leans," Poley said, nodding at Nick.

"Leans?"

"Politically. Religiously. Socially. Anything you like."

A good job no one ever approached Nick Skeres for a career in intelligence. His thoughts played clear in his eyes. Nick knew Marlowe, though God knew how. Schoolmates, maybe—Marlowe was said to be a Cambridge man—though it sounded like "friends" would be stretching matters. And Nick knew something that could hurt him. Frizer saw the moment Nick decided he didn't care. He could follow the thoughts as if they were his own. Marlowe, lording his poetic celebrity over London, while Nick scraped out half a living as a bondsman in the suburbs. In some cases, betrayal made good business sense. Frizer had worked hard to teach Nick that lesson.

"We never discussed politics," Nick said, "but he was reckless, wild, even then. Nothing seemed to matter to him."

Poley nodded. "Hasn't changed much, I see. Still dancing his way out of choosing a side."

Nick looked between Poley and Frizer. "Side?"

Poley laughed as if Nick had told a clever joke. "Your old school friend Marlowe is one of the queen's best spies, Nick. And your business partner here has been helping me with the rougher parts of that work for years."

The idea that Christopher Marlowe might be a spy for the queen was a shock to Frizer, but nothing like the thunderclap it seemed to be for Nick. He wasn't sure which revelation surprised Nick more: that a rogue like Marlowe could be trusted with state secrets, or that a petty criminal like Frizer could. But Nick recovered fast. The next words out of his mouth were confident, as if he'd belonged in this world all his life.

"If you're asking if I think he'd betray the crown, I'm certain he would."

Poley folded his hands, resting them on his taut belly. "And what makes you think that?"

"He's a liar and an atheist and a thief," Nick said with a laugh, as if he'd waited years to say it. "Do you trust a man like that to know right from wrong?"

Frizer saw hunger flash in Poley's eyes and knew at once where it came from. Atheism was a heavy charge. Valuable leverage, if a man without scruples could get his hands on it.

"You're certain?" Poley said.

Nick's congealed bitterness had started to flow. He leaned forward, gesturing broadly as if drunk. He couldn't seem to stop talking. "He told me Christ and John the Evangelist fucked each other six ways to Sunday after the Last Supper. That while Joseph was out whoring in Nazareth, the Virgin Mary met a neighbor's cock and not the Holy Spirit. Shall I go on?"

Poley raised a finger. He snatched Nick's ledger and flipped to a new page, on which he began to scribble, blotting lines across the grid. "Say that again," he said. "Christ and John the Evangelist?"

"The disciple Jesus loved, he said."

Poley laughed. "God above. It's Christmas for Baines."

"Poley, what does any of that matter?" Frizer said.

"He's a traitor, Ingram," Poley said, still writing. "When you want to get rid of a traitor, you take anything you can get."

Frizer glanced over Poley's shoulder. Poley shuffled Nick's words as he wrote, shifting the syntax, extemporizing wildly when needed. *Regarding the damnable beliefs of Christopher Marlowe . . . That Christ was a bastard and his mother dishonest . . . That Saint John used Christ like the sinners of Sodom . . .* Perhaps Poley ought to have gone after a career in the theater himself. He certainly knew how to turn a phrase.

"What do you mean," Nick said, watching Poley's flowing pen, "when you say 'get rid of'?"

Frizer closed his eyes. "What," he said, "do you think he means?"

The panic in Nick's voice was almost laughable. "What if I take back what I've said? What if I—"

"Nick, my good man," Poley said, scribbling down a final word and tearing the page from the book, "you could say nothing else and this business would have your name all over it."

Frizer pressed two fingers to the bridge of his nose, considering. Marlowe's arrest meant nothing to him, just another unfortunate soul who'd fallen afoul of Robert Poley's ruthless drive to cut away his competition. And where Poley needed help, Frizer saw his opportunity. He could show Cecil that Ingram Frizer was worth more than the occasional threatening word and right hook in a tavern fight. He could earn a regular commission from Cecil, the same as Poley did, and turn his back on this filthy business once and for all. Live respectably, or close to it. The life of one stranger was worth that. He'd have damned fifty for it.

"You'll need more than that to make a case," Frizer said. "Confirmation. From someone who knew him recently."

Poley smirked. "One step ahead of you there."

Well, let him think so. Poley was used to this business, but Frizer planned his moves three steps ahead. You didn't live long south of the river otherwise.

"Who's your man?" Frizer asked.

"Marlowe lived with a man in Shoreditch," Poley said. "A scrivener, part-time actor, something of a poet. Thomas Kyd. You know him?"

Nick paled, but Frizer ignored this. If the man wanted to make his living in this world, he'd need a stronger stomach.

"No," Frizer said, "but I'm happy to meet him."

"He should have something to say, at least," Poley said.

"I think he will," Frizer said, smiling. "I'm persuasive."

Forty-Five

London's seven gates shut and locked at sundown. Once darkness fell, citizens were left to the authority of night watchmen, non-Londoners to fend for themselves beyond the walls. Past midnight, then, was not the ideal time to make this journey so far from Gregory's home near Aldgate. But city curfew had never stopped him before.

The boatman waited for him at the jetty off Thames Street, the only ferryman still on the water at this hour. Gregory had used this fellow before, when business took him afield late at night. Always good to know a scoundrel with a boat who needed money. Gregory clambered in and passed the man a purse that sounded as heavy as it was.

"Deptford dockyard," he said. His voice reached the boatman's ear and not an inch farther.

The boatman nodded and pushed off into the Thames.

London felt macabre this late at night, as if it wasn't meant to be seen after sundown. The moon reflected seamlessly in the black river, unbroken by light save from the boatman's lantern, unbroken by sound save from the waves rippling along the banks. South of the water, Gregory saw the dingy walls of the playhouses, dark smudges against the darker night. He shook his head, setting his eyes instead on the lantern, its narrow light barely illuminating what came before him.

Now was not the time for this. He was being sentimental enough as it was.

Arthur Gregory was an agent of the queen. That responsibility wasn't one to throw away lightly. And for many—for most—it wasn't one that lasted long. Few but Gregory could boast a tenure of more than two decades. Keep queen and country safe, and stay alive doing it. That was a job he could do under any administration. Nothing at all had changed, in that respect.

Some things, though, had changed.

He closed his eyes, but he still saw the figures that haunted him, clearer now if anything. Marlowe back at Cambridge, sharp-eyed and weak as a starved dog, with all the infuriating self-confidence of twenty-one and more skill to back it up than a spy with twice his experience. Unraveling Mary Stuart's plots, earning Lord Strange's confidence. Baines and Poley, in a Whitehall alcove, like rats scrapping for a mouthful. Both men looking up, catching Gregory's eye, and falling silent at once. The slick curve of Poley's smile. Thomas Watson, sick and pale and near dying in Newgate, taking Marlowe's letter from Gregory's hand, and the way he'd said the boy's name, *Kit*, the name of a friend, as if it meant something.

Gregory knew the danger Marlowe courted, knew what Cecil and his men didn't say when they spoke of *the resolution*, or *curtailment of risk*. But in this business, it was every man in charge of his own soul. It had to be. No surviving otherwise. No safety in allegiance to anyone but the crown, not when allegiance looked like treason in the wrong light. In doing even this much, he was doing more than any reasonable person could have expected. He couldn't do more.

He could have spoken to Marlowe directly, could have turned up at his lodgings with money for passage to France and driven him onto the ship at knifepoint, could have—

He was doing what he could, he thought, as the boatman tossed out a rope and secured his craft to the dock. The ghosts of half-built ships loomed above and around, timbers creaking in the soft wind. As Gregory stood, his not-inconsiderable bulk caused the boat to sway like an Eastcheap drunk. He climbed onto the dock, leaving the boatman to glare.

"Am I to wait?" the man asked.

"I won't be long."

"Another shilling for my trouble, at least."

Gregory scoffed and tossed the man a rude gesture. "I'll douse you in the river for your trouble," he said. "You've been overpaid already."

He crossed the dock with confidence, or at least with speed. After dark in this neighborhood, it didn't do to tarry, but a fellow with business could usually count on being left to his own devices. Masts without sails creaked around him, a forest halfway between sea and sky. Soon, the timbers faded, replaced by darkened buildings and streets smelling of fish and piss. There was something comforting in that vulgarity, something intimate. It was hardly his first time here.

Gregory had only pounded twice on the tavern door before Eleanor Bull yanked it open with death in her eyes. It was late, he supposed. And in this suburb, surprises late at night rarely ended in good news, least of all for a widow who must have made a fair number of enemies. The owner of the Bull and Boar wore a heavy shawl over a nightgown, but from her sharp eyes and the lingering smell of sherry, Gregory knew she hadn't been in bed. She held a candle in one hand, which underlit her strangely beneath the chin.

"Good evening, Mistress Bull," he said.

She tried to shut the door in his face, but she was a slightly drunk middle-aged woman and he had once thrown a man through a second-story window. He caught the door in one hand and forced it open, stepping into the tavern's front room.

"My thanks for the warm welcome," he said. "But I can't stay long."

"Have you any idea what time it is?" Eleanor snapped the door shut behind him. Neither the movement nor the words made enough noise to carry up the stairs, Gregory noted with distant approval. A shame neither Walsingham nor Cecil had gone in for hiring women. A natural talent. They could have used someone like this.

"Past one, I think," he said. "So the polite thing would be to offer me a chair."

She folded her arms and stood firm. He sighed, then crossed to the corner table. Like all the others, its chairs rested on it upside down so Eleanor's boys could sweep. He took one down in each hand and sat with something more than his usual irritation. She set her candle on the table but made no move to join him. Gregory, unperturbed, kicked his feet up on the other chair. His heel caught the table leg, causing the candle to waver, shuddering the light. He cracked his right knuckles with his left palm. It was a nervous habit, not a threat, but if Eleanor flinched at the sound, there were worse outcomes.

"You'll have visitors tomorrow, Mistress Bull," Gregory said.

Eleanor laughed. "I run a public house, Master Gregory. Visitors are my trade."

"Visitors of my sort."

At this, Eleanor shoved his feet aside and sat down.

"They'll want the private room upstairs," Gregory said. "To meet a man. But their sort of business, you don't want any part of it."

The flash of shock that had crossed her face was gone now. In the unstable candlelight, he couldn't tell if she was afraid or eager. "They'll pay, I expect?"

"Not enough. When they come round tomorrow to ask you, say yes if you like. I know what you risk by saying no. But you warn that man, when he comes. You tell him it's not safe. You tell him to run and never come back. Understood?"

He reached into his pocket and produced a second purse. It rang like a plague bell as he dropped it on the table. Her eyes flicked across the gold inside—it was gold, of course, none of the cheap silver with which he'd placated the boatman. Gregory had no doubt Eleanor tallied its contents at a glance, and even less doubt that her figure was accurate.

"A widow's life is precarious, Master Gregory," Eleanor said. "Vulnerable to all kinds of accidents. You understand, I need to watch out for me and mine."

"This isn't a bargain you want to make," Gregory said sharply. He stood, towering above her. Even when she stood in turn, that didn't change. "A man's life depends on it. Whatever they offer, remember they're asking your soul in return."

"And a soul is a precious thing," she said.

"You understand me?"

"Quite. It's always a pleasure to see you, Master Gregory." In a moment, Gregory's purse had disappeared, and even he hadn't seen where she put it. "Be careful making your way home. It's after curfew."

Gregory paused. Looking deep into her eyes. Trying to see the soul beneath, if indeed there was one. He came to no conclusion at all.

"Yes," he said finally. "I will. Remember your duty, Mistress Bull."

"I always do," she said, watching him go.

The boatman was still waiting at the dock. Money made anyone loyal, Gregory thought, climbing back in. A precept he'd once believed, and wanted to believe again.

He'd done everything he could do. Cecil would have Marlowe's lodgings under surveillance, ears pricked for any hint that events might not unfold according to plan. One late-night visit and Cecil would know Gregory had thwarted the meeting—aided and abetted a traitor—and soon the hangman would be readying two nooses instead of one. A man who valued his own life above all couldn't do more than what Gregory had done.

And while Gregory would sacrifice many things for what he believed in, he would not sacrifice his life.

As the unstable boat fought the current toward London proper, the water dragging velvet fingers against the prow, Gregory closed his eyes and crossed himself. He hadn't prayed properly in years, but it was late, and the city was dark, and it was the sort of night a man wanted God on his side.

"Good luck, you blasted idiot," he murmured to the river.

"What?" the boatman said.

Gregory shook his head. "Nothing."

Forty-Six

Night stretched across the Fleet. The moonless sky hung with matte stars, cold and distant, the May air motionless. They lay together, Tom with his head on Kit's bare shoulder. Kit looked up at the ceiling, the blanket slung across his hips, silent. Without the shimmer of moonlight, his face looked paler than Tom remembered. The room's shadows seemed to pool beneath his eyes.

This was all Tom had ever wanted: to be close to Kit. During their careful years of living apart, the long months Kit spent in Mary Stuart's service, even those cold months in Newgate—those months he would not think about, not tonight—even when he'd hated Kit the most, his thoughts had always come back to this. Having Kit here, always here in bed beside him, the taste of their kiss on his lips.

Listening to Kit's soft breathing, he realized he should have known better. Though Kit's touch had been tender that night, it came with new hesitation. As if he feared moving too fast would make Tom disappear, like a dream shattered by a dog's bark in the distance. They could never just be alone together, the two of them. There was always something else.

Tom kissed the hollow of Kit's collarbone. "Are you all right?"

Kit paused. "No." He didn't look away from the ceiling.

Tom leaned up on one elbow. "You're safe here," he said. "I promise."

God knew what faces Kit saw in the ceiling. "He had Strange killed, Tom. Without even telling me."

This was true. But Kit had given so much to the crown. Kit had risked everything: love, safety, career, happiness, life itself. And Tom, Tom had risked it too. Surely that was enough sacrifice. And if Strange had been eliminated in the end, what did it matter? Wasn't that what they'd asked for?

"What can I do?" Tom said.

Kit closed his eyes. From his tone, he might have addressed the inside of his eyelids. "Just don't leave. Not tonight."

Tom winced. It would have been easier to hear Kit talk this way if he couldn't remember Cambridge. If he couldn't remember Bankside, spilling into London's streets drunk on poetic triumph. If he couldn't remember the Kit who laughed without fear, who made the darkness sing with threats of erotic sonnets. Miles removed, now, from this pale, quiet man who jumped at shadows.

"I'm not leaving," Tom said. "I live here," he added, after a pause.

Tom didn't believe Kit's laugh as they sat up, first Kit and then Tom a beat later. The blanket slipped down to Kit's waist, revealing his chest, the curve of his hipbones. Tom couldn't remember when Kit had become so thin.

"Do you think I'm damned, Tom?" he asked, as if he'd been thinking of nothing else.

There was no good answer to that question. If he said no, Kit would call him a liar. If he said yes, he would be lying. "You don't believe in hell," he said at last.

"That's not what I asked." Kit's voice rose, magnified by the dark. He spoke too fast, his spine too straight. Even as they sat close enough to feel the ghost of the other's breath, Tom felt Kit leave him. He saw the flash in Kit's eyes, heard the soft crack in his words, and knew he had gone, but didn't know where. Somewhere he couldn't follow. "Heaven, all right, heaven's a lie, but hell, Tom, sometimes I think I'm wrong, not about all of it, but about that, and what I've done, Tom, what I've done to—"

"Kit," Tom said, the word like a slap. "Stop." His hand moved to take Kit's, pressed that cold hand against his own cheek. "Stay with me. Here. With me."

Kit's breath caught. Not a gasp, but a jerk awake. At least night-mares gave the comfort of sleep first. Not like this, raw, the panic of imagination rolling into the panic of waking life without a breath of peace in between.

Tom didn't know how much longer he could do this.

He didn't know how to do anything else.

Kit looked down at the scars ringing his wrists. They had healed after his return from the Low Countries, but a tangled mess of white ridges remained. God, what they'd become. Two men shy of thirty, scarred and scared and hunted. Kit's hair streaked with gray, deep shadows always under his eyes. Tom, closing his eyes to see Evan Lloyd's neck snap on the gallows, the twitch of his feet. Perhaps they'd always be like this. Perhaps there'd never been another way.

Tom loved Kit so much it frightened him. He wished the fact meant more, that it changed anything.

He brought a hand to Kit's chin, softly guiding him to look up. He smiled, as best he knew how, and let his hand brush Kit's cheek, to cup his head and bring him closer. They kissed, and Tom clung to it, fighting to shut out the world. The only fight worth winning. Only this. This feeling, Kit's lips against his, the faint trembling sense that neither of them could let go, that if they let go, the other would fall. Not an embrace but a shipwreck, hanging on against the waves.

They lingered there, close enough that Tom felt Kit's heartbeat like his own. Janus's two faces reversed, nose to nose and not back to back, keeping the present trapped in the breath between them.

"I'm sorry," Kit said. "It's worse at night."

"You say that." Tom traced the ring of scars on Kit's wrist with his thumb. "But it's the same in the morning."

The offer occurred to him, though he knew even then it wouldn't help. But he had to try something. He couldn't sit here helpless, not while he felt Kit drifting, far away, impossibly far. And it had been the only thing that helped him, these weeks and months since Newgate, the only place that could block out the memories for an hour at a time.

"Come to church with me," Tom said. "Sunday. It—"

"Church?" Kit repeated with a laugh, as Tom had known he would. "Of course. Should I start with confession? They'll drag me to hell from the pews."

Tom flushed. "Don't be dramatic. They canonized Paul, and he went about stoning people."

Kit shook his head. "Tom. Don't. God's a lie, I'm a murderer, and the other end of prayer is the devil, mocking me." He laughed and flung himself back against the bed, landing with a soft thump to gaze again at the ceiling. "And you wonder why I dream."

Tom rested his head in the space between the halves of Kit's ribcage. It felt like home still, despite everything. "Get some sleep," he said. "Remember what tomorrow is."

"Wednesday?"

Never too dark or too late for Kit to revel in missing the point. "Yes, Wednesday. When *Faustus* opens."

Kit raked his fingers backward through his hair. "Ah, Christ. That's tomorrow."

Tom hadn't read a word of *Doctor Faustus*, though he'd heard Kit rage against the censor, watched him stay awake long into the night, lit by the flickering orange of a dying candle, blotting eight lines of every ten. God knew what he'd bring to the Rose tomorrow.

"I can't go," Kit said.

Tom frowned. That wasn't like Kit. The first time *The Jew of Malta* took the stage, yes, Kit had thrown up behind the theater from nerves, but then he shoved his way to the front of the pit, to get the best possible view. "Why not?"

"Henslowe will run it all summer," Kit said. "My name makes him money. I have time."

"Why not?" Tom said again.

Kit sighed. "I have an appointment."

Tom shifted onto his side to look at him. When Kit made appointments, he disappeared for months and came back haunted, half-healed scars whittled into his wrists, meeting strangers at the scaffold.

Kit smiled. It was the most open Tom had seen him in days. The most like his old self. Tom knew at once that he was lying. "It's not like that," Kit said. "I'm only going to Deptford. Deliver a report, get shouted at by Robert Poley, come home. I'll be back before dark."

Tom wanted to believe that. But even if Kit wouldn't tell him the truth, there was nothing he could do. Secrets were woven into the fabric of them now. Look what happened the last time he demanded the truth. He could only pretend it didn't hurt, which was impossible, and love Kit, which was the simplest thing in the world.

"Just try to sleep tonight." Tom brushed Kit's hair off his forehead, then, smiling at the shameless way Kit leaned into his touch, kissed the hollow of his throat. Kit's breath caught. The simplest thing in the world. "Unless you'd rather pass the time some other way."

"You have a case in the morning," Kit said. *Yes*, said the faint strain in his voice.

"And you have an appointment," Tom said, his voice a low purr beneath Kit's ear. Kit's breathing rasped with longing. Nothing mattered but that, this familiar hunger, and the press of Kit's body yearning against his own. "But I care more about this."

Forty-Seven

Kit didn't remember falling asleep. He remembered Tom's body, warm and familiar in the dark, Tom's gentle touch, the wave of pleasure that silenced his thoughts. He remembered the soft glow of after, Tom stroking Kit's hair, Kit lazily bathing him with kisses, tasting the salt of Tom's sweat sharp on his tongue. Relaxed, for the first time in weeks. And then hours passed, hours he didn't remember losing, leaving him foggy, with Tom nudging him awake. Tom's beauty was agonizing in the golden hour of morning. Blurred through a slight haze, the sunrise cast a sort of corona around his edges. Almost enough to make Kit consider waking with the sun more often, for more mornings like this.

"I'm off." Tom's voice was rough, unused for hours.

Kit stretched and snaked out of bed. Tom had dressed for the courts, while Kit wore nothing but a worn pair of breeches, but that didn't matter. The light shifted as he moved, and Tom looked ordinary again, human.

"I'll be at the Rose this afternoon," Tom said. "After my case. If you change your mind."

Kit's mind wasn't his to change. "Tell me how it goes," he said.

"Of course." Tom twined an arm around Kit's waist, pulling him closer. "I'll give you a glowing report of your own genius."

"Scene by scene."

"Line by line, you arrogant disaster," Tom said, smiling. "Be careful today."

"Aren't I always?"

Tom's eyebrows arched skyward. "You're lucky I love you."

Kit said nothing. After the night before, words evaded him. He had nothing to say, nothing but *I love you*, which even in his mind felt pathetic. *I love you*. As if that were ever enough. He'd have words again that night, after the play, after all this. It didn't matter if he couldn't find them now.

They kissed, soft and brief, like the dregs of a dream.

Tom ran the pad of his thumb along the bow of Kit's lips, then gave a boyish smile. "I'll be back tonight," he said, kissed him once more like a door closing, and slipped into the hall.

Kit heard his footfalls on the stairs. Heard him exchange empty words with the landlady, rendered unintelligible by the two floors between them. Heard the building's door snap shut. He stood motionless, feeling more tired and lost than before he'd slept. He glanced at the hearth, where the ashes of a recent unsigned letter rested against the stone.

The Bull and Boar. Deptford Strand. Wednesday at ten. Come alone.

The ashes rippled with his movement as he paced to the window. He watched Tom, below, merging with the crowd until he disappeared down an alley toward Temple Bar. Kit turned and reached for a shirt, as the morning light wiped the heel of its palm across the room's shadows and smudged them into day.

Deptford. Very well, then.

Forty-Eight

I t would rain soon. Eleanor Bull could tell.

So close to the river, dotted with ships waiting to sail for Gravesend and to sea, Deptford's business swelled and ebbed with the sky. She could feel the thick, damp air in her bones, and in the rhythm of the dockhands drifting through the tavern. Outside, the river reflected metallic sheets of cloud. As Eleanor scrubbed at a sticky smudge of beer on a back table, she could hear the dull rumble of thunder, a faint thrumming somewhere far off. It would rain soon, and a crush of sailors would flee the river to her house, to drink and curse and brawl and wait out the storm. She sighed, tired at the thought. Bad form to curse God for too much business, though. And she'd take the custom of anyone who could pay.

The best way to do business. Palm open, eyes closed.

She repeated the thought as the door opened. The salt smell of fish and rotting timber crept in at the man's heels, with the musk of clouds about to burst. She abandoned the table, staring. The man looked back, aware of being stared at.

From the way they'd carried on, those smooth-smiling fellows from Whitehall, she'd expected their man to be the devil himself. But this fellow was nothing. This small, slim man with gray-flecked brown hair and that easy, catlike way of moving, dressed poorly as any sailor dropped from a French ship. Gregory must be going soft in his old age. Five years ago he'd have recognized a losing cause when he saw one. Five years ago he'd have remembered how easy it was to outbid a single man.

Spotting her across the room, the young man approached, drifting more than walking. The sailors' eyes slid over him unseeing. The kind of face no one remembered. The kind of man prone to disappearances.

"Marlowe?" she said.

He nodded without a word.

"They're waiting upstairs," Eleanor said, gesturing with the rag. "The private room. You need anything, come find me," she added, though she didn't know why. She wiped both hands on her apron. Her fingers brushed against the curve of a gold sovereign, which she'd left there in the pocket, as a reminder.

The man turned. "Thank you."

Eleanor watched as he disappeared to the floor above. Then she turned back to the stain on the table, scrubbing until her elbow ached.

Palm open, eyes closed, after all.

———

Standing in the pit at the Rose, Tom took another half step back. When the play began, he'd been one row of bodies away from the boards. Tom could have touched Ned Alleyn's boot as he strode onstage, book in hand, to deliver his opening speech. By now, Tom stood nearly in the street. He couldn't bear being closer. It was like standing inside Kit's mind.

So these were his monsters in the ceiling.

So this was why Kit screamed in his sleep.

"It strikes!" cried Ned onstage—cried Faustus in Wittenberg. "Now, body, turn to air, or Lucifer will bear thee quick to hell." He sank to his knees, began to raise his hands in prayer, then let them fall heavy to his sides. Useless. Prayer offered nothing now.

The Rose echoed with the sound of a tolling bell, unseen and everywhere.

One.

Two.

————

Kit had found himself among strange combinations of people before, but never a trio quite like this. He stepped inside the Bull and Boar's private room, trying to make sense of the group waiting for him.

Robert Poley, well-dressed and smirking, seated at the table, where an ignored game of backgammon had been set. A man Kit didn't recognize, dressed with the cheap flash of a Southwark native, tawny hair streaming, rangy limbs sprawling from the chair. And the third, a copper-haired man who'd been standing at the window with his back to the door, and who, as Kit entered, turned.

For a long moment, Kit was certain he'd lost his mind.

Poley he'd expected. The second fellow was a shock—if Poley was enlisting fresh faces from the seedier parts of the city, it couldn't spell anything good. But there was no explanation on earth or in hell for what brought Nick Skeres to Deptford.

"Nick?" Kit said, laughing, not because it was funny, but because his mind didn't know what else to do. Nick Skeres, arrogant, privileged Nick, holed up in Deptford with the queen's spies? Nick belonged in some country estate, doing whatever people with money did. Not with men like these. Or, for that matter, with men like Kit.

Nick moved to sit at the edge of the bed. "You sound surprised," he said.

"You don't sound surprised enough," Kit said.

"We keep the same circles, it seems."

No one kept the circles Kit kept. Even as he spoke, Nick wouldn't meet Kit's eyes. Instead, he looked intently at his hands clasped between his knees, as if expecting them to do something more interesting than continue to be hands.

"Well, this is a charming reunion," the tawny-haired man cut in.

Kit turned around to face the other two, heart humming. He

couldn't afford to be distracted, not even by Nick. Poley wasn't a man you turned your back on. Neither was this new fellow, who carried on seeming comfortable as anything, watching the scene with mild interest.

"Kit Marlowe," Kit said to the stranger with a pointed nod. "Though I imagine you knew that already."

"Who among us doesn't know the morning star of Bankside?" the man said smoothly. "Ingram Frizer. Friend of both your fellows here. An honor, really."

Kit wiped his palms against his breeches, then took a vacant chair and edged it back, widening the distance between himself and Frizer. The duration of his acquaintance with this man could be counted in seconds, but there was something about Ingram Frizer that made him want to keep three arms' lengths away. "Right. You don't mind if I smoke, do you?"

"By all means," Frizer said. "Make yourself comfortable."

One more reason tobacco was God's incense. Filling and lighting a pipe kept Kit's hands occupied and his face impassive. Every public house worth its salt had the accoutrements on hand now, for which he had the glamour surrounding Sir Walter Raleigh to thank. Frizer filled a pipe of his own, raising the lit bowl in a wry toast. Kit inhaled, willing the tobacco to soothe his nerves. Though it always had before, it wouldn't now.

"What can I do for you?" Kit said, words cool through the smoke.

"Rushing into business so quickly?" Poley said with enough condescension to choke on. "Take your time. No need to be common."

Common. The word touched something painful in Kit's consciousness, a bruise he'd thought had healed. Maybe it wasn't so surprising Nick had fallen into Poley's company.

"Shall I call for a drink?" Poley asked, glancing toward the door Kit had left open.

"If you like." Kit shrugged. "I don't drink while working."

Poley laughed. "Never took you for a sober fellow. As you like.

354 + A TIP FOR THE HANGMAN

A glass for the rest of us." He rose and stuck his head out the door. "Francis!" he shouted.

Kit flinched, startled by the strength of Poley's voice. Nick jumped halfway out of his skin.

Francis—the tapster, presumably—did not materialize, but Kit heard movement below. He took another pull from his pipe, letting his fingers brush the knife handle against his hip. A trail of smoke stretched toward the ceiling and out, splaying tendrils against the closed window before turning back into the room.

A spy, a criminal, and a Cambridge graduate. Kit's mind spun, trying to work out the point at which those three spheres could intersect.

You, said a voice in Kit's head. It's you.

———

Three.

As if summoned, masked men, hands and arms and faces smeared with soot and filth from the river, flowed onstage. Their arms stretched for Faustus, who knelt with his back to them. In one of the demons, Tom could make out Will's dark hair and raven eyes through the grime. Even so, he shivered. A dozen devils stood onstage, borrowing the form of Will Shakespeare or not.

Four.

———

"Forgive the question," Kit said. "But do you three know each other?"

Frizer smiled. A leonine smile, and one Kit did not trust. "Your master made introductions."

That mockery in Frizer's voice sent a thrill of alarm through Kit. He hadn't been this edgy since Flushing—playing both sides, each while the other looked on. Frizer took up a backgammon piece and turned it between his forefinger and thumb, a banker checking a coin for authenticity. Kit watched Frizer's hands. It still seemed unwise to look away from them.

"Ah!" Poley turned to the door as a boy entered with a bottle and glasses. "Excellent. Thank you, Francis."

The boy set his burden on the table. Nervous, he knocked against Kit's shoulder as he passed. Kit felt the nudge like a shock through his chest. The boy stammered out an apology, keeping his shamed gaze on the floor. Kit focused on his breath and shook his head. Don't apologize. It's nothing. Frizer beckoned the boy closer with a crooked finger and slipped a shilling into his palm. An exorbitant payment for carrying a bottle upstairs, but the boy didn't protest the extravagance. When the boy left, he shut the door behind him. Kit heard a key turn in the lock.

Not until then did he feel the hollow against his thigh where his knife should have rested. In the same moment, he saw Frizer slip something into the pocket of his doublet.

Kit sat up straighter. A pickpocket, and a child at that. He had to be better than this. He draped one arm over the back of the chair, circling the bowl of his pipe with the other thumb. He hoped it looked insolent, relaxed. Unafraid. He was a writer, not an actor, but Christ, the stakes for this performance were high.

Poley poured out three glasses of sack. He tilted an empty one in Kit's direction, then shrugged as Kit shook his head. Nick drew up a chair and joined them, a nervous phantom at the edge of the quartet. Kit didn't look at him. One threat at a time.

"So," Kit said to Frizer, taking too deep a pull on the pipe, "you've been working with Master Poley here, I take it."

Frizer grinned. "We've a bit of a history. Robert usually calls me in for the dirtier parts of the business, but circumstances change. He's coming to see the full range of my talents."

Kit felt the loss of his knife like the severing of a limb. "And you?" he said, turning to Nick. "Something happen to your circumstances too?"

Kit had seen that smirk spread across Poley's face before. "It's fair to say he's become useful," Poley said.

"Information is my trade, Poley," Kit said, his words brittle, "the same as yours. I'd appreciate some at this point."

"So would I," Poley said.

Kit would not ask Poley to clarify. If they wanted him to understand, that was their responsibility.

Poley, receiving no response, sighed and took a long drink. "Cecil's unable to take your report tomorrow," he said. "Busy man, you understand. Indisposed. Deliver it to us, and we'll convey it to him."

Kit wasn't fooled for a moment. The list of Cecil's responsibilities was endless, but no man was that busy. Still, Cecil was an arrogant bastard, and that was Kit's saving grace. The spymaster would never relinquish command to a slick peacock like Robert Poley and a slippery swindler like Ingram Frizer. And down-on-his-luck Cambridge scholar Nick Skeres? Not likely. No, if Cecil decided Kit's risk outweighed his reward, he would deal with it in person.

This was another test, Kit decided, drawing confidence from the thought. Gathering other opinions of his trustworthiness. It helped to explain this motley crew of inquisitors. Three men who could judge Kit in three walks of life: the spy, the scholar, the Bankside rat. Three men who could tell when he was lying. Who could tell when he was afraid.

Kit swallowed. The hand holding his pipe trembled.

But he was a poet and a spy. Hard to conjure a pair of professions better suited to lying.

"Of course," Kit said—his smile, at least, was steady. "Stop me if you need context," he added wryly, to Nick.

He spoke easily and without strain. He'd learned nothing in the past week that would be of use to Cecil, not since Anne's rejection. But the longer he spoke—the more forthcoming he appeared—the higher his value, and the better his odds. He told them everything, repeating information he'd given Cecil weeks ago, hazarding speculations, sketching motives. A poet to the core, spinning out stories and the thread of his life for a little longer.

Kit had no idea how long he spoke. His nerves made time

feel unreal. If food could mark the passage of a day, they talked through the full bottle of sack and a pork-and-rabbit pie brought by Francis, who would not meet Kit's gaze and locked them back in as he left. Kit, for his part, had no appetite. He ate nothing, drank nothing, smoked a great deal.

"Impressive," Frizer said, as Kit finished. He had taken Kit's knife from his pocket and cleaned his fingernails with it, flicking out small specks of dirt. "All that without notes? Your memory must be a thing of beauty."

"Infinite riches in a little room," Kit said, tapping his temple. "Part of the trade."

"True enough," Poley said, draining his glass.

Kit set down his pipe, empty now, the dregs lightly smoking. "Now then. You've asked your questions. Can I ask one of mine?"

Frizer's smile reflected back in the blade of Kit's knife. "That's your job, isn't it? Asking questions?"

Neither Frizer nor Poley had any reason to give Kit a straight answer about their motives, but there was another person in this room. One Kit thought he could work to his advantage. He turned sideways to look at Nick and leaned forward, hands on his knees. Willing Nick to look up and meet his eyes. This could still end well. This could still all be a test. But for Kit to believe that, Nick had to look at him.

"Nick," he said.

"What?" Nick looked at the floor.

"What did they promise you?" Kit said, gesturing at Frizer and Poley as if they couldn't hear. "Money? Power? Influence? What was it?"

Nick hated Kit, it seemed. Well, Kit hated him too. But they'd been friends once, or if not, closer to that than to other things. If Kit had to trust his life with one of these men, these three men who hated him and couldn't be trusted, he was least afraid of Nick.

"I know his sort," Kit continued, nodding at Poley, when Nick said nothing. His knees were four inches from Nick's. He could have reached out and taken Nick's face in one hand, forced his head up, demanded that Nick look at him. "I know what they can promise. But it isn't worth it. Selling yourself for that."

"Oh, it can be," Poley said. "When the cause is just."

But it was Frizer who stood. Kit's knife hung in his left hand like an extension of his arm.

"And what cause is that?" Kit said.

Frizer grinned. "You."

———

Five.

The demons pressed closer, then parted, allowing their leader, Mephistopheles, to step to the front. Cloaked and masked, Mephistopheles hovered two feet behind Faustus. Tom could read the demon's thoughts—Kit's thoughts—in the set of those shoulders, in the angle of that brow, in the wordless shake of that head.

You signed yourself to me, said the silent Mephistopheles. I warned you, what this would cost. You can't cheat the devil. He's the best artificer and double-dealer, better by far than you.

You can't cheat the devil at his own game.

Six.

———

Kit had held on to hope long after he stopped believing in it. That hope was gone now. He ran his open palm across the top of his now-unarmed thigh. "Me," he said.

Poley draped both arms over the chair back, as comfortable as a country gentleman at his estate. "Strange wasn't the only one who's given Cecil cause to worry," he said. "You've made dangerous connections, you have to know that."

"Are you calling me a traitor?" Kit asked.

Frizer took a step forward. "He's not the only one," he said. "Your friend Tom had plenty to say on the subject. He was a forthcoming fellow, after some convincing."

Tom.

Kit's bones flashed cold. The chair crashed against the floor as he stood. His hands clenched in anticipation of a fight he was destined to lose, but he'd fight it, God damn the world but he'd fight it. He could hardly understand what Frizer said. Tom. Tom would never betray him. Not unless he had no choice. *After some convincing.*

"If you laid a hand on Tom," Kit said, voice shaking, "I swear to the devil I'll kill you."

"Don't worry." Poley dismissed him with a wave of his hand. "His scrivening might suffer a little, but he's fine. Or will be. Most likely."

Kit's knees buckled; he barely caught himself on the table. He could have wept. He wondered, distantly, if he might still. A scrivener. Thomas Kyd. Of course they'd go to him. Poley had been angling toward this for some time, he'd know where Kit had lived, and with whom. And Kit had seen Tom that morning. He wasn't thinking clearly, jumping to idiot conclusions. He couldn't fall apart.

"Your friend was a godsend," Poley went on. "Sang like a starling. Underhand allegiances, heresy, secret meetings with traitors in that dingy little suburban room of yours. And those screams, Marlowe, as each of his fingers broke joint by joint. It's a sound I won't soon forget."

Poley's words thudded into his gut, replacing relief with horror. Jesus. Poor, pathetic, nervous, innocent Thomas Kyd. Interrogated and broken, all for knowing him. Another name lengthening the list of people he'd damned.

Kit turned to Nick, who watched him now with wide, owlish eyes. Nick knew what lay behind Kit's panic. Kit could see him remembering. Three young men in a Cambridge dormitory, air heady with smoke. A blush at a misplaced hand, a wink and a turn away. An offhand comment in a tavern and a broken nose for his trouble. Sounds, drifting through thin walls, when desire made Kit reckless, every moan and gasp and movement perfectly audible. Never a doubt. Not really. Nick had always known.

"Please," Kit said, letting the rest hang.

Don't tell them. Let them do what they will to me. I don't care, not anymore. Don't let them hurt Tom. Anything, anyone else.

Nick nodded. Kit took him at his word. He had to. He had nothing else left.

Francis had locked the door. They were twenty feet off the ground, the window overlooking a hard fall to unforgiving stones. Kit took a step back toward the wall. His heart beat an iambic warning in his ears. *Get out. Get out.* But there was no getting out. Not from this.

Frizer took two steps forward. Kit took another step back. The wall pressed against his shoulders.

"Everything I've done," Kit said, "I've done on Cecil's orders." His voice was oddly level—a saving grace that surprised him. Theater to the end.

"Perhaps," Poley said. He still had not risen. He looked like a spider in the center of a web, winding in the threads. "Perhaps not."

"I'm on your side," Kit said, pleading now.

Frizer's grin revealed every one of his startlingly white teeth. "No one's on anyone's side but their own, Marlowe," he said. "You have to know that by now."

———

Seven.

Faustus shook his head. A disagreement to no one, bargaining with a God who wasn't listening. "I'll burn my books," he whispered.

Behind him, Mephistopheles laughed. Almost like a sigh, a caress. Soft as it was, it carried through the theater, which waited breathless as a tomb.

Faustus looked. Man and demon regarded each other in profile, half of each face shadowed, the other half to the audience. Even partly hidden, Faustus's resigned smile made Tom want to retch. He knew that smile. Ned copied it from life.

"Ah," Faustus said, in quiet recognition, like spotting an old friend. "Mephistopheles."

Eight.

———

One moment the wall was at his back, and the next he was on the floor, breath knocked from lungs, brain reeling from Frizer's blow, the hilt of the knife to his head. He gasped. Drowning. The wood boards pressed against his cheek. He felt the cold pressure of a nail beneath his eye.

Everything moved too fast. Nick stood by the door, behind which no one was listening. No use calling for help. Eleanor Bull, downstairs, scrubbed away at sticky tables, hearing without listening. She knew already.

Animal instinct flooded him. Like he was a child again, wild and reckless, and Frizer a fourteen-year-old brawler in Canterbury streets. Kit fought desperate, fought dirty. Anything went. Anything fair. He felt blood beneath his nails where his fingers raked Frizer's face. Landed a blow, two, heard Frizer howl, bent double. But Poley, moving at last, seized Kit's wrist and twisted backward.

Kit heard himself scream. The crunch through the fog was the bone in his arm breaking.

He crumpled to the ground, clutching the shattered ruin of his arm. The room blurred, lost to a blackness sharpening at the edges. Unreal. He thought his arm had fallen from the shoulder. The twisted remains spooling toward his fingers belonged to someone else. Poley grabbed him by the collar with both hands and wrenched him to his feet again.

With his good arm, Kit reached for his knife. He'd kill them. Kill them all, to live, and to hell with the damnation that followed. His fingers closed on empty air. Remembering a second too late. Poley pinned Kit's arms behind his back. He screamed against the searing pressure on splintered bone.

———

Nine.

Mephistopheles extended a hand. Faustus stared, then held out his arm, the same arm he'd slashed three acts ago, spilling blood to sign away his soul. Mephistopheles gripped it, hard enough to bruise, and dragged Faustus to his feet. The trapdoor in the stage opened. Faustus made no sound.

It would have been less horrifying if he'd screamed.

Ten.

The entire stage, the entire theater, had gone silent. Mephistopheles and Faustus stared at each other, demon hand around human wrist. Eye to eye, man to not-quite-man. It might have been intimate, if not for the lesser demons circling, silent vultures, breathless.

Mephistopheles closed his eyes and flung Faustus forward.

Eleven.

For a minute, pinned and fading, looking at Frizer, Kit saw the flash of a Cambridge office, and a man behind a desk, and eyes like ink watching him over steepled fingers. The knife shone like five gold crowns winking in the lamplight. It shone as bright as Frizer's glittering smile.

"Wait," Nick said from the door, to no one.

And Frizer plunged the blade through Kit's eye, hilt-deep.

Twelve.

Forty-Nine

Nick pressed his back against the door. He watched as the body's limbs buckled and it sank, slowly, as if suspended, to the floor. He called it *the body*, in his head. He refused to think of it as *him*.

Frizer tugged at the knife until it gave, then wiped the blade against the thigh of his breeches. It left a dull smear like the path of a slug. He twirled the knife between his fingers, letting the blade catch the light.

"Well," Poley said. "There you are. Easy as breathing."

Frizer continued watching the knife as it darted back and forth, flipping dragonfly-like between his fingers. Nick could look at nothing but the body. He had nothing to say.

Nick, my good man, came the echo of Poley's voice. *You could say nothing else and this business would have your name all over it.*

"The watch will be here soon," Poley said, a reminder.

Frizer nodded. This had all been part of the plan. They would be arrested for the murder of Kit Marlowe, reckless blasphemer, Bankside heretic. They would be arrested, tossed in prison for the night, and tried the next day in a court overseen by the very men who had tacitly condoned the murder. Come tomorrow afternoon, they would stand there as the court pardoned Robert Poley, Ingram Frizer, and Nicholas Skeres for killing an unarmed man in self-defense.

Nick could hear Poley's voice telling him the story for the hundredth time, as he'd done all morning, repeating it until the moment Kit walked into the room. Marlowe had charged them with the knife, they would say. He drank too much (Kit drank nothing) and grew aggressive and violent (Frizer attacked first) in an argument over the bill (they came that day to kill him, there was never a chance he wouldn't die).

No one would be surprised. Kit had never been trustworthy. He'd never been respectable. The dangerous, reckless son of a shoemaker, known the city over for his empty pockets, daring blasphemy, and debauched friends. Some, Poley said, would think he deserved it. The clergy. The master of revels. Richard Baines. And Sir Robert Cecil's servants weren't condemned for following orders. There would be a brief flurry of interest, a penniless poet or two penning an unimpressive elegy in Marlowe's honor. And then within six months, no one would remember a thing.

No one would remember a thing.

Nick would remember.

He stared at the body on the floor, blind and silent and motionless. Through the locked door, he heard voices shouting in the tavern, Eleanor Bull's unconvincing protest, and the thundering of booted feet against the stairs.

Frizer tossed the blade aside. It landed on the floor beside the body with a soft clang, like the striking of a bell. He glanced first at Poley, then at Nick, and smiled.

Then Frizer turned to the door, and the three murderers waited together, listening as a soldier clicked a key into the lock.

Fifty

Faustus's fall seemed to take an age. He no longer appeared quite human, no longer quite alive. He arced forward, curiously suspended, as if the air had thickened to water. The hem of his robe vanished last, a lingering snatch of fabric swallowed by the black. The swarm of soot-blasted demons moved as one, a shadowed wave that clambered down into the pit after.

Mephistopheles stood alone now. His November eyes passed over the crowd. Not looking so much as watching. Not wondering so much as waiting.

Who's next? he seemed to say.

And he turned away, through the doors at the back of the stage, and was gone.

The silence in the theater stretched a full ten seconds. The applause, when it came, shredded Tom's nerves. A whistle from the second tier of seats ached his teeth like grinding metal. They were right to cheer, of course: *Faustus* was a triumph. London had never seen anything like it. Something so close, so strong, so immediate that, for a moment, for two hours, the city forgot it was fiction.

Tom hadn't forgotten the truth of it, not for a moment.

He pressed his hands deep into his pockets, hunching his shoulders. The weather had been in a state of turning for two hours, though the rain refused to break. A wind rippled Tom's hair, warm and thick. Traces of applause ringing behind, he turned from the stage. On another day, he'd have waited for Kit to give his ebullient notes to the actors, equal parts wild cursing and useful suggestions. Then, an arm around Kit's waist, savoring second-hand excitement, they'd drift toward the Mermaid to drown their victory in drink. But though Tom needed a drink more now than most nights, Kit wasn't here, and Tom couldn't bear any company but his. Ned would have to celebrate his latest triumph alone.

Tom wove around the few latecomers behind him, most of them whispering, though there was no reason but awe to keep their voices down. He forced his way into the street. In that moment, he wanted nothing more and nothing less than to be alone.

Small wonder Kit hadn't come, he thought, walking along the Thames. Appointment or not, how could Kit stand there and watch demons speak his own nightmares to an uncomprehending London? Of course he hadn't shown it to Tom beforehand. Nearly ten years Tom had loved this man, and still there were some things Kit wouldn't tell him.

Maybe someday soon.

Not today, though. He wouldn't ask today. Kit wouldn't tell, and Tom couldn't bear being lied to, not again, not after what he'd seen.

The sky opened, and it began to rain. Slow at first, and then, with an almost-audible sigh, all at once. A jagged slice of lightning streaked from the clouds, bleaching the street. Theatergoers, tradesmen, apprentices, children pushed past Tom, hurrying toward shelter. He let them go. The rain drenched him through, until his shirt clung to his chest and his hair sluiced water across his brow and into his eyes, but it didn't matter. He would be wet anyway, whether he ran or walked.

Kit would be back from Deptford by sundown. Then Tom would do exactly what he'd promised. He'd tell Kit *Faustus* was a stroke of genius (true) and that it shook London to its foundations (also true). If Tom kissed Kit deeper, held him closer, let his touch linger an extra moment, Kit would attribute it to celebration. Literary awe. For tonight, Tom would let him think that. Tom would love him as if nothing had changed, as if Kit were still that ambitious Cambridge scholar with greatness in his grasp and the world to prove it to. That man with a smirk that meant everything, and none of it good. That man who trailed behind him a cloud of tobacco and innuendo and youthful indifference. Loving that man, as if he still existed, instead of flickering in and out of sight for ten years. Loving him as best Tom knew how. That would be enough. It had to be. He didn't have anything else.

I'll burn my books, Faustus had challenged God.

Tom would burn anything, if it would do them any good.

Beside him, the river shuddered, its surface tattered into erratic waves, edged in white lightning. Tom pushed his wet hair from his forehead, squinting through the rain. He turned his back on the theater, toward home. Soon, nothing remained for Bankside to observe but the battering rhythm of rain against the river, the fading silhouette of a soaked man walking alone, and, after the thunder, silence.

Author's Note

A Tip for the Hangman is largely based on historical fact, but there are many places where I've chosen to value a good story over a true event. I hope no one is using this novel as a study guide for their Early Modern History and Politics exam, but just in case, here are some of the major divergences between fact and fiction.

Was Christopher Marlowe a spy? We think so, yes. There are strong signs indicating Marlowe was well connected with people high up in Elizabethan intelligence circles, and for a job that depends on keeping a low profile, "strong signs" are all we're likely to get. Burghley's note to Corpus Christi College is the most famous of these signs, though allusions to a "Marley," "Morley," "Marlin," or "Merlin" appear in association with a number of covert operations, including the surveillance of Lady Arbella Stuart. Historians looking for proof also get deep into Marlowe's spending habits at Cambridge, but you probably didn't come here to hear me shout about ledger-book entries from 1585, so let's leave that there.

That said, Marlowe was almost certainly not involved in exposing Mary Stuart, though the involvement of Arthur Gregory and Robert Poley is well documented. Kit's role in this book is closest to that of Thomas Phelippes, a linguist and Walsingham's chief code breaker. Still, the possibility of getting Kit involved in such a high-profile case was too good for me to pass up, especially as Kit's last years at Cambridge mapped so perfectly onto its timeline. The Babington plot itself unfolded more or less as described, though I've left out some of the more convoluted details for the sake of not making this book nine hundred pages long. There's an anecdote about Mary smuggling out coded letters inside of wine barrels that I wanted desperately to include, but alas.

Lord Strange probably wasn't actively plotting to depose Queen Elizabeth, although there's a factual foundation for the story I've offered. Ferdinando Stanley, Lord Strange, was one of many in the running as Elizabeth I's successor, and numerous historians describe his communications with exiled English Catholics who wanted him to overthrow the queen. Strange is thought to have declined their offer, and it's believed that his Catholic would-be conspirators may have had him assassinated in retaliation. My version of the Strange plot, then, is more of a *What if he'd said yes?* scenario, although numerous elements—Kit's journey to Flushing, for example—are taken from fact. Strange did indeed die by poison, but not until a year after Marlowe's own death, in 1594.

The motives of Marlowe's murderers are famously difficult to pin down. What's certain is that Marlowe arrived at a Deptford tavern owned by Eleanor Bull on May 30, 1593. He spent several hours in conversation with Robert Poley, Ingram Frizer, and Nicholas Skeres. At some point, a brawl broke out, and Frizer stabbed Marlowe through the eye with Marlowe's own knife. I've provided one fictional explanation by involving Sir Robert Cecil, which, though unconfirmed, seems more likely to me than Marlowe faking his own death and adopting the pen name of William Shakespeare. (No offense to any anti-Stratfordians who may be reading.)

I've also done a bit of conflating and rearranging of individual characters to suit my story, which is worth noting. First, Tom. The historical Thomas Watson, though an intimate friend of Marlowe's, was some nine years older than him, and so they definitely did not study at Cambridge together. He was a moderately successful tragic poet, too, writing mostly in Latin. Watson faded from public view in the mid- to late 1580s after his imprisonment in Newgate for the murder of William Bradley, and he died in 1592 at the age of thirty-seven. It's probably most accurate to think of my Tom as an amalgamation of many people in the historical Marlowe's life—friend, classmate, cellmate, lover—rather than a one-to-one representation of a real person.

Nick Skeres, too, looks a little different in the record than he does here. Nicholas Skeres almost certainly didn't attend Cambridge with Marlowe (history's money is on Furnival's Inn, a London law school), and he may have been involved in Whitehall's schemes significantly earlier than May 1593. I've flexed my authorial privilege a little by giving Nick and Kit a more personal relationship here than the professional one they probably had.

Christopher Marlowe and Thomas Watson were indeed arrested for the murder of William Bradley, but Bradley was of no relation to the historical Marlowe, and definitely not his brother-in-law. In reality, Margaret Marlowe married John Jordan, a Canterbury tailor, in 1590. I chose to invent the Kit-Bradley connection for a number of reasons: some boring and logistical, some "Let's give Kit more opportunities to make stupid decisions."

Many of the documents referenced in this book—including the letters between Mary Stuart and Anthony Babington, Burghley's letter to the Cambridge fellows, and Richard Baines's deposition—exist in the public record, and while I've borrowed heavily from them, I haven't quoted them verbatim. This is mostly because the Elizabethans were, among many things, verbose. The original texts are available online through the National Archives and the British Library, and I highly recommend reading them, if only for proof that the historical Richard Baines is indeed the worst.

Finally, there were some places where the historical timeline conflicted with my narrative timeline in small, annoying ways that would have blown cannonball-sized holes in this book. In those cases, I've erred on the side of nudging dates a couple of years in either direction. These include the election of Sir Robert Cecil to the Privy Council, the Hog Lane murder of William Bradley, the deaths of Jane Marlowe and Sir Francis Walsingham, the first recorded performances of Marlowe's plays (especially *Edward II* and *Doctor Faustus*), and a few other minor events.

It's my hope that the clearer reading experience makes up for the slight inaccuracy.

I've no doubt that some sharp-eyed reader or another will note other errors or inaccuracies in this book, and I take complete and sole responsibility for those mistakes. Although, since Shakespeare gave Bohemia a seacoast and Marlowe had no idea where Damascus was, at least I'm in good company.

Acknowledgments

This book wouldn't exist without the support and hard work of so many wonderful people, and while it's practically guaranteed that I'll forget somebody, I'll try not to.

Huge gratitude and the thirteen-dollerest bottle of wine to my agent Bridget Smith, whose unwavering belief in Kit is the reason he made it to print. Further thanks and a standing ovation to my editor Carolyn Williams, who understood this book immediately and showed me what it needed to work. Both Bridget and Carolyn have shown me endless trust and enthusiasm, given me freedom to try and fail, and generously tolerated my puns along the way. They're all a writer could want from their team.

A major shout-out to everyone at Doubleday for showing so much care to a debut author's book about theater spies. Special thanks are due to Amy Ryan, copy editor and oracle of truth, and Mike Windsor, who created the absolutely stunning cover art. This book truly could not have found a better home.

Endless gratitude to Laura Hulthen Thomas, at the University of Michigan's Residential College, whose patience, enthusiasm, and endless exhortations to "do something about the sexual tension" are why this book ever got drafted. You're a goddess, Laura. And the word *nostril* isn't in this book once—I checked.

Thanks also to my Northwestern MFA mentors, Juan Martinez and Christine Sneed, who taught me more about craft, discipline, and generosity than I can hope to repay.

I'm raising a glass to the wonderful writing groups who read drafts, offered critiques, and helped me believe someone might read my words someday: the U of M Writers' Community, the Oak Park Collective (especially the late E. J. Shumak), the Team B Slack channel, and my Northwestern MFA cohort (especially the Ren Faire Group Text). You all inspire me every day, and I hope I haven't sullied our good names.

A second, overflowing glass gets raised for the friends and loved ones who supported me, distracted me, and overanalyzed *Edward II* with me as I wrote, especially Aubyn Keefe, Audrey Fierberg, Ben Levy, Ed Utter, Henry Sullivan, Jessica Ross, Katie Brill, Kim Ellsworth, Kristen Field, and Nina Kryza (who defied the seven-year curse). Thanks for being the best people in the world to yell about good news with, and for being so understanding when it took me a hundred years to answer texts. Much love.

This book would still be a daydream and a handful of index cards if not for my incredible family. Thanks to my brother, Adam, the best hype man in the world, and my sister, Danielle, the first person I ever wanted to impress. Thanks to Jason for saying, "This looks like a book I would read," when he saw the cover, which I promised to use as a blurb. Thanks to the full Epstein-Milliman clan, especially Nancy Epstein and Alan Epstein, who've believed in me since I was five years old scribbling in a Winnie-the-Pooh notebook. Warmest gratitude also to the late Richard and Donna Milliman, who would have been front-row at the book launch shaking a water bottle full of pennies.

To Ida Epstein, a big hug and a signed copy, with all my love.

Last, to my parents, Ann Marie Milliman and Michael Epstein. For plopping me in front of a bookshelf at age two. For not getting mad when I was reading so intently I missed my stop on the kindergarten bus. For looking at my stories and early drafts, for the dramatic phone calls, for the family vacations to historical battle sites, for being there always, and for being the first people I want to share good news with. You're the best, and I love you.